Mon cher Theo,   merci de ta bonne lettre
ainsi que du billet de 50 francs.

Je ne trouve pas jusqu'à présent la vie
ici aussi avantageuse que j'eusse pu l'espérer
seulement j'ai trois études de faites ce qu'à
Paris de ces jours-ci probablement je n'aurais
pas su faire

J'étais content de ce que les nouvelles
de la Hollande étaient assez satisfaisantes
Pour ce que est de Reid je serais peu
étonné de ce qu'il ait pourtant — il
prît de mauvaise part que je l'aie devancé
dans le midi — de notre part que
nous n'aurions jamais eu avantage à le
connaître serait relativement injuste
puisque 1: il nous a fait cadeau
d'un très-beau tableau (lequel tableau
soit dit entre parenthèse on avait l'intention
d'acquérir) 2: Reid a fait monter les
Monticelli de valeur et puisqu'on en possède
5 il en résulte pour nous que ces tableaux
ont haussé en tant que valeur. 3 il a
été de bonne et agréable compagnie
dans les premiers mois —

Maintenant de notre côté on a
voulu le faire participer à une affaire
plus importante que celle des Monticelli
et il a fait semblant de n'y pas comprendre
grand'chose.

Il me semble que pour avoir davantage
encore le droit de rester maîtres de
notre terrain en tant que quant aux
~~offrir de prix~~ impressionistes. —
pour qu'il n'y puisse avoir de doute
concernant notre bonne foi ~~concernant agir~~
à l'égard de Reid — on pourrait
le laisser agir sans intervenir comme
bon lui semblera pour les Monticelli
de Marseille. Résistant que,
                                            sur ceux
les peintres décédés nous intéressent
qu'indirectement au point de vue
argent.

Et si tu es d'accord en ceci à la rigueur
tu peux de ma part aussi lui
dire que s'il a l'intention de
venir à Marseille pour y acheter des
Monticelli il n'a rien à craindre de nous
mais qu'on a le droit de lui demander
ses intentions à cet égard vu qu'on l'a
devancé sur cette toile —

Vincent and Theo

THE VAN GOGH BROTHERS

DEBORAH HEILIGMAN

SQUARE FISH

Godwin Books

HENRY HOLT AND COMPANY • NEW YORK

moins de remettre à circuler

cela n'ayant pas été le cas dans
les derniers temps à Paris je n'en pouvais
véritablement plus.

Il faut que je prenne mes couleurs et
mes toiles soit chez un épicier soit chez un
libraire qui n'ont pas tout ce qui serait
désirable. Il faudra bien que j'aille
à Marseille pour voir comment
l'état de ces choses serait par là
j'avais espérer trouver du beaubleu
et en somme je ne m'en désespère pas vu
qu'à Marseille on doit pouvoir acheter
les matières brutes de première main.
Et je voudrais pouvoir faire des
bleus comme Ziem — qui ne
bougent pas tant que les autres
enfin nous verrons —
Ne t'embête pas et donne
une poignée de main aux
copains pour moi. b.t

Vincent

les études que j'ai sont une vieille
femme Arlésienne un paysage avec de la neige
une vue d'un bout de trottoir avec la boutique
d'un charcutier. Les femmes sont
bien belles ici c'est pas une blague au
contraire le musée d'Arles est abrué et une
blague et digne d'être à Tarascon — il y a aussi

For Aaron and Benjamin—
dear brothers, exemplary sons

SQUARE
FISH

An imprint of Macmillan Publishing Group, LLC
120 Broadway, New York, NY 10271
fiercereads.com

Our books may be purchased in bulk for promotional, educational, or business use.
Please contact your local bookseller or the Macmillan Corporate and Premium Sales Department
at (800) 221-7945 ext. 5442 or by email at MacmillanSpecialMarkets@macmillan.com.

The Van Gogh Museum, Amsterdam, is gratefully acknowledged for permission to use
the following images: Letter from Vincent van Gogh to Theo van Gogh, Auvers-sur-Oise (pp. i–iv);
View from the Apartment in the Rue Lepic, Paris (pp. x–1); *La Crau Seen from Montmajour*,
Arles (pp. 8–9); Letter from Vincent van Gogh to Theo van Gogh (pp. 52–53); *View of Royal Road,
Ramsgate*, Ramsgate (pp. 74–75); *Coke Factory in the Borinage*, Flénu (pp. 108–109); *Sorrow*,
The Hague (pp. 124–125); *View of the Sea at Scheveningen*, The Hague (pp. 158–159);
Letter from Vincent van Gogh to Theo van Gogh with sketches of Post for Perspective,
The Hague (p. 170); *A Sunday in Eindhoven*, Nuenen (pp. 190–191); *View of Paris with Notre-Dame
and the Panthéon*, Paris (pp. 216–217); *Gate in the Paris Ramparts*, Paris (pp. 244–245); *Landscape
with Windmills at Fontvieille*, Arles (pp. 262–263); *Trees with Ivy in the Garden of the Asylum*,
Saint-Rémy-de-Provence (pp. 304–305); *Interior with Tables and Chairs, and a Sketch of
'The Bedroom,'* Auvers-sur-Oise (pp. 336–337); *The Wall Enclosing the Wheatfield near the Asylum*,
Saint-Rémy-de-Provence (pp. 358–359); *Studies of a Dead Sparrow*, Saint-Rémy-de-Provence (pp. 388–389);
Letter from Vincent van Gogh to Theo van Gogh, Auvers-sur-Oise, 23 July 1890 (pp. 404–405).

Farm and Wagon Shed (pp. 14–15) courtesy of Wikiart.

Library of Congress Cataloging-in-Publication Data
Names: Heiligman, Deborah, author.
Title: Vincent and Theo : the Van Gogh brothers / Deborah Heiligman.
Description: New York : Henry Holt and Company, 2017.
Identifiers: LCCN 2016009017 (print) | LCCN 2016016667 (ebook) |
ISBN 978-1-250-21106-4 (paperback) | ISBN 978-1-250-10969-9 (ebook)
Subjects: LCSH: Gogh, Vincent van, 1853–1890. |
Painters—Netherlands—Biography. | Gogh, Theo van, 1857–1891—Family. |
Brothers—Biography. | BISAC: JUVENILE NONFICTION / Biography &
Autobiography / Art. | JUVENILE NONFICTION / Family / Siblings.
Classification: LCC ND653.G7 H39 2017 (print) | LCC ND653.G7 (ebook) |
DDC 759.9492 [B]—dc23
LC record available at https://lccn.loc.gov/2016009017

Originally published in the United States by Laura Godwin Books/Henry Holt and Company
First Square Fish edition, 2019
Book designed by Anna Booth
Square Fish logo designed by Filomena Tuosto

1 3 5 7 9 10 8 6 4 2

AR: 6.4 / LEXILE: 900L

Vincent van Gogh
1853–1890

Theo van Gogh
1857–1891

The world would not have Vincent
without Theo.

Contents

Threshold

1.

TWO BROTHERS, ONE APARTMENT, PARIS, 1887

---

*There was a time when I loved Vincent
very much, and he was my best friend,
but that's over now.*

—Theo van Gogh to his sister Willemien, March 14, 1887

THEO'S BROTHER VINCENT has been living with him for just over a year, and Theo cannot take it anymore.

It is "almost intolerable for me at home," he writes to their sister Wil in March 1887. Even though Theo has moved them to a larger apartment, this one still feels too small to hold Vincent's outsized personality and Theo's desperate need for quiet. He's dying to tell Vincent to move out, but he knows if he does, Vincent will just be more determined to stay.

Dogged. Contrary. Stubborn. Vincent.

Theo van Gogh is the manager of Goupil & Cie, a successful art gallery on the fashionable Boulevard Montmartre in Paris. Theo is good at his job, but it's terrifically frustrating for him right now. The owners of the gallery want him to sell paintings in the traditional style because they're popular and bring in money. Though Theo certainly needs to make money—he has to support himself *and* Vincent *and* help their mother—he wants to sell art that is truly exciting to him, paintings by the Impressionists and their crowd, friends of his and Vincent's: Émile Bernard, Paul Gauguin, Claude Monet, and Henri de Toulouse-Lautrec. Soon, maybe even paintings by Vincent himself.

But these modern painters don't bring in enough money, so it's a constant battle with his bosses. Theo *has* persuaded them to let him set up a little display of Impressionists on the entresol. The entresol is not the ground floor, and it's not the first floor. It's the floor in between. It's as if the paintings are there, but not quite yet, a glimpse into the future. It's a start. But he spends his days working hard and comes back to the apartment at 54 Rue Lepic exasperated and exhausted. What he needs at home is rest and *peace*, but instead he gets VINCENT.

Theo loves his brother's brilliant mind, his gregariousness, even his fiery temperament. Vincent can be a good antidote to Theo's own inwardness and tendency to melancholy.

But after so many months of the cold Parisian winter spent indoors with Vincent, Theo is a wreck both mentally and physically. A few months back, in December, he was actually paralyzed—he couldn't move at all for a few days. Although Theo knows he can't blame his bad health on his brother, to get better he needs a break from Vincent's gusts, his squalls, his constant talking and lecturing.

And, to make matters worse, lately Vincent has been furious at *him*. "He loses no opportunity to let me see that he despises me and I inspire aversion in him," Theo tells Wil.

A portrait done of the brothers at this time would be sizzling with streaks of red-orange paint.

———

WHEN VINCENT AND THEO were young, growing up in the village of Zundert in the Netherlands, their father, a pastor, had written a special prayer. All the Van Gogh children had to memorize it and recite it when they left home:

"O Lord, join us intimately to one another and let our love for Thee make that bond ever stronger."

Theo has valiantly been living up to that prayer. He's been Vincent's best friend for most of the last fifteen years, ever since they made a pledge to each other on a walk. And through many ups and downs and storms, for the past seven years, Theo has been giving Vincent money for paint, pencils and pens, ink, canvases, paper, clothing, food, and, until he moved in, rent.

On March 30 Vincent turns thirty-four; on May 1 Theo will be thirty. They've made it this far in their journey together—how can Theo kick him out now?

———

VINCENT AND THEO VAN GOGH look a lot alike: They both have red hair, though Vincent's is redder, Theo's more reddish blond. Vincent has freckles; Theo does not. They are both medium height—around five feet seven—but Vincent is broader, bigger; Theo slighter, thinner. They have pale blue eyes that sometimes darken to greenish blue. They are definitely brothers.

But they couldn't give more different impressions.

Vincent in his workman's clothes spends his days painting, outside if it's not too cold, or inside the apartment. He is covered with Parisian soot and grime, overlaid with splatters and spatters of paint: ochre, brick red, orange, lemon chrome, cobalt blue, green, black, zinc white.

He doesn't bathe often, which is typical for a nineteenth-century man, but it's even less often than he *should*. He *stinks*—of body odor, dirt, food, paint, turpentine, wine, and tobacco. He usually has a pipe in his mouth, though he has very few teeth left, and those that are left are rotten.

And yet Vincent looks healthy: he's robust, sturdy, and vehemently alive. Passion pours from him, as if the world he's trying to capture is inside him, bursting to come out.

Theo is tidy, well dressed in a suit, looking very much the proper Parisian businessman. His features are finer, more refined. He would be handsome if he weren't so sick: he's thin and pale; he looks as though the life is being sucked out of him. He feels that way, too.

IN MANY WAYS, Vincent's move to Paris has been good for both brothers. Thanks to Theo's influence, to the artists he's met, and to his own tenacious work, Vincent's paintings are better than ever: they are imbued with color and light and Vincent's own particular style.

And Vincent has given Theo more of a life. He'd been lonely in Paris, *so lonely*, and now, even though he doesn't have a wife and family, Theo at least has a circle of friends through Vincent. For that he is grateful. So even though he's desperate, Theo doesn't kick out his brother. Yet.

In April, Theo acknowledges to another sister, Lies, that he's been ill, "particularly in my spirit, and have had a great struggle with myself." If he were well, he could deal with Vincent.

In fact both brothers do better with sun and warm air and hours spent outside. The Parisian days are getting longer—by minutes, anyway. If only spring would arrive! But there's still too much gloom outside and in.

Gloom *and* fire.

It's as if there are two Vincents, Theo has told Wil. He knows both sides of his brother very well. Sometimes Vincent is ebulliently happy and kind, sometimes furiously angry and difficult. He has a huge heart, but he's stubborn and argumentative.

Vincent argues not only with Theo, and with himself, but also with friends and people he admires. One cold and fiery night in the near future, Vincent will fight with another roommate. And that argument will end in blood.

Entresol

A GLIMPSE INTO THE FUTURE

2.

TWO BROTHERS, A HOSPITAL BED

––––––––––

 IS A YEAR and a half later, the end of December 1888. Vincent is no longer in Paris; he is in Arles, a town in the South of France, living with a painter friend.

Theo is in Paris, happier than he's ever been.

The brothers are separated by almost five hundred miles.

The day before Christmas, Theo receives a telegram.

Vincent is gravely wounded.

Theo goes to his brother at once, on the night train from Paris to Arles. The journey takes sixteen hours. When Theo arrives at his brother's hospital bed, Vincent is barely conscious. He's got a bandage wound around his head to stop blood seeping from a severed ear.

The brothers talk as Vincent drifts in and out of consciousness. He is sometimes delirious. It is not certain he will live.

Theo is bereft. He lays his head next to his brother's on the pillow.

Vincent feels Theo next to him. Almost drained of life, he is transported back to their childhood in the Netherlands, to their small town, to a time he remembers as simple and pure and beautiful, a time when the two brothers shared an attic room, a life, a future.

He whispers into Theo's ear, "Just like in Zundert."

Beginnings

1852–1872

3.

TWO VINCENTS

VINCENT AND THEO'S FAMILY began with death.

There was an older brother.

Their mother, Anna van Gogh-Carbentus, gave birth to her first child on March 30, 1852. The baby was stillborn. *Levenloos*, the Dutch word for "lifeless," is written on the registry in the Zundert town hall. Next to this the father signed his own name: Theodorus van Gogh. There is no name recorded for the baby.

But they *had* given him a name: Vincent, after his father's father, and they buried him in the cemetery next to the church where Theodorus was the pastor. He was the first stillborn baby to be buried in that cemetery.

Anna and Dorus lived in the parsonage right next to the church and cemetery, and there, in their bedroom, exactly one year later on March 30, 1853, at eleven in the morning, Anna gave birth to another baby boy, this one alive and healthy.

They named *him* Vincent, too. The eldest son, named after his father's father, like his dead brother. His middle name was Willem, after his mother's father. Theodorus registered this baby, too, in the Zundert town hall. The serial number happened to be twenty-nine, just as his dead brother's had been the year before. But this time there was a name filled in: Vincent Willem van Gogh.

And, unlike his dead brother, Vincent Willem van Gogh was baptized, three and a half weeks later, on April 24. Although according to the Christian faith this ceremony gave him a clean slate, he did not have a blank canvas on which to paint his life. The first Vincent was always there, in the family history and on the gravestone in the churchyard right next door:

VINCENT VAN GOGH
1852
SUFFER THE LITTLE CHILDREN TO COME UNTO ME, FOR SUCH
IS THE KINGDOM OF GOD.

It's almost as if there were two portraits, side by side, two Vincent van Goghs. One stayed a newborn, frozen in time, while the other grew from a baby to a toddler to a freckled, redheaded little boy.

But there was just one Vincent—the eldest living son, upon whom, traditionally, parents placed their hopes. The first baby Vincent is a pentimento, a ghostly image under the second Vincent's portrait, the picture of a child who might have been.

When an artist paints over an image, the first painting is often gone forever, never to reappear. But the portrait of the first Vincent will become more and more visible as the living Vincent grows up.

4.

THOSE DAYS

AFTER VINCENT CAME FIVE more babies, all born healthy and at home: Anna (1855); Theodorus, called Theo (1857); Elisabeth, called Lies (1859); Willemien, called Wil (1862); and fourteen years after Vincent, the youngest, Cornelis, called Cor (1867).

The house at 26 Markt was tiny, and with each new baby, more crowded. But Anna and Dorus didn't mind; they wanted their family to be close now, and forever.

The closer they were, the easier it was to preserve their own values. The Van Gogh home and church community was a small island of Protestantism in the much larger Catholic community of Zundert, and all North Brabant, the province in the southern Netherlands where they lived. Reverend Van Gogh and Anna felt strongly about bringing up their children with a sense of duty, charity, and morality. They were determined to insulate them from what they thought of as the rougher and wilder Catholic community. Dorus wrote the family prayer to embody their values and hopes for their children: that they should be joined intimately to each other and that their love of God would make the familial bond strong, always.

Anna and Dorus van Gogh placed as much importance on this world as the next and valued hard work. They wanted to bring up their sons to be self-sufficient. And they raised all their children not only to help those in need but also to revere culture, society, reputation, and all the niceties that came with it.

They felt strongly that their children should be well educated in both the arts and the sciences; they saw God as a father who educated people through people. So although they wanted Vincent, Anna, Theo, and the younger siblings to adhere to their values, they did not want to close them off from the world. To encourage them all to learn about other cultures and to develop their talents, Anna and Dorus had magazines and newspapers delivered to the house.

The Van Goghs' parsonage was fancier and more decorated than most other village houses. They had fine furniture, and Anna filled their home with flower cuttings from the garden and nearby fields. Since Anna was an excellent artist, and specialized, like a lot of women of the time, in painting flowers and plants, she hung her own beautiful botanical watercolors on the walls. She also crocheted and embroidered, and her handiwork was on display around the house.

Dorus reserved the biggest room in the front on the first floor for his duties as the pastor. That's where he held meetings, Bible study, coffee hour after church on Sundays, and catechisms when the church was too cold in the winter. The front room had its own fireplace, floors made of pine instead of the usual tile, and wallpaper.

Aside from the public part of the house, the only other luxury was the privy in a shed attached to the house; the Van Goghs didn't have to walk outside to use the bathroom. The rest of 26 Markt was a simple and cozy home for Vincent and his sisters and brothers. Lying wounded and sick in that hospital bed in Arles years later, Vincent could see the parsonage vividly, the details of his childhood home indelibly etched in his mind's eye, a particularly rendered painting, staying the same always.

"I again saw each room in the house at Zundert," he wrote to Theo, "each path, each plant in the garden, the views round about, the fields, the neighbours, the cemetery, the church, our kitchen garden behind—right up to the magpies' nest in a tall acacia in the cemetery."

The front part of the house was at least 225 years old when Dorus moved in. (He wasn't yet married when he became Zundert's pastor.) Other parts of the house were old, too, but had been added later as needed. It was narrow—the first floor of the house was only as wide as two windows and a door. Dorus and Anna slept in the middle room on the first floor. From there you could go down to the basement or up to the second floor. The second floor, essentially an attic, was even narrower than the first, the house tapering under a slanted roof. It was in a room under the eaves that Vincent slept, and Theo, too, when he was old enough, the two brothers in a bed under the eaves, their heads together.

Eventually all the children slept on the second floor, and a maid, and later a governess, Dorus and Anna putting up walls to divide already small rooms into smaller ones. Pa wrote his sermons in another room under the eaves, a room filled with books and prints that Vincent would always remember.

———

IN THE MORNINGS the children climbed out of bed and went downstairs to the back room for breakfast, maybe a cup of hot chocolate. This room had a well pump, a fireplace, an oven, and a stove. When he was cold, Vincent would wrap his arms around the stovepipe to get warm.

The family spent most of their time here: they ate their meals, played games, and read novels and fairy tales together in the evenings. The room faced the yard and overlooked the long, sloping garden, which was filled with flowers: bright red geraniums, sweet-smelling mignonette, and purslane with red, orange, yellow, and pink blossoms. The garden had fruit trees, too, and berries, herbs, and pea vines in one corner. A beech hedge fenced in the garden. There were more vegetables, including potatoes, in a larger vegetable garden farther behind the house, next to a field of rye. A hired gardener helped them with the harvest. The family also kept three goats.

When it was warm enough, Vincent and Theo and their sisters Anna and Lies played in the kitchen garden. They ran, climbed, and dug in the sandy dirt, building sand castles as if they were at the beach. Vincent invented games for the younger children, and one day they had so much fun that Anna, Theo, and Lies declared the most beautiful rosebush in the garden now belonged to Vincent, a thank-you gift.

The happy intimacy of his childhood home stayed with Vincent forever. Wounded in Arles, hovering in that space between life and death, his head was filled with "primitive memories of all of you, of those days."

5.

NATURE'S ROOTS

———————

When Dorus had moved into the house at 26 Markt in 1849, Zundert was a market town thick with commerce, a gateway into the Netherlands from next-door Belgium. Carriages, carts, and wagons carrying merchants, goods for sale, and travelers—the outside world—passed by the parsonage every day. Stagecoaches and mail coaches changed horses at the market square, just down the street. Servants gathered at the town pump to get water and gossip. On many days the square jammed with so much traffic that nothing could move. Townsfolk complained about the congestion, the noise, and, when it was dry, the dust clouds the traffic stirred up, making the air so thick and dirty they couldn't open the windows of their houses.

On Sundays, when the square was much quieter, the constable read the village news on the steps of the town hall, followed by the clerk, who read the legal news from the notary's office.

By the time Vincent's name was entered into the ledger in the town hall, his existence recorded and announced, a railroad had diverted some of the traffic away from Zundert. With fewer travelers passing through, the town quieted down a bit, though the parsonage fronted on the main street, which was still crowded and busy.

And yet Vincent and Theo always thought of themselves as country boys because the back of the house was on the edge of town, and Zundert was surrounded by, as Vincent later wrote, "black fields with the young green wheat," fields of rye and corn, and heath-covered moors.

A boy could walk out through the garden gate and straight into the rye, and beyond that into meadows strewn with wildflowers to pick, pine forests to ramble in, and streams to follow. Vincent loved to wander, to discover, to collect. He often left home with a fishnet and a bottle, and came back with treasures from nature: a bird's nest or an egg, stones, and unusual wildflowers that he had a knack for finding when no one else in the family could. He especially enjoyed catching beetles and water bugs from the streams, but above all else, he was passionate about collecting itself.

Though Vincent mostly walked alone, Theo often rambled with him, once he was old enough and allowed to go. He didn't have Vincent's passion for collecting, nor did the other children. But they always wanted to know what treasures their big brother had found, crowding around him to see his trophies when he came back through the garden gate.

After showing Theo and his sisters what he'd gotten, Vincent would go to his little attic room to organize his collection and mount the bugs. He'd carefully pin them in a box, which he'd lined with clean white paper. And then he'd neatly label the insects with their Latin names.

"Copying nature absolutely isn't the ideal," Vincent wrote to Theo when he finally found his way to being a painter. "But knowing nature in such a way that what one does is fresh and true—that's what many now lack. . . . You will say, but everyone has surely seen landscapes and figures from childhood. . . . Question: did everyone who saw them—heath, grassland, fields, woods—also love them, and the snow and the rain and the storm?"

Vincent knew and loved nature in all her moods.

When he was a lost young man, he would walk for miles and miles without money or food, the rain pouring down on him. He would sleep outside, in the cold, and in the heat.

Years later he would paint under the hot sun day after day for hours and hours to capture fields, flowers, the sun itself. He battled the fierce mistral winds in the South of France, only giving up when his easel would not stay anchored.

Nature was part of him; its extremes were part of his very being.

He would rush to a storm to see it up close, to be inside it.

Vincent adored a good storm.

His parents did not.

6.

DORUS AND ANNA:
THE PASTOR AND HIS PARTNER

Our father and our mother have been
exemplary as married people.

—Vincent to Theo, January 22, 1889

ANNA AND DORUS did like nature and the outdoors. They planted the abundant garden behind the house, and Anna filled 26 Markt with cut flowers. She and Dorus took the family out for an hour's walk every day around the village. But those walks were disciplined; they were not meanders of discovery like Vincent's on the heath.

As a young man, Dorus had once walked forty-five miles and become seriously ill. He didn't take such long walks after that, but he still walked whenever he could and encouraged his sons to do the same. Dorus did not have a penchant for extremes, though, either in action or in nature. He and Anna liked *order*, structure, tranquility, good behavior. They were strict with themselves and their children. They believed in dressing well, behaving properly, and being friends with the *right* people.

Vincent would grow up to think most of that was nonsense. But as a child, he did not question his parents' values; he loved Ma and Pa, unconditionally, wholly, separately and together.

Portrait of Pa

THEODORUS VAN GOGH, thirty-one when the second Vincent was born, was a short man, small framed and good-looking. He had a long, strong nose, high cheekbones, a square jaw. Villagers called him "the handsome domi-nie." Not all ministers were so attractive! His sandy blond hair turned grey prematurely, which many thought made him look even more dignified.

He was, like many fathers, a complex man. Although set in his be-liefs and ways, he was kind to others, gentle, and exceptionally generous. He took food to the sick and poor, no matter if they were parishioners or their Catholic neighbors. He gave money to those who would accept it, and secretly paid the grocer for people who couldn't pay their bills. Sometimes the elders of the church council thought he was too generous with the church's money, but his big heart meant that he was loved not only by his parish but also by the Catholics in Zundert and the country surrounding it.

"We thought so much of him," a Catholic woman remembered years later. "We would have gone through fire and water for him."

But Dorus did have a temper—which he lost sometimes at home with his children, and even with his parishioners. When a member of his congre-gation did not show up at church, he went straight to his home after ser-vices and yelled at him. Years later the mayor of Zundert (a Catholic) remembered him as "severe" and "a proper little Protestant pope."

Dorus himself would have admitted to a different fault: he was a lousy speaker. His sermons were dull, his speaking voice weak. Vincent and the other children didn't realize this—they didn't have anyone to compare him to. But Dorus knew his limitations, and was content to be a pastor in the small community of Zundert, in a church that was part of a small move-ment in the new, less rigid Dutch Protestantism. His own father was a pastor, a much more successful one, but Dorus was not striving to be like his father; he was not ambitious for himself.

He had brothers who were ambitious, and much more successful in their own fields. He was one of eleven children, five sons, the only son to follow in his father's footsteps. One of his brothers, Jan, was an admiral in the Dutch navy. The other three brothers—Hendrik, Cornelis, and Vincent—were successful art dealers. His brother Vincent was the most successful, a partner in the famous Goupil art dealers. He married Anna's sister Cornelia, and since they had no children of their own and lived nearby, Uncle Cent and Aunt Cornelie—especially Uncle Cent—played a big role in Vincent's and Theo's lives from the time they were little.

Dorus welcomed his brother's influence in his sons' lives. And so as the boys grew up, it was as though they had two sets of parents, especially two fathers. Dorus and Cent would guide them, demand of them, give them advice (sometimes asked for, sometimes not). But it was their father Vincent and Theo looked up to, judged themselves against, willingly or not, favorably—or not.

Theo took after their father in looks and also in personality, except for the temper. Vincent got that. But in most ways, Vincent took after their mother.

Portrait of Ma

ANNA CARBENTUS was a few years older than Dorus; she was already thirty-four when she gave birth to Vincent. She was artistic, smart, strong, outgoing, and practical. From the beginning of their marriage she was a partner with Dorus in his professional life—going with him to visit parishioners and to bring food to the sick. She also helped him very much behind the scenes with plans for the church and the community.

Anna inherited her artistic talent from her father, Willem Carbentus, who was a renowned bookbinder. He'd bound the first constitution of the Netherlands and thereafter was known as "the Bookbinder to the King." Anna was also a good writer and a faithful correspondent. Her daughter-in-law would later remember her letters fondly—and also her knitting, Anna moving the needles fast and furiously to the end of her life.

Vincent got his talents in art and writing from his mother. And he resembled her in looks. He was strong, sturdy, broad like Anna. He inherited other traits from her as well: Anna was gregarious and opinionated, and had a strong sense of right and wrong. She was also stubborn.

7.

VINCENT:
THE REDHEADED BOY

---

*It is better to be fervent in spirit, even if one
accordingly makes more mistakes, than narrow-minded
and overly cautious.*

—Vincent to Theo, April 3, 1878

*A*FTER HE DIED, Vincent van Gogh was remembered by Zundert neighbors as both the boy who took long walks alone on the heath and the boy who stayed inside reading all the time.

He was remembered as

a loner

a bad boy

strange

good-natured

ugly (red hair and freckles were thought to be unattractive!)

quiet

Who a person becomes later in life, how he lives, how he dies, clouds people's memories of him, spinning and skewing—distorting—their portraits of him as a child. But we will draw Vincent as clearly as we can using not only impressions but also strong lines, sharp details. A picture will emerge.

Vincent, Book in Hand

ALTHOUGH HE SPENT many hours walking and collecting, Vincent also loved books, starting at an early age. As a small child, in the evenings in the back room overlooking the garden, he drank in the stories that Pa read aloud, especially fairy tales, especially those by Hans Christian Andersen, dark and primal and complex.

Once Vincent could read, he did so voraciously, mostly fairy tales and novels. The love of books and reading stayed with him always, and as he grew, he had the constant desire to learn, so he read books of all kinds. Reading, like bread, was necessary for sustenance, he said. But there was a difference: food to Vincent was an unavoidable necessity; most of the time he didn't care what—or if—he ate. But he had a "more or less irresistible passion for books" that started in Zundert.

Vincent, Drawing

HERE IS VINCENT at the table, drawing. Ma gave him her drawing manuals and encouraged him to learn from them. She also gave him her own drawings of flower bouquets to copy. He spent hours at the table making pictures, but interestingly, Vincent's family did not think of him as a particularly gifted artist as a child, though he clearly showed prowess early on. When the family talked about his artistic endeavors, the stories went to his temper, not his talent.

The Curious Incidents of the Cat and the Elephant

WHEN HE WAS ABOUT EIGHT, Vincent drew a picture of a cat climbing a tree. Ma praised him up and down for it. Rather than being pleased,

Vincent became annoyed by his mother's enthusiasm. He ripped up the drawing.

Around the same time, Vincent took some putty from a house painter who was working around the parsonage. He made an elephant from the clay. When family members fussed over how good the elephant was, Vincent destroyed it.

SO, VINCENT, the young boy:

Red haired. Freckled. Temperamental. Smart. Talented. Stubborn. Quiet. Passionate. Kind. Solitary. Self-critical. Opinionated. Unusual.

The oldest child in a big family, but not a typical firstborn "good boy." That child, perhaps, lay in the cemetery next door.

8.

THE OUTSIDE WORLD

IN 1861, when Vincent was eight and Anna was six, Ma and Pa decided
to try the village school. It was right across the street from their house, but
it was another world from the strict and mannered Van Gogh home.

The front of the school looked out onto the busy market square. Behind the school was a courtyard with a water pump and a toilet. Inside, the
floors and walls were lined with blue tiles. The one room had twenty-one
desks and nine benches, not nearly enough for the 150 children who were
usually there. And when there was no planting, weeding, or harvesting to
be done on the nearby farms, the number swelled to 260, bodies cramming
the benches and overloaded desks. Each desk had three inkwells and one
drawer stuffed with schoolbooks, which the students weren't allowed to
take home without permission from the headmaster. Many days the children ended up fighting for space and air, and often fighting each other.

On rainy days, the room smelled musty and dank from all the coats
hanging in the back, soaking wet from their owners having walked miles in
the rain to get there.

The headmaster was known to have a drinking problem.

It was into this world that Ma and Pa sent their two oldest children from eight thirty to four o'clock, with a two-hour break at home for lunch.

Vincent studied geography, history, and nature. Anna, in the youngest group, learned reading, writing, and arithmetic. She sang songs, recited poems. They used slates for writing, and abacuses, weights, and measures for math.

Their parents gave it ten months but decided that they didn't like the influence of the rough-and-tumble children from outside the Protestant world. Anna and Dorus withdrew Vincent and Anna, choosing instead to hire a governess to educate them at home, along with the younger Van Goghs when they were ready. Pa gave them some lessons, too. And Ma worked with Vincent on his drawing. Again the tiny house was full all day, the children close to one another and their parents.

But it wouldn't last forever. Vincent needed a better education if he was going to be independent and to make his mark in the world.

9.

A CHILDHOOD VIEW

A MONTH BEFORE HE turned eleven, Vincent took a piece of wove paper, smoother than ribbed laid paper, and with a pencil carefully drew a scene from Zundert. In the background is a small farmhouse with a tree next to it. In the foreground is an open barn shed with a farm wagon inside. He gave this picture to his father for his forty-second birthday.

On the back Dorus wrote the date, which was February 8, 1864, and "Vincent." Then he proudly framed his son's picture. It's an unusually good drawing for a boy his age, the first piece of art we can definitely attribute to Vincent, and it is a view from his childhood, from the home he would soon have to leave.

10.

A YELLOW CARRIAGE
IN THE RAIN

I wish I didn't love home so much.

—Lies to Theo, January 10, 1875

*E*IGHT MONTHS AFTER Pa's birthday drawing, it is a rainy, grey autumn day, October 1, 1864. Vincent and his parents climb into a yellow horse-drawn carriage. The carriage pulls away from the little house at 26 Markt.

Dorus and Anna have decided it is time for Vincent to go to boarding school. He is eleven and a half. Money is tight, as it always is in the Van Gogh household, but education is a priority. And Vincent is the eldest son.

The school, run by a Mr. Jan Provily, is in a town called Zevenbergen. It is only fifteen miles from Zundert, but it is still wrenching for Vincent to leave the parsonage, and Theo, and his sisters, his parents—all he has ever known. Home.

It will always be a rupture for the Van Gogh children to leave home. On this overcast day Vincent is the first to leave, for the first time.

And the first to watch his parents leave him.

"I stood on the front steps of Mr. Provily's school, watching the carriage drive away that Pa and Ma rode home in," he told Theo later. "One could see that yellow carriage in the distance on the long road—wet after the rain, with thin trees on either side—running through the meadows. The grey sky above it all was reflected in the puddles."

Vincent isn't yet an artist when he writes those words to Theo, but he paints the scene perfectly, with color, light, composition, emotion—a landscape of memory.

We see the sad trees, with their autumnal leaves dripping rain, the grey sky reflected in the puddles on the road. We feel the chill in the cold, damp air. We watch the yellow carriage getting smaller and smaller, fading away into the distance, the little boy standing on the steps outside the school, watching his parents vanish. We don't have to see his face to know how Vincent is feeling.

11.

THEO: SOME CROQUIS

WHEN VINCENT LEAVES HOME that first time, Theo is a little boy of seven, four years younger than Vincent. But he's the second-oldest child in the parsonage now, the oldest boy. And he is named after his father.

He's been there all along, of course, next to Vincent, looking up to him, his big brother, his only brother. (Cor won't be born for three more years.) If they were royalty, Theo would be the spare to the heir. And in some ways he is just that.

We have contrasting pictures of Vincent as a boy; about Theo we have only glimpses. After Vincent died, and became *the* Vincent van Gogh, writers interviewed the neighbors from Zundert. People hardly talked about Theo at all. It would not be until much later that some, and only a few, would realize that Theo should not have been ignored.

So Theo appears to us in a series of croquis.

A croquis is a sketch. Artists make croquis for different reasons. While learning how to draw the human figure, an artist uses each croquis to concentrate on a different part of the body, a different pose: how an arm bends throwing a ball, what the hand looks like when grasping a paintbrush or a fishing pole or a lover's hand. A croquis is made quickly, the artist drawing for just a few minutes, while the model holds one pose. Then the model changes position, and the artist draws again. It's easier on the model than posing for a painting, holding the same position for hours at a time.

Sometimes the artist fills a sketchbook with pieces of a person, and uses the drawings as a foundation for a finished painting. Or the sketches might remain just that—sketches, never creating a whole. Artists often use croquis for subjects who won't or can't stay still—like a feral cat or a small child, someone whose whole being cannot be captured on paper in one steady view. Like young Theo.

Theo, Croquis #1

THEO IS SITTING at the table with his family, ready to eat a stew of potatoes, carrots, a little meat. He's one of a pack of siblings, the second son, a younger brother, a proper and well-behaved middle child.

Theo has just lifted his head from grace before the meal. His blue eyes have darkened a bit, to a greenish blue.

Theo, Croquis #2

THEO IS AN EASY CHILD, much easier than Vincent. Easier in the sense that he doesn't have outbursts like his brother. He's not a troublemaker. He's a "good boy."

But sometimes a person who seems easy is one whose calm outside belies a troubled and turbulent inside. By the time he becomes a teenager,

Theo has bouts of melancholy. Did this depression of his start in childhood?

Maybe he's quiet because he's sad.

This sketch of Theo the boy is full of cross-outs, erasures, holes, blank spaces.

Theo, Croquis #3

SCENE: the countryside in Brabant, just outside the village of Zundert. You can see the fields, the summer sky. There is a boy. His back is to us. He is walking with his older brother in a field. From the set of his shoulders we can see he is pleased to be with his brother, happy to go along with him on his adventure.

Theo, Croquis #4

THEO IS PLAYING in the garden with Anna and Lies. Vincent is away at school. It will be months before Theo can follow his big brother out the garden gate again. But he looks happy now, happy enough. And yet . . .

We can see more; we know what will come later. It is sometimes the gift of the artist to know more about her subject than he himself does, to go beyond the moment. So while Theo is playing contentedly in the garden with his sisters, we draw a tinge of melancholy into his countenance, a slight frown, a worried brow. It's cheating, really. But we capture his sadness. And then Theo turns away.

12.

DUSK

VINCENT HAS BEEN at Mr. Provily's school for two weeks.

He is standing in a corner of the playground. It is evening, the light fading into dusk.

Vincent is alone.

Then—he later wrote Theo—"they came to tell me that someone was asking after me."

The someone wasn't identified, but he knows.

He *knows.*

And a moment later he is flinging his arms around Pa's neck.

For these minutes Vincent is no longer alone. In the crepuscular light, he is connected again, bound to his father and, through him, to all the family back in Zundert.

Pa has come to see him.

But Dorus can stay only a short time, and soon Vincent is alone again.

He is on his own journey, one that will be arduous and long, filled with missteps and stumbles.

He has years of pilgrimage ahead of him.

13.

VINCENT WALKING

————————

Walk 1

VINCENT IS, like his father, a walker of great distances. On this day he is walking for three hours, returning to Zundert from school.

Vincent is no longer at Mr. Provily's school. When he was thirteen, he'd moved to Tilburg, a town about thirty miles northeast of Zundert, to attend the public King Willem II secondary school. Like other boys who don't live nearby, Vincent boards with a local family. The newly opened King Willem II is a secular high school housed in a palace built by the Dutch royal family. There are thirty-six students, all boys. Vincent takes classes in German, Dutch, math, history, geography, botany, zoology, gym—and drawing. The drawing master is excellent, and art is considered important in the school. The Netherlands and nearby Belgium are known for their great art masters and their reverence for painting. There is mechanical drawing and calligraphy, and each student spends four hours a week on freehand drawing.

There are no drawings extant from this time. Did the teacher look at Vincent's work and recognize his genius? Did any of his classmates? There are no records, no evidence of an early reputation. He was not yet *the* Vincent van Gogh the world came to know. But certainly seeds were being planted.

To get home, Vincent first took a train to the town of Breda. From there it's still a long walk to Zundert, about nine miles. Another boy walks with him. Pa had asked the oldest son of their neighbors, the Honcoops, to fetch Vincent at the station. Vincent is carrying a large, heavy parcel filled with what he needs for a visit home: probably books and clothes. Likely more books than clothes, knowing Vincent.

After they've been walking for a while, the Honcoop boy offers to carry Vincent's bundle. It's a long walk to carry such a heavy load.

"No, thank you," Vincent says. "Everyone must carry his own parcel."

When the Honcoop boy relays the conversation to his parents, "Everyone must carry his own parcel" becomes a saying in the Honcoop family and within the Protestant community in Zundert, an adage extolling strength and self-reliance. From Vincent.

In the years to come, Vincent will take many long walks, for many different reasons, in different moods. It will be years before he figures out where he's going. He will often crave company, demand help, plead for both. But this day he knows where he's going, and he's carrying his own parcel.

Walk 2

JUST BEFORE HIS FIFTEENTH BIRTHDAY, Vincent walks home from high school for the last time. He hasn't graduated. He was one of the better students—he and only four others of the ten in his class had been promoted after the first year. But he has decided he doesn't want to go to school anymore. We don't know why, but he's done.

Back home in Zundert, he spends his time as he used to when he was a boy. He reads, he walks on the moors, in the fields. He's content.

But he can't stay home forever. Ma and Pa want Vincent to go out into the world, get a job. It is time for him to support himself, and maybe soon, help the family. Dorus and Anna and Dorus's brother Vincent, Uncle Cent, will decide what Vincent should do. He could follow in his father's and grandfather's footsteps and become a pastor. Or he could follow Uncle Cent and other uncles into the art business. God or art?

They've all been thinking about Vincent's career since he was a boy. But they still don't know where he will fit best.

It's not easy.

Vincent is moody. He holds himself bent over. He's stubborn and (too) sure of himself. Anna and Dorus think he's awkward, that he doesn't present himself well. They worry that he doesn't have the right social graces to fit in—at either job. He doesn't seem well suited to the life of a pastor, where you should be even-tempered and sociable. But would he be able to maneuver in the world of art dealers and buyers?

Vincent himself doesn't have much, if any, say in the matter. He wants to please his parents and do what they think is best. But he doesn't want to leave home. He would be happy to stay in Zundert with the family, reading and walking. Very happy.

Finally, after more than a year of discussions, in the summer of 1869, Vincent's parents and uncle make a decision. With Dorus's special family prayer memorized—"O Lord, join us intimately to one another and let our love for Thee make that bond ever stronger"—Vincent is sent off into the world.

14.

ART, NOT GOD

---

*F*OUR MONTHS AFTER he turns sixteen, Vincent becomes a junior apprentice at Goupil's, Uncle Cent's firm in The Hague.

The art business, like his uncles, not the God business, like his father.

Dorus and Anna take him to The Hague and find him a room with Willem Marinus Roos and his wife, Dina Margrieta van Roos-Van Aalst. The Rooses have no children and take in boarders. They are good, simple folks who will provide Vincent with a safe place to live, food to eat, and company. But Ma and Pa encourage him to spend time with Uncle Cent, who will help him make good connections with other well-placed people in the city. They tell him good-bye and go back to Zundert and their other children.

Vincent is on his own, truly, for the first time, in a big city, with his first job.

Goupil's sells fine art and reproductions to middle-class people all over the world. Its headquarters is in Paris, where there are also two branches of the gallery. And in addition to the branch in The Hague, where Vincent will be working, there are branches in Brussels, London, and New York. The Hague gallery is furnished like the home of someone from the new wealthy middle class: with upholstered wooden furniture, fancy, well made, and ornate. Heavy draperies with brocade and tassels hang on the windows and separate the rooms; paintings in gilded frames hang close together on the walls. The ambience is meant to encourage customers to feel comfortable and to spend money; it is not at all like the tiny house in Zundert, not even the fine front room.

In this unfamiliar setting Vincent has to learn about art and how to sell it—prints, paintings, reproductions, old art, newer art, art of different styles. He has to emulate the other gallery staff as they help clients, advising people on what they should buy.

Vincent learns very quickly, absorbing more and more about art every day. He becomes an expert on what clients will (and will not) like. His bosses are happy with his progress, and he enjoys the work. He also loves the art and starts his own collection. No bugs this time: Goupil prints of traditional art by Old Masters, as well as prints and photoengravings. Photography is a new art, and Vincent will never like photographs as much as paintings, but he wants to expand his knowledge of all art.

He learns more about where he's living, too. During his off-hours, Vincent learns how to navigate the city, which is a huge change from tiny Zundert. The Hague is the seat of the Dutch monarchy. The royal family lives here, although the government is based in Amsterdam, the capital. Already a big city, The Hague's population is exploding. Newcomers keep arriving—by ship, canal boat, and stagecoach. More and more buildings are needed to accommodate them, so the city is expanding into the countryside. But fortunately for Vincent, it is still easy to get away from the congestion. He can walk about three miles to the North Sea coast and stroll on the beach and into the sand dunes. Heading inland, it is a short walk out of the city into a landscape that is reminiscent of his childhood in Zundert: fields and farms, windmills. He needs that; although he is adjusting, and doing his job well, he is often homesick and lonely.

Life at the Roos house is not enough for him. The accommodations are perfectly fine—his room is comfortable; the food, as little as it matters to him, is good. Vincent is great at making friends wherever he is, and the Rooses and the other boarders are pleasant, but they're not like his family, and they aren't intellectually stimulating.

So Vincent looks for connection and stimulation elsewhere. Through Uncle Cent he meets a family of cousins, the Haanebeeks. He spends a good deal of time at their house and becomes interested in one of their daughters, Caroline. As the months pass, his admiration for Caroline grows stronger.

Yet even with the diversion of a young lady and her family, he still is homesick. Sometimes he just wants to go home—to the parsonage, the walks on the heath. Zundert.

But a year and a half after he's left home, he gets the news that his father has been reassigned; Dorus is going to be the pastor in Helvoirt, a town not far from Tilburg, where Vincent had gone to high school. Ma and Pa and Vincent's younger sisters and brothers are moving.

The house in Zundert with the attic bedroom and the room overlooking the garden, the garden itself—none of it is theirs anymore. It's all now just memories.

15.

VINCENT AND THEO WALKING, 1872

THE SETTING: a Dutch landscape, low-lying land, a dirt road along a canal. The September sky is grey from days of rain. It is drizzling now. Two figures walk away from the city into the nearby countryside.

Vincent and Theo. Vincent is nineteen; Theo, fifteen.

We walked "through the raindrops," Vincent wrote afterward, in his very first letter to Theo.

Vincent has been living in The Hague for three years now. This is the first time his brother has visited him; Theo is just about grown up.

There is nothing to cure loneliness like family. Vincent is treasuring every minute with his brother. When he's not working at the gallery, he shows Theo around the city. The two spend days exploring together and talking, getting to know each other away from the rest of the family, becoming more than brothers.

This walk in the rain seals their friendship, deepens it. Later both brothers will refer to it as a meeting of the minds, of the time they made a pledge to each other. They will always remember this day. Theo will use the walk in arguments. So will Vincent. The brothers will come back to it again and again. It is an anchor, a promise of the future, a touchstone.

They'd left Vincent's room in the Roos house, near the center of town, and headed out to the countryside along the Trekweg road, next to an old canal. Water not only falls from above, it also lies beneath the ground they tread. Much of the land in and around The Hague is polder, land reclaimed from the sea with dams and dikes. Polder is in constant danger of flooding, and of disappearing back into the sea. Windmills power pumps that drain the water so the land is not swallowed up. The land has to be solid enough to build on.

It doesn't take long for the brothers to get out of the city and breathe clean country air, Zundert-like air. Walking through the raindrops, they talk about their futures, separately and together.

Theo is still in high school, four miles from his parents' house. He walks there and back every day, no matter the weather. He likes his classes in French, German, English, and math. But he's not a great student. Dorus is not impressed by his progress, and since there are fees to pay, he thinks Theo should leave school at the end of the year and go to work. Having Theo contribute to the family funds would be a big help.

What work will Theo do? Will he follow in Vincent's footsteps? The brothers talk about Theo's career, about Vincent's.

"Both you and I thought then about becoming painters, but so deeply that we didn't dare to say it straight out then, even to each other," Vincent will write later.

Did Theo really want to become an artist? Perhaps this is Vincent looking back through his own painter's eyes, thinking they both wanted the same thing. They do talk about art and how much they love it. They talk about life and love. Vincent is in love with Caroline Haanebeek, though she does not return his feelings. She is in love with another man. During this visit Vincent will bring Theo to a party where they will see the

Haanebeeks, including Caroline and her beau, and also her younger sister, Annet.

But now, on the walk, it's only Vincent and Theo. The brothers arrive at a polder windmill in Rijswijk just as the rain stops. They see a sign in the window of the mill: milk for sale, one cent a glass, and also fried eels.

Vincent and Theo each buy a glass of milk. No eels.

They drink their milk and make a pledge to each other.

They promise to always be close, to keep the bond between them strong and intimate. They always will walk together. They will be more than brothers, more than friends. They will be companions in the search for meaning in life and meaning in art. Together they will achieve lives filled with a purpose. And they will, when needed, carry each other's parcels.

When Theo returns home, he will write Vincent a thank-you note for the visit. Vincent will write back to say how much he misses his brother. "It was strange for me not to find you when I came home in the afternoon."

Those letters begin their lifelong correspondence.

Except for Vincent's last hours alive, this walk through the raindrops to the windmill will be the brothers' least complicated time together. Vincent will paint this mill years later, at a time when he is scared of losing Theo. But now there is no fear, only closeness. So let's stay here for a while and enjoy the scene:

Vincent and Theo, nineteen and fifteen, outside the mill, standing together, talking. The milk is fresh, the rain has stopped, the ground beneath them is solid.

Dangers

1873–1875

*The years between 20 and 30 are full of
all sorts of dangers, full of great danger, yea,
the danger of sin and death.*

—Vincent to Theo, early September 1876

16.

PASSIONATE SEAS

---

*But precisely because love is so strong, we are,
especially in our youth (I mean now, 17, 18, 20 years old),
usually not strong enough to maintain a straight course.*

—Vincent to Theo, November 12, 1881

PA HAS WITHDRAWN THEO from high school. He will be following in Vincent's footsteps and working at Goupil's. Uncle Cent has arranged it. But Theo won't be moving to The Hague to work with Vincent. He's been assigned to work at the Goupil branch in Brussels, Belgium.

Although Vincent would have liked Theo closer, he is thrilled that they are now officially on the same path. "My dear Theo," he writes in his second letter to his brother with what will become his standard salutation. "That was good news that I just read in Pa's letter. My hearty congratulations." It's a short letter, with a promise of many more. "We must correspond often," he says.

Theo starts work in January 1873, the youngest salesman at the Brussels branch; he won't turn sixteen for four months. Like The Hague, Brussels is a big city, its population exploding, too. It's a promising place to start a career in art dealing. The economy is strong, and people are willing to spend money: there are more than thirty galleries in a city where art is revered and has had a long, magnificent history. As good a placement as it is, Theo, still a real country boy, finds the city overwhelming.

Anna and Dorus tell him, "Be brave. You have now taken the first steps which may lead to an independent life, should God give you his blessing."

And Vincent, now almost twenty, enthusiastically takes on the role of sage older brother and mentor. He will give Theo the benefit of his experience and his life wisdom. But he also wants to learn *from* and *with* Theo. They should always share their opinions about the paintings and drawings they see, he writes. From The Hague to Brussels, he puts his arm around his younger brother and says, Let's do this together. Theo agrees; their walk to the mill will continue, even at a distance.

PA AND MA watch both sons closely, giving advice and intervening when they have to. Back in North Brabant, a notice arrives that Vincent has been drafted for peacetime military service. For him to be exempt Pa has to pay 625 guilders for a replacement—another man will join the army in his place. Considering that Dorus makes a little over a thousand guilders a year, it's a huge expense for the Van Gogh family, one Dorus will later incur for Theo and Cor as well.

But Pa can't fix everything, can't save Vincent from every danger, every hurt.

Although work is going well, Vincent's personal life is not. He is heartsick.

Caroline Haanebeek is marrying. Vincent doesn't confide his heartbreak to anyone, but he hints at his sadness to Theo, couching it in advice that Pa gave to him and he is now passing along: "Theo, I must again recommend that you start smoking a pipe. It does you a lot of good when you're out of spirits, as I quite often am nowadays."

Uncle Cent notices something is wrong with Vincent, and so do Ma and Pa, even from afar. He is withdrawn, remote, sullen. It starts to show at work. Ma and Pa think he should socialize more, make more profitable connections. The only connection he wants is with Caroline.

He does try to help himself: he spends time with the other boarders at the Roos house, and he reads and takes long walks, as always. He tells Theo, "It's cold here, and people are already skating on the flooded fields. I go walking as much as I can."

But as Caroline's wedding approaches—she is to be married April 30, 1873—Vincent is more and more swamped by his sadness. He feels unmoored from himself, from home—and from his parents' values.

For the first time he realizes that his father doesn't know everything, that not all his parents say is indisputable. In a great break from what he learned at 26 Markt, in a potentially cataclysmic departure from his parents' beliefs, he tells his fellow boarders that he is an atheist.

Then he does something else that goes against his parents' values. We can't paint a complete picture because he doesn't, but Vincent has gotten into trouble, and he needs help. Has he rejected everything from the parsonage in Zundert? When he gave up God, did he also give up the strict morality he learned at home? Or is he just a young man with needs and no other way to satisfy them?

There's a neighborhood in The Hague with many brothels, where it's common for young unmarried men to visit prostitutes. Perhaps Vincent is short of money because he paid too many prostitutes. Maybe he caught a disease. Something . . . he has done something. Although his own father had some youthful "experiences," Vincent is sure he can't go to him or his mother, or to Uncle Cent or another uncle in the art business, Cornelis van

Gogh. He is scared of their judgment, their wrath. So he seeks out the advice of his boss at Goupil's, Hermanus Gijsbertus Tersteeg.

H. G. Tersteeg is only eight years older than Vincent, and they are very friendly. Tersteeg is settled down—married, with a baby girl, Betsy, whom Vincent adores. But when Vincent asks for advice, Tersteeg gets very angry with him.

Vincent immediately regrets confiding in him and worries that his boss will tell Uncle Cent and that Ma and Pa will find out. He will write to Theo a few years later that at this time a fear swept over him, that he was terrified of his family. He has gone from being the obedient firstborn son to being scared of his own parents.

He is right to be afraid. Tersteeg does betray his confidence, and when the news of his indiscretion gets back to his family, Ma and Pa are horrified. Furious. On a visit home Pa lectures him against sin and sends him back to The Hague with religious missives to read. But Vincent isn't repentant. When he returns to the Roos house, one of the boarders will later report, he takes a pamphlet and burns it, throwing it page by page into the fire.

Uncle Cent and the other directors of Goupil's decide that Vincent must leave The Hague. Vincent writes to Theo, "You'll have heard that I'm going to London, and probably very soon. I do hope we'll be able to see each other before then."

The new job in London is not in a gallery; it's a stockroom that supplies stores with wholesale reproductions of popular and famous paintings. It will broaden his experience in some ways, but it will also curtail his contact with clients. He hasn't been doing so well with them lately.

"I'm only just noticing how attached I am to The Hague," Vincent writes to Theo, "now that it's been decided I must go away. Still, it can't be helped, and I intend not to take things too hard. I think it's wonderful for my English, which I understand well, though I don't speak it nearly as well as I'd like."

Theo was first to go live in a new country, but Belgium is right next door to the Netherlands and most people there speak Dutch. England is across the North Sea, so Vincent will have to make part of the journey by boat. And he will be living in a different culture, speaking a new language. But with Theo he puts up a good front, acting as though his own boat isn't about to flood.

17.

A TOP HAT, A STEAM TRAIN, LONDON

---

*O*N HIS WAY from the Netherlands to London, Vincent stops in Paris. He sees beautiful paintings at the Louvre, at the Musée du Luxembourg, and at the Salon, the French Academy's annual exhibition of "living masters" of the current art world. But not of all the current art world. The academy has chosen to ignore several independent artists who paint in a different style. The art establishment finds these artists too avant-garde in their use of light, a bright palette, visible brushstrokes, unusual composition, and strange angles. The art establishment also objects to "the new painting" for what the artists paint: contemporary subjects such as train stations, cafés, bridges. These independent artists will hold their first exhibition in 1874, and eventually they will be called Impressionists, after Claude Monet's painting *Impression, Sunrise*. So in May 1873, Vincent does not see these modern paintings, and will not for many years. He has no idea what he's missing.

WHEN HE ARRIVES IN ENGLAND, Vincent buys a top hat. "You cannot be in London without one," Pa tells Theo, relieved that Vincent is out of The Hague, starting over. A letter from Mr. and Mrs. Roos praising Vincent makes Ma and Pa happy. They worry about him all the time now—about his moods, his appearance, his lack of social graces. So a nice word from the Rooses about Vincent's time boarding with them means a lot to Anna and Dorus, and gives them hope that Vincent will be all right.

Even though he was reluctant to come, Vincent loves his new city. At first he lives on the outskirts, and takes a little steam train into town every day to go to Goupil's at 17 Southampton Street, in central London, near the Strand and Covent Garden, just a short walk from the Thames River.

He spends his first months learning all about English art. There's a lot he doesn't know, but studying art makes Vincent happy. And he is fine with the new job, even though it's just a stockroom. For one thing, his hours aren't as long as they were in The Hague. He's finished at six o'clock, which leaves him time to do what he loves: read, write letters, and take long walks.

At the end of the summer Vincent moves closer to work, to a boarding-house on Hackford Road, Brixton, in south London, where he lodges with a mother and daughter. Ursula Loyer, and her daughter, Eugenie, who at nineteen is a year younger than Vincent, run a school for little boys next door to their house.

Now he can walk to work, about an hour each way, forty-five minutes if he walks very fast. His route takes him through the streets of south London up to the Thames, along the river until he crosses it to get into central London and to Goupil's.

London is damp, misty, grey. The streets are filled with horse poop, the atmosphere smoky. But Vincent loves London; he finds it charming, picturesque. The city's range of colors, its palette, is similar to that of the Netherlands. He rows on the Thames with two Englishmen and reports to Theo, "It was glorious."

For now, at least, he is distracted enough not to be heartsick. Leaving The Hague, leaving Caroline, seems to have been a good move. For him, and also for Theo.

18.

IN HIS BROTHER'S FOOTSTEPS

THEO HAS DONE VERY WELL at Goupil's in Brussels. He learned fast, impressing his bosses. He is a good salesman, and when his bosses gave him some managerial duties, he proved to be good at those as well. Ma and Pa are very proud and hope that soon he'll be able to completely support himself. Maybe he can even help with the family budget.

Like Vincent, he has spent much of his free time taking long walks into the countryside outside the city, past fields of wheat, inhaling the familiar aromas of hay and potatoes. He's comforted to be reminded of home.

Now, after only ten months in Brussels, he is going back to his homeland. He is being sent to work in Vincent's old branch in The Hague.

Theo moves into the Roos house, just as Vincent had, and he takes long walks into the polder, just as he and Vincent had two years earlier when they walked to the windmill. He acclimates quickly to the work at this Goupil branch.

And just as Vincent had, Theo starts spending time with the Haanebeek family. Ma and Pa have suggested it, not knowing, of course, that spending time there was not all happiness for Vincent. The Haanebeeks will be a good influence on Theo, they think, as he makes his way into the society of The Hague. They are perhaps even more wily than that, hoping for a match. Vincent also suggests that Theo visit the Haanebeeks, in fact, but for his own reasons—he is eager for news of Caroline. And he wants Theo to tell *them* about *him*, about how well he's doing in London. Theo visits the family every week, and just as Vincent had done, he falls for one of the Haanebeek daughters—Caroline's younger sister, Annet.

By the time Theo turns seventeen on May 1, 1874, he is deeply in love with her. Vincent approves. He tells Theo to read a book he just read, and loves, *L'amour* by Jules Michelet. It is essentially a guide to women and love. "The Family rests upon Love, and Society upon the family. Hence Love goes before everything," Michelet declares in the introduction.

Theo reads the book, and he and Vincent write back and forth about it. "A book like that at least teaches one to see that there's a lot more to love than people usually think," Vincent writes.

Vincent is a romantic. So is Theo. But just as Caroline had not returned Vincent's love, Annet does not return Theo's.

Still Theo keeps going to see her.

Vincent encourages him in his passion because, he tells him, "a woman and a man can become *one*, that is, *one whole* and not two halves, that I believe."

19.

VINCENT AT TWENTY-ONE:
A PORTRAIT

I gave up on a girl and she married someone else, and I went far away from her and kept her in my thoughts anyway. Fatal.

—Vincent to Theo, November 12, 1881

VINCENT CROSSES WESTMINSTER BRIDGE every morning and evening, enjoying "when the sun's setting behind Westminster Abbey and the Houses of Parliament, and what it's like early in the morning," and as the year ends, "in the winter with snow and fog." London's air is, on many days, pea-soup thick, the coal smoke from factories mixing with fog. The word *smog* won't be coined until early the next century, but the air is so toxic that hundreds of Londoners die from bronchitis the year Vincent arrives.

In this dreary winter weather, Vincent becomes sad and lonely. He misses Caroline terribly, and romanticizes her as the ideal woman. He writes her letters and sends her photographs of artwork for her scrapbook. He even sends her and her husband a passage from *L'amour*'s "Autumnal Aspirations" about a beautiful woman never forgotten. Michelet argues that a woman can only be truly happy if she's married—and to the right man. It should be a vigorous love, an active love, a divine union.

Vincent asks Theo repeatedly about Caroline and all the Haanebeeks, but Theo doesn't realize why. Vincent is miserable, lonely, and humiliated in his heartache.

His family can see his mood darkening off and on, and they wonder what is wrong. Later they will decide that Vincent had been in love with his landlady's daughter, Eugenie. The error will be perpetuated for decades in books and even a movie. But it was a misunderstanding, though unintentional, like a painting erroneously attributed to a master.

Vincent *is* very fond of Ursula and Eugenie Loyer, in some ways too fond. Just as he idealizes Caroline, he paints the Loyers as the perfect mother and daughter. He sees them through a lens of homesickness, through his memories of Zundert and the closeness of 26 Markt. Maybe he even wishes he had a closer relationship with his mother and father now, like the one he used to have, or wishes Ursula were his mother, too. But it is not a romantic love for Eugenie. His heart still longs for Caroline.

And something else is wrong with Vincent. Something inherited, he thinks. Vincent knows there are members of the family who suffer from melancholia, from mood swings, extreme behavior, eccentricities. He's always been *different*. Even odd. Now, as a young man, he fears he is suffering from some kind of problem in his mind. Vincent is right. He has inherited something. We can't go back in time and diagnose him, but from here it looks like a form of epilepsy or, most likely, the beginnings of bipolar disorder, which is also known as manic depression.

So there cannot be just one portrait of Vincent at twenty-one. He has mood swings: he is very sad some days, low, tired, angry. Other days he's full of energy, ideas, vigor, hope.

One portrait of Vincent at twenty-one: dark colors, dark shadows, lethargy, pessimism.

Another portrait: Vincent in sunlight with Passion! Energy! Fascinations!

At this time there is little understanding of mental illness. Sigmund Freud, who will make advances in its study and treatment, is three years younger than Vincent. There is no medicine to treat his condition, and people know little, if anything, about what helps and what hurts. So Vincent unknowingly makes it worse. He eats too little for the amount he walks. He doesn't sleep enough. He smokes tobacco.

He misses Theo and doesn't have anyone close right now. No woman, no friend, nobody to help steady his moods. And he is so far away from his family. But that might change. Vincent's sister Anna is thinking of coming to London to work. Perhaps having her nearby will help.

20.

TURBULENCE

VINCENT IS NOT CLOSE to Anna the way he is to Theo. But, he writes to Caroline, he hopes that he'll get to know his sister better.

Early summer 1874, Vincent goes home to the Netherlands. He sees Theo and the rest of the family, and he brings Anna back to London with him. She moves into another room at the Loyers'.

Vincent shows his sister art and takes her around London. Every day the two of them look in the newspaper to find her a job. "Anna is managing well," he writes to Theo. "We go on wonderful walks together." Having Anna with him does Vincent good. She makes sure he eats better, and he feels good being her mentor. She's not Theo, but she's family.

At the end of the summer they move out of the Loyer house, and soon after that, Anna finds a teaching job and moves thirty miles north of London. They'll still see each other more often than if she lived back in the Netherlands, but it's not the same. Ma worries that Vincent won't eat enough now that Anna is gone. She's right to worry. When Anna sees him next, her reports back home are not encouraging. It's not just his physical appearance: he's sadder, less friendly.

Reports from Goupil's aren't good either. Vincent is moody and erratic, and not doing well at his job. At the end of October, his bosses send him to Paris for two months, during which time he doesn't write home at all. Ma and Pa have no idea how he is. When he comes back to London, he goes to work in a new gallery that Goupil's has bought. But he's still not happy. He's apathetic. Cranky. Melancholy. Dark. Blurry. Depressed.

Anna goes to see him; they fight, and both feel miserable. Anna writes to Theo that Vincent "has illusions about people and judges people before he knows them, and then when he finds out what they're really like and they don't live up to the opinion he formed of them prematurely, he's so disappointed that he throws them away like a bouquet of wilted flowers. . . . I'm very sorry that I visited him."

Vincent turns twenty-two on March 30, 1875, and in early May he's sent back to Paris to work at the Goupil headquarters. Rather than a promotion, the move seems like an attempt by Uncle Cent to salvage Vincent's plummeting art-dealing career.

21.

BROTHERS TWICE OVER

VINCENT DOESN'T WANT TO TALK about the bad visit with Anna. He will another time, he tells Theo, but for now "I hope and believe I'm not what many think me to be at present. . . . People will probably say the same about you in a couple of years; at least if you continue to be what you are: my brother in two senses of the word."

Two brothers in love with two sisters.

Unrequited love.

Theo is in love with Annet. But Theo's misery is incurable. Unless love can bridge the other world with this one, there is no chance for Theo and Annet because Annet is fatally ill.

Life is perilous in the nineteenth century. Many people don't live past their forties. (Antibiotics won't be discovered until the next century.) Both Vincent and Theo are acutely aware of the dangers.

"HOW IS THE PATIENT?" Vincent asks Theo. "I'd already heard from Pa that she was ill, but I didn't know that it was as bad as you said. Write to me about this soon, if you will."

Their sister Lies writes to Theo that Annet is "still so young to have to die. Gosh, it would cost me a lot if already now I had to part from a world where there is so much to be enjoyed."

Poor Theo is already in mourning. A close friend and housemate at the Rooses', Johannes Wilhelmus Weehuizen, died suddenly after being sick for only a few days. Theo had spent a lot of time with him before his illness, talking about Michelet's *L'amour*, which his friend had also read. "He thought it so beautiful," Theo tells Vincent. Theo wasn't with him when he died, and he feels terribly guilty about that.

Then on June 14, 1875, Annet dies.

Theo is bereft.

Vincent writes the very next day with sympathy, and assurance that Annet will be with Theo always. He won't ever forget her, or the tragedy of her death. Alluding to their beloved Michelet's lost love, Vincent writes, "She stayed with me 30 years, returning to me incessantly."

Vincent tells Theo to leave The Hague. Too many memories. Dorus advises him not to spend so much time at the Haanebeek house. He should go out, his father says, spend time with other people. Being sad for too long could cause lasting damage, he says. "Giving in to melancholy is not conducive to the generation of energy." He tells Theo that young people are supposed to be "happy and jolly."

Then, three months after Annet's death, another of Theo's housemates, Willem Laurens Kiehl, dies suddenly.

"We are hard hit by the news of Kiehl's death," Pa writes. "I can imagine that you're very conscious of it and feel it deeply. . . . Dying pathetically. So young."

Theo is devastated. Pa tells him to pray. It will give him strength. He also tries to console him with religious precepts, reminding him that every life has its "trials and tribulations."

But Theo finds no solace in religion. None at all.

Brothers twice over, yes, in some ways, but not in every way. Certainly not in their feelings for art and God.

In Paris, Vincent has done a complete turnaround from his days in The Hague as an atheist. He has lost all passion for the art business and has replaced it with a religious fanaticism unlike anything they had learned as boys in Zundert. Quotes from the Bible and religious precepts have been creeping into his letters to Theo. There is no explanation for this change. And now, after this last death, he writes Theo a letter *filled* with quotes from the Bible. He tries to persuade Theo to turn to God for strength. "Let us trust in God with all our heart and lean not unto our own understanding."

But Theo does not turn to God. He tries to heal himself by reading poetry and working hard. He fails, and he falls into a deep depression.

"Be careful, old boy," Vincent tells his brother. "Don't lose your resilience."

Missteps, Stumbles

1875–1879

After all, we're in the midst of life—
well then, we must fight a good fight—
and we must become men.

—Vincent to Theo, May 31, 1877

22.

THE ROSE AND THE THORN

VINCENT TRIES TO BUOY Theo's spirits from afar. He writes from Paris, giving him all kinds of advice: don't go out if you don't want to. Though Vincent himself never eats enough, he tells Theo to eat bread; it's the staff of life. And in a real departure: give away all your books except the Bible. Even *L'amour* by Michelet!

He wishes Theo were closer so they could "breakfast together or drink a cup of chocolate in my room."

Vincent writes many letters to Theo, day after day, mailing them in yellow envelopes. He is generous with advice (Have you tried it yet? Eating bread?) and consolation. He ends his letters warmly, "I shake your hand heartily in thought," and "Your most loving brother." But he's also overly generous with Bible quotes, sometimes whole letters of just Bible quotes, which are of no interest to Theo.

Though Theo is in terrible shape, Ma and Pa are more concerned about Vincent. Theo's sadness seems justified, caused by real tragedies. But Vincent's newfound religious zeal really worries them.

Their worry turns to anger when they find out that Vincent is neglecting his work at Goupil's. As he was in London, he is in Paris, unenthusiastic, apathetic.

They complain about him to Theo, calling him "eccentric" and "strange." Vincent should be working harder; he should be more normal.

Then Theo has another setback. He stumbles and falls on an icy street in The Hague and badly hurts his foot. What more can poor Theo endure? Vincent writes to him as soon as he finds out. He wishes he could be close by to do something for his brother. He will come home for Christmas and hopes Theo will, too. He writes to him, begging Theo to let him know how his foot is, what the doctor says. And he sends him some chocolate. "The packages of chocolate marked X are for you, the other two are for Mrs. Roos." Vincent also sends chocolate—and art prints—to his sisters Anna and Wil, who are living in England and won't be home for Christmas.

THOSE MEMBERS OF THE FAMILY who do gather together for Christmas— Ma and Pa, Vincent and Theo, Lies and Cor—have a good time. But Theo leaves to go back to work before Vincent, and at New Year's Vincent confides in his parents that he might quit his job.

Pa thinks Vincent should stay at Goupil's for a while longer, and resign in a few months. Vincent also talks to Pa's brother Cornelis, because he is in the art business but doesn't work for Goupil's. Uncle Cor agrees. So Vincent heads back to Paris determined to tough it out for a while longer.

"You can imagine that we are very anxious," Pa tells Theo. "There is always something strange about him, despite his many good points."

WHEN HE GETS BACK TO PARIS, Vincent walks into his boss's office. Hello, he tells his boss. Happy New Year! But his boss does not respond in kind.

He's furious that Vincent has been gone so long. He'd told him not to take so much time off! Christmas and New Year's is a busy time for art galleries! He had been needed!

The conversation goes from bad to worse.

Vincent is fired. His boss tells Vincent he can stay on until April 1, but then he'll have to leave.

Vincent writes to Pa with the news, and Pa says to apologize. Vincent does. But his boss doesn't relent. Vincent will be out of a job in a few months.

Vincent's not entirely sorry. It seems to him now that selling art is not the way to give something to the world, to make a difference. God is. Teaching, preaching the gospel. God, not art.

WHEN HIS JOB at Goupil's ends, Vincent goes home to the Netherlands, to Etten, where his parents are now living. (Pa had been transferred again.) Vincent won't be there for long. He has found a new job, not in Paris or the Netherlands, not in art or preaching, but in teaching, at a boys' boarding school run by a minister on the eastern coast of England.

When Pa and Cor, the youngest Van Gogh, take Vincent to the depot for the four o'clock train, parting is difficult again.

"Through the small window I saw Pa and little brother in the road, watching the train leave."

Ma and Pa have trouble saying good-bye, too. They are worried about what will become of their firstborn.

"And now we picture him in our minds at his destination," Ma tells Theo, "and long to hear how he was received. We have good memories of his stay here, and now just hope that God will help him find something that is right for him. We felt pity for him when he left, going alone into the wide world. We think of him with melancholy."

Vincent's life is as unpredictable as his eccentricities. To his parents it's as if he is deliberately wearing a crown of thorns, giving himself pain.

But how happy they are that Theo takes pleasures in *his* work, Pa says. On Theo's nineteenth birthday, Dorus writes that they think of him as their crown, their honor, their pride and joy. They let their worries about his last traumatic year fade as their faith in his future blossoms, like a halo of roses on his head:

"When you were baptized you were adorned with the first May rose to bloom in Zundert. The christening gown which was decorated with the tiny rose no longer fits you and the rose is long since wilted; nevertheless it remains a symbol of the great charm and great affability which may, we pray be qualities granted to you in life."

It's as though the image of the first baby Vincent emerges from under Vincent's, a pentimento uncovered, and in their parents' eyes the portrait of that hoped-for "good boy" melds with Theo's.

And thus Anna and Dorus transfer their hopes to Theo, the second-born son.

23.

VINCENT WALKING, II

---

*He walks great distances for many hours and I fear that
his appearance will suffer and that he will become
even less presentable.*

—Pa to Theo, July 1, 1876

ᐁINCENT IS TWENTY-THREE. He's moved to Ramsgate, England, a seaside town on the far east coast of England, south of Margate, north of Sandwich, near where the North Sea meets the Strait of Dover. He loves living near the water, near the harbor "full of all kinds of ships, closed in by stone jetties running into the sea on which one can walk," he writes to Theo when he first arrives. "And further out one sees the sea in its natural state, and that's beautiful. Yesterday everything was grey."

He watches the ocean in a storm and paints the scene in a letter to Theo: "The sea was yellowish, especially close to the beach; a streak of light on the horizon and, above this, tremendously huge dark grey clouds from which one saw the rain coming down in slanting streaks."

While teaching at Mr. William Port Stokes's school, Vincent identifies with the young boys, which makes him miss his childhood, his home. He remembers the garden in Zundert as he builds a sand castle on the beach with the boys. He worries that Mr. Stokes is too hard on his pupils, withholding their food and drink in the evening if they've been too boisterous.

And he looks on with empathy as the boys watch their parents going back to the train station after a visit, just as he did on the steps of Mr. Provily's school, watching the yellow carriage fade away.

Not able to give up art entirely, he creates it himself. When he first moved to London, he made a book of drawings for Tersteeg's little girl, Betsy, back in The Hague. (He didn't hold a grudge against his old boss.) Now he makes one of the first of many drawings and sketches he will send to Theo in a letter. With pen and ink, he draws the boys' view from the school: a winding road, with a streetlamp on the right, and a little park beyond that, a building at the far end on the left, and beyond it all the sea, with boats on the water. "Many a boy will never forget that view from the window."

He describes for Theo the view from his own room, too, looking out on Spencer Square: "I looked out of the window of my room onto the roofs of the houses one sees from there and the tops of the elms, dark against the night sky. Above those roofs, one single star, but a nice, big friendly one. And I thought of us all, and I thought of the years of my life that had already passed, and of our home, and the words and feeling came to me, 'Keep me from being a son that causeth shame.'"

Quoting Proverbs to Theo, he admits he does not want to disgrace their parents. He knows they worry. He knows, and he's trying. He takes a very long walk.

VINCENT WALKS FROM RAMSGATE to London. It's a journey of seventy-five miles, and it's a quest, and a pilgrimage. He is looking for work with the church. He knows Dorus doesn't approve of these long walks, and it is quite hot out, but he's making so little money, there's no other way to get to London.

He walks and walks, in the hot June sun, and well into the warm evening. He arrives in Canterbury, and then walks a little more. As the sun sets, he goes to sleep next to a pond, under beech and elm trees. The birds wake him at three in the morning, and so he continues his journey. In the afternoon he arrives in Chatham, and through the grey fog he can see the ships on the river Thames. He's about halfway to London.

He gets a ride on a horse-drawn cart for a little while, but when the driver stops at an inn, Vincent walks on. He doesn't want to wait, and he has no money to buy food, anyway. On and on he treads, through the suburbs and finally into the city.

He stays for two days with the parents of a friend from his Paris days and looks for work. He writes to a London preacher whose church he'd attended when he lived in London. "A clergyman's son," he writes, "who, because he must work to earn a living, has no money and no time to study . . . would, in spite of everything, dearly like to find a situation connected with the church." He knows it's a long shot since he has no training, but he hopes his experiences—traveling, living in other countries, working in a gallery and doing manual labor, knowing different kinds of people (religious and not)—will help him find a post. And he speaks Dutch, French, English, and German.

He ends the letter with a plea: "I am asking you for a recommendation in my search for a situation, and to keep a fatherly eye on me should I find such a situation."

Vincent does find a new job, at a school near London run by Reverend Thomas Slade-Jones. He will teach and preach some, but much of his time will be spent running errands, collecting money from the students' parents. Ma and Pa don't like the sound of this. They don't like the way he seems, worrying to Theo that Vincent is "exaggerated and overwrought, quoting at random from the Bible. . . . It is a bitter, bitter shame."

But Theo is worried about himself.

24.

LET THERE BE LIGHT

THEO HAS DONE SOMETHING "BAD" in The Hague, just like his big brother. He confesses to Vincent.

Vincent writes, "Don't worry about your wanton life, as you call it, just go quietly on your way. You're purer than I, and will probably get there sooner and better."

What did Theo do? Putting himself back together after the deaths of Annet and his two friends, and his foot injury, he likely sought solace and comfort—not in religion but in prostitutes. Three months after his confession to his brother, Theo falls seriously ill. He's weak and runs a fever off and on. It's not just a cold; he doesn't get better. It could be serious. Vincent is worried. "How much I'd like to be with you, my boy," Vincent writes. "Oh why are we all so far apart? But what shall we do about it?"

Ma and Pa are concerned, too, and close enough to do something: they take turns going to The Hague to nurse him. Vincent offers to come while Ma is there. "Besides wanting so much to sit at Theo's bedside, I should also like so very much to talk to my Mother, and if possible to go to Etten once more to see and speak to my Father again. It would be but a short visit, I could stay with you one or two days."

Let me come home.

But Ma tells him no. Do not come home. They will see each other in a few months, at Christmastime back in Etten.

Is she thinking of Vincent, and how hard it would be to make such a long trip for such a short time? Is she trying to protect Theo from Vincent? Or is she thinking about herself, not wanting to worry about two sons at once, and not wanting the complication of Vincent?

Vincent doesn't force the issue; he stays in England and focuses on God. In God there is comfort and solace. And light.

A few weeks later Vincent gives his first public sermon. He loves the experience. "When I stood in the pulpit I felt like someone emerging from a dark, underground vault into the friendly daylight," he tells Theo, "and it's a wonderful thought that from now on, wherever I go, I'll be preaching the gospel. . . . God says, Let there be light: and there is light."

Back in the Netherlands there is light, too. Theo has taken a turn for the better.

Ma and Pa bring him home to Etten to finish his recovery there. It's good to be able to help a son.

25.

DOING WHAT IS RIGHT

————————————

VINCENT DOES GO to the Netherlands for Christmas, and while he's there, Ma and Pa persuade him not to go back to England. Why should he? His job is mostly collecting school fees from parents. If he really wants to focus on God, he can do so closer to home. When he agrees, Uncle Cent finds him a job in Dordrecht, a town eighty-six miles from Pa and Ma in Etten and, even better for Vincent, only about thirty miles from Theo in The Hague.

In January 1877, Vincent begins work at Blussé & Van Braam, a shop that sells books, magazines, office supplies, maps, and prints, including re-productions of famous paintings produced by Goupil's. Vincent is a jack of all trades: he supervises shipments, keeps the account books, runs errands, and does whatever other odd jobs need doing. He starts at eight in the morning and doesn't get back to his lodgings until late—often one o'clock the next morning. He's not particularly good at some parts of his job (like keeping the books), and his heart isn't in it—it's with God and the Bible. But he needs to make money and he likes being busy.

He also likes his room and the view from his window: gardens with pine trees and poplars, and a large old house covered with ivy. Vincent lives with three other boarders, including his roommate, schoolteacher Paulus Coenraad Görlitz. Fifteen years later, in response to an article about Vincent, Görlitz will write a letter with a picture of Vincent at this time.

Görlitz's Portrait of Vincent

VINCENT SOMETIMES COMES HOME EARLY, around nine o'clock. When he does, he lights his pipe and reads his Bible. Görlitz watches as Vincent copies out passages to learn them by heart. Vincent also writes religious essays.

Görlitz likes Vincent but thinks he is ugly. Yet as soon as Vincent talks about religion—or art—his face lights up, his eyes sparkle. Then Vincent's face is no longer ugly to Görlitz.

After about a month living together, Vincent asks Görlitz if he can decorate their room with Bible pictures. Görlitz says yes, and under each picture of Jesus, Vincent writes, "Ever sorrowful, but always rejoicing," which is exactly how Görlitz sees Vincent.

Sometimes Vincent reads the Bible aloud to the other boarders. Görlitz enjoys it, but the youngest housemate laughs at him. Vincent doesn't care. He believes reading the Bible is the right thing to do.

At mealtimes, Görlitz and the other two boarders eat like famished wolves, but Vincent eats very little and refuses meat. "Vegetable food is sufficient, all the rest is luxury," he says. On Sundays his landlady urges him over and over again to eat some meat, so he eats a little. To Görlitz it looks like "four potatoes with a suspicion of gravy and a mouthful of vegetables."

Although Vincent cares little about food for himself, one Saturday afternoon, out walking with Görlitz, Vincent sees a starving dog. He has hardly any money left for the rest of the month, but he uses most of it to buy some rolls for the dog. He feeds it, but when he sees the dog is still hungry, he goes back into the bakery and empties his pockets to buy more bread for the dog. He has nothing left to buy tobacco for his pipe, the only luxury he allows himself.

DURING THIS TIME, Vincent learns that one of their old neighbors in Zundert is dying. He borrows money from Görlitz to go back and see him. He takes the train and then travels ten miles in the dark on foot. As Vincent walks on the familiar heath, stars poke out from behind the clouds, lighting his way. He passes the old house on Markt and stops in the cemetery where the first baby Vincent lies.

As he stands at the grave, he thinks of his father, and how hard it must have been to lose his firstborn son. Later that year Tersteeg will lose a three-month-old infant, and Vincent will write to him about his father's loss. He contemplates the "bond that never lets go of us, not even when we suffer the most, the bond of God's love." For Vincent, God is ever present, guiding him in all ways, helping him do what is right.

When Vincent arrives at the neighbor's house, the man has already died. Vincent stays and prays with the family. Görlitz is sad for him when he hears Vincent went all that way only to find the man had died. But Vincent reassures Görlitz that visiting with the family was the right thing to do.

SOON AFTER THAT WALK, Theo comes to visit, with big news: he's in love. And this time, unlike with Annet, the woman loves him back. But Theo knows Ma and Pa will not approve of her: she's lower class and has a child. Vincent, though, is happy for Theo, and especially pleased that Theo has shared this news with him. We should have as "few secrets as possible," he writes. "We're brothers, after all."

Coming home from work a few nights later, through the still quiet of snow falling, the only sound the watchman with his rattle, calling out the hour, Vincent thinks of Theo. As he walks through the snowflakes, he reflects on how lucky they are to have been blessed by God to have each other, "two brothers who slept together for so long in the little upstairs room in their parents' house."

But when those parents find out Theo's secret, they're distraught. For once it is Theo who gets Ma's wrath. She tells him that he can't stay with this woman, that he's still getting over the loss of Annet and his friends, and that he's acting rashly. As Job from the Bible was tested and lost everything, Theo will be tested. Ma says he will lose everything, too. He will be brought down by the woman, both in society and maybe in his own health. Ma is right to worry about the latter: Theo is not strong; his body is vulnerable. If he hasn't already caught something . . .

Ma tells him he has to do *what is right*.

A rift between Theo and their parents would be terrible, so Vincent, surprisingly, takes his parents' side. He hopes his brother will see his own way to the solution, but he should remember that their father loves him more than this woman does. "Your heart will need to trust itself and to pour forth—you'll be torn between the two."

Theo *is* torn. The family prayer binds him to his parents, but what if a person no longer believes in prayer? Theo *does* believe in family, but he is lonely. He doesn't know if he will do what his parents think is right.

26.

APPEARANCES

---

*We have improved his appearance a little bit
with the help of the best tailor in Breda.*

—Pa to Theo, May 7, 1877

AFTER ONLY A FEW MONTHS, Vincent quits his job, moves out of the room he shares with Görlitz, and goes home. He wants to focus completely on God. He's decided to go to theology school in Amsterdam. He's twenty-four.

In Amsterdam, he'll stay with another of his father's brothers, Jan, the director of the naval dockyard. Dorus and Anna hope and pray that being a preacher is the answer for him, but they are not happy they have to pay for this school. Self-sufficiency does not seem to be anywhere in Vincent's near future. Still, they do spend money on new clothes for him— appearances matter. And since Vincent will be stopping in The Hague on the way to Amsterdam, they ask Theo to help with Vincent's appearance, too.

"Would you be so kind as to do another work of mercy and have his hair metamorphosed by a clever barber—here in Etten we don't have such people. I suppose a Hague hairdresser might be able to do something about it, therefore coax him into coming with you to one."

Pa also asks Theo to make sure Vincent sees various people in The Hague, including his old boss, Tersteeg, and a man named Anton Mauve. Mauve is a relative—he's married to Vincent and Theo's cousin Jet. Mauve is fifteen years older than Vincent and a well-known painter, a member of the Hague school of artists. They paint in a realistic style using somber colors—browns, greys, dark greens, colors typical of the Netherlands. Mauve favors outdoor scenes: peasants in fields, men on horseback on a beach, flocks of sheep. Ma and Pa would like Vincent to see Mauve not because he's a successful *painter*, but because he's *successful* and a member of good society. He will be a useful contact for Vincent once he's ordained as a minister. Vincent and Theo visit Mauve, they go to the barber, and then Vincent is on his way to Amsterdam.

While Ma and Pa are trying to have faith in Vincent's new path, Uncle Cent can't forgive him for his failure. He's pinning all his hopes on Theo. Ma tells Theo to "write him from time to time; that will give him pleasure, and tell him about everything."

But Theo absolutely cannot tell his uncle everything. Though he's better at keeping up appearances than Vincent, he has not given up his girlfriend. He tries to keep this a secret, but it's a small community, and soon his parents find out he hasn't broken up with the woman. They're furious. This is not how it's supposed to be—not who Theo is supposed to be! He's the good son, the one they can trust to behave well!

If you're this weak, Ma tells him, avoid her, avoid the danger. "Your love is based on sensuality, and you must open your eyes to the danger in order to flee it all the more forcefully."

Pa writes to him, too, bringing up a tragic example in their family: one of Ma's brothers had fallen for a woman of ill repute, and his life ended disastrously, presumably by his own hand. Such a relationship—based on sensual desire—is loathsome. And, Pa warns Theo, being seen with someone like her will ruin Theo's reputation. "You can and must have pleasure and diversion, only I beg you, do not seek it in people of that kind. Your whole future depends on it."

Theo is distraught that he's upsetting his parents so. "I should really like to get away from everything," he tells Vincent. "I'm the cause of everything and only make others sad, I alone have caused all this misery to myself and others."

Theo knows the only way to give up the woman is to leave The Hague. Maybe he could move to the Goupil branch in Paris, he tells Vincent. Vincent agrees it might work, but leaving your home country comes with a sacrifice. There's a lot to love about Paris and London, Vincent tells Theo, but you can't love those cities "as much as the hedges of thorn-bush and the green grass and the little grey churches" of their childhood landscape.

The most important thing, Vincent tells his younger brother, is that they have to *live*. They have to *stay alive*. We must "both make sure that we survive the time between now and the age of 30 or so—and we must beware of sin. . . . We must become men—which we aren't yet, neither of us—there is something greater in store for us."

The twenties have proved to be perilous years. Annet died. Theo's friends died. The younger sister of a friend of Vincent's died after falling off a horse. And sleeping with prostitutes can lead to illness—syphilis and gonorrhea. If Vincent and Theo stay healthy and safe, they will live to be parents, grandparents. They will live to give something to the world. *They have something to give to the world.* This is the pledge they made on their walk to the mill. This is what keeps Vincent going when he is unmoored. He and Theo are here for a reason, both of them.

Vincent now thinks that his path is with God. And no matter what, God will help us, Vincent tells his brother.

But Theo does not agree. He needs to help himself. He asks for a transfer out of The Hague to another Goupil branch. But both Uncle Cent and Tersteeg tell him that there is nothing available abroad. There might be in the future. They will keep Theo's request in mind. But for now, Theo will have to stay put. Pa warns him: "Don't spoil things in the meantime by acting too hastily."

THAT FALL, Goupil's sends Theo on sales trips around the Netherlands. "Who knows," writes Ma, "on your travels you may just meet the girl meant for you."

He doesn't meet anyone, but the distance gives him perspective. That winter, Theo's letters home are happier, lighter. He seems to have broken it off with the woman. Ma and Pa are greatly relieved—about Theo.

27.

THE WORST OF TIMES

---

*May Vincent not only have blessing on his work,
but also become more normal. There is so much good in him,
it would be such a shame.*

—Ma to Theo, January 6, 1878

VINCENT AND THEO go home for Christmas as usual. And after Theo returns to The Hague, Vincent has another New Year's chat with his parents, just as he did the year before, when he wanted to quit Goupil's and ended up being fired. He tells Ma and Pa that he hates the theology school in Amsterdam. He is trying to make the best of it because he wants to work in the church, but he thinks the classes are dumb; he must study things he doesn't need. He's not doing well because he doesn't care. He just wants to be out helping people.

Go back to school, Dorus and Anna say. Try harder.

Vincent leaves, and on his way back to Amsterdam, he visits Theo in The Hague. Ma and Pa hope Theo can help Vincent stay on his path.

It has been more than five years since Theo visited Vincent in The Hague and they walked together to the mill. Back then it was the older brother looking out for the younger one. But now their roles are reversed— at least that is how Ma and Pa see it.

Theo and Vincent have a nice visit, and Theo reports home that his brother seems fine. But unlike them, Theo accepts Vincent for who he is. He does not wish that Vincent dressed better or acted in a more "normal" way. Since that walk to the windmill, Theo has pledged himself to Vincent. He has committed himself to Vincent as *Vincent*, not as some ideal first son their parents still—in spite of it all—hope for.

So Ma and Pa are not convinced by Theo's report. "He is so awfully impractical," Ma worries to Theo, "but we will hope for the best."

THE NEXT MONTH Pa visits Vincent to "put my mind at ease a little about Vincent's future." They walk around the city. They visit family and friends together. The visit doesn't entirely put Pa's worries to rest. But for his part, Vincent loves their days together, having so much time alone with his father. They spend a whole morning in Vincent's study looking over his schoolwork and talking about religion, theology, and God. It is a connection they have—again.

But then it's so hard for Vincent to say good-bye.

He takes Pa to the station and watches as the train pulls away, stays as it disappears down the tracks, so all that's left is the smoke. He stands there until the smoke vanishes, too. When he goes back to his room and he sees the chair his father sat in, the one by his desk with all his notebooks still out from their talk the day before, he breaks down and cries like a child.

The yellow carriage has ridden away again.

Now he's even more homesick. And still miserable at the school.

A year later, when Vincent's life will seem a lot more hopeless than it does right now, he will tell Theo that his time at this school in Amsterdam was "the worst time I've ever gone through."

28.

CITY MOUSE, COUNTRY LION

WHILE VINCENT IS SO DOWNCAST in Amsterdam, Theo gets the news
that he's going to *Paris*. Finally! It's a temporary assignment, but on his
twenty-first birthday, May 1, 1878, he leaves The Hague. He'll be working at the Goupil stand during the World Exhibition. He spends his first
few days roaming around the city. Paris is hot and crowded and initially
Theo is overwhelmed by the number of people, the chaos, and the confu-
sion. Neither The Hague nor Brussels has prepared him for life in this big
city. But Paris is alive with hope and beauty, joy and optimism. Since the
end of the Franco-Prussian War, the arts have been flourishing—painting
and theater and literature. So once he acclimates, Theo is overjoyed to be
in Paris, the City of Light.

The Exposition Universelle in 1878 is a celebration of Paris's re-
emergence as a cultural capital after a time preoccupied with war and recovery. The theme this year is New Technologies. The enormous Palais du
Champ de Mars houses a Street of Nations and a Gallery of Machines,
where visitors can see innovations and art from around the world.

Across the Seine, the newly built Palais du Trocadéro hosts art exhibits, concerts, and meetings. Most major countries—about three dozen—have exhibits. An estimated sixteen million visitors come to see the new inventions, including a solar oven, American porcelain teeth, Alexander Graham Bell's telephone, Thomas Edison's phonograph and his megaphone, modified to help the hard of hearing. Fittingly, in June a switch is thrown, and electric light illuminates the exhibitions for the first time. Voilà! Let there be light!

Before long Theo knows he wants to stay in Paris permanently.

VINCENT WISHES he could go visit Theo and see the exhibition.

He has quit theology school. He's moved back home with his parents. He is twenty-five.

And now, strange as it seems, he wants to go to another school. He and Pa have decided he'll go to a training college for evangelists. Vincent is willing to try it because this school in Brussels will teach him exactly what he wants to do—preach to and help poor people. He's especially interested in going to the Borinage, a very poor mining region in Belgium. Although the school is for Belgians, they are willing to take Vincent on for a trial period.

Another try at a career on the God path.

But Vincent wants to stay home for the family's first wedding: Anna is getting married in August.

Anna would rather Vincent just left. He's getting on her nerves. She complains to Theo that Vincent is stubborn, irritating, "more of a wooden lion than ever and is very annoyed at the preparations."

In fact, Vincent is worrying about Anna! He thinks she's strained over the wedding preparations. He writes to Theo that she's "far from being as one would like to see her, sometimes she still looks so pale and tense, and is always so weak." He hopes she'll make it to the ceremony!

When he's not worrying about Anna—or as she sees it, getting in her way—he's spending time with his little brother Cor and working on some sermons.

He's also making sketches in pencil, and drawings in pen and ink.

Four days after Anna's wedding, Vincent moves to Brussels for his trial period at the school. If he succeeds, he will be well along on his path to becoming an evangelist.

If not, nobody knows what will become of Vincent.

29.

DIVERGENT PATHS

THEO IS ON HIS WAY back to the Netherlands, having done splendidly at the Exposition Universelle. He worked hard and learned a lot. His bosses are once again impressed and pleased. But to his great disappointment there is no good job for him at Goupil's in Paris. Living in Paris had expanded Theo's world. He knows more about not just art but also theater, music, food, fashion, city life. He's cosmopolitan now. He chafes at the idea of going back to the Netherlands. But Uncle Cent and the other Goupil directors feel he would benefit from more time working at the branch in The Hague, learning still more about the business. And they assure him that in the future a more senior position will be available in Paris. There's nothing he can do about it. Theo will just work hard in The Hague and bide his time.

He stops in Brussels to see Vincent on his way back to the Netherlands.

Oh, how different the brothers are now, what different roads they travel. Their paths are not even parallel. Vincent wants to bring Jesus to the poorest of the poor. His passion is to preach to "those who work in the darkness, in the heart of the earth . . . , are very moved by the message of the gospel and also believe it."

Theo wants to sell art in Paris.

At least they still have the love of art in common. They visit the art museum in Brussels and talk about the paintings they see. And before he leaves, Theo gives Vincent some prints as a present. One is an etching of three windmills. Vincent tries to give it back to him—he should keep it! But Theo wants his brother to have it.

After the visit, Vincent writes to Theo and admits to him that he'd love to sketch what he sees along his journeys. But he's worried drawing will interfere with his real work—the work of the church. So it's better he doesn't begin.

But in fact he does make a sketch, of a little building with a café. He sends it to Theo. "How much there is in art that is beautiful, if only one can remember what one has seen, one is never empty or truly lonely, and never alone."

One is never truly alone if one has art. He says that, but he doesn't know it yet, not really, not in his heart.

"I wish you well," Vincent writes to his brother. "May you thrive in your work and encounter many good things on your path in life."

Vincent doesn't send the letter right away. A few days later he adds a postscript: he's not going to be kept on at the school. He's been told there are spots only for natives of Belgium. But he's determined to continue with his plan, so he sets off for the Borinage without a job.

And Theo goes back to The Hague, hoping to return to Paris soon.

Windmills, art, their shared history—they still have a lot in common. But their differences are huge. And neither brother's path is smooth at the moment.

Vincent needs art. He needs Theo. The boys walking to the windmill.

But here he is heading to the Borinage, where there will be no art, and no Theo.

As long as they can stay connected to each other, all should be fine.

30.
GNARLED ROOTS

VINCENT MOVES TO THE BORINAGE and lives with a colporteur, an evange-list who also sells devotional literature (like the pamphlet Vincent threw into the fire at the Roos house). His determination to work pays off. He receives an appointment from the Belgian Evangelization Committee of the Associated Churches and starts work as an evangelist on February 1, 1879. It's a six-month trial; if he does well, he'll get a permanent position.

He enjoys his responsibilities: Bible readings, teaching the word of Jesus, visiting the sick. And the colporteur helps Vincent find permanent lodging with a farming family in Wasmes, the community he's serving.

The Borinage has farms as well as mines (the name comes from the word *boeren*, farmers), but it's not a farming landscape like the one Vincent is used to. It's stark.

"There are sunken roads here, overgrown with thorn-bushes and with old, twisted trees with their gnarled roots, which look exactly like that road in the etching by Dürer," Vincent tells Theo, referring to *Knight, Death and the Devil.*

The coal miners are "completely black when they come out of the dark mines into the daylight again, they look just like chimney-sweeps." They live in huts scattered along the sunken roads, in the woods, and against the slopes of the hills.

Vincent is drawn to the darkness and the poverty, so much so that he decides to live more like the miners live. The farmer's house is too luxurious.

He moves to an empty hut—there isn't even a bed. He forgoes soap, and soon his face is as black as the coal miners'. He gives away most of his clothes to those who need them more, leaving him with little to wear, none of it clean. And because he eats only bread with nothing on it, he loses a lot of weight.

The village people already think he's strange. They have trouble understanding his French because of his Dutch accent. Now his actions make him even more foreign to them. And his host family is terribly worried about him. He's so skinny and dirty that he's putting himself at risk for typhoid, which is rampant in the community. Church elders worry, too, and what's more, they vehemently disapprove. Nobody told him to take a vow of poverty.

Ma writes to Theo that she and Pa received "a very grim letter from him." It "confirmed all our worries that he had no bed, no bed-clothes, no one to wash his things. But he wasn't complaining at all, saying instead that it didn't concern anyone and so on." Although Vincent says he's fine, they think he's lost touch with reality. They were about to send him a package; Dorus decides to take it to Vincent himself.

While Dorus is on his way to the Borinage, a letter arrives from Evangelization Committee elders. They've given Vincent an ultimatum: he has to go back to the house where he'd been living or he'll lose his post.

When Dorus arrives and sees Vincent and his hut, he knows his son is in terrible shape physically and mentally. Neighbors have been hearing him cry out at night. Pa gives him a stern lecture about taking care of himself. He has to eat well, wash, sleep. Finally Dorus persuades Vincent to use the hut only during the day. He will sleep in a bed in the farmer's house. That's about as far as Pa gets with him, but it's something. What agony it is for Dorus, to see his son like this. But he can do no more for him. He goes back home.

Though Pa feels that Vincent's behavior is not "normal" religious passion, he probably doesn't realize that Vincent's extreme religious zeal is likely a sign of mental illness. One thing is certain: if Vincent continues to live like this, he will not survive into his thirties, as he told Theo they must.

Theo knows about Vincent's condition only from his parents. Vincent does not tell him. He writes to Theo only about art, about how he tries to see beauty in the bleak surroundings. He tells him he misses going to museums and galleries. He asks after their cousin's husband, Mauve, the painter, and others in The Hague. And he tells Theo about this adventure:

One spring day, Vincent decides to see for himself what the miners' underground world is like. He goes down into the most dangerous mine in the area. Many people have died in it—from suffocation and gas explosions and floods and cave-ins.

It's not pleasant going down, he tells Theo, "in a kind of basket or cage like a bucket in a well," a well "500-700 metres deep, so that down there, looking upward, the daylight appears to be about as big as a star in the sky."

He spends six hours down there and paints the picture for Theo: it is like a beehive, with all its cells, or a dark underground prison. Someone should make a painting of it, he says.

That somebody might be him, for Vincent is starting to draw what he sees. He's actually written to Tersteeg in The Hague and asked him (not Theo) to send a box of paints and a sketchbook.

"Have you seen anything beautiful recently?" Vincent asks his brother.

THEO CERTAINLY HAS BEEN seeing a lot of beautiful art, but he's not happy in The Hague. Compared with Paris, it's so dull. But at least Tersteeg's made a deal with him to share the profits of the gallery.

While Vincent is rejoicing in poverty, shedding his clothes, his possessions, his membership in middle-class society, Theo is honing his talents as an art dealer and becoming more and more ambitious.

Vincent is also discovering a talent for and fulfillment in ministering to the sick and injured. He's a terrific nurse: against odds and expectations, he nurses back to health a man who'd been terribly burnt in a gas explosion.

And so the differences between the brothers grow. Vincent misses Theo, but he feels alienated from him. He tells him so in a letter. What can he say to him anymore? he asks. What do they have in common? Yet he still wants Theo to come visit.

Theo will be passing right by the Borinage at the end of the summer. He is going back to Paris to work at Goupil's for six weeks. "Wouldn't you consider spending a day here, or longer if possible?" Vincent writes. "I'd so much like you to know this country, because there's so very much that's unique to be noticed by those who look at things closely."

Theo tells Vincent he will think about it. He knows Ma has been to see Vincent recently and was not reassured at all. He looked terrible, and when she was leaving, he was so sad, she writes Theo, it was "as though it were for the first time but could also be the last time."

Ma also tells Theo she thinks it's doubtful Vincent will get a permanent position. He probably won't "adhere to the conventions, as requested. . . . If he would just get a grip on himself for once, how much could still be put to rights. Poor chap, what a difficult, young life with so little fulfillment and so much deprivation, what will become of him?"

Vincent is wondering the same thing. He takes another very long walk.

31.

VINCENT WALKING, III

---

*I*T IS A HOT, hot summer day. Vincent leaves the Borinage and walks north to visit Reverend Abraham van der Waeyen Pieterszen. Pieterszen is a member of the Evangelization Committee and also a painter.

The distance is thirty-three miles. Vincent walks most of the way.

He knocks on the door of Pieterszen's house. The reverend's daughter opens it up to see an exhausted, very thin redheaded man dressed in rags, covered with dirt and sweat. She runs back into the house, terrified. Someone else comes to the door to tell Vincent that Pieterszen isn't home; he is in Brussels.

So Vincent goes to Brussels.

He really needs advice. His six-month trial is over. He has not been reappointed as an evangelist.

Vincent and Pieterszen talk about religion and art. Vincent has been drawing, staying up late at night "to have some keepsakes and to strengthen thoughts that automatically spring to mind upon seeing the things." The reverend asks for one of Vincent's sketches of a coal miner, which Vincent gives him.

Before he leaves Brussels, Vincent visits a bookseller's shop, where he buys a large sketchbook made with old Dutch paper. Art *and* God?

WHEN THEY HEAR THE NEWS that Vincent was not reappointed, Ma and Pa are distraught. They see it as another failure.

But Vincent doesn't. He doesn't care. He moves to Cuesmes, a village not far from where he's been living. He concentrates on his drawing.

He begs Theo to come visit on his way to Paris. He wants to show him some drawings he's made, of "types from here, not that they alone make it worth your while to get off the train," but he also wants to share with his brother where he's been living and what he's been doing. What his passion is now.

Theo does indeed decide to go to the Borinage to visit Vincent. But his agenda is not art; it is not social. It's business. Family business. Vincent has no idea what's coming.

GALLERY FOUR

Fissures

1879–1880

32.

VINCENT AND THEO WALKING, 1879

ON AUGUST 10, 1879, Theo arrives in the Borinage.

The brothers take a long walk together.

Theo, the art dealer, hoping soon to move to Paris.

Vincent, the erstwhile evangelist, now living with a baker, spending his time drawing.

Vincent takes Theo for a walk near an old mine called Petite Sorciére, little witch. It has fallen into disuse. Vincent has been eager to show Theo the stark beauty of the area; later he hopes to show him the drawings he's been making.

But as they walk through the bleak countryside, Theo reminds Vincent of the time they walked together near the old canal to the Rijswijk mill. It has been seven years.

Back then we agreed about so much, Theo says. But now, Vincent, you've changed. You're not the same. I am angry and frustrated. So are Ma and Pa. The whole family is.

You have to pull yourself together, Theo says. Walk on a straighter path. You must find a job, support yourself.

He suggests Vincent could be a lithographer, design letterheads. He tells him Anna thinks he could be a baker, learn the trade from the man he's boarding with.

Vincent is blindsided, furious.

STOP IDLING! says Theo, and walks away from Vincent.

He leaves, cutting his visit short.

VINCENT IS DEVASTATED. He walks some more; then he goes back to his house and draws a portrait. And he writes to Theo.

It's like going to that school in Amsterdam, he argues—people telling him what to do, how to live, who to be. He was miserable then, when people gave him "wise counsel given with the best of intentions." His use of "wise" is sarcastic.

"If," he writes, "you think that I thought I would do well to take your advice literally and become a lithographer of invoice headings and visiting cards, or a bookkeeper or a carpenter's apprentice—likewise that of my very dear sister Anna to devote myself to the baker's trade or many other things of that kind (quite remarkably diverse and mutually exclusive)—which it was suggested I pursue, you would also be mistaken."

Anna doesn't understand him. Forget her! But Theo, how can Theo misunderstand him so?

He *has been* trying to find his way. Trying to be a good member of the family.

"If I must seriously feel that I'm annoying or burdensome to you or those at home, useful for neither one thing nor another, and were to go on being forced to feel like an intruder or a fifth wheel in your presence, so that it would be better I weren't there," he writes, "then I'm overcome by a feeling of sorrow and I must struggle against despair."

The family prayer says they should be joined intimately to one another. Vincent feels not drawn in but pushed out.

If this is true, he tells Theo, if he's really being pushed out of the family, he'd rather die.

It's a nightmare for Vincent. To be the family outcast, this is the worst thing he can imagine.

He must do something to get back in the good graces of his family. He's determined he will.

But he is furious at Theo for the visit, for what he said.

He cannot forgive him.

33.

NOT HIS BROTHER'S BROTHER

---

*I*T IS A FEW DAYS after Theo's visit with Vincent. Anna and Dorus are home alone. Lies and Wil, the two daughters who still live with them, are out boating with another family.

All of a sudden they hear Vincent's voice:

"Hello, Father, hello, Mother." I am here.

Ma and Pa had been urging him to come home since he had no job anymore in the Borinage. But they are surprised he has.

Their surprise turns to shock when they see him. He's pale, thin, dirty, in tatters.

Vincent knows he's taking a chance coming home. He knows they're impatient with him, that he is causing them shame. But he needs them. He needs to know they still love him.

When the prodigal son comes home in Luke 15:20, "His father saw him and was filled with compassion for him; he ran to his son, threw his arms around him and kissed him."

Like the evening in the playground at Mr. Provily's school.

It is not the Van Gogh style to hug and kiss, but Dorus and Anna are generous, compassionate people. He is their son, and they are relieved to be able to help him.

They give him better clothes: a new, cherished jacket of Pa's, some of Theo's old socks and underwear. They feed him. They buy him a new pair of boots.

Within a couple of days he looks much better.

But he doesn't seem emotionally healthy. He does nothing but read all day—Charles Dickens's novels. He keeps to himself and speaks only when they ask him a question. Sometimes he answers correctly, often oddly. Reading Dickens gives him solace; nothing else seems to. He doesn't talk about his past, or his future.

He passionately wants to make something of his life, to make an offering to the world. And to his family.

He doesn't want to make letterheads! How can he be true to himself and keep the bond with his family?

But he doesn't say any of this. He remains silent.

Pa takes him for a long walk to visit some family. Ma hopes Vincent will speak his heart to his father as they walk.

But Vincent is silent the whole time.

Ma and Pa are in no hurry for him to leave. They want him to recover, get back to himself.

But after only a short time at home, Vincent goes back to the Borinage. They still don't know what he is thinking.

And the silence continues.

For the next year, he sends no letters home, and he writes no letters to Theo.

———

THERE HAD BEEN YEARS when art filled Vincent's life: beautiful paintings and drawings he had seen in The Hague, in London, in Brussels, and in Paris. There were years when religion gave him purpose. Tending to the coal miners, healing the sick and wounded, had fulfilled him, too. But now the life of service no longer seems an option. He has failed at everything.

As summer turns to fall, Vincent, at twenty-six, is alone.

He has turned away from God. He has put down the drawing pencil he'd picked up the summer before.

His life is as dark as an unlit coal mine; he's trapped in the prison of his own fear, anger, agony, despair.

He is not his father's son.

He is not the Father's son.

He is not his brother's brother.

34.

NEGATIVE SPACE

————————

WHILE VINCENT IS ALONE in his darkness and despair, Theo's life has taken a turn for the better. He has been offered a permanent position in Paris. It's not a high-level job, but he accepts. He's more than ready to leave The Hague and move back to the City of Light.

He starts as an assistant at Goupil's oldest Parisian branch, at 19 Boulevard Montmartre, in November 1879. Modern art is booming, and Paris is the hub. The gallery is in a fancy part of Paris, close to the stock exchange and the opera house. People with money to spend pass by every day.

Theo is just where he wants to be.

For the first time since their walk to the windmill, there are no letters between Vincent and Theo. Month after month after month.

Negative space.

Sometimes in a painting, negative space is intentional; sometimes it is an accident of composition. Empty space can create a meaningful image, or it can just be empty.

35.

VINCENT WALKING, IV

---

*I*T IS EARLY MARCH 1880. Vincent is broke, hungry, alone. But he has pulled himself out of his darkness enough to take yet another very long walk.

He is traveling from the Borinage to Courrières, a coal-mining town in northern France. It is about fifty miles away.

He doesn't have a real plan. He just feels he must see Courrières. Maybe he'll find work. He hopes to meet a painter who lives there. He has only ten francs and uses almost all of it to buy a train ticket to take him partway. Then he walks the rest of the distance, some twenty-two miles, trudging "rather painfully."

When he arrives in Courrières, he looks for the studio of the painter, Jules Breton. Vincent finds the studio, but he just stands outside looking at the building. The facade disappoints him. It is new, made of brick. It doesn't look to Vincent the way an artist's studio should look; it seems to him cold and inhospitable.

He admires Breton. He should knock, he knows. But he can't summon the courage to introduce himself.

And so he walks away from Breton's studio, not even trying to meet the man he came to see. Instead he looks around town for other traces of the artist. He finds none of Breton's paintings, only a picture of him at a photographer's shop.

With only two francs left, he cannot take a train back to his home in the Borinage. So he walks the whole fifty miles. It rains; it is windy. He has to bivouac out in the open for three nights.

He is at the end of his possibilities and, as he will tell Theo later, is at "a point of destitution such that one doesn't even have a roof over one's head and must tramp on and tramp on like a vagabond into infinity without finding either rest or food or shelter anywhere, moreover without the possibility of doing any work."

But.

Vincent has brought with him some drawings he made. Those drawings become his currency.

"I earned a few crusts of bread en route here and there in exchange for some drawings that I had in my suitcase."

Vincent has just begun his art career.

But he doesn't know it yet.

No one does.

36.

DISTRESSING DARKNESS

Oh, Theo, if only some light would shine on
that distressing darkness of Vincent.

—Dorus to Theo, March 11, 1880

SOON AFTER HIS WALK to Courrières, Vincent goes to see his parents again.
He looks terrible; he's moody.

Dorus and Anna are worried about his health, his sanity, his future.
They're concerned about their own finances, too. How can they continue
to support him? He's now twenty-seven, and there's no indication that he
will ever be able to support himself. He's unwilling to bend to their conventions. But he stays.

Pa writes to Theo, "Vincent is still here. But oh, it is a struggle and
nothing else."

Theo is still angry at his brother. They are not writing to each other.
Theo hates to see Vincent cause his parents so much unhappiness—yet again.
So he secretly sends Pa fifty guilders to help. The money is useful, but it
doesn't ease the anxiety Anna and Dorus feel.

The tension in the parsonage grows.

Yet Vincent stays.

Over the next few months, Ma and Pa and Vincent argue heatedly and repeatedly. Pa's temper, Vincent's temper, flaring again and again.

And again.

The lowest point: Dorus tells Vincent that he wants to have him declared a ward of the state. He wants to commit him to a psychiatric hospital in Geel, Belgium, known for the good care and supervised freedom given to its patients.

Freedom or no, Vincent is beyond furious. A mental institution? A ward of the state? It is to Vincent a betrayal so severe he declares he'll never forget it, never forgive his father.

He decides to leave. Pa asks him to stay nearby. But Vincent refuses. He flees back to the Borinage.

And still, silence remains between the brothers.

The Quest

1880–1882

Sorrow

37.

A WAY BACK HOME

Everything has changed for me.

—Vincent to Theo, September 24, 1880

*E*ND OF JUNE 1880.

Back in the Borinage, in the darkness, Vincent remembers art. He picks up his pencil. He starts drawing again.

Light. Resurrection. Life.

And after a year of silence, he writes to Theo.

"It's with some reluctance that I write to you not having done so for so long, and that for many a reason. Up to a certain point you've become a stranger to me, and I too am one to you, perhaps more than you think; perhaps it would be better for us not to go on this way."

The ostensible reason for the letter is to thank Theo for the money he'd given Pa. He's still angry with Theo, but he can't tolerate the separation anymore. He wants to be welcomed back into that intimate bond. He knows that it will be hard to regain the trust of the whole family, but he's "not utterly without hope that little by little, slowly and surely, a good understanding may be re-established with this person and that."

He wants them all back, but especially Theo. And Pa.

A year earlier, during that awful visit in the Borinage, Theo had suggested that Vincent use his artistic ability and become a lithographer or a
draftsman. At the time Vincent took that as a serious insult. He did not
want to be someone who made calling cards! He didn't want to be someone
who drew for money!

But now he knows that he is happiest when he's drawing. Theo's advice
had been right. If he gets good enough, he can earn money by being a
draftsman. He has to be skilled enough to draw accurate pictures of machines, houses, furniture, whatever people need. If he's a working draftsman, he can become independent *and* contribute. He can reestablish
himself with the family. Some artists are fortunate enough to come from
wealthy families or to have patrons. But Vincent does not come from such
a family or have any connections with the kind of people who could be
patrons. He has Theo's help, but he hopes to become self-reliant. Not completely eschewing the values he was taught at 26 Markt.

So with passion and perseverance, he spends day after day filling pages
of notebooks made of old Dutch paper like the one he bought from the
bookseller in Brussels. He sketches in graphite and reed pen. He experiments with watercolor and sepia ink. He copies plates from Charles Bar-
gue's *Cours de dessin* (*Drawing Course*). He's attacking art with the force and
fury of a storm, and the tenacity of a tradesman learning a craft. By late
August he has news to report to Theo: "You should know that I'm sketching large drawings after Millet. . . . Well, if you saw them perhaps you
wouldn't be too unhappy with them."

And a request: Will Theo please send him any prints he has by some
artists Vincent admires, including Jean-François Millet and Jules Breton,
on whose studio door he was too timid to knock. "Don't buy any spe-
cially, but lend me what you may have." He tells his brother that if he can
go on drawing, he will recover. "I'm writing to you while drawing and I'm

in a hurry to get back to it, so good-night, and send the sheets as soon as possible."

Theo sends the prints, and a letter. Vincent has Theo back.

Soon Vincent is able to look back at his journey through despair and poverty and loss, and the long walk to Courrières, and see what all of it had actually meant. He tells Theo that it was when he was making this painful trip that he was able to notice the beauty in nature, "the Courrières countryside then, the haystacks, the brown farmland or the almost coffee-coloured marly soil." He started to see the world through the eyes of an artist.

And once he started to make art again, he says, everything changed for him. And now his pencil is becoming more and more obedient every day.

He is going to contribute to the family, and go home again, be a help, not a burden. To do that he needs to learn as much as he can, as fast as he can. He has to draw and draw and draw. But he needs help. Although he received his calling at his lowest and poorest, he tells Theo, as an old proverb says, "Poverty prevents good minds succeeding."

He is going to need money.

38.

THEO CARRYING THE PARCEL

---

*F*EBRUARY 1881, PARIS. Theo gets a promotion. He's no longer just an assistant at Goupil's. He's now the general manager, the *gérant*, of the Paris Goupil branch at 19 Boulevard Montmartre.

The Boulevard Montmartre teems with rich and fancy people day and night. Just before Theo got this job, a cartoonist made a drawing of celebrities who were likely to stroll on the boulevard right in front of the gallery, including the world-famous actress Sarah Bernhardt. This branch and the main gallery are at the center of the art world in Paris, which is the center of art in Europe. This promotion is a great honor—and a great responsibility. Theo is twenty-three years old.

With the promotion comes more money.

Theo's parents are thrilled at his success. But when Pa writes to Theo to congratulate him, his pride is tempered by worry about Vincent. Again. Still.

To them it seems as though Vincent is pursuing another path that will inevitably fail. But Vincent is confident in his plan. He's moved from the mining region of the Borinage back to Brussels. Brussels, Vincent figures, is a great place for someone who wants to be an artist.

In Brussels, Vincent makes a new friend, as he does everywhere he goes. This man, Anthon van Rappard, is a painter and draftsman, and although at twenty-two he's five years younger than Vincent, he's farther along in his career. Vincent and Van Rappard talk about art, and Vincent asks Van Rappard to teach him more about drafting. Vincent hopes that he will get good enough to be hired. He meets other artists through Van Rappard and begins taking lessons from another painter. He's making progress and is living as cheaply as he can—on Pa's money.

Pa is not only worried about Vincent, he's skeptical too, and he's not happy he still has to send his eldest son money every month.

Vincent knows he's a burden. He knows he's been one since the day five years earlier when he was fired from Goupil's. But he's sure he's finally on the right path, and he wants his parents to know that, to be convinced of it.

He writes home telling Ma and Pa how hard he's working to learn his craft. He knows he can make money as an artist. He's not being impractical! And he's *good*.

He tells them he'd asked an established painter if he could borrow a skeleton from his studio and take it home. The painter hesitated—afraid, Vincent thought, that he'd keep it for too long. But Vincent returned it in a couple of days, and the painter "thought my drawing good, and in fact it isn't that bad."

Vincent tries to reassure them about another of their worries: he is dressing better. He's bought some secondhand clothes—trousers and jackets. He includes some pieces of the material so they can see for themselves. He will switch between two suits so each will last. But none of this reassures

Ma and Pa as much as an offer from Theo to help support Vincent, now that he's making more money.

It's a huge relief to Vincent, too. "For this accept my heartfelt thanks," he writes his brother. "I have every confidence that you won't regret it."

39.

OUT OF PROPORTION

----

*T*HAT SPRING, Vincent works in Van Rappard's studio in Brussels. But when he and Theo go home for Easter, they and their parents decide that it would be best if Vincent moved back in with them. Although the last time he'd lived at home it had been a disaster, he is so much better now. And he can work on his art there, saving everyone money. Van Rappard is leaving Brussels soon anyway.

Vincent moves back to Etten and gets to work immediately, sketching outside when the weather is good. He uses black chalk, pencil, and pen to draw fields and laborers. He sometimes uses watercolor, and experiments with using watercolor in chalk drawings. He makes several of his drawings on grey paper instead of plain. He likes to play with how things are usually done, even as he is still learning his craft. And he's serious about learning the craft—he wants to get paying work as soon as possible. But he's struggling with both proportion and perspective.

He asks Theo to keep an ear open for jobs as a draftsman, and also to let him know what's going on in the art world. He wants Theo's advice, too, on what to draw. He wants Theo to critique his art. "Sometimes I'll find it useful, sometimes perhaps not, but don't hesitate to tell me one thing and another."

––––––––

IN MID-JUNE, Van Rappard comes to visit in Etten. Ma and Pa and Vincent take him on a walk the first evening, along little paths through the fields. Vincent and Van Rappard paint together, talk, and walk some more. It is a lovely visit.

But another visit that summer causes serious trouble.

Vincent and Theo's first cousin Kee Vos comes with her eight-year-old son. Her husband has recently died. Vincent knew them when he lived in Amsterdam; he'd spent time with her and her husband. He had no romantic thoughts about her then, but now widowed and grief-stricken, Kee unwittingly presents a romantic figure to Vincent.

She needs company, and so the two spend a lot of time together. Vincent finds her a great confidant and kindred spirit. He assumes she's feeling the same way, and one day speaks his heart to her. He's in love and feels she is the closest person to him and he, the closest to her. He wants to marry her.

No, she says. She can't separate her past and her future; she will never get over her husband, will never love another man. Vincent is distraught. Another unrequited love, just like Caroline. But Kee doesn't have a husband, so Vincent refuses to give up. He tries to convince her that he's right. They belong together. She's adamant and refuses over and over.

Even after she leaves, Vincent continues trying to persuade her. Ma and Pa are deeply embarrassed. Only Uncle Cent is at all encouraging (maybe he sees this as a way to get Vincent off their hands), but everyone else in the family takes her side and tells Vincent to stay away from her.

Vincent tries to persuade Theo to take his side, and to help. If Kee would only correspond with him, get to know him, she'd fall in love, too. "Theo, aren't you in love, too, at times?" he writes. "I wish you were. . . . Sometimes one is desolate, there are moments when one is in hell, as it were, but—it also brings with it other and better things."

Vincent tells Theo there are three stages of love: first, not loving and not being loved; second, loving and not being loved; third loving and being loved. He knows he can bring Kee around, he tells his brother. But please, he begs, don't say anything to the others about the way I'm (still) feeling.

But of course Ma and Pa know. Pa loses his temper at Vincent, actually curses at him. He threatens to kick Vincent out if he continues to pursue Kee.

Vincent goes silent. He doesn't talk to his parents for days, making Pa even angrier.

Vincent knows that Dorus and Anna think he's going crazy, but he remains steadfast in his feelings. Borrowing from his beloved Michelet, he writes: "I love her, her and no other."

Throughout all this heated drama, Vincent keeps drawing, and sending his sketches to Theo. "I'm sorry to say that there's still something stiff and severe in my drawings, and I think that *she*, namely *her* influence will be needed to soften that."

Vincent asks Theo for some money to go to Amsterdam to see Kee. In exchange he promises to keep the peace with their parents. Maybe Theo could help? Could he put in a good word with Ma and Pa? If Vincent can win Kee, he writes, his art will continue to reach a "higher artistic level, *without* her I am nothing, but *with* her there's a chance."

Theo sends the money.

40.

FLAMES 1, 2, 3, 4

1.

VINCENT ARRIVES at Kee's house, where she and her son live with her parents. They are all—except for Kee—sitting around the dining table.

Where's Kee?

She's not here.

When she heard that Vincent had arrived, she left the table.

Kee's father had already told Vincent that there would never be anything between them. They are cousins; they could never be more than brother and sister! Otherwise it would be shameful.

Shame. A word Vincent hates. He feels their looks of contempt, and yet he cannot help himself.

He puts his fingers in the flame of the lamp on the table. "Let me see her for as long as I hold my hand in the flame," he tells them.

But they blow out the lamp and declare, "You shall not see her."

Vincent walks around Amsterdam aimlessly for the next three days, feeling "damned miserable." Until he finally finds himself tedious and decides to put an end to it.

He goes down to The Hague, and with his heart beating quickly, he arrives at his cousin-in-law Anton Mauve's place. A leading member of the Hague school of painters, Mauve can teach Vincent a lot. He'd already offered to come to Etten to give Vincent lessons in watercolor and oil painting. But arriving at his door, Vincent asks if they can do it here instead. Mauve agrees. Vincent stays with him for a month.

2.

AT CHRISTMAS, Vincent goes back home to his parents' house. He and Pa get into another big fight, ostensibly about Vincent not going to church, and about religion, morality. But it is really about Kee. Pa (and Ma) are concerned about appearances—how Vincent (and they, because they are his parents) look to others in the extended family. Vincent thinks his parents are petty. He refuses to go to Christmas services with them, and they take that as the ultimate act of betrayal.

Vincent gets angrier at Dorus than he remembers ever being in his life. He tells Pa that he finds the whole system of religion loathsome. Vincent looks back on the time when he focused on religion so much—too much—and sees his zeal as a symptom of his melancholic misery.

His father tells him it would be better if he left home.

Vincent leaves that very day, packing up just what he needs: his painter's tools, his watercolors, his portfolio with drawings, and some clothes.

Even as Vincent is leaving in a fury and a huff, Pa offers him money. But he refuses.

He goes back to The Hague, away from his parents' life, religion, God. Art, *not* God.

3.

THEO HAS BEEN supporting Vincent by giving Pa money to then pass on to Vincent. So from now on, Theo sends money directly to his brother to protect Pa from Vincent's storms.

Buffering their father, Theo becomes the first line of defense.

In The Hague, Vincent borrows a hundred guilders from Mauve, because the money Theo has sent is not enough. He uses it to rent a place to live and work in, a room and an alcove, with bright light from a large southern-facing window. It's in Schenkweg, on the outskirts of The Hague, a half-hour walk from where he'd lived at the Roos house. He buys some furniture (in, he assures Theo, a respectable style), including a sturdy kitchen table and chairs. He's feeling optimistic. With Mauve as a mentor right there, and his old boss, Tersteeg, in town, he will be near people who, like Theo, and unlike his parents, understand art.

"Pa isn't the kind of man for whom I can feel what I feel for you, for example, or for Mauve," Vincent tells Theo. "I really do love Pa and Ma, but it's a very different feeling from what I feel for you or Mauve." As long as he can stay close to Theo, he doesn't care that much if he's at odds with Pa.

But is Theo still on his side? Not squarely. He's tired of his brother making life miserable for their parents, and he tells him so.

"I think it very good that you're permanently installed in The Hague," Theo writes, "and hope to do as much as I can to help you until you can start earning yourself, but what I don't like is the way you've contrived to leave Pa and Ma.

"Pa can't survive if there's bad blood between the two of you," Theo tells him. "It's your *duty* to set things straight at all costs." Pa is fifty-nine. Both sons are aware that he might not live much longer.

Also, Theo thinks, Vincent is too focused on Mauve and is idealizing him, as he is wont to do with people. If someone isn't like Mauve, he's not a good person. You can't look for the same qualities in everyone! Does Pa's life count for nothing?

"I don't understand you!" Theo tells Vincent. "Write to me again when you can."

4.

VINCENT WRITES BACK IMMEDIATELY, furiously, in a white heat. He sends back Theo's letter with the various points numbered, and next to them why Theo is wrong about each one.

"You mustn't think that I'm sending the letter back to insult you," Vincent writes, "but I find this the quickest way to answer it clearly. And if you didn't have your letter back, you wouldn't be able to understand what my answer refers to, whereas now the numbers guide you. I have no time, I'm waiting for a model today."

These are the points Vincent makes, vehemently:

1. I didn't want to leave home. I wanted to stay in Etten. It's much harder for me here. I don't know how I will survive.
2. You say I am making Pa and Ma's life miserable. Pa always says stuff like that! If you say something to Pa he doesn't like, he'll answer, "You'll be the death of me," while calmly reading the newspaper and smoking his pipe. Pa gets angry and hurt too easily, and he's so used to getting his own way!
3. Because Pa is an old man, I've tolerated so much that is truly intolerable!
4. I'm being nice to them, for the sake of appearances. But it's not just up to me. I won't apologize, but I'm not asking for an apology, either. If they take it all back, I will take it all back. But that won't happen!
5. Sure, they can't stand it if there's bad blood. Well, it's their fault, and they are the ones who are going to be miserable, and alone.
6. I used to feel worse about how much I was upsetting them, but I don't anymore. Pa told me to leave, and so I did! I'm sorry—for you—because it's more expensive this way.

7.   You say I put too much on Mauve. I like him, and his work,
     but I'm not going to follow him blindly. I also like others
     who are very different and whose work is very different.

"I don't understand you!" Theo had said.

Vincent says they will have to have patience with each other, and keep writing letters, until they can see each other again.

Without Theo as his companion, his journey makes no sense. Theo taking Ma and Pa's side is not only hurtful, it is terrifying.

He cannot lose Theo.

After this angry response, he writes softer letters, focused on the art, telling Theo of his progress with his watercolors and sketches.

Theo does not stay angry. In fact, when he gets a raise—he's now earning four thousand francs a year—he sends about a third of it to Vincent. Every month he takes 100 francs from the 330 he gets and sends it to his brother.

They now have an arrangement, an understanding. Vincent will keep working hard; Theo will keep sending him money. And Vincent will keep the peace with his parents, and with Theo.

Sometimes that will mean hiding the truth.

41.

SORROW

VINCENT KNOWS he has to improve his craft. He continues to copy works of the masters, to talk with and learn from other artists, especially Mauve, and to use lessons from art instruction manuals. He finds watercolors difficult, but with Mauve's tutelage he perseveres. He knows he has to draw the human form better. He needs to *perfect* it. He has an instruction manual with sixty plates of the male figure. He copies the figures over and over again, and by the end of this year he will have copied the whole book four times. He reports on his progress to Theo, including sketches to show him what he's doing.

But he feels the best way to learn how to draw people is from live models, not from pictures or artists' statues. He'd be happy to stand outside and sketch people on the street, especially peasants, laborers, poor people, like the miners in the Borinage. But the winter is "so damned cold," and he can't "draw as fast as more practised draughtsmen."

He sometimes sits in the third-class waiting room at the Rhijnspoor train station, near his flat, and sketches people there. Since he often eats at the soup kitchen, he sketches people there, too. Sometimes he invites people back to his studio so he can pose them and draw them more slowly and carefully. That's what he really wants to do all the time. But you have to pay models. Even with Theo's help, Vincent doesn't have enough money. He's eating very little. His clothes are wearing out, and so are his boots. But he doesn't care much about any of that. He is using most of his money for paint, pencils, paper.

But he's found someone he thinks will be a perfect model for him. She's about thirty, is pregnant, and has a little girl who is four years old. The father of her unborn baby has abandoned her. She and her family are very poor, and she'd been working as a prostitute. She also has a mother and a younger sister who are willing to pose. Her name is Clasina Maria Hoornik. Vincent calls her Christien or Sien. She needs the money and agrees to pose for him. He has to train her, but she's a fast study, Vincent tells Theo.

But Vincent doesn't tell Theo everything. He doesn't tell him, for example, that she'd been a prostitute. And soon there will be more he won't divulge.

VINCENT DOES WRITE to Theo with some good news. He's sold a drawing to Tersteeg. And Uncle Cor has commissioned him to draw a dozen views of The Hague.

Vincent finishes those drawings quickly, and when he gives them to Uncle Cor, his uncle likes them so much he commissions a second series of cityscapes.

Vincent predicts to Theo that in a year he'll be making drawings and watercolors that are salable, and not just to a friend or relative.

Vincent begins to feel so good about his life as an artist that he starts a campaign for Theo to become an artist, too. He wants his brother *right next* to him. "I sometimes suspect you of keeping a great landscapist hidden inside you. It seems to me you'd be extremely good at drawing birch trunks and sketching the furrows of a field or stubble field, and painting snow and sky &c. Just between you and me."

He pictures the two of them going out to paint together, carrying their easels and palettes. It is anything but practical. Who would support the two of them?

Theo is not interested. His life is going how he wants it to, mostly (he'd like a wife and a family). He's doing well at Goupil's, and he's now living in a new apartment, at 25 Rue Laval in Montmartre.

Again Vincent isn't telling Theo everything. He wants Theo to join him on his path because he's lonely. Vincent usually has a male friend or two. But he doesn't now—because he's had a fight with Mauve. He tells Theo that the fight was over plaster casts. And it was, sort of. Mauve told Vincent he should use plaster casts to draw from, instead of using Sien as a model. The tradition in academic training has been, since the late seventeenth century, to draw first from plaster casts and then turn to models. As usual, Vincent wants to do things his own way.

Vincent told Mauve, "Old chap, don't speak to me of plaster casts any more, because I can't stand it."

But that wasn't the only reason Mauve was angry. He was suspicious about Vincent's relationship with Sien. Mauve told Vincent he wouldn't see him for two months.

Vincent went home and furiously "threw the poor plaster mouldings into the coal-scuttle, broken."

Vincent tells Theo most of this. He omits Mauve's misgivings about Sien.

———

ON APRIL 10, 1882, Vincent sends Theo a drawing of a woman. He's made three versions. "The enclosed is, I think, the best figure I've drawn, that's why I thought I'd send it to you."

In the drawing, the woman is naked. She sits, bent over, her knees pulled up, her crossed arms on her knees, her head in her arms, her face hidden, her long hair straggling down her back. Her pendulous breasts hang over her rounded (pregnant) stomach. Vincent calls the drawing *Sorrow*.

The drawing is striking, well executed, poignant, melancholic, beautiful—but not in a traditional sense. In fact, it would likely offend traditional artists and critics. Vincent has not drawn an idealized woman; he has rendered her the way he sees her. He's drawn a real person. And even though you can't see her face, you feel you *know* her.

It is Sien.

Theo likes it.

"I'm very glad that you saw something in the drawing I sent, I also thought there was something in it," Vincent writes.

Sorrow. Sorrow because Mauve is furious at him. Sorrow because he knows that if Ma and Pa find out what's really going on between him and Sien, there will be even more of a break.

Sorrow because he's hiding the truth from Theo.

That is a real sorrow.

42.

APPEARANCES, II

What is more cultured, more sensitive, more manly:
to forsake a woman or to take on a forsaken one?

—Vincent to Theo, May 7, 1882

/T IS OBVIOUS to anyone who visits Vincent at his studio that Vincent and Sien are more than just painter and model. They are lovers.

Tersteeg, who knows about Vincent's situation from Mauve, goes to see for himself. Vincent thinks he's giving him dirty looks, staring at his hand—the hand that he'd held in the flame for Kee. Tersteeg indeed is angry at Vincent, just as he was back when Vincent was working under him at the Goupil branch in The Hague and asked for help with some trouble he was in. That time Tersteeg had told Vincent's family. Now Tersteeg threatens to tell Theo to stop supporting him.

Vincent is terrified that Tersteeg and Mauve will tell Theo what's going on and Theo will take their side. And Vincent will be all alone.

He decides to try to win back Mauve. He asks him to come to his studio. "I certainly won't come to see you, it's over and done with," Mauve replies.

But Vincent persuades Tersteeg to meet in the sand dunes at the north end of The Hague. The conversation does not go well. The way Vincent later reports it to Theo:

"You have a vicious character," Mauve says.

Vincent turns around and walks home.

"Mauve and I have parted ways for ever," he tells his brother. And then finally he comes clean, arguing his case.

He'd met Sien when she was roaming the streets. The only way to save her, Vincent tells his brother, was to share his food with her, make her bathe, and take her to the hospital where she would have the baby. "No wonder she was ill, the child was the wrong way round and she had to have an operation which entailed turning the child with forceps."

Uncle Cor once had asked Vincent if he would feel anything for a woman or a girl who was beautiful, "but I said I would have more feeling for and would prefer to be involved with one who was ugly or old or impoverished or in some way unhappy, who had acquired understanding and a soul through experience of life and trial and error, or sorrow."

When he first met Sien, he didn't think it would be a permanent relationship, but now he does. "I can marry only once," he tells Theo, "and when would be a better time to do it than with her."

Theo doesn't write back right away. The delay worries Vincent, so he writes again, begging Theo not to tell Ma and Pa about Sien. He also defends the relationship some more, arguing, among other things, how much good he is doing Sien: when he first met her, she was pale and sick. "I'm amazed at the sight of her getting stronger and more cheerful every day." She has a speech impediment, bad moods, and "a couple of peculiar habits that many would find repellent," he tells Theo. But Vincent can understand her and isn't bothered by any of this. Besides, "she understands my own temper, and we have a tacit agreement, as it were, not to carp at each other."

And as far as the art is concerned, she's learning how to pose better every day, and doesn't ask for much: she's fine with nothing but bread and coffee, as Vincent is. A good match, and no extra trouble for Theo.

Though there is another thing. Vincent does want to rent the studio next door, which would be large enough to accommodate all of them—Vincent, Sien, her daughter, Maria, and the new baby. But it's more expensive, so he'll need more money from Theo.

Theo still doesn't write back.

Vincent writes another letter, again stating his case, saying he's not being frivolous, not trying to live off Theo in an irresponsible way. And he's not being impetuous, thinking of marriage. Sien is good for his work. "I feel that my work lies in the heart of the people, that I must keep close to the ground, that I must delve deeply into life and must get ahead by coping with great cares and difficulties."

He begs Theo to write back to him. He couldn't stand it if his dear brother went the way of Mauve. He ends with a prayer: "I hope that the air stays clear between you and me."

THEO FINALLY WRITES to Vincent. He's not abandoned him, but he's not happy, either. Theo doesn't look down on Vincent for being with someone from a lower class, having done so himself. "One would have to be narrow-minded or have a misplaced sense of guilt to put one class absolutely above the other," Theo agrees. But why flaunt your lifestyle? Theo knows how to appear one way to the outside world, but please himself. He suggests Vincent do the same. Don't marry her, he says.

It's not unusual for a young man to sleep with a prostitute or have an affair with a woman of "ill repute." What is unusual is that Vincent wants to *marry* Sien.

But Vincent wants to be better than the man who had gotten her pregnant and then abandoned her. That man, who had a higher standing in society, was guilty before God for abandoning her to keep his social status. How could that be honorable?

Yet Theo has another point: Vincent was supposed to have loved Kee Vos so much. How can he so quickly love another?

Vincent can't answer that quite yet.

Instead he asks for more money, maybe even a weekly allowance. And he wants to move to the bigger flat with Sien and the children when the baby comes.

Please consider it! he says, and ends with humor: "Adieu, old chap, but before you strike the blow and chop off my head *and Christien's and the child's too* . . . sleep on it again. But again—if you must—then in God's name '*off with my head.*' But preferably not, I need it for drawing. (And Christien and the child couldn't pose *without heads.*)"

The next day he writes again, once more pleading his case about his love for Sien. He describes what happened with Kee Vos and her family in Amsterdam. The refusal, the flame, the humiliation.

He admits that if Kee hadn't refused him, he wouldn't be with Sien. But he's with her now, and he wants Theo on his side. He doesn't want to abide by conventions. He writes he's not with Sien without thought, frivolously, but "*in damned earnest.*"

Vincent's letter is in Dutch, but this phrase he writes in English, in very large letters, "damned" underline twice and the whole phrase underlined with a paintbrush dipped in ink.

Theo goes silent again.

43.

LONGING AND MEMORIES

MAIL IS DELIVERED QUICKLY from Paris to The Hague. When Theo mails a letter, Vincent gets it in a day or two at most. Day after day Vincent waits. Nothing comes. He doesn't hear from Theo. He's in terrible suspense. Has he persuaded Theo to his side, or will his brother abandon him?

Vincent keeps working even though he's anxious, weak, and sleepless. He gets up early every morning and goes outside to paint by four o'clock. It's spring, and "during the day it's too difficult to be on the street on account of the passers-by and the urchins, and because that's the best time to see the broad outlines while things still have tone." Work saves him—from disapproving eyes and his own angry thoughts. He sends Theo more drawings, including another version of *Sorrow*.

Still no word from his brother.

He longs for a letter.

It's nearing the end of the month, and money is running out. He writes again, asking for more money, asking if he should rent the bigger place, asking Theo to please write and say whether he's received the drawings.

His friend Van Rappard comes to visit and gives Vincent a little money to fix a tear in a drawing. He wants to give him more, but Vincent won't take it. Instead he gives Van Rappard a pile of woodcuts and a drawing—still another version of *Sorrow*. Van Rappard likes Vincent's drawings, which cheers him up. But he's still feeling weak and worrying about Theo. He writes to him again.

He confesses that he's used some of Theo's allowance to buy linen for Sien and the baby for when she goes to deliver. They are living on dry black bread and a little coffee. It's been two weeks since Theo's last letter, which to Vincent is an eternity. When you live with a pregnant woman, Vincent tells him, an hour seems a day; a day, a week.

The rent is due the next day. Vincent writes again, begging Theo for the money. "I work day and night and have a small drawing ready for you which I'll send bye and bye. I have no more money for a stamp, excuse the postcard."

THEIR LETTERS CROSS in the mail. Theo's letter and money arrive just in time for Vincent to pay the rent. But Theo is not happy about Sien. What would Pa do if he found out about her? Would he once again think about trying to make Vincent a ward of the state? Commit him to an asylum? Theo thinks this is a possibility. And from his point of view it looks like Sien has cast a spell on Vincent, bewitching him into thinking he loves her.

Vincent writes back immediately, denying that Sien has deceived him—another girl tried that once, and he'd closed the door firmly in her face. And Sien is a true helpmate. Even though she's very pregnant, she comes with him when he wants to sketch the people who live near the dunes. They camped in the dunes "for days on end from morning till evening like true bohemians. We took bread and a small bag of coffee, and fetched hot water from a water and coals woman in Scheveningen."

She's so much better than Kee would have been for him. She "takes on all the toil and worry of the painter's life and is so willing to pose, I believe I'll be a better artist with her than if I had won Kee Vos."

If for nothing else, be on my side for art's sake, Theo. Please, Vincent pleads. And please help me with Pa and Ma.

The next day Vincent writes again, hammering home the strong bond between the brothers, with a memory, *the* memory that is the most important touchstone in their lives so far. "I've thought of you so often these past few days, and also occasionally about the time long ago when, as you will remember, you visited me in The Hague and we walked along Trekweg to Rijswijk and drank milk at the mill there."

He recently did some drawings set near there, he tells Theo, and he's the same person he was then.

We made a pledge to each other then—we are still pledged. Don't leave me. We are both in charge of our own paths, our own destinies. Together we will make a difference in the world. Don't leave me.

The next letter Vincent writes to Theo is from a hospital bed.

44.

DICKENS

He remains singular, and I have no great expectations.

—Pa to Theo, June 14, 1882

ABOVE HIS USUAL SALUTATION of "My Dear Theo," Vincent writes: "Municipal hospital (4th class, Ward 6, no. 9) Brouwersgracht." The sleeplessness he has been suffering, along with a chronic fever, pain while urinating, and probably his feeling of weakness (though that could have been from lack of nourishment), are all symptoms of "a very mild case of what's known as 'a dose of the clap.'"

Vincent has gonorrhea.

The treatment is bed rest, which he desperately needs anyway, injections of zinc sulfate, and quinine tablets. Also painful examinations.

He's brought with him to the hospital books on drawing perspective and a few novels by Charles Dickens, including *The Mystery of Edwin Drood*, which Dickens had left unfinished when he died twelve years earlier. "There's perspective in Dickens, too," he tells Theo. "By Jove, what an artist. There's no one to match him."

Sien comes to visit him with a package that had arrived at the flat from Ma and Pa: clothing, underwear, cigars, and even some money. They still don't know about Sien, but it gives him reassurance, which he also desperately needs. He writes to thank them, and he tells them he's in the hospital.

Vincent's letter arrives at Etten on Saturday evening, and Pa leaves for The Hague on Monday morning, which is as soon as he can after his church obligations.

When Dorus arrives at Vincent's room, he thinks Vincent "was somewhat surprised to see me, a little touchy," he tells Theo afterward. But Vincent calms down. They talk about his work—Vincent tells him that Uncle Cor didn't like his second set of drawings as much as the first but that his friend Van Rappard thought they were good.

Pa encourages him to come back home when he gets out of the hospital. But Vincent says no, he needs to get back to work. He doesn't, of course, tell Pa he can't come home because of Sien.

Dorus notices that when it comes time for visitors outside of family to arrive, Vincent looks toward the door uneasily. Pa wonders to Theo, "Can it be that he was expecting a visitor, someone that he would rather I did not meet?" Pa asks. "Can there be any danger in that so-called model?"

VINCENT THOUGHT he'd be in the hospital only for a fortnight, but he doesn't get better as quickly as he and the doctors had hoped, so the two weeks stretch into three and a half.

Vincent tells Theo that here in the lower-class ward they treat patients worse than in the higher-class ones: "They're less hesitant about inflicting a little pain on the patients . . . and more ready, for example, to stick a catheter in someone's bladder" without good manners.

And yet, he likes being in this ward. It's as good as being in the third-class train station waiting room. If only he could draw his fellow patients, he'd be happy! But he's glad that Theo has seen something in the drawings he'd sent before going to the hospital: a fish-drying barn in the dunes, done in pen and pencil, and the view from his studio of a carpenter's yard with a clothesline, done in black and white chalk.

Tersteeg is nice enough to come visit, even though he's angry at Vincent. They don't talk about Theo's financial support—another thing to cheer Vincent. But he wants to get out of there. He's worried about Sien. He tried to stay calm when she came to see him before going to the maternity hospital to wait for the baby. But he broke down crying. Vincent is miserable separated from her, he in his hospital bed, she in hers.

Back in Etten, Pa has written to Theo admitting that Vincent is still so strange; he has no great expectations of him.

There is an entire Dickens novel in what Pa does not know about Vincent's life.

45.

HOMECOMING

I have a sense of being at home when I'm with her.

—Vincent to Theo, July 6, 1882

WHEN VINCENT FINALLY LEAVES the hospital, walking home through the streets of The Hague, he sees everything differently: the light is brighter, the spaces larger. Every tree, building, person, seems imbued with significance. It's a beautiful world, and he's thrilled to be back in it.

He goes to see Sien at the hospital with her mother and little Maria.

"You can imagine how tense we were," Vincent wrote to Theo afterward, "not knowing what we'd hear when we enquired after her." But by the time they get there, Sien has given birth to a "very nice little boy," and mother and baby are recovering. Though the birth had been traumatic and baby Willem had been delivered by forceps, they'll both be fine.

Vincent's so happy to see her, and "ah, old chap, she had such a look on her face and she was so glad to see us." Sien is feeling good; she assures Vincent they'll soon be drawing again.

Vincent rents the bigger apartment. While Sien recovers, Vincent and her mother get it ready. He also paints a watercolor and makes a drawing for the doctor who treated him.

Two weeks later, Vincent brings Sien and the baby home. "It really was a lovely homecoming," Vincent tells Theo. Sien loves seeing the cradle, her wicker chair, and especially Maria.

Vincent can't wait for Theo to come visit; he is certain meeting Sien will reassure him. He even wants Pa to come. He tells Theo, "I want to show him Sien and her baby, which he won't be expecting, as well as the house bright and the studio with all manner of work in progress."

Vincent wants the family bond to extend to his new little circle. He desperately wants Ma and Pa's approval. But it is highly unlikely they would ever approve of Sien, of the whole situation.

A few days after he's settled them all in, Vincent receives a visitor who vehemently disapproves and threatens to divulge all to Dorus and Anna.

Storms

1882–1883

46.

HIS OWN CARRIAGE

TERSTEEG DROPS BY to see how Vincent is feeling. But when he sees Sien is living there with her daughter and the newborn, Willem, he is furious.

Vincent sees his reaction but hopes that he will act friendly, if not for his sake, then for Sien's, who has so recently given birth.

But Tersteeg does not hide his fury, Vincent tells Theo afterward. He challenges Vincent: what is the meaning of this woman and that child?

Where on earth did Vincent get the idea of living with a woman, and with children, too?! He is making no money of his own, being supported by his brother!

It is as ridiculous as if Vincent were to drive about the city in his own carriage! As if he were a wealthy man!

No, says Vincent, it is a different matter entirely.

Tersteeg doesn't buy it. Are you not right in the head? he yells. You are obviously sick in mind as well as body! You'll make her unhappy anyway!

He threatens to tell Uncle Cent and Pa.

Vincent stays calm to protect Sien, he reports to Theo. He tries to distract Tersteeg by showing him his drawings. Tersteeg then calms down, too, and looks around the studio. But he dismisses what he sees. Those are just the old drawings; he's seen them already.

Vincent tells him he has made new drawings, though most of them are with Theo or Uncle Cor.

Tersteeg has no interest in seeing any drawings, and he leaves.

Vincent is worried Tersteeg will tell Ma and Pa and his uncles how he's living, ruining the peaceful relationship they all have at the moment. "It's so rotten of Tersteeg to be such a troublemaker."

Vincent reports all to Theo right away. He needs Theo to buy his arguments and not side with Tersteeg, who is in his "police officer mood." He prays that Theo will think it reasonable for Vincent to live with Sien and her children and for Theo to be supporting all of them.

He's terrified Theo will pull away from him not only financially but also emotionally. He wants Theo to understand. "I don't want to leave Sien in the lurch. If I don't have her I'll be broken, and then I would also be broken in my work and everything else." But he needs Theo by his side, walking right next to *him*, not with Tersteeg and Mauve, and the closed-mindedness they represent. Of course he'd prefer that he had Tersteeg on his side—he is a member of the art establishment who could help him, who could sell his work eventually. It would be good to have Mauve, too. Both of them.

But Theo is the most important one.

He tries to persuade Theo not only with words but with art. He paints a memory that has great meaning for both of them. The picture is a declaration and a plea.

47.

THEIR WINDMILL

---

*There really is a sympathy between you and me
in many things, and it seems to me, Theo, that all your
trouble and all my trouble won't be in vain.*

—Vincent to Theo, July 18, 1882

To BE A GOOD ART DEALER, Theo must know how to interact with wealthy clients, how to deal with his bosses, the whole art establishment. To be a good art dealer, he must dress well, speak well, present himself well. But Theo's not only the hardworking art dealer and "good" son his parents think he is. He's living in *Paris*. He does not go home every night and have a cup of hot chocolate. He goes out and finds entertainment for himself the way young men do in a nineteenth-century city. Paris is not just the City of Light; it is a city of fun. Young single men go out for drinks, to the theater, to shows with music and dancing girls. And they visit prostitutes. Theo is a man of the world, and he understands how to navigate the line between passion and presentation; Vincent does not. Being Vincent's brother and supporter, Theo is caught between his brother's needs and their parents' concern about appearances. He does not think Vincent should marry Sien. No. He is not squarely on his brother's side.

Vincent feels the distance between them. He misses the simplicity of the intimacy they had a decade earlier. He longs for that time—the walk to the mill, the declaration of shared ambition, of understanding.

Because Sien is still recovering from the birth of her son and not yet able to pose, Vincent is working on landscapes, scenes from around The Hague.

He paints their windmill.

The Laakmolen near The Hague (The Windmill)

IT IS NOT a well-known image. Surprisingly, it rarely shows up in books about Vincent. Scholars probably consider it a practice drawing, maybe for his cityscapes for Uncle Cor. Vincent might have referred to it as a drawing, not a painting, as he often did when he used watercolors. Paintings, to him, were those made with oil. And Vincent barely mentions it in his letters to Theo, even though he often does write about the mill, and their walk to it.

But it is *the* image of Vincent's relationship with Theo, *the* piece of art depicting the most important relationship in Vincent's life. It should be one of his most famous.

FOR THIS PIECE, Vincent uses watercolor, pencil, and pen and ink on paper. Although it's of an iconic Dutch structure—a windmill—he paints just the bottom part; you can't see the sails in the wind. This could be to say: I'm not buying into all things Dutch, all things the establishment stands for. Certainly he wants the viewer to focus on two figures: two men standing close together.

There are four figures in the painting, but the most prominent are these two men standing together.

The men are in workers' clothes, not fancy establishment garb. One of the men is thinner than the other, of a slighter stature. He stands straight and neat. The other man is bigger and maybe taller, but he is slouching, so he looks shorter. He's messier, and he is leaning into the other man, his right knee bent toward the other man's leg, his right foot forward, touching, or almost touching, the other man's left foot.

It makes sense to see the men as Vincent and Theo.

Vincent leaning into Theo.

The bigger man could be talking.

Making a point.

Vincent is always making a point of some kind.

At this moment, it could be a plea: stay close to me, stick with me. We are in this together!

There is a sign on the mill, next to the door, MILK FOR SALE. Just as there had been when Vincent and Theo took their walk.

There is a woman standing in the doorway, looking at the two men.

There is another figure, faded, behind them. A woman perhaps, a man, probably. The figure is barely painted, all in one color, a light ecru. The figure is walking away, his back to the viewer. He is not looking at the two men.

Who is that?

Vincent makes this painting in July, when the letters between the brothers are all about Sien, Tersteeg's disapproval, Theo's disapprobation. At this time Vincent writes to his brother:

"I also repeat that I long for you so much, isolated from everything and everyone else, because I need sympathy and warmth."

And:

"I would so much like to take a walk with you—*even though the Rijswijk mill isn't there any more.* Oh well."

The mill, in fact, is still there.

Why does he say it isn't?

There *are* plans to replace it with a steam-pumping station. These plans come to nothing, but alterations are made to the mill around now. Perhaps Vincent thinks they are tearing it down, not renovating it. Or perhaps he means it's closed because of the work.

No glasses of milk for sale.

Maybe he means symbolically it isn't there.

How does he paint it? The mill is not close to his flat, so maybe he paints it from memory, or from a photograph. But it is so very accurate, as if he is standing right next to it.

And he chooses a very particular point of view.

He paints it showing a path that ends at the fence surrounding the mill. There are many places to stand and paint the mill from different angles. Why does he paint it from this perspective? With a fence blocking the path? Is the path leading away from something, or leading *to*?

And although we focus on the two men at first, our eyes soon go from the lower part of the mill to a hut on the left, to a bird flying between the hut and the mill, back to the two men, to the woman in the doorway, and finally to the fading figure walking away.

So many questions are unanswered. Who is the woman in the doorway? Is it their mother? Or just the woman selling milk? Who is the shadow figure walking past the mill? Mauve? Tersteeg? Pa? Sien, walking away?

LOOKING AT THE PAINTING AGAIN, we see something else. The part of the sail we see looks like a ladder. It draws the viewer's eye to the two men. A ladder is a support; it's also a way up.

The Laakmolen near the Hague is a message to Theo. Reaching back to their walk, reaching forward to the future. It is a picture of support. Of friendship. They are more than brothers. It is a plea. Stay with me. Stay by me.

The painting is a personal statement, an allegory, and it is also a glimpse into the future. Vincent's future. He takes traditions from the Hague School and plays with them, makes them his own. Vincent is still learning, but already he is forging new paths for himself and those who will follow, though he doesn't know it yet.

THEO PLANS TO VISIT Vincent the following month, August.

Vincent writes, in anticipation of the visit, "Do you think we could agree that while you're here we'll spend the time together that's left after your business and visits and then do our best, on both sides, to be in the same sort of mood as in the past at the Rijswijk mill?"

Vincent hasn't shown Theo the painting yet. But he tells him "what has reawakened deep inside me is the belief that there's something good and that it's worthwhile making an effort and doing one's best to take life seriously. This is now perhaps, or rather certainly, more firmly rooted in me than in the past, when I had experienced less. For me the point now is to express the poetry of those days in drawings."

He writes to Theo about art, and color, and how he is trying to capture it all, to give something of himself to the world, to their family.

WHEN THEO COMES, he brings a generosity of spirit—and money. He tells Vincent he'll keep supporting him. And Vincent agrees that he will not mention Sien or his situation to their parents. And for now he won't think about marriage.

He does not mention Sien again to Theo for six months.

Vincent's bond with Theo is more important than any other he has. More important than the one with Sien. By agreeing not to write home about her, he will not put Theo in the middle.

He tells Theo he's working hard and fast, making up for lost time because he had started making art so late. He tells Theo how grateful he is for his help. He knows he's "privileged above a thousand others in that you remove so many barriers in my way."

WHEN THEO LEAVES, Vincent buys new brushes, a watercolor box that he will use when painting outside, watercolors, and oil paints. Vincent sends Theo a sketch of the palette, and a list of the colors he bought: "ochre (red, yellow, brown), cobalt and Prussian blue, Naples yellow, terra sienna, black and white, supplemented with some carmine, sepia, vermilion, ultramarine, gamboge."

Vincent realizes that Theo does not have to be *exactly like him* for them to be close, for Theo to help him carry his parcel. It's a hard-won understanding for Vincent, and one that he will forget in the future.

But the brothers are connected by their differences as much as their similarities. One is neat and straight-standing, the other messy, leaning.

They are part of each other, interstitial: lodged between each other's cells. Theo is the invisible glue that holds Vincent together. But Vincent also holds Theo together, even if it doesn't always seem that way to either of them. They have helped each other set their goals, and they will prod each other into reaching them.

Here, in the summer of 1882, it is as if they are standing by the mill once again, the ground beneath them solid, at least for now.

48.

THE PERSPECTIVE FRAME

VINCENT HAS BEEN WORKING HARD to teach himself the fundamentals of art: anatomy, perspective, and color. For now he's focusing on drawing; color will have to wait.

But he's having trouble with perspective.

In June he'd gotten himself an artist's tool called a perspective frame, but then he had to go into the hospital. He took books on perspective with him but was too weak to work.

Now, just after Theo's visit, he takes out his perspective frame again. Modeled after one made by the famous German painter Albrecht Dürer, and depicted in Vincent's art manuals, it's an open rectangle made of wood, strung with horizontal and vertical threads to make a grid. Vincent adds diagonal threads from the corners to create an X through the middle, so it looks like the Union Jack British flag, or a six-pointed asterisk.

He takes it to a blacksmith and has him put iron corners on the frame, and iron spikes on the legs so he can stand it up outside next to his easel. This way, he tells Theo, "on the beach or in a meadow or a field you have a view *as if through a window*." He draws a sketch so Theo can see it: "The perpendicular and horizontal lines of the frame, together with the diagonals and the cross" form a grid. Sometimes Vincent even draws a grid of squares right on his paper before he starts a scene. With the perspective frame, he feels confident making a drawing with a firm hand, the outlines and proportions being correct.

Vincent knows that to earn money as a draftsman, he has to have all the basics down. And—he can't help but think—if he's ever to become a true artist, he has to hone all his skills to perfection. At times he already feels like an artist and has even begun to sign some of his works—just his first name, "Vincent," often in bright red letters. He underscores it with a flourish. But he doesn't refer to himself as an artist, just as a draftsman. He wants to fulfill his promise to Theo that he will be selling his art by the end of the year.

He knows he has more to learn about perspective, "why and how perspective appears to change the direction of lines and the size of masses and planes. Without that, the frame is little or no help, and makes your head *spin* when you look through it."

To be able to understand the perspective of a scene, you have to know what you're looking at *and* where you are standing. You have to understand how moving this way or that changes a picture—how objects far away look smaller, objects closer look bigger. Being too close can make something seem larger than it is.

Look through a window. Move an inch and the view is different. Depending on where you stand, you see a view differently. Even with a frame around it.

Distance can change your perspective, too. So can time.

49.

POETRY IN THE STORM

_____

DORUS AND ANNA have moved again. Theo goes to see them in Nuenen, another small town in the Brabant region of the Netherlands. Theo suggests Vincent might like to paint it one day, and Vincent replies yes, he'd like to try "doing that kind of old church and churchyard with sandy graves and old wooden crosses," with "a stretch of heath and a pine-wood nearby."

Reminiscent of Zundert.

Theo keeps the peace. He reassures Pa and Ma about Vincent, and he extols *their* virtues to Vincent. Vincent writes back that he agrees, that their parents are special and should be appreciated. But he knows he's not cut from the same cloth as they are, and he knows their worries about him are not over. He is sure that if they saw him, they would be upset.

Since he's spending all his time either with Sien or alone working, he has let his appearance go. Ma and Pa wouldn't understand that, or his life-style, or his art.

Vincent sees art and poetry in the storms of life and in the storms of nature, unlike his parents. It's been stormy and stormily beautiful to Vincent in Scheveningen lately, and into the squalls he goes. He is just starting to paint with oils and is not used to them yet, but he takes oil paints into the storm to paint the beach, the waves crashing one after the other, the wind blowing, the sea the color of dirty dishwater. He makes one of his first oil paintings, *View of the Sea at Scheveningen*, with a fishing boat and several figures on the beach. The wind is fierce, kicking up the sand. Sand sticks to the thick, wet paint.

Vincent loves capturing the turbulence of a storm. "There's something infinite about painting," he tells his brother. "I can't quite explain—but especially for expressing a mood, it's a joy."

A few days later, on a quieter day, he sketches the beach. Sending the sketch to Theo, he describes "a blond, soft effect, and in the woods a more sombre, serious mood. I'm glad that both of these exist in life."

Wild and somber. Room for both. Room for all.

Vincent finds oils easier to paint with than watercolors, and loves to lay the paint on thickly, a technique called impasto. But because oil paint is expensive, he continues to use other media: he draws with charcoal and a carpenter's pencil. He adds black and white chalk to his watercolors.

By October he's drawn one hundred studies of figures—all since Theo's August visit. He can't quite capture on paper what he has in his head, but he's learning. "Success is sometimes the outcome of a whole string of failures," he tells Theo.

In November he decides to learn the art of lithography, Theo's suggestion long ago, so that he can become an illustrator. He draws using lithographic crayon and ink, sometimes adding those media to his drawings in graphite. He experiments, drawing with lithographic crayon over carpenter's pencil, and uses a mixture of milk and water to fix the drawings to the paper. This creates a matte finish, which he likes. He makes lithographs of *Sorrow* as well.

He's excited by his progress all around. But by the end of the year he knows he hasn't produced a salable drawing. He apologizes to Theo, tells him he appreciates his help and friendship, and keeps on working.

50.

LITTLE HOPE

WINTER IN THE HAGUE. Vincent is lonely. Living with Sien and her children, he's isolated from everyone else. And now tensions are growing with Sien.

Meanwhile in Paris, Theo has met a woman. Marie. It was a dramatic meeting, as Theo describes it to Vincent. She was alone, sick in body (she had a tumor in her foot) and soul (she was, Theo tells his brother, the victim of a man who took advantage of her). She is Roman Catholic, born on the coast of Brittany. And like the woman he loved back in The Hague, she is from a lower class. Theo falls for her immediately and hard.

He pays for her operation, and for the first few months Theo is consumed with taking care of her. When he tells Vincent, Vincent is all for it. He encourages Theo to marry her, or at least to think of it as a marriage. They should have a child together!

Theo does consider marriage and weighs when to break the news to his parents. He and Vincent discuss all of this in letters. "What a mystery life is, and love is a mystery within a mystery," Vincent says.

By the summer, July of 1883, Theo is overwhelmed financially. He's now supporting Marie, Vincent, and Sien and her two children, and he's sending money to Ma and Pa and to Wil.

He writes to Vincent, "As for the future, I can give you little hope."

Vincent panics: "I don't know how you intended those words, nor can I know. Your letter is too brief, but it gave me an unexpected blow right in the chest." He posts that letter and then writes another the same day. Theo will often get more than one letter from him in a day—mail is delivered several times a day in Paris, even on Sundays.

Vincent's feeling sick. He doesn't know if it's a fever or a reaction to what Theo said. He begs Theo to write back soon. "I don't really have any friends except for you."

Is Theo going to stop supporting him? Or has he lost hope for the future of Vincent's art? The first he can live with; the second, not.

"I've set my whole heart on it," he tells Theo.

The next day he writes again. He'd gone for a walk, and been up all night. He's worried sick. He sends Theo photographs of some recent drawings he's done: peat diggers in dunes, potato grubbers, and a sower.

He begs for more time. He knows he's not there yet, but . . .

If Theo is going to abandon him, he wishes he'd never taken up art; he wishes he'd died when he was in the Borinage.

51.

TORN MONEY

IT'S NOT about the art. It's about the money. Theo's letter arrives the next day. He points out how many people he's supporting. Rather remarkable.

Vincent snipes back that sure, that's remarkable, but isn't it remarkable, too, that he's dividing the money Theo gives him between four "living beings" and all the expenses for models, drawing and painting materials, and rent?

He doesn't like being dependent on Theo, either. As it is right now, Vincent says, he has to fast until the next installment of money.

Vincent has a proposal: the next time Theo comes to visit—soon, he hopes—they should make a real effort to sell his work. Vincent follows this proposal with a letter the next day, making sure that Theo understands that they are partners: "My studies and everything in the way of work in the studio is definitely your property."

By the end of that week, Theo sends money. But it's a banknote, paper money, and it's torn. Vincent's bank won't give him the full amount. They give him some, and he has to send the note to Paris for the rest of the money.

Theo has sent a letter, too. It explains more about what's been going on with him. Theo's worry is not just about the money. He's conflicted about his love life. Just like his brother.

52.

UNFORTUNATE CONSEQUENCES
OF GOOD DEEDS

---

*T*HEO LOVES MARIE. But he doesn't know if he should marry her. It would be the honorable thing to do—for her. But Ma and Pa would be upset if Theo married a Catholic, lower-class woman. Appearances.

He writes to Vincent, asking his advice.

Vincent is sympathetic, empathetic: "What you write in your letter about the conflict one can have over the question of whether one is accountable for the unfortunate consequences of a good deed . . . that conflict is familiar to me too."

How do you balance your feelings with the way you look to society? And what if the honorable thing actually would look bad to others? Would it be better to act in a way that goes against your conscience but is better for your appearance?

Both the brothers are plagued with the consequences of their "good deeds."

Theo is overwhelmed with money worries and by his ambivalence about Marie, but at least he has colleagues at the gallery, clients he speaks to regularly, painters he spends time with. Vincent is isolated. He has no one but Sien, the children, and Sien's family. And Sien's family is a problem now. Her mother especially, Vincent says. She keeps interfering in a negative and controlling way.

Being with Sien might not be worth it anymore. But he wants to be honorable to her. And there are the children.

Willem, the baby, adores him; he wants to be with Vincent all the time. "If I'm working he comes up to tug at my jacket or works his way up my leg until I take him on my lap." When he's in the studio, he "crows about everything" and can sit for hours with a bit of string or an old paintbrush. He's such a happy baby, and the way he is now, he will grow up to be "cleverer than I am."

Vincent worries about his situation with Sien, plus he's got a fatigue he can't shake, and bouts of melancholy. Even so, he works assiduously. He has the same mission as always, and a new reason for working fast: he's feeling so weak he "can't count on living for a great many years." He gives himself six or ten years at the most.

As he had the summer before, he works especially hard on his oil painting. He's happy with his progress, and he starts to refer to himself as an *artiste-peintre*, a painter. He will keep drawing—and by the end of his life the number of drawings will equal the number of paintings—but by calling himself an *artiste-peintre* he means he's not just a draftsman. He thinks of himself as someone who is responding to a higher calling. It's not just about making money anymore. Because he's "walked the earth for 30 years," he wants to "leave a certain souvenir in the form of drawings or paintings in gratitude."

Theo writes that he is coming to visit. Vincent is excited: he can't wait to see what Theo thinks about his work. But Vincent is worried, too. He knows that Theo is his most severe critic . . . after Vincent himself. And Theo's the one whose opinion matters most.

WHEN THEO ARRIVES in The Hague and Vincent shows him his art, Theo doesn't see enough progress; there is nothing good enough for him to sell. Vincent is disappointed, but he is willing to work harder. He knows he has to.

But that isn't the worst part of the visit.

They argue about Sien.

Theo had heard from others how terrible Vincent looked. Now he sees it for himself. Vincent is gaunt, badly dressed, clearly not well. Theo is dismayed. He tells Vincent that living with Sien and her children, the insufficient money, the lack of food, the worries—it's all taking a terrific toll on him.

Vincent admits that he hasn't bothered with clothes or appearances at all recently. "This year I've been completely outside any kind of social circle, so to speak."

Theo gives him a suit, but it's not just about appearances. He begs Vincent to take better care of himself.

He tells him to leave Sien. Life would be so much easier if he did. Vincent would be able to work better without her in his life. And Theo would have an easier time with fewer people to support.

Vincent tells him he has a sense of duty to Sien and her children.

Theo says he thinks Sien's motives are financial—she's in it for the money.

Vincent says no, Sien is honorable. Though her mother *is* a bad influence.

Theo has a way for Vincent to end it with Sien. He says Vincent's work *has* progressed enough that he could get work as an illustrator in London. He could move there. Besides, he argues, separating from Sien would be better not only for Vincent's work but also for Sien.

Vincent disagrees. He says he doesn't want to leave her. He would rather leave The Hague and move to the country with Sien and the children. He could move her away from her mother and that bad influence. And they'd reduce expenses by living outside the city. He is certain that if he leaves her, she'll go back to being a prostitute. And there is little Willem. . . .

They argue about Pa, too. Theo says Vincent is too cool toward Pa. But Vincent actually longs for his father. He wishes that he could go to Nuenen when Theo does, and walk through the old country churchyard with Theo and Pa. His "heart yearns to be together."

Theo tells him to consider the consequences of staying with Sien, and of leaving her. And then he goes home to their parents.

AFTER THEO'S VISIT, Vincent asks Sien to stay away from her mother, but she refuses. Her family is pressuring her to leave Vincent because they are so poor.

Vincent and Sien argue and argue.

Back home, Theo doesn't tell Ma and Pa everything that is going on with Vincent, but he does ask Uncle Cor for help with their financial problems. Uncle Cor helps by taking more than twenty of Vincent's drawings on consignment. If he sells them, he will pay Vincent. Vincent is grateful for Theo's intervention and Uncle Cor's help, but he tells Theo that this cannot be contingent on his leaving Sien. He's not ready to make that decision, even though there is now a real lack of trust between him and Sien, no true understanding anymore.

Vincent reports to Theo a conversation he and Sien have had:

She told Vincent he expects too much of her. "I am indifferent and lazy," Sien said, "and I always have been and there's nothing to be done about it. . . . It's bound to end up with me jumping into the water."

53.

DISAPPEARING

I can't help but make progress precisely through learning by doing; every drawing one makes, every study one paints is a step. It's true that it's like going along a road, one can see the steeple in the distance, but the land undulates, so that when one thinks one is there, there's another stretch that one didn't see at first and which is added on. However, one does get nearer.

—Vincent to Theo, October 15, 1883

*D*O YOU KNOW what I've done?" Vincent writes to Theo soon after Theo's visit. He's told Sien that he is leaving The Hague. He wants to go to Drenthe to paint. Drenthe is in the northeast of the Netherlands; it's rural and very few people live there. Vincent's friend Anthon van Rappard has been there, painting, and he loves it. He visited Vincent and told him all about it.

At first Vincent had thought he'd take Sien and the children with him. They've been living together as a family for over a year. But, Vincent reports to Theo, they sensibly decided to separate.

We have only Vincent's side. We see Sien, and this moment, only from his perspective: Vincent and Sien, equal partners in this discussion, both with the same point of view.

Vincent and Sien talk calmly. It would be better for both of them, for all of them, they agree.

Sien tells Vincent she'd already been planning to leave him.

"Go as straight as possible," Vincent says to her. Always remember that you are the children's mother. No matter how you support them, that is the most important thing.

He says he had wanted to marry her, but now there is no other way but to separate.

They end the conversation, parting as friends.

VINCENT LEAVES THE HAGUE and moves to Drenthe. He thinks he will be happy painting there.

But he is not. Van Rappard is no longer there. Vincent paints and tries to stay optimistic, but he is terribly lonely.

In Paris, Theo is unhappy, too. He has told his parents he is going to marry Marie, and they strongly disapprove. He doesn't know what to do. And he's starting to have more and more disagreements with his bosses at Goupil's. He's thinking about quitting his job and moving to America. He tells Vincent he wants to disappear.

Vincent writes him long, long letters from Drenthe, filled with advice and ideas about Marie and about work. He tells Theo that he, too, sometimes thinks of disappearing, but that neither of them should. "Neither you nor I must *ever* do that, any more than a suicide."

I am sometimes melancholy, too, Vincent tells his brother, and I, too, think of disappearing. But when you have those feelings, you must BEWARE. Suicide, disappearing, these are not things we Van Gogh brothers would do.

Vincent has another answer. The one he falls back on when he's lonely: Theo should quit his job and come be a painter with him. "If something in you yourself says 'you aren't a painter'—*it's then that you should paint*, old chap, and that voice will be silenced too, but precisely because of that."

Vincent thinks he's talking about Theo, but he's thinking about himself: for him, painting is the answer to his misery, to his lack of confidence, to his feelings of being at sea in the world. Not so for Theo. He tells Vincent so. Theo says he will not become a painter; he has no talent.

Vincent writes back, argues. He tells Theo he can learn. Back when Vincent drew some pictures in London, they were bad. But if someone had just taught him a little about perspective, he'd be much farther along now. He could teach Theo. Come paint on the heath with me!

Theo responds again: no.

Vincent doesn't give up. He even writes with an ultimatum: he will take no more money if Theo keeps working at Goupil's.

Theo responds by not responding. He disappears.

Day after day Vincent waits for a letter from his brother. Nothing comes. He is lonely, isolated, in a place he doesn't know, away from everyone. No Theo. No friends. No Sien. No baby Willem. It is winter, his worst time. Vincent disappears again into darkness.

54.

DIRTY DOG

---

*There's a similar reluctance about taking me into
the house as there would be about having a large,
shaggy dog in the house.*

—Vincent to Theo, December 15, 1883

WHEN A LETTER from Theo finally comes, after three weeks, Vincent quickly answers. He tells Theo he hadn't meant to give him an ultimatum. He just doesn't want to be a burden. He—and Marie and their parents and Wil—don't want Theo to stay in his job if he's unhappy just so he can support all of them. He tells Theo he will do what he can to help; he will go back home. If he lives with Ma and Pa again, he reasons, it will save money.

This is Vincent's way of apologizing. (Though he won't give up for quite a while trying to persuade Theo to be an artist with him.)

But the truth is also that Vincent wants to go home. He *needs* to go home. He is depressed, and he craves the intimate bond of his family again, no matter how imperfect that can be.

Vincent writes to Pa. He begs him for help.

Pa immediately sends him money for a train.

IT IS A STORMY December afternoon. Vincent gathers his brushes and his paints, his canvases and his easels, all the painting supplies he'd taken to

Drenthe from The Hague, and he walks. He treks for six hours across the heath in the snow and the rain to get to the train. He arrives in Nuenen, at his parents' house, again filthy, exhausted, a wreck. He knows it. He knows he's like a dog, a big, shaggy, dog with muddy, wet paws. It can't be easy for them to let him in. The dog will "get in everyone's way. *And he barks so loudly.*" He is, he tells Theo, "a dirty animal."

"At first it seemed to be hopeless," Pa writes to Theo, "but it has gradually got better, particularly since we agreed that he will stay with us for the time being, to make studies here."

Vincent is clean and fed. He is not alone. But sometimes he still feels so unbearably lonely, he wishes he had stayed on the heath.

In Paris, Theo hears what a difficult time it is for all of them. But he's glad his brother has moved in with their parents, where he can be watched over, and away from Sien. The expenses will go down, too, thank goodness.

Ma and Pa try to make Vincent's life with them as good as they can. They turn the mangle room, where wet clothes are wrung out to dry, into a studio so he can paint and draw at home. They make space for him to store some paintings as well. Pa tells Theo that they set up the room as Vincent wanted it—not as he and Ma thought it should be. The creation of the studio in the parsonage, a room the way Vincent wants it, is a sign that they are encouraging his work as an artist.

Ma and Pa even vow not to bother him about his "eccentricities of dress etc." People in Nuenen have already seen him. He *is* eccentric, and there is no changing that.

———————

IN LATE DECEMBER, Vincent goes back to The Hague to collect his things. And to see Sien. She is weak, sick. At least she's not working as a prostitute, but as a washerwoman. Still, Vincent fears "very much for her well-being," he tells Theo. "And the poor baby, which I cared for as if it were my own, is no longer what it was either."

Vincent feels deep regret. He is still attached to Sien, and he is sure he put her and her children in great danger by leaving. He'd made the wrong decision. Sien. Little Maria. Baby Willem. How could he have done that?

He goes back to Nuenen, sits down with a piece of paper, and rails at Theo. It's Theo's fault! Theo pressured him in so many ways during that August visit, pushing him into deserting Sien and the children. "What is crueler than to deprive such an unfortunate, withered woman and her little child of support?" he writes. Who is the dirty animal now?

It is a sad letter to end the year, 1883. "Sad for me to write," Vincent says. And sad for Theo to receive, "but it's worse for the poor woman." Vincent is sure she will die soon.

In fact, Sien will live twenty more years. In 1904, long after Vincent's death, she will commit suicide by jumping into the water, just as she had once predicted.

But Vincent doesn't know that, of course. He writes more angry letters to Theo. Theo writes angry letters back. Their relationship is again strained to the point of breakage.

Endings and Beginnings

1884–1885

55.

FRACTURES AND IMPRESSIONS

I do so hope that his work might find some approbation.
For he works so much it is exemplary.

—Pa to Theo, February 10, 1884

VINCENT HAS BEEN LIVING in Nuenen for six weeks. Even with some tension at home and a lot of long-distance tension with Theo, he's been working well. He's begun a series of paintings of peasants weaving. He's already made four paintings.

One day he's out painting in the fields when he is summoned home. There's been an accident. Ma has fractured her right thighbone getting off a train. Although there is no immediate danger, it will be a long recovery, and given her age, sixty-four, there could be serious, even fatal, complications.

The crisis brings out the very best in Vincent. He immediately writes to Theo and tells him the money he sends will go to Ma and Pa, not for his painting supplies. He nurses Ma with the kindness he showed the miners in the Borinage. Pa appreciates how helpful he is around the house. His relationship with both of his parents improves dramatically.

When he's not helping his parents, he still works on his art, painting weavers and winter landscapes and gardens and views around the village of

Nuenen. He can paint in oil, since his expenses are reduced by living at home, but he also keeps drawing—in pencil, black chalk, and colored ink—and uses watercolor. He keeps working on perfecting the human figure using all these media and opaque white paint.

Pa tells Theo how happy he is with Vincent. "Vincent remains exemplary in nursing and is also working with the greatest ambition on drawing and painting."

Finally Pa isn't complaining about Vincent to Theo but praising him. He also tells Theo to be nicer to Vincent.

BUT THEO IS STILL ANGRY at his brother, not just because of Vincent's accusations about Sien, but also because he thinks Vincent isn't making enough progress with his art. Vincent is furious back at him for that. He declares not for the first time that theirs should be only a business relationship; whatever he makes officially belongs to Theo. Vincent adamantly does not want Theo's money to be a gift, or worse, charity. He will send work every month, in exchange.

The argument gets heated. Although Vincent says he wants the critiques from Theo, he is angry that Theo still doesn't think his work is worth selling. It's frustrating, and embarrassing! People in town make comments, wondering what Vincent is playing at.

"You have *never yet* sold *a single thing* of mine—not for a lot or a little—and IN FACT HAVEN'T TRIED TO YET. As you can see, I'm not getting *angry* about it—but—there's no need to beat about the bush."

It is Theo's role to help Vincent's paintings sell, and therefore to tell him how to improve so they *will* sell. Theo has some very specific thoughts. In letters, and on a visit home in early June 1884, he tries to persuade Vincent to paint with lighter, brighter colors. He criticizes Vincent's dark palette and describes to him the work of some painters he's seeing in Paris.

They are Impressionists: Edgar Degas, Camille Pissarro, Claude Monet, Pierre-Auguste Renoir, and others.

At the Goupil gallery he's also trying to persuade his bosses to see the value of this new Impressionist style: the use of color, light, brushstrokes, the freedom, the originality. He's so frustrated with his bosses, who won't let him sell modern art in the gallery. They just don't understand.

But Vincent, ever eager to improve, puts aside his hurt feelings and tries to understand what Theo is talking about. From what Theo tells him, he's beginning to grasp that the style is "something different from what I thought it was, but it's still not entirely clear to me what one should understand by it." But to understand Impressionism, you have to *see* the light, the brushstrokes, the unusual points of view, the *suggestion* of a boat, a bridge, water, sky, the use of light as a *subject*. These paintings are not being mass reproduced yet, so Vincent cannot see them in Nuenen. He has no idea what they look like.

He begins to read and study books about color theory. The books are by Dutch painters, who painted in a muted palette, so although he absorbs some of what Theo is trying to tell him, Vincent's color range remains more Dutch than French. He is trying to make the darker colors seem light, but he can't help but paint in somber shades of brown and grey.

And yet Vincent's life is anything but muted right now. His world is bright, hot. Red hot. For, once again, Vincent is in love.

56.

POISON

MA IS RECOVERING NICELY. Vincent is working hard in a studio he's rented away from the house.

He is also spending a lot of time with the woman next door.

Before Ma broke her leg, she had been holding a sewing class in the house. While she was laid up, a neighbor, Margot Begemann, taught the class for her. She's also been helping out with Ma, and so Margot and Vincent have gotten to know each other. She's the youngest of three daughters; her father was the pastor of the village for many years but died eight years earlier. She is, according to Vincent, smart and compassionate and a good businesswoman; she is a partner with her brother, Louis, in a linen mill. Although she is twelve years older, forty-three to Vincent's thirty-one, the two have fallen in love.

After spending a lot of time with her for the past months, Vincent has decided he wants to marry her. And she wants to marry him!

They both talk to their families.

Margot's family is vehemently opposed to the idea. Her sisters, older and not married, belittle her, treating the whole idea of the marriage scornfully, Vincent reports to Theo.

Theo comes to visit late in the summer. Vincent expects Theo to be supportive of his romance, but he's not. He does not think Vincent should marry Margot. The brothers argue. Vincent is, in the moment, furious.

At her house, Margot's family lashes out at her about the idea, too. Whereas Vincent is used to being at odds with his family, Margot is not. She becomes distraught.

In the days that follow, Vincent grows more and more concerned about Margot. She is acting oddly, and Vincent recognizes the symptoms of depression. In many ways he knows how she is feeling, and he is very worried about what might happen to her. He wants to help. So he goes to a doctor, describes her symptoms, and asks for advice. Then he talks to her brother, Louis, and warns him that she might be heading toward a nervous collapse. He tells Louis the family "acted extremely imprudently by speaking to her as they did."

But Louis does nothing to help Margot; instead the family tells Vincent he must wait two years if he wants to marry her. Vincent does not want to wait! If they are to marry, it will be soon.

Summer turns to fall, and as they walk together through the fields around Nuenen, Margot makes ominous declarations to Vincent. "I wish I could die now," she tells him. Vincent wishes he could be with her every moment so nothing bad will happen.

And then one morning, as they're walking, Margot collapses in the field.

At first Vincent thinks she's just weak. But then her stomach starts cramping, and she seems to be having convulsions. "She lost the power of speech and mumbled all sorts of only half-comprehensible things," Vincent told Theo afterward.

Vincent thinks maybe it's a nervous fit, but he realizes all at once it's quite different.

"Have you taken something by any chance?" he asks her.

"Yes!" she screams. She asks him to swear he won't tell anyone about it.

"Fine," says Vincent, "I'll swear anything you want but on condition that you vomit that stuff up immediately—stick your finger down your throat until you vomit, otherwise I'll call the others."

Margot vomits some, but not enough to cure her. Vincent takes her to Louis, and gets him to give her an emetic so she will vomit more. Then Vincent rushes her to the Van Gogh family doctor, who gives her an antidote. Her life is saved, but she needs more medical and psychological help than she can get in a small village.

Louis takes her to a doctor in Utrecht, a large city sixty miles to the north. She will stay there until she recovers. Her attempted suicide is kept a secret. Louis tells everyone she's on a business trip.

Vincent still wants to marry her, but her doctor counsels patience. She would be too weak to marry for at least two years. But a breakup would devastate her. So Vincent and Margot write letters back and forth. (Vincent and Margot correspond for a few years. She is not allowed to utter his name in front of her family, and she burns all his letters. Margot has some of Vincent's early work, and in 1889, Vincent will ask his sister Wil to give Margot one of his paintings, but Wil never does. Margot will live until 1907.)

Theo disapproves that Vincent is still in touch with Margot. Vincent is hurt by that. And he's hurt that Theo has broken it off with Marie and hasn't told him why.

The brothers had been doing better since Ma's fracture—because Vincent helped so much and Theo was grateful. But now their goodwill has all but disappeared. Theo thinks Vincent is once again causing his parents too much distress with the Margot affair.

He thinks Vincent should leave Nuenen for the sake of Ma and Pa.

Then Theo tells Vincent he doesn't think he will be able to sell anything of his for two years. But Vincent is working harder than ever; he needs to buy more supplies. He needs more money from Theo. It's exceedingly awkward. Vincent feels Theo doesn't understand him or his work. They have such different views of the way life should be lived. And yet Vincent needs Theo's money.

Theo answers back. He is suspicious that Vincent keeps running short of money. What is he really using it for? Vincent is indignant. He tells Theo they have clashing ideologies. Theo is part of the stodgy establishment, a company man, while Vincent is the passionate worker, the artist.

There is a coldness between them—and a fiery heat—as autumn turns to winter. They are so angry at each other, their relationship tainted as if *it*, too, has been poisoned.

In the second week of December 1884, Vincent writes to Theo: "It seems to me that we must split up—*in both our interests*."

57.

BLACK AND WHITE

---

*I*T'S THE BEGINNING of 1885. Vincent has been working hard at his art for almost five years. He thinks he's getting better.

Theo is not convinced.

Without Theo's faith in him, it's hard to keep going.

But then Theo tells him they should stop arguing; Vincent would do better to spend his time painting more pictures. He says that would be better not only for the two of them but also for the world. He does still have faith in him. In fact, in addition to that declaration of confidence, Theo also proposes increasing Vincent's monthly allowance.

In spite of the reprieve from fighting with Theo, Vincent feels gloomy. Winter in Nuenen. Too much time indoors. But still he works hard. He paints during the day; at night he draws a series of thirty heads, up close.

Vincent still isn't doing what Theo wishes he would: paint in lighter, brighter colors. He *is* experimenting, but with black, and black and white.

He is trying to perfect his use of chiaroscuro, the interplay of light and dark, *without* regard to color.

———————

PA AND MA notice his gloominess. Pa tells Theo that Vincent is moody and often unresponsive, spending very little time with them. On February 19, Pa writes to Theo that he's worried Vincent is becoming estranged from him and Ma again. "His short temper prevents any talking and that in itself is enough to prove that he isn't normal. It's certainly not easy for me to be passive. And yet previous experience has taught me that one doesn't win by opposition and it doesn't improve matters."

Pa doesn't want the rift to grow, so after writing to Theo, he goes and finds Vincent. He talks to him, tells his son about his concern for him. The talk does not turn into a fight, and Dorus writes a postscript to Theo the next day. Vincent has assured him that he is fine, that he is not depressed, and that there would be no reason for him to be. Pa is relieved but, as always, worried about what the future will bring for Vincent. Still. He tells Theo, "We will just have to wait and see."

In March, Vincent and Theo write only a few letters. They are impersonal, businesslike, focused on the art.

But on March 27, Vincent sends Theo three telegrams, one right after the other:

The first one he sends to the Goupil branch where he thinks Theo might be:

SUDDEN DEATH, COME, VAN GOGH. It arrives at 6 a.m.

To the same branch, at 7:35: OUR FATHER FATAL STROKE, COME, BUT IT IS OVER. VAN GOGH

To the other Goupil branch, at 7:58, just in case Theo is there: OUR FATHER FATAL STROKE. VAN GOGH

Pa had died on the threshold of their house the evening before, at 7:30.

Wil was the only eyewitness: "Pa went out in the morning healthy and in the evening he came home and as he came in the door he collapsed without giving any further sign of life. It was terrible. I shall never forget that night."

Alive one minute, dead the next. Black and white.

58.

STILL LIFE WITH HONESTY

---

*P*A WAS SIXTY-THREE. He was, as far as anyone knew, in good health. He'd just taken a long walk across the heath. Theo had received a letter from Pa the day before. All had been fine.

And now Theo is going home to his father's funeral; he leaves Paris the same day he receives the news. He'll arrive in Nuenen the next, March 28. A friend of Theo's, fellow Dutchman Andries Bonger, takes him to the train station for the first part of his journey. "Never have I taken a friend to the Gare du Nord in more melancholy circumstances," Andries writes his father. He is worried about Theo, who was already sickly and "not very strong; so you can understand the state he was in when he left."

DORUS IS BURIED on Monday, March 30, Vincent's thirty-second birthday.

Vincent and Theo haven't seen each other since the previous August. They fought then and have been fighting ever since. But seeing each other in person over their father's coffin goes a long way toward mending their relationship. A clasping of hands, a rejoining of hearts.

And they have time while Theo is home to look over Vincent's recent work together. The news is good there. Theo likes some of Vincent's paintings well enough to take them back to Paris: oil paintings of peasant women and a still life of flowers in a vase. There are several kinds of flowers in the painting; one is called honesty.

After Theo returns to Paris on the afternoon of Wednesday, April 1, Vincent makes another painting similar to the one with flowers in a vase, but in the new one he includes a pipe and tobacco pouch of Pa's. Pa was the one who had told Vincent to smoke a pipe when he was sad, and Vincent had passed on that advice to Theo.

In a letter Vincent offers this painting to Theo, but Theo tells Vincent to keep it, and for some reason Vincent soon paints over it—a basket with apples.

Again work helps Vincent cope with sadness in his life. He tells Theo, "I'm still very much under the impression of what has just happened—I just kept painting these two Sundays."

In Paris, Theo consoles himself with a new girlfriend, someone he'd met a few months earlier, "S." He also spends a lot of time with his friend Andries Bonger. Though Theo met Dries when Theo had first moved to Paris five years earlier, they haven't spent much time together. But Dries always liked Theo, and now he wants to help him. He tells his parents in a letter that Theo is very sad about his father's death but is still very good company. "He is a charming companion," Dries writes.

Although Dries is in the insurance business, he likes art. He and Theo go to museums together, and on long walks; they talk inexhaustibly about art. Theo is still incredibly shaken, but Dries's company helps ease his grief.

In Nuenen, Vincent is not visibly grief-stricken, other than being more withdrawn than usual. He's trying to stay away from everyone, especially his sister Anna, who came home for the funeral with her children and a nanny and is staying on for a while. Over the years Anna has grown to despise Vincent. She is furious at him for how hard he's made life for their parents. She thinks he gives in "to all his desires," sparing "nothing and no one. How Pa must have suffered."

One day Vincent and Anna have a huge fight, and Vincent considers moving out of the house. He's already renting an outside studio to work in; he has been since the previous spring. It's big enough that he could live there, too.

He knows that many in the family do not like him. To make peace he's offered to give most of his share of his inheritance from Pa to Wil and Lies, reserving just a little bit for himself, to ease Theo's burden, since Theo has had to pay for the funeral and other expenses. They have to think of the future: Ma, as the parson's widow, is allowed to stay in the house only for a year. Then she'll have to move out.

The future is on Vincent's mind for many reasons. For one, he now truly believes he will someday amount to something. He is finally on the right path. His path.

He has started sketches and studies for an oil painting he thinks just might be worthwhile. It is a scene of peasants sitting around a table eating potatoes. He prays this painting will make enough of an impression on Theo and others in Paris that he can begin to sell his work. He sends Theo a study of it and waits eagerly for his response.

59.
A FAMILY

---

*T*HEO REALLY LIKES Vincent's study of the family. He thinks it's good enough to get the opinion of another art dealer in Paris, Alphonse Portier. Portier sees things he likes in the study, and Theo is optimistic that others will, too. Theo writes Ma immediately that he's "quite glad that I could give Vincent good news recently, I don't think it will amount to much for the time being, but the person who gave me his opinion of his work is someone of great experience and on whose judgement one can count. . . .

"What I should wish," Theo tells Ma, "is that he started to see the fruits of his work. Many before him have had to struggle for a long time before they sold something. It's not necessary, though, for everyone to have to wait so long and so I very much hope that he will get satisfaction from his works within a short time."

For the first time since Vincent picked up his artist's pencil, Theo is optimistic that he will be able to sell Vincent's art.

Vincent is pleased with Theo's reaction, and Portier's reaction, and encouraged enough to make the actual oil painting. But he remains guarded, skeptical, practical.

He is worried that less savvy people won't like his work and that maybe Portier will change his mind.

Still he works hard on the painting, being careful not to spoil it as he puts on the finishing touches. "The last days are always hazardous. . . . Changes have to be made very coolly and calmly with a small brush," he tells Theo.

He makes himself walk away from it.

As the paint dries on *The Potato Eaters*, Vincent has another huge fight with Anna. On the same day that he moves completely out of the family house and into his studio, he sends the painting to Theo.

Just weeks after Dorus's death, with his father no longer there to please—or displease—Vincent has made a painting of a family. It's a family of peasants sitting around a table eating. There is much about it that is unskilled. Vincent is still learning how to paint well in oil, and struggling with faces and figures. The people's features are coarse, exaggerated. Vincent knows that. He expects some will think the people ugly, unfinished, but he hopes they will be seen as real people, and the painting as *sincere*. He painted it from the heart: the scene harks back to his time in the Borinage, and it reflects his attachment to his own family and to the idea of family, to the ideal family.

Join us intimately to one another.

The painting is startling. The people sit around the table as if suspended, like props in a play, or puppets on strings. The colors are in the Dutch palette, the overall effect dark and muddy. Theo tells him it's too dark, and once again encourages Vincent to lighten up. And yet it's a breakthrough for Vincent. Theo sees a lot in it and knows others will, too. And they do. They see the life and the feeling that Vincent meant to evoke, of real people, in a family, with faults, eating around a table, peasant life, real life, unromanticized. All of this is there.

Vincent still can't make the paintbrush do exactly what he wants, so he will keep working on his craft, diligently, tirelessly.

This whole summer after his father dies he works as hard as he can. He paints outdoors—farmworkers, peasants, landscapes. What he sees and what is inside him burst onto the canvas. When he is tired from painting, he draws—a series of the wheat harvest. He is confident, passionate. He's thrilled with his work.

But not everyone is.

60.
SUMMER 1885:
A BREAK

VINCENT KNOWS he still has to improve his people. He's had trouble with
the human figure since the beginning. He has a plan to draw at least a hundred figures like one he's already made of a peasant woman pitching hay.
But he's very proud of *The Potato Eaters*, so he sends a copy to his friend
Anthon van Rappard. As an artist and a friend, Van Rappard will understand what Vincent means by this painting.

Before Pa's death, Van Rappard had been to visit twice in Nuenen.
Both were long and pleasant visits. The latest was just in November, a helpful distraction from Vincent's worries and woes about Margot. The two
men painted side by side and talked about art, including Impressionist
painting. They'd had an artists' commune of two, and when Van Rappard
left, Vincent knew he wanted that camaraderie again, with Van Rappard,
and someday with others.

When Vincent receives Rappard's response to *The Potato Eaters*, he's
shocked. Rappard *hates it*. His friend is also upset that he got a printed
notice of Dorus's death, not a personal letter. But Van Rappard writes

mostly about the painting. "You'll agree with me that such work isn't intended seriously. You can do better than this—fortunately; but why, then, observe and treat everything so superficially?"

He accuses Vincent of not studying how people move, and criticizes in great detail the way Vincent painted the figures, and pretty much everything else: "That coquettish little hand of that woman at the back, how untrue! And what connection is there between the coffeepot, the table and the hand lying on top of the handle? What's that pot doing, for that matter; it isn't standing, it isn't being held, but what then? And why may that man on the right not have a knee or a belly or lungs? Or are they in his back? And why must his arm be a metre too short? And why must he lack half of his nose? And why must the woman on the left have a sort of little pipe stem with a cube on it for a nose?"

Vincent sends the letter back to Van Rappard the next day, but unlike the one he'd sent back to Theo a few years earlier, all marked, this one he just sends back, with a short note: "I just received your letter—to my surprise. You hereby get it back."

While others were seeing the emotion, the expression, in Vincent's painting just as he had hoped, his *friend* was seeing only the flaws. "How dare you to invoke the names of Millet and Breton?" Van Rappard had written. He knows Vincent admires and emulates those two. How could Van Rappard say that? Another painter, Charles Serret, recently told Theo that Vincent might surpass Millet!

How could his friend, the painter he felt closest to, deal him such hard judgment? Vincent is eager for helpful criticism and thinks Van Rappard has made reasonable points about the execution, but the tone is so awful! And how can he misunderstand Vincent so? How can he accuse Vincent of being cavalier in his painting? *Cavalier?!* Vincent? He works so hard, in anything but a cavalier manner.

Vincent takes almost two months to write Van Rappard again. But when he does, and angry though he still is, he says this disagreement is no reason to break off their relationship. He wants them to remain collegial friends. He even invites Van Rappard to come to Nuenen and stay in his studio. He has a spare room, he tells him. They should forget this disagreement and be together as before, painting, talking.

Although they write back and forth a few more times and Vincent really does want to make up, they don't. In August, Vincent defends his art, his process, and takes Van Rappard to task for his judgmental nature. He says he cannot accept what Van Rappard has said—that Vincent's work is extremely weak, that the faults outnumber his strengths. "I'm too absolutely and utterly convinced that I am, after all, on the right path—when I want to paint what I feel and feel what I paint—to worry too much about what people say of me."

He tells Van Rappard that as he goes forward with his own art and gets better, he should not be conventional; he should be bold. It is what Vincent wants for himself eventually, when he is skilled enough—to defy convention and to be bold.

Vincent will not be deterred by the criticism. He tells Van Rappard, "I keep on making *what I can't do yet* in order to learn to be able to do it."

61.

SUMMER 1885:
A MEETING

---

*A*FTER DORUS DIED, one of the things Theo and his friend Andries Bonger did together was to visit the memorial exhibit of a French painter, Eugène Delacroix, who had died twenty-two years earlier. Both Vincent and Theo knew and liked his work, and Delacroix's use of brushstrokes and color influenced the Impressionist painters.

After that visit Dries wrote to his parents that the paintings of Delacroix were "an inexhaustible topic of discussion" for him and Theo. They went back again the next day.

Theo had sent Vincent a book about artists, including Delacroix. Delacroix "wanted life; life at all costs, life everywhere, in the fields, in the skies, around his figures." When Vincent had tried to make up with Van Rappard, he'd asked him if he knew about Delacroix, who painted "like a lion devouring his piece of flesh."

Delacroix is known for his use of color and also for his passion. Both appeal to Vincent and to Theo.

THEO AND DRIES decide to take their summer holidays at the same time, and spend part of the time together. First they see some museums: in Lille, France, and in Ghent and Antwerp in Belgium. Then they go to Nuenen, where Theo introduces Andries to Vincent. Theo and Vincent are getting along so much better now, but upon meeting him for the first time, Dries is struck by Vincent's eccentricity, his lack of social graces. He figures it's because he's lived for so long outside of "society."

Both Theo and Dries consider their families extremely important. Theo, like Vincent, feels that Zundert, and all he learned there, shaped the man he has become. He is glad to introduce his friend to his family—minus Pa, of course. When Andries leaves to go to his family in Amsterdam, where Theo will join him soon, Theo chases him with a letter: "Even if the world is the greatest school, family life as we have known it since childhood was the ABC for it."

He's eager to go to Amsterdam, to meet the Bongers and also to see the just-opened Rijksmuseum there. "Won't it be enriching to absorb the work of such masters, and there are so many there to be seen."

Theo and Dries do go to the museum together, and although they don't like the building—they much prefer the Louvre in Paris—they love the art.

But it isn't art that makes the biggest impression on Theo in Amsterdam.

On Friday evening, August 7, 1885, Theo arrives at 121 Weteringschans, the Bonger family apartment. It's on a beautiful street just a three-minute walk across a canal from the new Rijksmuseum. The Bongers are a cultured middle-class family, wealthier than the Van Goghs. Mr. Bonger is an insurance broker with enough money to send seven children to private school. (But not enough to send them all to university—only the youngest would go.) They are all musical; the father plays the violin; the oldest son, the cello. Three of the daughters, Lien, Mien, and Johanna, play the piano.

When Theo arrives at the apartment, most of the family is there. Andries's parents like Theo very much right away. But a cousin, Willem, is also visiting, and holding court. So everyone focuses on him. But not Theo. He's mesmerized by Andries's favorite sister, Johanna. Her family calls her Net, but she's known as Jo to everyone else. She's twenty-two.

While the others listen to the cousin—that silly man, as Theo thinks of him—he can't take his eyes off Jo. Does he see immediately that she's intelligent, sensitive, emotional? He likes the look of her: hair pulled up and back, bangs low on her forehead accentuating her dark eyes; square jaw, broad nose, full lips—features that all together create a soft and yet also striking appearance. He knows no more about her than about her sisters, but she steals his heart then and there. She has something he's been seeking for a long time but hasn't found. Until now. He knows that this meeting will have, as he will tell her later, "far-reaching consequences."

Jo barely notices Theo. She's hopelessly in love with another man.

An Expanded Palette

1885–1887

When his work comes right he will be a great man.

—Theo to Lies, October 13, 1885

62.

COMPLEMENTARY COLORS

$\mathcal{B}$ACK IN PARIS, Dries goes over to Theo's most evenings. Dries tells his parents of Theo: "The longer you know him the more you like him, and I am learning to appreciate his great gifts and talents more every day." They work side by side, read, and talk—about art, and also about love, and marriage—with all its benefits and drawbacks. Theo hasn't confessed his infatuation with Jo to Dries—he's still seeing S., after all. Dries already worries about Theo being so much in the art world, with its loose ideas about sex.

Theo hopes that one day Jo will grow to like—even love—him. But for now he keeps his love secret. For a while Dries keeps a secret, too. On their trip back home, Dries became privately engaged to a woman named Annie. He'd known her since childhood, and he'd introduced her to Theo in Amsterdam.

Once the engagement is public, Theo confides in his sister Lies that he doesn't know how happy his friend will be with Annie. Though Annie seems to have a "flawless character," Theo tells Lies she might be "too out of the ordinary to become a good housewife." Her appearance is so different from Jo's; Annie is "slim & blonde & rather English-looking." Not for him.

He's happy for Dries, but his friend's engagement makes him feel alone again in Paris. "The streets are full of people yet one feels lonelier than one would in a village." Unlike Vincent, who makes friends wherever he lives, Theo is not so easily social.

So he focuses on work, learning more and more about art and sharing what he learns with Dries, and with Vincent by letter. He tells Vincent more about Impressionism, and new uses of color and brushstrokes. Once again he encourages him to experiment with moving away from the dark, muddy palette of the Dutch masters.

Vincent hears him. He devotes a large part of his time to reading about color. He learns about color theory, and especially about complementary colors. As ever, he wants to keep learning, improving his skills as an artist. And, he figures, if he can please Theo, he will please others and his work will start to sell. One way to help that along would be to use more color. He loves the darker palette and isn't sure how to make his lighter, but he does add more colors.

———————

IN OCTOBER 1885, Vincent takes himself to the Rijksmuseum in Amsterdam. He spends three days there, and his visit is a revelation.

Looking at art in those three days expands his view of color in painting in a way that reading about it could not. He still hasn't seen any Impressionist paintings, but there is an older painting at the Rijksmuseum, *The Meagre Company* by Frans Hals and Pieter Codde, from 1637, that he tells Theo made "the trip to Amsterdam well worth while, especially for a colourist."

In the days that follow, Vincent and Theo write many letters to each other about color. Vincent sends Theo some paintings he made while he was in Amsterdam—paintings with more color. Once back in Nuenen he makes some more paintings and sends them to Theo: baskets of apples and of potatoes. The one Theo likes best has more red in it. Although the palette isn't bright, Theo sees that Vincent is using more color. He gives him a critique of the basket of apples, and although he doesn't say it's perfect, Vincent is thrilled.

"Here we are on the way to agreeing more about colors," Vincent says, and asks Theo to think more deeply about questions of pigment, shades, hues. "Just to say how that study was painted—quite simply this. Green and red are complementary. Well there's a particular—red in the apples, very coarse in itself—and greenish things as well." He points out pink in the apples, and the association between the red and the green.

From Paris to Nuenen and back, Vincent and Theo send each other books about color and color theory. They read about the phenomenon of simultaneous contrast of colors, about complementary colors. Complementary colors, the brothers read, when they are placed next to each other, reinforce each other. They make each other stronger.

63.

BLACK. AND BLACK AND WHITE.
AND COLOR.

My palette is thawing, and the bleakness
of the earliest beginnings has gone.

—Vincent to Theo, October 28, 1885

THE BROTHERS WRITE LETTERS to each other about black, too. And about black and white. Though Vincent is trying to lighten his palette, he still wants to use black. Is that allowed? he asks Theo. Theo says yes, to Vincent's relief. "I read your letter about black with great pleasure," Vincent writes. "And it convinces me accordingly that you aren't prejudiced against black."

With his answer, Theo sends Vincent an analysis of a painting by Édouard Manet, *The Dead Toreador*, painted more than twenty years earlier. In it, a bullfighter lies on his back, blood seeping from his left shoulder. The ground is an olive green, the toreador's cloth is a light pink. His flesh is pale beige. But the rest of the painting has stark contrasts of black and white: the toreador's clothes are black, his shoes are black; his pants come to just below his knees and he is wearing bright white stockings. He has a bright white shirt, covered only partially by his jacket.

Vincent finds Theo's letter not only a great analysis but also a beautiful piece of writing. "If you put your mind to it you can paint something in words," Vincent tells his brother, not for the first time.

Although his palette is thawing, Vincent still is not sure how to put more color into his paintings. But he knows he wants to. He still wants to paint what is real and true. But with more color. He is beginning to think about varieties of one single color, differences of tone, for example, in the same family of yellow.

A symphony in yellow.

He compares his newfound sense of color to tulip mania, when the Dutch were so obsessed with tulips that everyone wanted them and the price of bulbs skyrocketed. But Vincent wants to plant seeds of all kinds.

He admires the painter Jules Dupré for his use of color:

Seascapes with delicate blue-greens, broken blue, and different whites in pearly tones.

Autumn landscapes with deep wine red, vivid green, bright orange to dark brown. The sky overhead with grey and lilac and blue and white.

Yellow leaves.

A sunset in black, violet, fiery red.

"*Colour expresses something in itself,*" he writes to Theo in big letters, underlined.

64.

STILL LIFE WITH BIBLE

---

*A*FTER READING THEO'S ANALYSIS of *The Dead Toreador*, Vincent makes a painting to show Theo what he can do with black, and with more color. The painting he makes, though, shows more than pigment. It's a still life with an open Bible, a novel, and some extinguished candles. He paints it seven months after Pa collapsed on the threshold. The Bible in the painting was Pa's, and it's opened to Isaiah 53, a passage that announces the arrival of the Messiah:

"Who hath believed our message? and to whom has the arm of the LORD been revealed?"

People do not recognize the Messiah when he comes:

"He was despised and rejected by mankind; a man of suffering, and familiar with pain . . . and we held him in low esteem."

Vincent paints, on the table next to the Bible, a novel he had read and loved just after Pa died—*La joie de vivre* (*The Joy of Life*) by Émile Zola. It had been serialized in a magazine in 1883, and was published as a book in early 1884. Pauline, a ten-year-old, has been orphaned and sent to live with some relatives, who mistreat her. Pauline has a hard life, yet Vincent finds comfort in the book. Even in times of sadness, he tells Theo, "one must work and be bold if one really wants to live."

Vincent lives by that motto.

Vincent does not write to Theo what the painting means. Are the extinguished candles a symbol of death, or of Pa's inability to be bold in life? Does it show the powerlessness of Christianity next to literature and art? Is Vincent thinking of himself as despised and rejected, esteemed not? Maybe some of this, maybe none. What he tells Theo is that he knows he's reached the point where "it really comes quite readily to me to paint a given object, whatever the shape or colour may be, without hesitation."

Objects he's got, color he's learning, but he's still feeling dissatisfied with the way he portrays the human figure. This grates on him. And he can't teach himself any more than he already has. He needs guidance, and he needs to be in a place where he can see art all the time.

A city. He's outgrowing Nuenen. And some in Nuenen are done with him: since September he's been having trouble with the Catholic clergymen. They tell him he has to stop using Catholic peasants and workers as models.

"What bad luck for Vincent!" Theo tells Ma. "If only he could find something else suitable soon! All the painters I show his work to say that there's a great deal in it and he must just keep going."

Vincent does keep going. How can he not? He is finally doing it. He knows it; others are starting to see it. Since he can't use the Catholic peasants as models, he turns to landscapes. But as summer turns to fall, which will turn to winter, he knows he has to leave.

In November 1885, eight months after Pa collapsed on the threshold, five years since Vincent started on his path as an artist, Vincent says goodbye to his mother, to his family home, and to the Netherlands for what will be the last time.

65.
ANTWERP: LIGHT AND DARKNESS

ƔINCENT MOVES TO ANTWERP, Belgium, and rents a small apartment above a paint merchant. He explores the city immediately; he doesn't care that it's pouring rain. He loves the docks and wharves, which remind him of popular Japanese art prints that he's begun collecting. He goes into museums and shops. He wonders, if Theo were with him, would they look at things the same way?

He decorates his apartment, pinning some Japanese prints on the walls, and he sets up a tiny studio—a "cubby-hole"—in the same building as his flat. He has some regret about leaving home, but he hopes to work well.

When he unpacks his work, he has another revelation about light and color.

The paintings he'd done in Nuenen look "darker here in the city than in the country." Is this "because the light isn't as bright anywhere in the city?" he asks Theo. Now he realizes why when Theo looked at the paintings in Paris, they seemed darker than they had to him. There is more open space in the country, more light to shine on his paintings. Still, surveying his work, Vincent is pleased. He *is* making progress. But he knows he needs to lighten up his palette even more.

He gets to work. He finds the best places in the city to buy oil paints and fine drawing brushes. He goes around to dealers and leaves some of his work with them. Maybe he'll sell something. He looks for models to hire but has trouble. Finally, by the middle of December, he finds some models, and he paints a head of a "splendid old man" in profile, filling up most of the canvas, a different style for him.

He is very low on money but full of ideas. He is inspired. He looks at photography with disdain. He thinks he and all painters have much more to offer than a photographer does. Painters can bring someone to life. To him people in photographs always seem to have "the same conventional eyes, noses, mouths, waxy and smooth and cold. It still always remains *dead*. And painted portraits have a life of their own that comes from deep in the soul of the painter and where the machine can't go."

The dealers say "they still think women's heads or figures of women are most likely to sell," he tells Theo. That's good news for him—he wants to work on people. That's why he came here.

But he's barely eating. He's spending almost everything Theo sends him to buy paint. He's weak and sick.

"I've only had some hot food 3 times," he tells Theo in the middle of December. He's living on bread. He leaves money at the baker's at the beginning of the month so that he can still eat at the end of the month.

He's smoking a lot so he won't feel hungry all the time; his teeth are breaking apart from decay.

Hungry, weak, in pain, he starts to crash into melancholy. What just a few weeks earlier had inspired him is now filling him with pessimism. He'll never be able to sell his work.

He pulls away from his family—all but Theo. Ma writes to him, but he doesn't write back. She and Wil are visiting Anna, whom he sarcastically refers to as his "charming sister," the one who despises him. Well, he doesn't need any of them. Just Theo. And his art.

His art.

As melancholy as he is, he keeps working. He sees many beautiful women in the city, and he wants to paint them. He still needs help with the human form. So he decides to set aside his disdain for institutional learning, left over from his days at theology school in Amsterdam, and enroll in a painting class at an art academy. He arranges to draw from plaster casts in the evenings. He joins drawing clubs so he can paint clothed and nude models.

He is determined to improve his skills. He works as much as he can.

But his body is a mess: his digestion is terrible, from poor nutrition; his teeth are getting worse by the day. He's lost "no fewer than 10 teeth," which makes him "look as though I'm over 40, which puts me at too much of a disadvantage," he tells Theo. He's only thirty-two. He decides to have many of his teeth pulled. It will be terribly expensive, so he pays half in advance.

The doctor who performs the extractions tells him he's smoking too much and eating too little. "I am most definitely literally exhausted and overworked," he writes to Theo. "Because it's not just the food, it's also all the worry and sorrow that one has."

Darkness again.

He knows what will help, though. Gone are the days when he tried to persuade Theo to quit his job to be a painter with him. He doesn't need that, but he needs to be near Theo. He wants to live in Paris. He makes hints. He tells Theo he wants to study with the painter Fernand Cormon, enroll in *his* studio in Paris.

Theo doesn't take the hint.

So Vincent stops hinting.

He tells him outright: I want to live with you. I can paint in the apartment. We won't have to rent a separate studio. That will save money!

Theo says it could work—but not yet. Maybe by the summer he'll be ready. Vincent should go back home to the Netherlands in the meanwhile.

But Vincent doesn't want to go back there.

And he can't wait.

His rent is due, and he doesn't have enough to pay it.

He has other bills he can't pay.

He is depressed, sick, lonely.

He needs Theo.

He leaves Antwerp quickly, without paying his bills.

66.
COMINGS AND GOINGS

ΥINCENT ARRIVES IN PARIS, February 28, 1886. Theo has no idea he's coming.

Sigmund Freud happens to be leaving Paris on the same day. The two men could have walked past each other in the train station, both with pipes in their mouths. Freud, just twenty-nine, wears a suit and a starched white shirt and has neatly parted hair, a long and tidy beard, and a mustache. He's a straight and proper young man, a new doctor. What would he make of Vincent, thirty-two but much older looking, gaunt, with broken, rotting, and missing teeth, his body dirty, his clothing ripped, a battered hat on his head?

Freud is eager to leave Paris. He's been in the city for four and a half months, but he didn't enjoy it. He ignored the famous wine, women, and song. He made no French friends. He is eager to get home to Vienna and his fiancée. He was in Paris to study, and that was successful. He's made some progress in his understanding of nervous breakdowns in men, male hysteria.

Vincent, on the verge of collapse, is relieved to be in Paris. He hopes Theo will take him in.

In the Gare du Nord train station, Vincent writes on a page of his sketchbook: "My dear Theo, Don't be cross with me that I've come all of a sudden. I've thought about it so much and I think we'll save time this way."

He tells Theo he'll wait for him from noon on at the Louvre, in the Salon Carré, the room filled with art of the masters of European painting.

"We'll sort things out, you'll see. So get there as soon as possible."

He's got some money left (since he didn't pay his bills) and could rent a place. But he hopes Theo will say he can move in with him.

He rips out the page, gives the note to a messenger.

Then he goes to the Louvre, and he waits for Theo.

67.

VAN GOGH'S BROTHER

A FEW WEEKS LATER, Dries Bonger writes home complaining that he hasn't seen much of Theo lately. "Van G.'s brother, who works as a painter, has arrived here."

And a few weeks after that: "Theo's brother is here for good, he's staying for at least three years to work in the studio of the painter Cormon." He reminds his parents what he told them last summer about Vincent, "what a solitary life" he'd lived. He has no social graces, and he fights with everyone. "So Theo has a great deal to put up with because of him."

It is *not* easy for Theo. Such a small space with such a large personality. After four months of sharing his small apartment with his brother, Theo decides to rent a larger one. This will help. He hopes. In early June the brothers move to 54 Rue Lepic in Montmartre. Their apartment is in the same building as the shop of Alphonse Portier, the dealer who liked Vincent's *The Potato Eaters*.

Dries tells his parents, "They now have a large, spacious apartment (by Parisian standards, anyway) and their own household. They have an excellent kitchen-maid" called Lucie. The apartment is on the third floor, with three decent-sized rooms, a tiny study, and a small kitchen. Vincent sleeps in the study, and behind that is the room he uses as his studio—a room with a window, though not a very large one.

VINCENT'S HAD HIS TEETH FIXED; he is eating better; he has energy. His health is much better than when he was in Antwerp.

But Dries is worried about Theo. He looks "awfully haggard. The poor fellow has a lot of worries. On top of that, his brother is still making life difficult for him, and accuses him of all sorts of things of which he's completely blameless."

From Dries's vantage point, Vincent's move to Paris is a disaster.

68.

IMPRESSIONS

---

*7*HE VIEW depends on the perspective.

FOR THEO, having Vincent there is not all bad all the time. It is very hard to live with him, but there are bright moments. Vincent brings to Theo social and intellectual stimulation—and that family connection.

For Vincent, living with Theo is necessary. He's come to Paris not only to be with his brother but also to sharpen his skills and further his career. Both brothers want that to happen. Vincent hopes to finally nail down drawing the human figure. Theo hopes Vincent will lighten his palette.

As the winter weather warms into spring in 1886, Theo introduces Vincent to modern painters, mainly the Impressionists. At galleries, salons, and museums, he shows his brother paintings by Edgar Degas, Mary Cassatt, Paul Gauguin, Pierre-Auguste Renoir, Camille Pissarro, Berthe Morisot, Claude Monet, and others. And he takes Vincent to the latest Impressionist exhibit.

Look, says Theo, and Vincent sees. He understands what Theo has been trying to tell him: light colors, bright palette, brightness.

Visible brushstrokes.

Dots. Dashes. Daubs. Slashes.

At this exhibit Vincent sees not only Impressionist paintings but also ones by Georges Seurat and Paul Signac—who create pictures made up of small dots. Their style will become known as pointillism. Seurat thinks of his work as more rigorous and meticulous than Impressionism. He and others will become part of a movement called Neo-Impressionism.

That impulse that Vincent has had all along to play with forms, to mix media, to be bold—it's affirmed.

There is so much in art to do, discover, explore.

Vincent is feeling healthy, charged, ready. Thanks to Theo.

As he'd planned, Vincent works at the studio of Fernand Cormon. He sits for hours on end drawing the human form from antique casts, and also from nudes. He meets many painters at the studio, including Henri de Toulouse-Lautrec and Émile Bernard.

Vincent and Bernard become close friends. Bernard marvels at Vincent's perseverance. When everyone else leaves for the day, Vincent stays and works, copying the forms with "angelic patience." He corrects himself, starting "again with passion," erasing, and finally wearing "a hole in the paper with the rubbing of the eraser."

But Vincent decides, after three months, to leave the studio. As he has before, he finds the instruction too academic, concentrating on the wrong things. Vincent has always been an autodidact, and within a few weeks, he finds a way to teach himself. He discovers a painter whose use of color and impasto makes a huge impression on him. Adolphe Monticelli, who lived in Marseille in the South of France, has just died. But his paintings become a guide for Vincent as he works to develop his own style of painting.

Vincent experiments with bright colors as well as complementary colors. He loads his brush with paint and lays it on thick, heavy. Sometimes he doesn't wait for the paint to dry, brushing wet paint onto wet paint.

He paints outside, scenes from their neighborhood in Montmartre, buildings, people strolling in nearby parks.

He also picks up a tip from his friend Henri de Toulouse-Lautrec and adds paint thinner to pigment, then paints in a style called *peinture à l'essence*, with feathery, sketchy brushstrokes.

When he paints inside, he paints flowers of all kinds—roses, zinnias, gladioli, asters, and sunflowers, his favorite flower. Some of these are *à l'essence*. He paints a pair of shoes, one sole up, one sole down, browns and tans, with light and white, though he is still using black.

His palette is lighter, brighter. The Impressionists have influenced him. So have the pointillists. All along he's been learning from masters and now from his contemporaries. But the work is Vincent's alone.

Theo writes to Ma that Vincent is making tremendous progress. Though he isn't selling anything yet, Vincent and Theo trade his paintings for paintings by other artists, some of them more established. In this way, the brothers are building a great art collection.

And Vincent is making friends. "Hardly a day passes without him being invited to visit the studios of painters of repute, or people come to him," Theo writes to Ma. Vincent has friends who send him "a beautiful delivery of flowers every week," which serve as a model for him to paint. "If we can keep this up then I think that his difficult period will be behind him."

Light is beginning to shine into the apartment.

But Theo doesn't tell Ma everything. He doesn't tell her how hard Vincent is to live with, though she certainly knows that firsthand.

And he doesn't tell her about his own problems.

69.

BEDFELLOWS

THEO HAS PAINTED himself into a corner with S., the woman he's been seeing. He desperately wants to end it with her, but she is fragile, unbalanced, and he's afraid that she might commit suicide if he breaks it off. Vincent and Dries try to help him figure out what to do.

He's also frustrated with work, again, still. His bosses give him little free rein; he has to fight to sell what he is most passionate about, the Impressionists. And then they bend only a little. He decides to go back to the Netherlands in August. It will be a break from living with his brother; he will put some distance between himself and S.; and he can also ask his uncles for help.

Although he was distraught after his father's death, he no longer has to look to him for approval. He is now, in effect, the head of the family, even though Vincent is the oldest. As if Theo's portrait has actually been painted over the stillborn first son.

Uncle Cent and Uncle Cor don't have the sway over him that his father had. He wants their approval and encouragement, certainly. But he doesn't *need* it. What he does need, though, is their financial help. He wants to set up his own gallery, where he can show the artists he wants, such as Claude Monet, whom he is representing already. He would sell Vincent's work, too, when he thinks it's ready. Vincent would help him figure out who else to represent, and is completely behind the idea. Andries Bonger is supportive, too, and wants to be a partner. But they need more money than Dries has or could raise.

While Theo is away, Dries moves into the apartment so Vincent won't be alone. Dries not only ends up taking care of Vincent, who gets sick, but also is drawn into the drama with S., who moves into the apartment, too, for part of the time.

Back in the Netherlands, it's not any easier for Theo. He has no success persuading Uncle Cent to give him money to set up his own gallery. Uncle Cor won't help, either. Theo reports back to Vincent and Dries. Vincent tells him to keep trying: "Courage and composure."

Dries tries to get some money for their venture, too, and fails.

Theo does report one piece of great news: Vincent's work is getting noticed by the art community in the Netherlands! Ma and Wil are pleased by this, too, of course. Wil especially, for she knows from Theo just how hard it's been in the apartment. She writes to a friend that Theo is telling her many "good things about Vincent. . . . His paintings are getting so much better and he is beginning to exchange them for ones by other painters, that's how it must gradually come about."

IN PARIS, the strangeness of bedfellows continues. Dries and Vincent talk about how to help Theo. What can he do about S.? The more time they spend with her, the more they both realize that not only does Theo need to break up with her, he has to do it in such a way that she won't do something awful to herself.

Both Vincent and Dries know Theo's secret by now, too: that he is in love with Johanna Bonger.

Vincent and Dries write Theo a letter together, offering sympathy about the predicament in his love life. If Theo breaks up with S. and she kills herself or goes crazy, Vincent says, "the effect of that on you would be tragic, of course, and could shatter you forever."

Vincent has a solution: he will take S. He would rather not *marry* her, but if he has to, he will. In any case, he will take her; they can fire Lucie, the maid, and S. can do the housekeeping. That way S. will be happy enough, and Theo can ask Jo to marry him.

Dries agrees only with one part: that Theo should break up with S. "The issue is to open S.'s eyes. She's not in love with you at all, but it's as if you've bewitched her. Morally she is seriously sick." But he doesn't agree with Vincent's solution! It's "unworkable, in my opinion."

Although Dries still finds Vincent eccentric, he likes him well enough, and when Theo comes back, he has dinner with them every evening. But Theo is discouraged and depressed. He enjoyed seeing the Bongers in Amsterdam, but because of his unresolved problems at work and home, he didn't tell Jo how he felt about her.

And as summer turns to fall, Theo's mood darkens. He is worried about his job and his life. Living with Vincent, he has no solitude, no quiet time.

Winter makes it all worse. The brothers are inside together more. Both of them suffer from the lack of sun and warmth. Vincent is more volatile and moody, Theo more melancholy.

By the end of the year, Theo is in terrible shape emotionally and physically. As 1886 ends and 1887 begins, he has an attack of paralysis and is unable to move for days. Theo is ill from syphilis he contracted earlier in his life, though it's not clear if he realizes what's wrong. Although it is known in the 1880s that venereal disease is transmitted by infected people having sex with others, little is known about the course of the disease, and there is no real treatment or cure. Someday antibiotics will revolutionize treatment of this illness, but that is still decades away. Theo has been living with the disease for a long time. Over the course of years it has been in his body, giving him fevers, making him tired, weak. Now the disease has gone to his nervous system. The episode of paralysis leaves him gaunt, weaker than ever, drained of life. He is afraid he won't live to his thirtieth birthday in May. Just as Vincent had worried years ago, Theo is in danger of not surviving his twenties.

70.

TWO BROTHERS, ONE APARTMENT, PARIS, 1887

CONTINUED

WHILE THEO STRUGGLES, Vincent paints.

Although he prefers to paint outside, during the cold weather he works hard inside the apartment. He concentrates on portraits, nudes, and still lifes. In some of his portraits he imitates the Japanese style he loves: framing the head in surprising ways, using strong colors. He paints a portrait of a woman, in some ways similar to one from two years earlier, but unlike that older one, this one is full of color: red background, green dress, blues, greens, browns, tans.

Complementary colors, analogous colors, vivid colors.

He also starts making self-portraits.

And he makes another still life of shoes, similar to the one of the year before. These are taller, workman's boots, but again one is sole up, the other unlaced, the lace this time reaching off the edge of the painting. The up-turned sole is worn; the upright boot is scuffed. He gives this painting more colors: blues and greens, browns and whites, orange.

This one he signs: *Vincent, '87.*

Two shoes, a pair. A pair that goes together, but one is up, the other down. Both are used, worn.

WHEN HE ISN'T at the apartment, Vincent is out with friends: Émile Bernard, Henri de Toulouse-Lautrec, and other artists. There is even a woman he's seeing, Agostina Segatori, who manages a restaurant. In February, Vincent organizes an exhibition of the Japanese prints he's been collecting. The exhibit is at Agostina's restaurant, Café du Tambourin.

In the apartment the atmosphere is tense—and has been for so long. Vincent can handle the storms; Theo cannot. He wants to kick Vincent out.

A friendship again strained to the point of breaking.

"It's a long time since you had a letter from me," Theo writes to Lies in April 1887. "But if you knew how life is here and the kind of situations I've been through this winter, it wouldn't surprise you that there was no desire to repeat everything that has been going on. . . . There's so much agitation and fighting that it would certainly not have been a good idea to disturb your tranquil life."

But he needs someone else from home to know. That's why he tells her, "I've been ill, particularly in my spirit, and have had a great struggle with myself."

He is lonely in the big city: "There's no family life. . . . Can you understand that it's sometimes difficult never to mix with anyone other than men who talk about business, with artists who are generally having a difficult time themselves, but never to know the intimate life with wife or children of the same class?"

He confides in her that he is going to propose to Jo Bonger, even though "it's true that I don't know her well enough to be able to tell you much about her." He still hasn't managed to break it off with S. Nothing is going smoothly for him.

But as the weather warms, Theo starts to feel optimistic. "Spring is slowly coming," he tells Lies. "It was raw and cold for oh so long. Now it's becoming lovely, and people, like nature, sometimes thaw out when the sun shines."

GALLERY NINE

Bonds

1887–1888

71.

THE VIEW FROM
THEO'S APARTMENT

VINCENT PAINTS the view from his room in Theo's apartment: a cityscape, blues and greens and whites, red shutters. Light, happy, pretty. His perspective, his point of view.

Would Theo have painted the same bright view? Unlikely. But as spring blooms, the atmosphere in the apartment does warm. The brothers are each much happier when the grey of winter fades and the colors of spring bloom: yellow sun; blue sky; purple, pink, red blossoms; green leaves; new life.

At the end of April Theo reports to Wil that he and Vincent have "made peace because it served no good to carry on in that way."

Paris in spring. A rapprochement.

Vincent is working outside again, and when he comes home, he's in a much better mood. He is still eccentric, sometimes maddeningly so, but when Theo is feeling stronger, he can deal with Vincent.

Theo needs their intimate bond. They both do.

They are on the path together again, and that makes both of them

VINCENT AND THEO

happy. Both of them. Not just Vincent. For Theo life is much fuller with Vincent next to him. They are so different, but their differences, when they are on the same path, complement each other, fill in spaces. They are more complex than they were on that walk to the windmill so many years ago, but they still have much in common, and their commonalities shine.

And being so close, they have learned from each other—and continue to.

Theo loves what he is seeing in Vincent's art. Vincent is painting scenes from their neighborhood—parks, street scenes, almost all of them within a short walk of the apartment. He paints another windmill, one right there in Montmartre, on top of a hill, in the Moulin de la Galette. He captures it from different perspectives, from many points of view: up close, far away, in the center, just part of the scene. One of the views, from a faraway perspective, shows spring in Paris: full of light and color, a palette bright with green grass, blue sky, the French flag flying atop the mill. There are three windmills nearby, and Vincent paints all of them while he lives with Theo.

Vincent is experimenting with different styles: aspects of pointillism, mixed with the more graphic approach of the Japanese paintings he loves. He uses some of his drawing techniques in his painting, too—dashes and strokes, working to find the painting style that he likes best. In May he starts loading his brush again, making thicker, fuller strokes. From the middle of May to the end of July he paints almost forty scenes of parks full of bright colors and thick paint.

He makes more self-portraits, too, many of them. In one, full of thick paint and lots of color, he is wearing a grey felt hat. He's in a brownish-green jacket, with hints of blue, against a blue background. His lips are red, and his orange-red beard is neat, closely cropped. His brow is furrowed, it seems, under his felt hat, his eyes green, staring out, intense, purposeful, determined.

"Vincent is still working hard and is making progress. His paintings are becoming lighter, and his great quest is to get sunlight into them," Theo tells Lies. Vincent wants to do nothing less than capture the sun.

"He's an odd fellow," Theo tells their sister, "but what a head he has on him, it's enviable."

Theo has hope for Vincent's future, and for his own, too. He is *feeling* so much better. He doesn't think about dying young anymore. He dreams of a life that will include Dries's sister Jo.

72.

A RINGING BELL

Myself—I feel I'm losing the desire for marriage and children,
and at times I'm quite melancholy to be like that at 35 when
I ought to feel quite differently. And sometimes I blame
this damned painting.

—Vincent to Theo, July 23, 1887

IT IS SUMMER 1887. Theo is off to visit Ma and Wil in Breda, where they now live. But visiting them is not the main purpose of his trip. With Vincent's encouragement, he is going to Amsterdam to see Jo. He'd been too discouraged last summer to tell her his feelings, but now he's ready. He wants a wife and a family; he wants *her*.

Never mind that he hasn't completely broken off with S., though there is some progress on that front. Never mind that Dries told him he should wait longer; he doesn't think the timing is quite right. Theo is determined.

He thinks about her all the time.

Theo has been writing to Lies about Jo, and about love. He's told Lies that Jo gives him "the impression that I can place my trust in her completely unreservedly, as I wouldn't with anyone else. I would be able to speak to her about *everything*."

He doesn't know if Jo feels the same about him, but he is certain that if they get to know each other better, she will. And to get to know each other better, he reasons, they should get engaged. He knows she might like a more romantic sweeping off her feet. But he thinks that is the stuff of fairy tales, not real life.

"You girls usually think that there are heroes of every kind in the world, and that the man who proposes to you naturally ought to be one of those beings," he argues to Lies, practicing for Jo. "But for my part I believe that many are taken in if they count on that. In any event, in this case I don't wish anyone to take me for what I am not."

He wants Jo to take him for who he is, what he has accomplished, and what he wants in life. And he plans to convince her that they would have a good life together.

———

ON FRIDAY, July 22, 1887, two years after he first met Jo, Theo van Gogh arrives in Amsterdam and heads from the train to the Bongers' house. Jo is twenty-four.

He arrives at two o'clock in the afternoon at 121 Weteringschans and rings the bell. The Bongers' apartment is upstairs in the redbrick building.

She knows he's coming, this friend of her brother's. She thinks it's just that—a visit from Dries's friend. "I was pleased he was coming," Jo writes in her diary afterward. "I pictured myself talking to him about literature and art, I gave him a warm welcome."

They sit down together and talk, Jo thinking nothing much of it, "and then suddenly he started to declare his love for me. If it had happened in a novel it would sound implausible—but it actually happened."

Theo tells Jo how their life together would be so happy: "He conjured up visions of the ideal I have always dreamed of," she says, "a rich life full of variation, full of intellectual stimulation, a circle of friends around us who are working for a good cause, who want to do something for the world."

If only she could open her heart to him, Jo thinks as he talks, maybe her "indefinable searching and longing" would be fulfilled.

But her heart is numb to Theo.

She is in love with someone else.

And she doesn't know Theo at all.

She is shocked that "after only 3 encounters, he wants to spend his whole life with me, he wants to allow his happiness to be dependent on me."

It's impossible, she tells him. She thinks two people should agree to marry only if they are already in love.

She doesn't tell him that there is a man she loves from afar, a man who does not love her. But she tries to turn him down as firmly as she can.

Theo does not take her refusal as a firm no. He asks if he can write to her, and she politely agrees to read his letter. He hopes they will start a correspondence and get to know each other that way. (Just as Vincent wanted to do with Kee Vos.)

But Jo has other plans. She's going away for a holiday, and she hopes that Theo will get over her quickly. "I am so terribly sorry that I had to cause him such sorrow," she writes in her diary after he leaves. "He had been longing to come here all year, and had such great expectations"—clearly he had told her everything!—"and now it has ended like this."

Jo worries he'll be depressed when he returns to Paris. "But I could not say 'yes' to something like that, could I?" she asks herself.

Theo continues on to Breda, to visit Ma and Wil. He writes to Vincent about his failure. Vincent has just broken off with his "Miss Segatori," the restaurant manager, and has resigned himself to a life alone. But Theo, he thinks, should marry, "for your health and business affairs."

As soon as Theo is settled in with his mother, he writes the letter to Jo. It's about the thing that has affected him the most.

73.

THEO'S LETTER: "THE THING THAT HAS AFFECTED ME VERY DEEPLY"

---

*H*AVING JUST FOUND a quiet space, the first thing is to start writing to you."

Theo wants Jo to know exactly who he is.

"I shall do all I can to present myself as I am, because I still nurture the hope that one day, when you no longer feel 'I don't know you,' we will have a rapport such as one does not encounter every day."

He firmly believes they are on the threshold of a new life, together. So he needs to tell her about the thing that has "affected me very deeply," the thing that has defined him:

"As you know, I have a brother," he writes. "He took me under his wing when I was just starting out (even though he lived in London & I in The Hague) & it is to him that I owe my love of art. I adored him more than anything imaginable & we were extremely close to one another for several years."

He tells her about Vincent's struggles and how they affected him and the whole family. He says that "everyone, without exception, people who

are considered pious, those he himself loved dearly, even his father &
mother, condemned him for his disregard of more temporal matters & his
refusal to yield to society as it is, be it at the expense of what was best in
him," he tells Jo.

"Perhaps you'll think that what I am telling you about him has nothing to do with us, at least when it comes to giving you a glimpse into my
heart. But having been through so much with him & having pondered his
views on life, I would feel I were concealing something important were I
not to tell you about my relationship with him from the start."

You can't have me without Vincent, he tells Jo in this letter.

But please, take me. At least give me a chance.

"I don't need to tell you I would be delighted to receive a few words
from you," he writes.

But Jo does not answer him while he is in the Netherlands. Theo goes
back to Paris.

74.

A CLOSED DOOR,
A CLOSENESS

$\mathcal{B}$ACK HOME with Vincent, Theo writes to Jo again. He knows from her father she's been away, but he hopes she is still thinking about what he said.

"I realise you haven't made up your mind yet, for if you had, you would not leave me in suspense for so long, but I am writing in the hope of hastening that decision, whatever it may turn out to be."

Her idea of being in complete harmony from the beginning, he writes, is "a very beautiful & very young idea, but it is not *true*. It is certainly a joy to *imagine* oneself totally compatible with another person, but it is only a dream, and one that is bound to be followed by a rude awakening."

He says they should reach out to each other, see the other's faults, and "forgive them & try to nurture whatever is good and noble in one another."

"Infatuation," he argues, "vanishes even more quickly than it comes."

And yet he concludes, clearly infatuated himself, "Know that not an hour passes without me thinking of you and hoping to hear from you. Times goes by so slowly when you're waiting."

After some time the wait is over. Jo tells him no, finally, definitively.

This time Theo believes her. He does not try again.

He focuses his attention back on his work and on Vincent.

The two brothers become closer than ever.

75.

REASSIGNED: PORTRAIT OF THEO

———————

*T*HERE'S A PORTRAIT from this time. For years people thought the man in the painting was Vincent, one of his three dozen self-portraits. It is very blue. Blue background, blue suit jacket, light blue stiff bow tie. Straw hat. Reddish hair. Blue-green eyes. There is a sadness in those eyes. The man has a melancholy about him.

It was called (by others) *Self-Portrait with Straw Hat* and is similar to another from the same time. As different as the brothers were, they were close enough to be confused by history.

But this man is definitely Theo. His hair is less red than Vincent's. His ears rounder. Vincent painted it right around this time, in the year 1887 in Paris. He painted a self-portrait, too, to match, both very small. Looking at the two paintings, it seems the brothers traded hats: Vincent is wearing a felt hat like Theo wore. Theo is wearing a straw hat, which is more Vincent's style. They must have meant the switch as a joke.

But from the sad look in Theo's eyes, Vincent surely painted it soon after Jo's refusal.

For well over a hundred years, everyone assumed Vincent hadn't painted Theo. It seemed odd that he would have neglected to paint his brother. He hadn't.

76.

DOUBLE PORTRAIT

---

*O*NE OF THEO'S BOSSES retires, giving Theo more freedom to display the paintings he most wants to show. He slowly starts turning the gallery branch he manages into one that sells not just the traditional Salon painters but also works by modern artists—the Impressionists, and now the post-Impressionists, too. In deference to his bosses, Theo hangs the more traditional paintings on the ground floor, and the modern paintings on the entresol. As if the newer paintings are on the threshold, but not quite in the gallery—yet. A step into the future. Although he is sad about Jo, and still not healthy, there's much in Theo's life that is good. Including Vincent.

This fall and winter, November and December 1887, Vincent is energized, in spite of his usual winter melancholy. He organizes an exhibition of painters he loves at the Grand Bouillon-Restaurant du Chalet. He hangs paintings by Bernard, Toulouse-Lautrec, and a few other artists—including himself. Georges Seurat and Paul Gauguin come to see the exhibit. Theo decides to take some of Gauguin's work on commission. Then Theo organizes an exhibition with Gauguin, Camille Pissarro, Edgar Degas, and others. The brothers' spirits are good this winter, kept up by each other and friends. They spend the evenings together in cafés in Montmartre with Georges Seurat, Armand Guillaumin, Camille Pissarro and his son, Lucien, and other painter friends who stop by. Vincent has brought this social life to Theo, who is so much happier because of it.

But there is one friend Theo isn't seeing: Andries Bonger. Not only would it be awkward because of Jo, but Dries also is judgmental about Theo's unconventional, artistic lifestyle, and he's staying away because he's about to be married.

Dries tells Jo he's concerned about Theo. He seems to be leading an unhealthful life, part of the "young painters' Bohemia." What is his lifestyle doing to his health? Staying up late, drinking—this could not be good for him! Back in the Netherlands, Jo worries that her refusal drove Theo to this behavior.

But Theo actually is focusing on work. He is building up a great art collection for the gallery and for himself. Vincent helps, advising him on which paintings to show and which to buy. Theo now has works by Gauguin, Toulouse-Lautrec, and Seurat in his private collection—in addition to all his brother's paintings.

The other artists in his collection are much farther along than Vincent; their work is already selling. But for the first time since they'd started on this path together, both brothers are certain Vincent will succeed.

"When he came here two years ago," Theo writes to Wil, "I never thought that we'd become so attached to each other." It's a shame none of their friends made a double portrait of the two of them at this time. Two brothers, side by side.

BUT THE TOGETHERNESS is not to last. Vincent grows tired of Paris life, and now of the cold, grey days. He feels weak and sick; he longs for sun and warmth. As much as Paris has given him for his art—the color, the experience, the association with other artists—as much as it could still give him, he has to leave. For his health. He doesn't want to leave Theo. But he has to leave the northern climate; he believes his health depends on it.

He wants to go south, to Marseille, where Monticelli, the painter he admires so, had lived. He will stop first in Arles, a town known for its warmth, beauty, and beautiful women.

Before he leaves, he decorates the apartment with art—Japanese prints and his own paintings. He wants Theo to feel as if he is still there when he's gone.

The day he leaves, the two brothers make a pilgrimage together. On February 19, 1888, they visit the studio of Georges Seurat, to see his latest work.

A few hours later, Vincent gets on the train to Arles.

Back at home in the apartment, Theo looks at the walls, at all of Vincent's paintings.

He feels a profound emptiness.

GALLERY TEN

Passions

1888

77.

FULL HEARTS

"DURING THE JOURNEY I thought at least as much about you as about the new country I was seeing," Vincent writes to Theo upon arriving in Arles. The trip had lasted a day and a night—Arles is about five hundred miles south of Paris.

He'd gone south for the sun, but when he arrived in Arles, there was almost two feet of snow on the ground! And it was still snowing. It had been the coldest winter in twenty-five years. But Vincent enjoyed the landscape from the train; it reminded him of winter scenes by Japanese artists.

In Arles, Vincent finds a place to stay—a little room in the Hotel Carrel, which also has a restaurant. He takes a short walk around town and finds an antiques dealer who says he has a painting by Monticelli. To be so near where Monticelli lived and painted, and to be able to paint in the air and the sun of the South of France! Vincent is excited. Arles and its surroundings look the way he imagines Japan. It's an old town, full of Roman artifacts, history, and ruins. But none of that interests Vincent. He is there for the light, the warmth, and the famous beauty of the women—the Arlésiennes, with their classic looks and bright clothes. He decides to stay in Arles instead of moving to Marseille.

There are only about twenty-three thousand people living in Arles, a huge change from the two million or so he just left in Paris. Most are southern French and Catholic. There is also a small community of a few hundred Italians. But Vincent is the only Dutch person. It will take him a while to get used to the food, the habits, the temperament of the southern French. They will need to get used to him, too. But he is mostly worried he won't find everything he needs—canvases and paints, especially. He is certain, though, that he will settle in and make a home for himself. "Don't worry," he writes Theo, "and give the pals a handshake for me."

In Paris, Theo feels Vincent's absence terribly. Alone but with Vincent's paintings everywhere, he can't stop thinking about his brother. He thinks he should get a roommate, he tells Wil, but "it's not easy to replace someone like Vincent." Theo's respect for Vincent's mind and his talent has reached new heights. "It's incredible how much he knows and what a clear view he has of the world," he tells Wil. "So I'm sure that if he has a certain number of years yet to live he'll make a name for himself."

As soon as Vincent had rested from his journey, he made three studies, even with the snow falling. "It seems to me that my blood is more or less ready to start circulating again, which wasn't the case lately in Paris, I really couldn't stand it any more," Vincent writes Theo. It's an apology: he was sad to leave Theo, but he is glad that he has, for the sake of his art. He knows Theo's lonely. He advises him to let their friend Arnold Koning, a painter, move into the apartment.

"He has such a big heart," Theo tells their sister. "He's always looking to do something for others," though sadly too often those people don't appreciate what he's trying to do for them; they don't understand him.

But Theo understands his brother. And Vincent understands him. Theo takes Vincent's advice. He lets Koning move in. "He isn't nearly as skillful as Vincent, but it will be more companionable than being on my own."

78.

SPRING 1888, NORTH AND SOUTH:
BLOSSOMS, STRONG WINDS

AS WINTER THAWS in both Paris and Arles, the brothers work hard—separately *and* together. Together they devise a plan to persuade Goupil's to champion their favorite artists not only in Paris but also in The Hague and in London.

Theo has already been displaying works by Paul Gauguin, Camille Pissarro, Auguste Rodin, Edgar Degas, and others in the gallery. Vincent encourages Theo to continue to take on even more new work, such as some of the latest paintings by Georges Seurat, which they'd both liked the day Vincent left. He also suggests that Theo write to Tersteeg about taking some of the modern paintings for their old branch in The Hague, too. Theo will. But he's also busy working for his brother. He's going to get Vincent's work more exposure. Which of Vincent's paintings should he put in the fourth Exhibition of the Independents? It will open in Paris at the end of March.

Vincent tells Theo it's up to him. He's looking not back but forward to what more he can do with his paint-loaded brush. "I'm inclined to place slightly more hopes in this year's work," he says.

But Vincent's painting already had gotten so much better while he was in Paris. Theo is eager to show him off. So he chooses three colorful, bright pieces for the exhibition: two of them are landscapes from near their apartment in Montmartre. One of them is a scene behind the windmill, with fenced-in gardens, the city down the hill in the distance; the other is of vegetable gardens in Montmartre, with the windmill's sails in the distance. The third painting is a pile of books—French novels—on a table. Next to the books are two pink roses in a glass. Behind the table is a colorful wallpaper background.

WHEN SPRING COMES to Arles, Vincent takes his easel and his paints outside. He loves plein air painting. He uses his old perspective frame often as he orients himself to the landscapes of his new home.

"I attach importance to the use of the frame," he tells Theo. He thinks more painters will start using it again, just as the old German, Italian, and Flemish painters had. Vincent loves the feeling of "us." For years he tried to get Theo to become an artist with him. Now he feels part of a larger group of painters, a community that includes people from different countries, who paint in all different styles. He is part of a painting tradition.

Someday he would love to create his own painting community, a studio where painters can live and work together. He wants to do it right there, in the South of France. But first he has to feel settled himself in Arles.

VINCENT'S PAINTING FLOURISHES with the warm weather, growing and changing as Arles fills with blossoming trees. His style has evolved many times already, and now taking with him what he'd learned in Paris, adding to it what he loves from Japanese prints, and expanding the colors in his palette, he experiments with line and color and thick paint. Away from other influences and the hustle and bustle of Paris, he paints dozens of pictures of blossoming trees, developing a style different from anyone else's, a mixture of all he has seen and loved recently. Years later Vincent will be called a Post-Impressionist along with other artists such as Paul Gauguin, Paul Cézanne, and Georges Seurat. But now he is one painter alone with his art.

One of his paintings, which he makes toward the end of March, is of two pink peach trees, one behind the other. He decides to give it to Jet Mauve, his cousin. Her husband, his old mentor and nemesis, Anton Mauve, had died in early February. Even though he had not been in touch since Mauve had left him angrily in the dunes—"You have a vicious character," Mauve had said to him—his death saddens Vincent greatly. He thinks of him every day. He tells Theo he wants to send the peach trees to Mauve's widow, and he signs it "Souvenir de Mauve, Vincent & Theo." But Theo feels it should be just from Vincent, one painter's homage to another, so Vincent removes Theo's name.

Although the painting is going well, Vincent can't find the supplies he needs in Arles. So he asks Theo to send him his colors: silver, white, lemon chrome yellow, vermilion, geranium lake, carmine, Prussian blue, very light cinnabar green, orange lead, emerald green, and more. He gives him two orders; one is urgent, and the other Theo should send only when he has the money.

Theo sends Vincent all he asked for—one hundred tubes of paint. Vincent is deeply grateful.

———————————

UP NORTH, there is progress, too. Tersteeg has agreed to help with their cause, so Theo sends him a group of paintings to show at the branch in The Hague: one each by Degas, Monet, Pissarro, Guillaumin, Gauguin, and Toulouse-Lautrec; two by Monticelli; and one by Vincent. It's the first time any Impressionist paintings are shown in the Netherlands.

And one by Vincent. In the gallery in The Hague where he had his first job.

VINCENT PAINTS FRUIT TREES in blossom, peach and pear orchards. He tells his friend Émile Bernard that he wishes he could paint more from his imagination, like Bernard can, but he's most comfortable painting outside in nature. He'd like to paint "a starry sky, for example, well—it's a thing that I'd like to try to do, just as in the daytime I'll try to paint a green meadow studded with dandelions." But for that he needs to develop his skills of fantasy.

He worries that he's using too much paint and that it will cost Theo too much money. He tells him that if there's a month or a fortnight when Theo feels pressed for money, he should let him know and he'll draw instead of paint. Vincent is deeply appreciative, more so than he's ever been, of all Theo has been doing for him. He is willing to alter his art in deference to Theo's bank balance.

Theo does not want him to do that, but nature takes matters into her own hands. The mistral, a strong, dry, cold wind coming from the north, starts to blow so fiercely in Arles that Vincent, never one to shy away from nature's furies, cannot keep his easel standing, even though he tries and tries.

So he goes inside and draws, modeling his work after the Japanese prints he loves so much. He concentrates on strong lines without shading, using a combination of pencil, pen, brown and black ink, and a reed pen that he made himself. Since he pledged himself to art, Vincent has gone back and forth between drawing and painting, learning about one from the other. He's energized.

Theo, however, is discouraged. His bosses are angry: they don't like that he's focusing on the Impressionists; they are not selling well enough. And in The Hague the paintings he sent have not moved; only one of the Monticellis sold.

Even so, Theo continues to exhibit the painters he wants to, despite what his bosses say. Vincent warns him not to fall out with "those gentlemen," though. It would be a rude shock for Theo, Vincent tells him, to be on his own; it would be disorienting, like leaving a prison after years of captivity. Unlike all those times he told Theo to quit, he now warns him not to make a change without a lot of thought, though he is suspicious that both of them will be "rooked by those . . . gentlemen."

———————

ON THE FIRST OF MAY, which happens to be Theo's thirty-first birthday, Vincent rents the east wing of a yellow house at 2 Place Lamartine, "which contains 4 rooms, or more precisely, two, with two little rooms. It's painted yellow outside, whitewashed inside—in the full sunshine." Sun and light inside and out.

He sets up his studio there, and he hopes to turn the room on the first floor into his bedroom at some point. But he can't afford to buy a bed, and he can't find one to rent. He can see getting a mattress and sleeping on the floor in the studio, but he isn't going to live the way he had in the Borinage. He wants a place to keep his clothes, and he wants to have his clothes cleaned and mended.

He wants the house to be nice, too. He thinks maybe he should have a housemate, maybe Paul Gauguin, a friend from Paris. They could room together, paint together, cook together.

He dreams more and more about establishing an artists' commune in Arles. In the north, he'd been suffering off and on physically from toothaches and stomachaches. But the clean air of the south, away from the soot of the city, is good not only for his art but for his health, too. He's getting out more; he's gone to some bullfights and visited a brothel. He is feeling pretty good.

But in Paris, something is wrong with Theo.

79.

EXTREME LASSITUDE

THEO IS EXHAUSTED. And worse. "My poor friend," Vincent writes to him, "our neurosis &c. surely also comes from our rather too artistic way of life—but it's also a fatal inheritance." The Van Goghs have been getting weaker from generation to generation, Vincent says. Even their sister Wil, who does *not* lead a Bohemian life at all, looks like a "madwoman" in a recent photograph. Vincent suggests Theo follow the advice of their doctor, David Gruby: "eat well, live well, see few women," and live as if you already have a brain disease.

A few weeks later, Theo goes to see the doctor. Gruby diagnoses a heart problem: that's what is causing his great exhaustion. But maybe his fatigue is exacerbated by the potassium iodide he's taking. It's prescribed for a persistent cough, which Theo has. It is also prescribed for cerebral syphilis.

"If you could now have just one year of living in the country and close to nature," Vincent tells him, "that would make Gruby's treatment much easier."

Vincent worries that Gruby is treating the wrong thing—that they should be concentrating more on Theo's nervous system, rather than his heart.

Feeling lousy, Theo often wants to give in to his fate. NO, Vincent says. Do not give up. Take care of yourself, he tells his brother.

Nothing matters to Vincent as much as Theo taking care of himself. He wouldn't mind if Theo went to America, as his bosses want him to. He wouldn't care if Theo quit Goupil's altogether. Nothing is important to Vincent besides Theo's well-being. He *has* to get better.

Vincent offers to go to America with him, if Theo wants. He encourages Theo to come south and visit him, since his own health is much better in Arles, though he does still "suffer from unaccountable, involuntary feelings, or a stupor on some days, but it's getting calmer."

There's one unequivocal piece of good news: the crate of two dozen paintings that Vincent had sent three weeks earlier, the first shipment from Arles, finally arrives in Paris. At least half of the paintings are of trees in blossom.

They are beautiful.

80.

A SENSE OF THE INFINITE

---

*At the same time that he's an excellent artist, he's a thinker,
because every one of his works contains an idea that
flashes on the eye of the man who looks for it.*

—Émile Bernard to his parents, about Vincent, July 1888

IN JUNE, Theo buys ten paintings by Claude Monet and shows them at his Montmartre gallery, on the entresol floor. One critic praises not only the show but the entresol itself, admiring the lack of "high class décor," no plush drapes or gilded cornices, as in the rest of the gallery. Theo is not only working through his illness; he's continuing to do things his own way. And well.

Vincent writes to him every other day, worrying, asking him often how he is feeling. He also writes about art, the art world, and their mutual goal of championing the Impressionists and other modern painters. He wants to help Paul Gauguin, who is broke. Gauguin should come to Arles, he thinks, and the two should live and paint together in the Yellow House. Theo could support Gauguin, too; supporting two painters who lived together would be economical.

Vincent needs more money, and supplies, and Theo sends him both. Vincent is painting up a storm. He *is* a storm. For most of June and July he paints landscapes, thick with impasto, textured, colorful. By the end of the summer he's made more than thirty-five landscapes: wheat fields, orchards, vineyards; ocean scenes, streets, and cottages from a trip to the seaside town Saintes-Maries-de-la-Mer; workers in fields, a sower, fields with flowers.

He often sends sketches or replicas of his work to friends, and sometimes when he does, he makes the painting a little different from the original, depending on whom he's sending it to. He is never unaware that his paintings are for people to look at and enjoy. And so, if he thinks one of his friends would like a version in a more Japanese style, for example, that's what he makes.

He does this even though his paintings are distinctly Vincent:

vivid colors

thick paint

textured fields and skies and flowers and trees and houses

all in blues and oranges and yellows and pinks and

whites and greens and reds.

He uses a lot of zinc white. He keeps running out of it.

Although he paints quickly and spontaneously, capturing what he sees on the spot, it is not as if he paints in a fever, he tells Theo. Even while he paints the picture on his easel, he is thinking about the next one—calculating it in a complicated way.

"And look," he tells his brother, thinking ahead, "when people say they're done too quickly you'll be able to reply that they looked at them too quickly. And besides, I'm now going over all the canvases a little more before sending them to you." He is anything but cavalier.

When the mistral kicks up again, he moves inside, drawing with pen and ink and working with watercolor.

His drawings are studies for paintings, studies after paintings, and also just drawings. He exchanges them with some of his painter friends. He sends studies for paintings to Émile Bernard: haystacks, fishing boats, a row of cottages, a sower with the setting sun, a harvest scene, and washerwomen at a canal with a bridge. He also sends him a drawing of a Zouave, a French soldier, which amazes Bernard. He tells his parents, "Vincent's becoming very good." But Vincent is not satisfied with this or his other Zouave paintings.

He doggedly continues to work on his technique, to improve his portraits. In late July he meets the postman Joseph Roulin. They become close friends, and Vincent paints and draws him many times. He is determined to *capture* people.

A death back home makes this feel urgent. Uncle Cent has died. Uncle Cent, who had been there so much in their childhood and in their adulthood, too. Uncle Cent, who had no children of his own, who disappointed both of the brothers, who was disappointed in Vincent, but who was the uncle they had been most tied to.

Theo goes to the funeral, and the brothers write about it for weeks afterward. Uncle Cent left Theo one thousand guilders (what Pa used to make as a yearly salary). He left Vincent nothing; he'd long ago given up on the nephew who shared his name.

But the lack of a legacy doesn't bother Vincent as much as it would have earlier. Uncle Cent's death makes him think more than ever about mortality—and immortality. Maybe there is an afterlife, maybe not. But if he paints someone well, that person is alive forever.

In the time he will spend in Arles—444 days—he'll make two hundred paintings and one hundred drawings, a huge number for an artist. He'll paint landscapes, still lifes, scenes of cafés at night, furniture, rooms, flowering trees, flowers—he is about to begin painting his favorite again, sunflowers. But painting portraits is the thing that moves him most deeply, that gives him "a sense of the infinite."

The 'Laakmolen' near The Hague, 1882

The Potato Eaters, 1885

A Pair of Boots, 1887

[The Cone Collection,
Baltimore Museum of Art]

View from Theo's Apartment,
1887

[Van Gogh Museum, Amsterdam]

Self-Portrait as a Painter, 1888

[Van Gogh Museum, Amsterdam]

The Bedroom, 1888
[Van Gogh Museum, Amsterdam]

Sunflowers, 1889
[Van Gogh Museum, Amsterdam]

Almond Blossom, 1890

[Van Gogh Museum, Amsterdam]

Self-Portrait, 1887
[Van Gogh Museum, Amsterdam]

*Portrait of
Theo van Gogh*, 1887
[Van Gogh Museum, Amsterdam]

81.

YELLOW NOTES, FIERCE WINDS, BIG NEWS

---

*E*VEN THOUGH he is working well, Vincent's moods fluctuate wildly. Like the mistral's fierce winds, his evaluations of his own worth are variable and unpredictable, and can be destructive. He works this summer often in a frenzy, with what he calls a high yellow note. Mania. Then he drops down and gets depressed about his future, the future of his work.

In August he writes to Theo, "You're enough of a judge of painting to see and to appreciate what originality I may have, and you're also enough of a judge to see the pointlessness of presenting to today's public what I'm doing, because the others surpass me in more precise brushwork."

Vincent blames the wind, his poverty, and his late start. But he doesn't want to quit. And he is profoundly grateful to Theo that he doesn't have to.

He reads Walt Whitman's poetry, which speaks to him of God in nature, of the future, of eternity. He writes to his sister Wil that Whitman "sees in the future, and even in the present, a world of health, of generous, frank carnal love—of friendship—of work, with the great starry firmament, something, in short, that one could only call God and eternity, put back in place above this world." Vincent has found a way to combine his two loves: God through art.

But while he paints, capturing the beauty of nature on the canvas, trying to give to the world what he once wanted to give through preaching, he worries about Theo's money.

So in September, he starts using less expensive paint, pigments that are less finely ground. To make up for it, he paints with even heavier strokes, the impasto thick and thicker.

And he paints furiously.

He has another reason for painting furiously now: the artist Paul Gauguin is coming to live with him, and Vincent wants to impress him. Gauguin is further along in his career, although he started late, too. Vincent wants to have work to show him, and to decorate the Yellow House.

When he's not painting, he furnishes the house. He buys two beds, one for each of their bedrooms, twelve chairs, a table for the kitchen. He buys a mirror, one good enough to use for self-portraits, because models are hard to hire, even in Arles. Practicing on himself will help him make those immortal portraits he so much wants to create, to give to the world the sense of the infinite.

Around the house he hangs the paintings he's made, ones he thinks Gauguin will like.

Early in October there is big news from Theo. He has sold a study of Vincent's to an art dealer in Paris named Athanase Bague. Vincent writes in response: "That's a really good one, about Bague," and underlines it three times.

Theo has sold a painting of Vincent's! Vincent had traded many of his paintings already, and had sold at least one to Julien Tanguy, a paint and art dealer in Paris, whose portrait he painted. But this sale—by Theo—feels different.

Vincent tells Theo to give Bague his best if he sees him, and he recommends two other paintings Bague might like: a vineyard and a night sky.

During this time, Vincent makes a portrait of Ma from a photograph. She is smiling, looking kindly off into the distance. When she and Wil changed houses in Breda, Ma put all his stuff—including his paintings—in storage with a carpenter in Breda. Those paintings will not survive. Ma clearly does not appreciate Vincent's art, but his quest is no longer for her, or for the memory of Pa. It is for himself, for the world. And Vincent loves her. He loved Pa, too. Pa, who *had* appreciated his art. He writes home and asks for a photograph of Dorus so he can make his portrait, too.

WITH THE FURNISHING OF THE HOUSE, in addition to his usual painting supplies, Vincent keeps needing more money. It really worries him. "I very often think that all the costs of painting weigh on you," Vincent writes to Theo. "You couldn't imagine what anxiety I have about it." He prays that the sale to Bague is the start of something.

Gauguin's impending arrival is making him think even more than usual about sales. Gauguin is quite ambitious, and he has agreed to make Theo his sole art representative, sending him at least twenty paintings. Vincent would love to see them. And he wants Theo to have success selling not only Gauguin's work but also his.

As always, Vincent continues working. A week before Gauguin is due to arrive, Vincent sends Theo a colored sketch of something he wants to paint on a big canvas: "This time it's simply my bedroom, but the colour has to do the job here," he writes. He wants it to be suggestive of rest and sleep. Although the finished painting will have slightly different objects than the sketch, the colors will be the same. Walls of pale violet, floor of red tiles. The bed and chairs of "fresh butter yellow." The linen "very bright lemon green" and the bedspread "scarlet red." He tells Theo that "looking at the painting should rest the mind, or rather the imagination."

Vincent is desperate for some rest. But he doesn't take it; he works harder. As Gauguin's arrival approaches, Vincent works himself into a state of utter exhaustion, fear, and guilt.

82.

GREAT DEBT, GREAT WORRY

---

*You talk about money that you owe me and that you wish
to pay back to me. I know nothing of that.*

—Theo to Vincent, October 27, 1888

VINCENT HAS SPENT so much of Theo's money getting the house ready,
he's sure that no matter how well he and Gauguin work, they will never
recoup the expenses.

When he adds these costs to how much Theo has given him for the
past eight years, he is overwhelmed. He feels himself spiraling down into
madness from the worry, the guilt, the responsibility. Finally he takes a few
days off from everything to rest and eat. He feels a little better, but the re-
alization of how much he owes Theo plagues him.

If only they could sell more of his paintings! He tells Theo he is upset.
He promises he will keep working as long and as hard as he can, and someday, someday—he will make it up to him.

But in the meantime, could Theo please send him more money and
more paints.

Theo immediately sends money, and a letter of great concern. He
doesn't want Vincent to neglect his health any more getting ready for
Gauguin. You are always doing for others, Theo says, at your own expense.

It distresses Theo. "I'd be very glad to see you more selfish until you're on an even keel."

Vincent thanks Theo immediately.

But he's still overwhelmed by the debt he owes his brother and is determined to pay it back, even though it means painting must take over his entire life. Clearly depressed, he tells his brother that it feels like he hasn't lived.

Theo writes him a heartfelt, strong, loving, insistent letter. "I can see that you're ill and that you're giving yourself masses of worries." He has a very different idea about the money, about Vincent. He *has* lived. And, "I must tell you something once and for all. To me it's as if the matter of money and sales of paintings and the whole financial side doesn't exist, or rather, that it exists like an illness."

Theo has been giving Vincent about 15 percent of his income. At times it has been a burden, of course, because he was also sending money home to his parents to help with their expenses, and to Wil, and to Cor. But he tells Vincent to stop thinking about the money.

All those fights over Vincent's progress. All those times Vincent had said, what I make is yours, your property. All the frustrations Theo has endured over the years. All of that is gone. What matters to Theo is that Vincent works happily, and lives, and that they stay close. Theo tells Vincent that if he wants to work hard for *himself*, he should. But not for him. He hopes that Gauguin's company will be good for him and that he will soon recover emotionally and physically.

THE THIRD WEEK of October 1888, Gauguin arrives. "He's very, very interesting as a man," Vincent writes, "and I have every confidence that with him we'll do a great many things. He'll probably produce a great deal here, and perhaps I shall too, I hope."

Vincent and Gauguin had exchanged self-portraits in anticipation of their new partnership. Vincent's self-portrait reflects how he feels about himself, that he has "something of a dual nature, something of both the monk and the painter." He's painted himself in the style of a bonze, looking a little bit Japanese. He likens himself to "a simple worshipper of the eternal Buddha," he tells both Theo and Gaugin.

Gauguin, in his self-portrait, looks like a wily rogue.

Apparently they have different ideas of what their time in the Yellow House will be like.

83.

ROOMMATES
NORTH AND SOUTH

THEO HAS A NEW ROOMMATE, too, another Dutch painter, Meijer de Haan. Theo is trying to make a community like Vincent does. But he is just not as good at it. He asks Vincent to "continue as in the past and create for us a circle of artists and friends, something which I'm utterly incapable of doing by myself."

Theo does like De Haan, though, and his work. He's a good artist, reminiscent of the great Dutch master Rembrandt. But his work lacks Vincent's fury. As does his personality! Still Theo enjoys him, and he's made friends with some of De Haan's friends. From what Theo tells Vincent about Meijer de Haan, and from seeing photographs of his drawings and paintings, Vincent approves. He wants to meet him and his friends someday.

But for Theo, it's not enough. Nobody can fill Vincent's shoes. And he still wishes he could have a wife and family of his own. He hasn't seen or heard from Jo Bonger since his unsuccessful proposal fifteen months earlier, and he hasn't seen Andries Bonger for almost a year, either.

Dries has gotten married, and although the marriage is rocky at best, a disaster at worst, he is living the life of a married man. Even if he wanted to see his old friend Theo, he wouldn't dare. He watches him from afar, judgmental and concerned. But Theo is not living a wild life; it's Vincent and Gauguin in Arles who are living a Bohemian lifestyle, with Gauguin taking the lead.

Paul Gauguin started painting when he was a stockbroker in Paris. After the French stock market crashed when he was thirty-four, he floundered. He wanted to paint full-time, but with a wife and five children to support, that was not practical. His wife did not approve. He had to sell his life insurance policy for the money, and then he moved with his wife and children to Denmark to live with her family. He took a job as a tarpaulin salesman, but he was miserable. In 1885, he and his oldest son moved back to Paris. That's where the Van Gogh brothers got to know him. At about the same time Vincent moved to Arles, Gauguin moved to Brittany, in northern France.

Gauguin is talented, and so far he is more successful than Vincent. He can be a difficult man—self-centered and selfish, brash and conceited. And he is wild; he drinks a lot, visits brothels often. Though he can hold his liquor better than Vincent, he has a temper. And when he gets angry and impassioned, he turns bellicose. He even carries weapons with him—he's a fencer and has brought his foils to Arles.

From the moment Gauguin arrives, the two paint together, learn from each other, and talk about art. Some of those discussions grow quite heated.

Though they have the same goal—to produce really good work—they discover that they have different ideas of how to paint and whose work to admire and emulate.

Gauguin is taken aback by what he sees as Vincent's disorderliness, both in painting and in life.

Vincent can talk a blue streak, even without drinking, and that drives Gauguin crazy.

Gauguin is a boaster—and he often boasts about his sexual prowess with the prostitutes they both visit. Vincent feels inferior to Gauguin in that way, and in other ways. He's in awe of the success Gauguin has already had with his painting.

When Gauguin drinks, he drinks a lot, and now so does Vincent. Alcohol makes the situation worse.

Neither one of them is easy to live with. But the arrangement is about the work, and Vincent still hopes Gauguin's influence will improve his painting.

Gauguin insists Vincent do things his way. His strong opinion is that they should paint from their imaginations, not from what they see, as Vincent likes to do. Although Vincent is in awe of Gauguin's talent, he maintains his ground, arguing that he much prefers to paint from life—from models, outside in nature, and inside, if necessary, but from objects placed on a table: fruit, flowers, books. He doesn't want to lose his own style, or his way of working. But after arguing with Gauguin for weeks, he finally capitulates. Gauguin, he tells Theo in November, "has proved to me a little that it was time for me to vary things a bit—I'm beginning to compose from memory."

The weather is getting too bad to paint outside, anyway, and they don't have enough money to hire many models—though they do sketch at the brothels sometimes. So Vincent tries painting from memory. In general the painting is going very well for him. Gauguin thinks so, too—he pays Vincent compliments, encourages him, and tells him he especially loves what he's doing with sunflowers. He tells Vincent that he'd seen a painting that Claude Monet "had made of sunflowers in a large Japanese vase, very fine." But he likes Vincent's better than Monet's. Monet, the founder of Impressionism!

Vincent and Gauguin are both prolific, and Theo is having success selling Gauguin's work. Soon, Vincent is sure, Theo will sell more of his, too.

The brothers' hard work is paying off.

Vincent is realizing his dream of the studio in the south.

Although he and Gauguin are not the easiest of companions and the arguments continue, it all really does seem to be working.

Until it isn't.

84.

ELECTRICITY

DECEMBER IN ARLES, 1888. It is cold, so Vincent and Gauguin are working inside. Vincent is working from the imagination, although he's not entirely happy or sure about it. He's also painting portraits of his friend the postman, Roulin, and Roulin's entire family. "And," he tells Theo, "if I manage to do *this entire family* even better, I'll have done at least one thing to my taste and personal."

There is tension in the Yellow House.

Gauguin is also working on a portrait—of Vincent. Watching him work on it, Vincent doesn't think it's bad. When he's done, Gauguin shows him the finished product.

Vincent says, "It is certainly me, but me gone mad."

It's Vincent at an easel, painting sunflowers. A year later Vincent will tell Theo, "It was indeed me, extremely tired and charged with electricity as I was then."

Charged with electricity, indeed. The two painters work all day, go to the café in the evenings, drink, argue, and then go to bed late.

The second week of December, Gauguin writes to Theo. He is fed up with Vincent. He wants to leave, go back to Paris.

"Vincent and I can absolutely not live side by side without trouble," Gauguin writes. They are of incompatible temperaments, and both need "tranquility for our work." He admits Vincent is "a man of remarkable intelligence, whom I greatly respect." He leaves him with regret, "but I repeat, it is necessary."

In the same envelope, Vincent encloses his own letter. He tells Theo that Gauguin will either "definitely go or he'll definitely stay." Gauguin is, he says, "disheartened by the good town of Arles, by the little yellow house where we work, and above all by me." He doesn't want Gauguin to leave. He knows his friend needs peace, but where and how? "Will he find it elsewhere if he doesn't find it here?"

Vincent persuades him to stay. They make a trip together, to a museum in Montpellier, about fifty miles to the west of Arles. When they return, they keep talking about art, the thing that connects them. They talk about Delacroix and Rembrandt. "The discussion is *excessively electric*. We sometimes emerge from it with tired minds, like an electric battery after it's run down," Vincent tells Theo.

Excessive electricity isn't always a bad thing—for Vincent. And he does love the communal living. He gets so much out of the support, even with the arguments. He thinks about Theo's roommate De Haan and his painter friends. He hopes they have a good community, too. He hopes to meet them someday, but for now he wants to give them encouragement. He asks Theo to tell them: Keep at it! Good work, good community—Vincent's ideal.

When Vincent writes this to Theo on December 18, 1888, as far as he knows, everything is the same in Paris. As far as he knows, his brother is working at Goupil's, living with De Haan, keeping company with him and other artists.

What Vincent doesn't know is that for more than a week, Theo has been keeping company with someone else.

There is electricity in Paris, too.

85.

ELECTRICITY, II

---

*D*ECEMBER IN PARIS, 1888. The past year has been terribly hard for Johanna Bonger. While Theo moved on from her rejection of him, she has been suffering from her own unrequited love. She'd kept trying to win the man's heart, but he kept rejecting her. She finally decided to take a teaching job away from Amsterdam, in Utrecht (where Vincent's Margot had gone to recover).

The job did not go well. She was distracted and distraught, depressed and weak. After only about four months, she was given an honorable discharge for "health reasons."

Back home in Amsterdam, she desperately needed a change of scene. She wrote to her brother Dries and asked if she could come stay with him in Paris. But his first year of marriage was going horribly. He found his wife dull and cold; they did not connect intellectually at all. He told Jo, "My married life so far has been torture." So he asked her not to come.

But when Jo finally realized that the man she loved would never commit to her and it was definitely over, she really needed her brother. Dries said she could come to Paris.

———————

SHE IS IN PARIS NOW. Since Dries and Theo don't see each other, Jo hasn't seen Theo. But she's heard of her brother's worries about him.

On top of her already fragile state, she is now terribly concerned—and feels guilty—about Theo. Convinced that her rejection has sent him on the path to ruin, she decides to find out for herself how he is. She also thinks it would be good for Dries to have his friend Theo back in his life. And she has doubts about her decision not to give Theo a chance.

So around December 10, Jo goes to Montmartre, Theo's neighborhood, and manages to run into him.

"Recently I wrote to you that when I met De Haan, I felt as if he had been sent to me, but now something even better has happened, much better," Theo writes to his mother. "Guess who I bumped into here a couple of days ago, Jo Bonger, whatever was I to do?"

Standing in the street, they just chat about this and that. And then Jo asks if she can have a word with him.

Is it my fault, she asks Theo, that you and Dries are no longer on good terms? Their chitchat goes deeper, and as they talk, Jo's heart, numb no longer, opens up to Theo.

Theo still likes her so much. He thinks they will be friends. But he doesn't dare hope for more. He's happy he will be able to renew his friendship with Dries.

The three start spending time together right away, and after just a few days Theo finds it impossible to be just friends with Jo. He takes a chance and tells her that he loves her, and to his great delight, she responds that she loves him, too!

Their feelings are true—and life-changing. Theo and Jo are passion-ately in love. Back when he first proposed and she rejected him, he wrote to her that the idea of being in complete harmony from the beginning was "a very beautiful & very young idea, but it is not *true*." But now this is exactly what is happening. They are in complete harmony. *This* is their real beginning.

They are passionate about each other, but also comfortable, happy, at ease. They spend time outside—and in the corner of Theo's room, where they enjoy "such peace together."

Within two weeks they know they want to marry.

Jo will take Theo just as he is, he tells his mother, announcing his wish to become engaged.

It is like a fairy tale. The life Theo had imagined for them—it is going to happen.

86.

PASSION IN ARLES

---

*Vincent and I do not find ourselves in
general agreement, especially in painting.*

—Paul Gauguin to Émile Bernard, December 1888

IN ARLES THERE IS PASSION, too, but not romance. The passions run
from creative joy to anger to frustration to inspiration to aspiration to com-
petition to rage.

While Theo is courting Jo, Vincent has written only once—about their
trip to the museum, and "electric" conversations about art. But nothing
since then.

Theo has been too busy to notice the absence of letters from his brother.
But if Vincent *had* written, Theo would have worried.

The situation in Arles has been getting more and more unstable.
Vincent and Gauguin have been drinking more, arguing more.

Vincent is not one to keep his mouth shut. The more he drinks, the
sadder, angrier, and more argumentative he becomes.

They each admire different artists, Gauguin writes to Émile Bernard.
The ones Vincent loves, Gauguin cannot endure. The ones he admires,
Vincent detests. "I answer: 'Corporal, you're right,' for the sake of peace."

It is hard to believe Gauguin always answers with such equanimity.

"He likes my paintings very much, but while I am doing them he always finds that I am doing this or that wrong," Gauguin says.

Even though Gauguin has been trying to push Vincent into doing things his way, Vincent has held on to his own ideas, his own style. He likes to play around with color, and he even includes bits of eggshells and coffee grounds that have dropped into the paint. Gauguin detests "messing about in the medium," he tells Bernard.

More than once, drinking at a table with Gauguin, Vincent has gotten over-the-top angry. He's been known to throw a drink in Gauguin's face.

And then, on December 23, 1888, as Theo and Jo are making their plans to marry, Theo happier than he's ever been, his personal path clear and certain, Vincent starts down a very different path—one strewn with blood and tears.

87.
TELLING THE NEWS

ON CHRISTMAS EVE, Theo writes to his sister Lies to tell her about his engagement. "You are one of the first to hear my great news which will be a turning point in my life."

After all these years of Theo's liaisons with "inappropriate" women, women his parents would never approve of, the woman he had set his eyes on three and a half years earlier, the woman whom his mother certainly approves of, the woman who had rejected him a year and a half ago, now this woman has promised to spend her life with him. Theo is overwhelmed with joy.

Theo and Jo are making plans for their official engagement announcement back in the Netherlands when a telegram arrives from Gauguin.

Vincent has been wounded. He is gravely ill.

88.

PASSION IN ARLES, II

DECEMBER 23–24, 1888, Arles, France. It is yet another tempestuous night at the Yellow House. Vincent and Gauguin have been drinking and talking, arguing electrically about art. About styles and methods and artists. About their shared and troubled finances. About the future of Vincent's dream, the studio of the south.

As reported later by Gauguin, the only eyewitness, this is what happens:

At some point Gauguin gets so angry, he storms out of the house, into the "shabby" streets of Arles.

Vincent goes looking for him. "Gauguin!" he calls. "Gauguin!" He's waving around a razor. Gauguin hears his name called, hears familiar footsteps. Vincent. He turns, they meet. They argue. Gauguin sees the razor and hurries away.

Later that night, quite late, Vincent appears at the door of a brothel that he and Gauguin have visited together. He asks for Rachel, his favorite prostitute. When she comes to the door, he hands her something wrapped in a piece of cloth. "Keep this object carefully," he tells her and leaves.

Rachel opens the package and falls in a faint on the floor. Wrapped in the cloth is Vincent's left ear. Human flesh and cartilage and blood.

Vincent goes home, gets into bed, passes out.

Gauguin has not slept at home. The next morning, the morning of Christmas Eve, he goes home and finds Vincent barely conscious. He might be dying. The police come, and Gauguin tells what happened between them, and what must have happened after they parted. Vincent cut off his left ear.

Gauguin was the only eyewitness, so this is how the story is usually told. But Gauguin was a fencer and had his sword with him in Arles. . . . Some historians postulate that Gauguin cut Vincent's ear (by accident) and Vincent agreed to keep quiet. It is unlikely, but we put this version here, next to the most often told story. Vincent *was* a nice enough person to cover up for a friend. It is unlikely, but just possible. . . .

No matter who cut the ear, Vincent is now near death.

He is taken to the hospital.

And Gauguin sends Theo the telegram.

TWO BROTHERS, A HOSPITAL BED

*T*HEO KNOWS he must go to Vincent. He hates to leave Paris and Jo, but it is just as he had said in that first letter he wrote to her: "I have a brother." You can't have me without Vincent. I am not me without Vincent.

He writes to her from work, "I received sad news today. Vincent is gravely ill. I don't know what's wrong, but I shall have to go there as my presence is required." He tells her he doesn't know how long he'll be; she should go home, back to Amsterdam. They had plans to go to the Netherlands soon anyway, and Annie, Dries's wife, is displeased with them for some reason, making Jo unhappy. She should just go now.

Jo agrees, but first she goes to Theo. She sees him off at the train station, standing on the platform in the chilly winter night, even though she has a cold. Theo says good-bye not knowing what he will find in Arles, or when he will see Jo again.

A night train south and he arrives in Arles the next day, Christmas Day, and goes to the hospital.

The doctors tell Theo that Vincent has been agitated off and on, has "been showing symptoms of that most dreadful illness, of madness."

Theo visits him in the ward, which Vincent will paint later: rows of beds, with curtains to pull around them for privacy. The walls are white, but the floor is brown, the bedspreads brown. Vincent is not always accurate about color—on purpose. But since this is the way he saw it, it's the way we see it, too.

Theo lays his head on the pillow next to his brother's. Vincent feels his brother next to him. Drained and exhausted, he is transported back to their childhood in the Netherlands, to a time he remembers as simple and pure and beautiful, a time when the two brothers shared a room, a life, a future.

Vincent whispers to Theo, "Just like in Zundert."

They visit for a while, talk. Theo tells him about his happiness with Jo. Theo sees the delirium for himself. "He seemed to be all right for a few minutes when I was with him, but lapsed shortly afterwards into his brooding about philosophy and theology," Theo writes to Jo later.

"It was terribly sad being there," he says. "From time to time all his grief would well up inside and he would try to weep, but couldn't. Poor fighter and poor, poor sufferer. Nothing can be done to relieve his anguish now, but it is deep and hard for him to bear. Had he just once found someone to whom he could pour his heart out, it might never have come to this."

If only he had found someone like I have—you.

———

THEO DOES NOT STAY with Vincent in Arles. He leaves that same day, taking Gauguin with him back to Paris.

When he gets home, Jo won't be there; she has already left for the Netherlands. He will follow ten days later.

"Will he remain insane?" Theo asks his beloved. "The doctors think it possible, but daren't yet say for certain. It should be apparent in a few days' time when he is rested; then we will see whether he is lucid again."

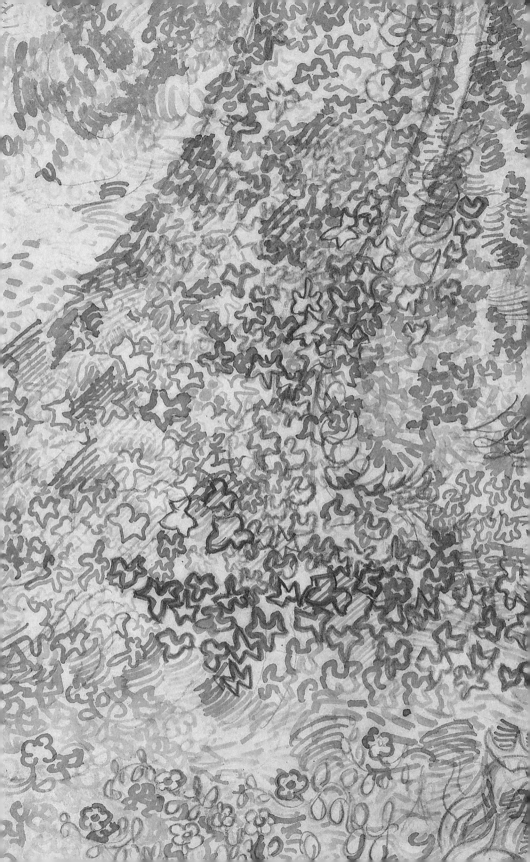

Abundances

1888–1889

I've been wavering between hope & fear.

—Theo to Jo, December 30, 1888

90.
PROSPECTS

WHEN THEO GETS BACK HOME to Paris, there's a letter from Jo waiting for him: "My thoughts were constantly with you on that long, tedious journey, but now I keep wondering, how will he have found his brother, how does he feel right now?"

How does Theo feel right now?

Bereft. Though he thinks of Jo with gratitude and relief, "the prospect of losing my brother, who has meant so much to me & has become so much a part of me, made me realize what a terrible emptiness I would feel if he were no longer there."

It's not clear if Vincent *will* survive. He's suffered a great trauma, which has left him weak both mentally and physically. He has a fever; he is often incoherent. And now the doctors are considering putting him in a mental asylum.

When he'd left Vincent to go back to Paris, Theo had asked Félix Rey, Vincent's doctor, to keep him posted about his brother's condition. The doctor already has written: Vincent's mental state has gotten worse. He'd gone to lie down in another patient's bed and would not leave it, despite the doctor's entreaties. "In his night-shirt he chased the Sister on duty and absolutely forbids anyone at all to go near his bed. Yesterday he got up and went to wash in the coal-box." The doctor has locked him in an isolation room.

On December 29, Rey writes, "Today, my superior issued a certificate of mental disturbance, reporting general delirium and requesting specialized care in an asylum."

Theo writes back with many questions, but Rey can't answer all of them. He tells Theo he still has some hope, though. He thinks Vincent will improve; he's a little better already. "My assessment," the doctor writes, "is that he will be able to recover in a short time, while retaining the extreme excitability that must form the essence of his character."

Theo reports all of this to Jo, and he tells her he couldn't get through this without her. "What would become of me without the knowledge that I have you, come what may."

And just as Rey predicted, Vincent does improve quickly. He is eating more and seems sane. Within a few days, they are treating only the wound.

On January 3, Theo writes to Jo that there is no more talk of commitment to an asylum. And he will be with her in the Netherlands soon: "Reception Wednesday!!!" Their engagement party.

He also tells her of a gift from Paul Gauguin: the portrait he'd made of Vincent painting sunflowers.

On January 4, Vincent leaves the hospital for a few hours. His friend Joseph Roulin picks him up. "He was pleased to see his paintings again," Roulin writes to Theo. "Don't worry; I will do all I can to give him some distraction; one of these days he will leave the hospital and go back to his paintings. That is all he thinks of, he is as sweet as a lamb."

While he's with Roulin, Vincent posts two letters: one to Theo, one to Gauguin. To Theo he apologizes that he had to make the trip. "I am, my dear brother, so *heartbroken* by your journey, I would have wished that you'd been spared that, for all in all no harm has come to me, and it wasn't worth troubling you." He also tells him how happy he is that Theo "made peace and even more than that with the Bongers." Not in this letter or ever, as far as we know, does Vincent write Theo about what happened that night in Arles. And Theo never disputes Gauguin's version.

To Gauguin, Vincent writes that he has thought a great deal about him while in the hospital. He'd sent word begging Gauguin to come visit, but Gauguin hadn't. "Tell me. Was my brother Theo's journey really necessary—my friend? Now at least reassure him completely, and yourself, please."

Gauguin writes back, asking Vincent for one of his paintings—sunflowers on a yellow background, "which I regard as a perfect page of an essential 'Vincent' style."

REASSURED THAT VINCENT is mending, Theo goes off to the Netherlands. On January 6 he and Jo send out an invitation to their party:

Engaged

Theodorus van Gogh

and

Johanna Bonger

January 1889 { Paris
Amsterdam

Reception Wednesday 9 January
Weteringschans 121

THE NEXT DAY, January 7, Vincent leaves the hospital with the help of Roulin. As soon as he is settled, Vincent promptly writes two letters: one to Theo and one to Ma and Wil. He tells Theo that being in the hospital was very interesting and that it is possible to learn how to live by being around the sick.

"I hope that I've just had a simple artist's bout of craziness and then a lot of fever" because of the wound. He assures Theo that he will get back to work tomorrow, beginning with one or two still lifes.

And he brings up some business: Theo had asked him to help choose which of his paintings to submit for the fifth Exhibition of the Independents coming up that autumn.

Vincent tells Theo it is his choice again. Theo chooses a night sky over the Rhone River, and a still life of irises.

To Ma and Wil, Vincent is much less forthcoming about his health. Writing in Dutch (he has been writing to Theo solely in French for two years now), he says, "Would you be so good as to take note that I'm dropping you this line in case Theo should have told you something about my being indisposed for a few days. . . . It wasn't worthwhile telling you about it." He says they shouldn't worry; he is fine. "It would please me very greatly if I were to get a letter from you one of these days," he writes. "I couldn't help thinking about you quite a lot these days."

Lying in his hospital bed in Arles, he'd remembered so well the parsonage in Zundert, "each path, each plant in the garden, the views round about, the fields, the neighbours, the cemetery, the church, our kitchen garden behind—right up to the magpies' nest in a tall acacia in the cemetery."

Theo had already told his mother and sister what had happened with Vincent, about the aftereffects, about the moment on the pillow, too.

Although Ma is thrilled about Theo's engagement, her worries about Vincent dominate her thoughts.

"Oh Theo, must the year end with such disaster?" Ma writes. "Such suffering for both of you, how he must feel it all, how touching about Zundert, together on one pillow."

91.

PORTRAIT OF HOPE,
PORTRAIT OF DESPAIR

---

*M*Y DEAREST THEO," Jo writes on January 13, 1889, from her family's apartment in Amsterdam. "As I sit here so quietly in my usual pleasant surroundings that wretched train is taking you further away from me by the minute; it's so empty now, so quiet, and you've only been gone for a couple of hours—how long the months will be!"

Jo and Theo have had their engagement party, but now Theo is on his way back to Paris to work. Jo will stay at home with her parents, and for the next two months she and Theo will be living in different cities, in different countries.

The distance will bring them closer. Over these months they will get to know each other intimately, writing seventy-eight letters back and forth. They will share everything from their innermost thoughts to their opinions about apartments and furniture.

But now is just the beginning, and as Jo writes to Theo, she gazes at his photograph and finds the words she hadn't been able to say to him in person before he left: "Thank you for all the joy you have given me, for all the love you show me, I feel so fortunate, so happy." In the week they were together in Amsterdam, she says, he taught her so much and inspired her to be something higher, less ordinary than she had been. "I'm quite sure that if I stay with you always, you might still be able to make <u>something</u> out of me."

But how is Vincent? she wants to know. She tells Theo not to hide his sadness from her, ever. Vincent had written to her directly, sending congratulations after receiving their engagement announcement in Arles. Though they haven't met yet, Jo feels guilty that in the "past wonderful week, I have thought far too much about myself and too little about him."

How *is* Vincent? He is trying to get back to his life and art in the Yellow House without Gauguin. He's writing to Theo and friends about art. He's painting. He paints two self-portraits showing his bandaged ear. He paints sunflowers. He will give one of the sunflower paintings to Gauguin, per his request. He needs more money.

Life as usual for Vincent.

But he's worried that people—his neighbors, his painter friends—will be afraid of him. And sadly, his good friend Roulin, who has been keeping close company with him, has been transferred to Marseille.

He is essentially alone.

————————————

FROM PARIS TO AMSTERDAM, Theo and Jo write back and forth almost daily, talking about their plans for their future, including where they should live. Theo wants to live in town, so he can go home for lunch with Jo. He finds an apartment less than a twenty-minute walk away, at 8 Cité Pigalle. They start writing about the furnishings they'll get for it. Theo shares news from the gallery, especially about an exhibit of Claude Monet's work that he is mounting.

As Theo writes a letter to Jo in his apartment, his roommate, Meijer de Haan, sketches a portrait of him, which Theo sends to Jo.

"I'm delighted with it," she writes. You see Theo writing a letter—and you can see words on his shirtsleeve. "What's my name doing there along with apartments and coffee and cokes—is that what was on your mind?" In fact it was! Theo has a habit of writing lists and notes to himself on his disposable shirt cuffs. He needs to buy coffee, get cokes for fuel, and write Jo a letter!

As time goes on and they grow closer, Theo and Jo confess their worries to each other. They worry not about the other but about themselves. Theo is moody. He writes to Jo that at times he loves everybody and at other times everything seems stupid, petty, superficial. He writes her during a bad mood like that and says he'd "like to lay my head in your lap & bask in your love. If you were here, I'd be able to accept the world as it is."

Jo confesses that she is still weak from her difficult years of longing for that other man. Theo tells her that "a person's state of mind affects their physical condition" and advises her to eat well and not worry. But she *is* worried—about how well she will keep house and cook and be that kind of a good wife to him. Theo reassures her and tells her not to focus on that. "Don't forget I am anything but spoilt when it comes to the ménage [house-keeping] and I shan't make things difficult for you." She should focus on being happy. He is evidence, he tells her, that the body responds to the state of mind: "I can tell you that for two years I had persistent fits of coughing every morning & since I started to be happy they have disappeared completely."

Theo doesn't think her weakness and other complaints will disappear all at once. But if they are truly happy together, her health will improve. Just as his had.

As for Vincent—Theo has sent her some letters Vincent had written, but not the last few. In the last few Vincent has seemed agitated again. Theo is worried.

———

ON FEBRUARY 3, Vincent writes to Theo that work is the best distraction for him. He is working on the sunflowers for Gauguin, and on another version of a portrait he'd done of Mrs. Roulin (Augustine-Alix Pellicot Roulin), called *La Berceuse*. It is his third version.

He is trying to get along with his Arles neighbors. Some of them like him and—he thinks—know of mental illness firsthand and so understand him. And some of them decidedly do not like or understand him.

Vincent pays a visit to the brothel, but not the usual kind of visit. "Yesterday I went back to see the girl I went to when I went out of my mind. I was told there that things like that aren't at all surprising around here." He tells Theo that he is reassured that Rachel, the woman he had given the wrapped ear to, has not been permanently damaged by his actions.

But he is not completely well. He has been delirious some of the time, and he has nightmares. He thinks he will always be mentally ill. "The local people who are ill like me indeed tell me the truth. You can live to be old or young, but you'll always have moments when you lose your head."

The day after he writes that letter, Vincent does indeed lose his head. He becomes terribly paranoid, convinced people are trying to poison him. His cleaning woman tries to take care of him, but he gets worse and worse: he stops eating, then stops speaking.

Theo knows nothing of this. He is busily working on his Monet show, writing to Jo, reading her letters, the two of them flirting by post. On February 6, on his office stationery, Theo writes to Jo: "I promise I shall stop making myself insufferable by telling you how grateful I am, but then you shall have to come here soon, because sitting before a sheet of paper is not the best way to make two people one."

On February 7, in Paris, Theo's Monet show goes up.

On February 7, in Arles, Vincent's housekeeper calls for help. She can't take care of him by herself anymore. Vincent is taken to the hospital, put in isolation.

Theo has no idea.

92.

A BROTHER'S LOVE

Let us keep our hopes up.

—Theo to Jo, February 12, 1889

THEO HADN'T WRITTEN to Jo for three days; he'd been too busy with his Monet show. Now he apologizes and tells her, "This afternoon I received bad news about Vincent again."

Theo has also been getting reports about Vincent from a reverend, Frédéric Salles. Reverend Salles has written to tell him that Vincent "has withdrawn into absolute muteness, hides himself under his bedcovers and sometimes cries without uttering a word." Salles thinks he needs to go to a mental hospital. "I regret, Sir, having to give you such distressing news." But he assures Theo he's watching out for Vincent. "Tonight I saw that a fire was lit in his cell, for it felt very cold to me, and that someone keeps it going all night." Salles hopes to get Vincent moved to a nicer room the next day.

Theo wonders what would be the best thing for Vincent. If he has to go to an asylum, would it be better for him to stay in the south, where it is sunnier, warmer? Or would it be better for them both if he were in Paris? He hopes Vincent will rest and recover and there will be no need to make a decision. But he doesn't fool himself. He knows it's unlikely Vincent will ever be cured, and certainly not completely.

Vincent's mind, he tells Jo, "had for so long been preoccupied with things our society today has made impossible to solve & which he, with his kind heart & tremendous energy, nevertheless fought against. His efforts have not been in vain, but he may never be able to witness their fruits, for it will be too late by the time people understand what he was expressing in his paintings."

He knows Vincent is a genius. He knows all his hard work will pay off. But when? Looking at Vincent's paintings, he tells Jo, "One first has to relinquish all one's conventional ideas in order to grasp what he means. But one day he will be understood. When? That is the question."

That *is* the question. At least it is not *if* in Theo's mind, but *when*. He himself doesn't always understand a work right away, but he has faith that Vincent's efforts will not be in vain. But will Vincent live to see it? Will Theo?

He tells Jo he's just written to Vincent and told him that no matter what happens to him, or what will happen next, "he should have the satisfaction of knowing he was one of those few great men who have discharged their duty to the full, without gaining any reward." He hopes that will help Vincent; he knows that is *the* thing that would make him feel better.

Their walk to the mill, the pledge they made, their intimate bond. Brothers through and through. Giving something of beauty to the world.

IN THEO'S GALLERY SHOW, he has included pieces by other artists in addition to Monet. There's a sculpture by Auguste Rodin—the head of John the Baptist on a platter—that Theo thinks looks just like Vincent, even though Rodin has never met him. "The same expression of suffering, that furrowed & contorted brow betraying a life of reflection and ascetism," he tells Jo.

Though Vincent's forehead slopes more, "the shape of the nose & the structure of the head are identical."

When Jo sees the sculpture later, she thinks it looks exactly like Theo.

———————————

OVER THE NEXT FEW WEEKS, Theo and Jo write back and forth, making plans, teasing each other, getting to know each other better and better. But Theo also worries and worries about Vincent. Jo offers him comfort. After all these years of carrying the burden alone, Jo is there. "Your letter came at exactly the right moment & made me so aware & feel so profoundly that I am no longer alone, but that far away someone is thinking of me, which is something I had so often longed for, but never found."

As Theo also gets updates from Arles, his thoughts go from Jo in Amsterdam to Vincent in the south. Theo aches for his brother.

After almost two weeks, Vincent is well enough to leave the hospital. He goes back to the Yellow House on February 18. Theo is relieved that Vincent is home again, with his own paintings, the art he loves, his books.

93.

A PETITION

---

*B*UT ALL IS NOT WELL at the Yellow House. Vincent never eats enough. He hasn't for years, not since he was a young man starting out. He drinks too much coffee, smokes too much tobacco, sleeps too little. With Gauguin, he got used to drinking too much liquor, especially absinthe, the strong, green-colored liqueur made from wine and wormwood.

None of this is good for his mental health. Home alone, he deteriorates. He has auditory and visual hallucinations—he hears voices, sees things that aren't there. When he drinks too much, he becomes overexcited and unpredictable, saying and doing things that scare his neighbors. In late February, thirty of them draw up a petition.

"Dear Mr Mayor," they write. "We the undersigned, residents of place Lamartine in the city of Arles, have the honour to inform you that for some time and on several occasions the man named Vood (Vincent), a landscape painter and a Dutch subject, living in the above square, has demonstrated that he is not in full possession of his mental faculties."

They declare that he is unpredictable and "a cause for fear to all the residents of the neighbourhood, and especially to the women and children." They say he is "prone to interfering with women"; one woman testified that she was "seized round the waist . . . and lifted off my feet."

They petition for him to be confined to a mental asylum.

Vincent feels the petition like "a hammer-blow full in the chest." He never meant to harm anyone. It breaks his heart that his neighbors have ganged up on him. He's sick, how could they . . . ?

Vincent is taken back to the hospital, not an asylum. But he is held at the hospital by order of the police.

———————

JO IS IN BREDA, meeting Theo's mother and sister Wil for the first time. Theo writes to her there. Ma and Wil respond immediately, as does Jo. Wil and Jo wonder if it might not be better if Vincent were to come home to the Netherlands. Wil wants to take care of him, wants him to come home to be with his family. "It's unnatural that other people should be tending him and looking after him while we do <u>nothing</u>. I <u>can't</u> bear it," she tells Theo. The family prayer remembered, echoing through the years.

But Ma disagrees. She does not think it would be a good idea for Vincent to come home.

So he stays in Arles. Reverend Salles keeps Theo informed, assuring him that his brother is getting good care. Vincent is too ill to write.

94.

BROTHERLY ANGUISH,
BROTHERLY LOVE

THEO IS GETTING READY for his wedding and his life with Jo in Paris. He is due to go to the Netherlands at the end of March and will stay there until April 18, their wedding day. In the middle of March he starts moving into the new apartment, at 8 Cité Pigalle, on the third floor to the left. He has not gotten a letter from Vincent for three weeks. He worries about him and misses him terribly. He does feel joy, though, as he hangs Vincent's paintings in the new flat. "In arranging my new apartment," he writes to his brother, "I see your paintings again with so much pleasure. They make the rooms so jolly, and there's such a note of truth, of real countryside in each one. It's just as you said sometimes of certain paintings by other artists, that they seem to come like that directly from the fields."

Black fields with young green wheat, fields of rye, corn, and moors of heath. Zundert.

Theo has no idea if Vincent will ever get better. "You've done so much for me," he writes to his brother, "that it breaks my heart to know that now that I'll probably have days of happiness with my dear Jo, you will actually have very bad days."

He tells Vincent that Jo wants to get to know him, too, that she hopes Vincent will be a brother to her "as you have always been for me."

Theo longs to visit Vincent, but it is far. "I'm short of time and I ask myself if my visit could be useful to you in any way."

But please send me news, Theo begs his brother. Apart from letters from Dr. Rey and Reverend Salles, "I don't know anything about you."

Vincent, ill as he is, understands what Theo is saying. He feels the magnitude of his brother's grief, reading between the lines. Vincent writes back, "I seemed to see so much restrained brotherly anguish in your kind letter that it seems to me to be my duty to break my silence. I write to you in full possession of my presence of mind and not like a madman but as the brother you know."

Vincent, once again after all these years and so sick, is the older brother, trying to take care of Theo.

95.

NEW HOMES

Your work and . . . brotherly affection . . .
is worth more than all the money I'll ever possess.

—Theo to Vincent, April 24, 1889

YINCENT KNOWS THEO NEEDS HIM, so he writes every few days as Theo prepares to leave for his wedding in the Netherlands. Theo writes back, and they discuss where Vincent should live after he is released from the hospital—they have agreed that he should not move back to the Yellow House, or even to that part of town.

Vincent is doing better, well enough to work again—in the hospital. He asks Theo to send him some tubes of paint before he leaves Paris: three of zinc white, four of veronese green, and a tube each of cobalt, ultramarine, emerald green, and orange lead.

Vincent knows that Dr. Rey is right: he has ruined his health by not eating regularly, by keeping himself going with coffee and alcohol. He tells Theo that he had wanted to "key myself up a bit to reach the high yellow note I reached this summer. That, after all, the artist is a man *at work*." He is more committed to being that artist than to taking regular care of himself. Theo is getting married, but he himself is getting old, Vincent says. He doesn't mind what happens to him—he'd even stay in the hospital—as long as he can keep working. He has given up hope of a wife and family for himself. His life is about his art. Not for his family, but for himself, and for Theo. Always Theo. (Though it would be nice if Ma appreciated his work.)

In early April he starts on what will become another series of paintings of blossoming orchards.

Theo sends Vincent the paints he asked for and some issues of a new magazine he thinks Vincent will like, and he leaves for the Netherlands to get married.

Theo has a happy heart and a heavy heart. In another scenario, Vincent would be going with him to witness his marriage.

IN THE NETHERLANDS, Ma desperately wants Theo and Jo to get married in a church. But Theo has no religious feelings at all and thinks it would be hypocritical. Lies begs him to reconsider—their mother is obsessing about it!—but Theo doesn't give in. Ma floats the idea of a wedding in the Bonger flat instead, but Theo and Jo get married on April 18 in the Amsterdam town hall. There is a reception afterward, and then the two leave for Paris, stopping for a day in Brussels.

When they arrive at the new apartment in Paris, they find that Aunt Cornelie, Uncle Cent's widow, had been there to set it up for them: there are flowers all over the flat, and the bed is all made up and ready for them. She also promises to give them a piano for Jo to play.

In their first days of marriage, the newlyweds are happy as can be, even though Jo has no idea how to keep house—"It's an absolute farce," she writes her sister Mien. But everything is running well, and she's managing to keep the apartment clean.

She finds their Paris neighborhood daunting, though: "The bustle and activity of people and omnibuses—well it is just awful." But she is happy with the apartment—there are so many doors, you could play hide-and-seek all day, she tells her sister. And already they have a routine. They get up at eight o'clock, Theo turns the gas on to boil the water; Jo makes the tea; it brews while they dress. Their milk and bread are delivered to the door.

Most of all she is ecstatic about Theo. "If only I could just fly over to tell you myself . . . how happy I am here!" Theo is so kind and so good to her. "We were used to each other from the very first moment," she confides to her sister, "nothing forced—nothing strange—he is so simple and natural, that makes it so easy and he says the same: I didn't think it would be so good."

IN THE SOUTH OF FRANCE, Vincent is contemplating a move, too. He writes with congratulations to Theo—wishing "you and your wife lots of happiness"—and tells him he wants to move to Saint-Rémy-de-Provence, a town not too far from Arles. There is a mental asylum there that Reverend Salles has looked at for him. It has forty-five patients and seems like a good place.

Theo writes to the doctor there, Théophile Peyron, to make sure that it will be good for Vincent. He asks that certain conditions be met: that Vincent can paint, that he can have wine with his meals, that he can leave whenever he wants (like the asylum in Geel, Belgium, that Pa had wanted to send Vincent to). The doctor grants all the conditions but one: Vincent cannot leave whenever he wants because he needs to be watched over carefully. But they will give him as much freedom as possible.

Before he leaves Arles, Vincent sends off two crates of his paintings. By the time the crates reach Paris, Vincent will be gone, but arriving at Theo's will be pieces of his life in Arles: *The Night Café, The Green Vineyard, The Red Vineyard, The Bedroom*, many paintings of fields, five paintings of sunflowers, four versions of Mrs. Roulin (*La Berceuse*), other portraits, including one of a baby, and many trees in blossom.

On May 8, 1889, with the help of Reverend Salles, and with Theo's blessing and financial support, Vincent checks himself into the Saint-Paul-de-Mausole asylum in Saint-Rémy-de-Provence. The place is not full, so he is given one room to sleep in and another one to use as his painting studio.

A new beginning for Vincent, too. He hopes he'll recover quickly and stay at the asylum for just a few months.

96.

VINCENT AND THEO AND JO

---

*T*HE DAY VINCENT CHECKS INTO Saint-Rémy, Jo writes him a letter: "It's high time your new little sister came to chat with you." She'd been waiting until she and Theo were married, but now she hopes Vincent would get to "know me a little and, if possible, love me a little."

Jo feels like she knows Vincent well. His paintings are everywhere. Each morning when she wakes up in the pink bedroom she shares with Theo, she tells Vincent in this first letter, she looks "straight at that beautiful flowering peach tree of yours." In the drawing room above the piano from Aunt Cornelie, they've hung a large landscape of Vincent's, one that Jo adores. He painted it in Arles, a harvest scene of yellows and greens and blues. "The dining room is full too, but Theo's not happy with the arrangement yet, and every Sunday morning is spent rehanging and arranging everything."

She tells him, "There are masses of things that are reminders of you, when I find a nice little jug or a vase or something, then it's always: Vincent bought that or V. liked that so much—scarcely a day passes when we don't speak of you."

Vincent writes back to Jo and to Theo the next day. He is settling in well and thinks he will be able to be calm at the asylum, and to paint well. This despite that he "continually hears shouts and terrible howls as though of the animals in a menagerie." But the people are friendly, and more polite than his neighbors in Arles. The other patients come to watch him as he paints in the garden.

Jo thinks it's so sad the way Vincent accepts his fate as one of the sick people. But Theo happily reports to Vincent that the crates from Arles have arrived, and there are some *superb* paintings in it.

Theo is sure the work Vincent is doing now will be appreciated someday. He can't predict when, but he is certain that Vincent will be appreciated. He can't tell him that too often.

ALL THROUGH MAY AND JUNE, Vincent paints and draws whenever he feels well. Theo sends more canvases, paints, brushes, and tobacco to keep him going. He sends Vincent chocolate, just as Vincent had done for him all those years ago when Theo was grieving for Annet and his two friends at the Roos house who had died.

Theo thinks a lot about Vincent's madness. He keeps looking at the paintings from Arles and wonders what making those paintings must have done to him. He puts off writing to him until he can articulate these thoughts, but finally, even though he isn't sure he will be able to, he gives it a try. "Your latest paintings have given me a great deal to think about as regards your state of mind when you made them," he writes to his brother. "All of them have a power of colour which you hadn't attained before, which in itself is a rare quality, but you have gone further." He can feel what

Vincent was thinking about nature and people by looking at his paintings. He can see how strongly attached he is to both. "But how hard your mind must have worked and how you endangered yourself to the extreme point where vertigo is inevitable."

Though he is happy Vincent is working hard right now, it worries him. "You mustn't put yourself at risk in these mysterious regions," he warns.

Theo is worrying about himself, too. The cough that had disappeared when he was first with Jo has come back. He has a lot of pain in his leg, and he is, Jo tells her sister, "dead tired in the evenings."

But he has so much to live for now, more than ever.

97.

COMPANIONS IN FATE

———————

ON JULY 5, Jo writes to Vincent: "This winter, around February probably, we're hoping to have a baby, a pretty little boy—whom we'll call Vincent if you'll consent to be his godfather."

A baby! Vincent is cheered by the news. He writes to Theo and Jo right away. He knows they're worried about Theo's health, and even Jo's, but he tells them that this baby will be more loved than one whose parents are healthy. He demurs about the name, though: wouldn't Ma be happier if they named him after Pa? He thinks it's funny they're so sure it will be a boy. It could be a girl—they should wait and see! The thought of a baby continues to comfort him as he spirals down into sadness.

A painting Vincent makes during his time at Saint-Rémy shows both his despair and his hope. He is looking through a window out into the garden of the asylum. You see the view through tree branches as if through prison bars. Vincent is still able to look out into the world and see its beauty. To see life. But he views it all from the prison of his hurting mind, as if the window of the asylum is his perspective frame.

THEO'S BODY IS A PRISON. As Jo's pregnancy progresses, his health deteriorates. His cough gets worse; he is pale and very thin, even though he has a tremendous appetite and eats like a wolf, Jo thinks. He starts every day with a raw egg in cognac, and a large cup of chocolate milk. He eats a good meal at noon, and one in the evening, with two helpings of meat. She gives him a piece of chocolate to eat at four o'clock at the office, but nothing helps. He keeps getting thinner.

Vincent is worried about Theo.

Theo is worried about Vincent.

There are days when each feels as though the end is near.

"Let's not be *too* concerned with each other," Vincent tells his brother. Although they are both ill, they are on the same path together, their dreams shared, just as they had imagined they would be when they were young men on that walk to the mill. They are—after all this time, from Zundert to now, through all their ups and downs, their divergent and convergent paths—bound together, brothers, friends. More than brothers, Vincent writes, more than friends—they are "companions in fate."

WHEN HE DOESN'T HEAR from Theo for a month, Vincent writes with great feeling and concern. Theo answers immediately, apologizing for his silence. He has been too exhausted to write.

The next day Vincent goes back to Arles with a friend. He still has paintings there. He collects some and sends them to Theo, along with pieces he's done at the asylum.

Theo writes enthusiastically to Vincent as soon as the paintings arrive. They are gorgeous! He raves about them, about the amazing work Vincent is now doing, *consistently*. If only Vincent were well. . . . "If you were living in surroundings entirely to your taste and you were surrounded by people you liked and who returned your friendship, I would be very pleased, for you cannot work better than you are doing."

But Vincent doesn't write back.

The last letter Theo had received from the doctor said Vincent was fine. But a day or two after the trip to Arles, a few days after Theo's letter telling of his exhaustion, Vincent had a severe breakdown. It seems he tried to poison himself by putting paint on his brushes and eating it.

VINCENT'S MENTAL HEALTH, as he himself had predicted, is unpredictable, volatile. Even as he struggles to hold on to his sanity, in September in Paris, the fifth Exhibition of the Independents goes up, and in it are two of Vincent's paintings: one of irises and the other a night sky over the Rhone.

People notice them. A critic calls him a diverting colorist. Finally, Vincent is a colorist.

And finally, after a month of illness, Vincent is well enough to paint again. He stays inside, working in his asylum studio painting self-portraits and touching up older canvases. When his health has improved even more, he goes outside to paint, capturing the garden of the asylum and, beyond that, olive trees and landscapes. He asks Theo to send more paint, more canvas.

He knows he can't paint when he is sick; so he paints as much as possible when he is well. And he is well now.

But Theo is not. *His* health continues to deteriorate. Theo and Jo don't know what's wrong with him. But they know it's bad when he takes a physical and is rejected for an insurance policy.

And then a flu epidemic hits Paris. Friends tell Jo they're worried about Theo. Jo can't stop agonizing. If Theo gets the flu, he will likely die.

She wants to keep him home all the time, but it's not possible. The second week of January 1890, Jo writes to her sister, "It's like a sword of Damocles forever hanging over our heads—I never really have a moment's peace."

There's only so much you can do to save a loved one from harm.

Theo knows that all too well.

In Saint-Rémy, Vincent again has eaten his paints.

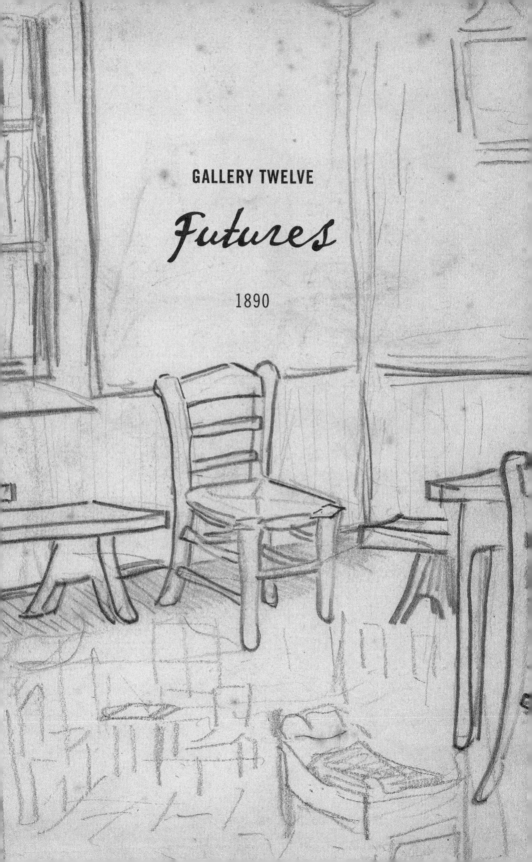

GALLERY TWELVE

Futures

1890

98.

JO WRITING A LETTER

---

*O*N WEDNESDAY NIGHT, January 29, 1890, at just midnight, Jo starts a letter. "Dear Vincent," she begins, "I've been meaning to write to you day after day since Christmas." She is sitting at the table in the apartment she shares with Theo. "There's even a half-finished letter to you in my writing-case."

Her mother, her husband, and her sister-in-law Wil are around the table, too. "And now—if I don't make haste to write this note you'd get the news that your namesake was here—before then I just want to bid you good-day."

Jo's water has broken. Her labor pains have begun. The doctor is there, too, in another room, sleeping for a while.

Jo feels she knows Vincent so well from his paintings, from all Theo has told her, from Wil, and from all the letters, which arrive so often in their yellow envelopes. But they still have not met. And yet here she sits at the table, in labor, with her husband and mother and sister-in-law, writing to Vincent on a piece of cream-colored paper, in Dutch, with black ink. Vincent has been in the asylum at Saint-Rémy for eight months. As far as she and Theo know, Vincent is doing better since his last attack, when he tried to poison himself with paint. Theo has advised him to stay away from the paints for a while; he should draw instead. He should stay away from Arles, too. But he's gone there again and had another breakdown. Theo and Jo don't know this yet.

"I can't write much—but I so much wanted just to talk to you for a moment." Ever since she rejected Theo's first proposal two and a half years earlier, and he chased it with that letter baring his heart and soul about his brother ("I would feel I were concealing something important were I not to tell you about my relationship with him from the start"), Vincent has been a part of them.

"Perhaps you'll think what I'm telling you about him has nothing to do with us," Theo wrote then. By now Jo knows that Vincent has everything to do with them.

So how can Jo not think of Vincent at this moment? She is about to risk her life giving birth to Theo's baby, Vincent's nephew and namesake. The baby is almost here, and Jo has something on her mind to tell Vincent. But first she has good news about his art.

There is an art show in Brussels, and a Belgian newspaper reported that the canvases people are most excited and curious about are by Paul Cézanne, Alfred Sisley, Auguste Renoir—and Vincent Van Gogh! Vincent had six canvases in the show, one of which sold for four hundred francs. That's about half of what Vincent needs for art supplies for a year. It's not a life-changing amount, but it is progress.

And there's more good news. "This morning Theo brought in the article in the *Mercure*, and after we'd read it Wil and I talked about you for a long time."

The article in the *Mercure* is a review—the first critical appraisal of Vincent's work, and an exuberantly positive one it is.

Albert Aurier has called Vincent's paintings "strange, intense and feverish" and Vincent a worthy successor to the seventeenth-century Dutch masters. He writes that Vincent's technique matches his temperament: "vigorous, exalted, brutal, intense." And his palette is "incredibly dazzling," his brushstrokes "fiery, very powerful and full of tension."

Theo and Jo are absolutely thrilled with the article.

Aurier has deemed Vincent an important person in the contemporary art world! He does, however, end the article by mourning what they all fear: that Van Gogh will never be completely understood, for he is "too simple and at the same time too subtle for the contemporary bourgeois mind."

But his genius *is* appreciated. It's what Vincent and Theo have been waiting for all these years.

Theo has sent Vincent several copies of the article, and a shortened version that appeared elsewhere. He also sent copies to their mother, and to Lies, and to another art critic he knows. Theo and Jo hope it will make Vincent happy.

But that is not the main point of Jo's letter. Her mission, as her contractions grow stronger, is to tell Vincent what Theo must know in case she dies.

"I've thought about it so much, whether I really have been able to do something to make Theo happy in his marriage. He's done it for me. He's been so good to me; so good—if things don't go well—if I have to leave him—you tell him—for there's no one in the world whom he loves as much—"

Waves of pain come over her.

"That he must never regret that we were married, because he's made me so happy."

By now Theo has gone to bed because he's so tired. She writes to Vincent, apologizing, "It sounds sentimental—a message like this—but *I* can't tell him now." It would be too upsetting for her to make this speech to her husband just before she gives birth. But she has to tell someone, and Vincent is the one.

There's more she'd like to say, but the pain is making it hard for her to think or write properly. "Oh if only I can just give him a dear, healthy little boy, wouldn't that make him happy?"

99.

DELIVERY

VINCENT WRITES BACK to Jo in the purple ink he often uses: "It touches me so much that you write to me so calmly and so much master of yourself on one of your difficult nights." He keeps the letter short because he's still recovering from his last attack, but he longs "to hear that you've come through safely and that your child lives."

He assures her that Theo will indeed be very happy if all goes well with her and the baby. "A new sun will rise in him when he sees you recovering."

The same day, Theo receives a letter from Dr. Peyron with the news about Vincent's most recent attack.

Theo writes back to Vincent with great sorrow, hoping that this episode will be short, as the previous one was. And he tells Vincent the happy news: Jo has "brought into the world a fine boy who cries a lot but who seems to be in good health."

The baby was born on January 31, 1890, and his name is Vincent Willem.

Another Vincent Willem van Gogh. "I'm making the wish," Theo writes to his brother, "that he may be as determined and as courageous as you."

Vincent has been so determined. *So* courageous. Fighting through the darkness to pick up his drawing pencil in the Borinage. Going without food. Working, working, working, now despite his illness.

Vincent is also generous, bighearted. Still recovering from his latest attack, he writes to Theo, "Today I've just received the news that you're a father at last, that the most critical moment has passed for Jo, finally that the little one is well." The arrival of this little one, he tells Theo, does him more good than he can express in words.

He is also modest, and still self-critical. About the Aurier review, he writes, "I feel mired in flattery." He thinks Aurier has exaggerated his importance and his skill.

He writes to Aurier, sending Theo the letter first to read and pass on to the critic. "Thank you very much," he writes. The article surprised him, and he thinks of it "very much as a work of art in itself, I feel that you create colours with your words; anyway I rediscover my canvases in your article, but better than they really are—richer, more significant."

He feels ill at ease with the praise, just as he had when he was a child and destroyed his drawing of the cat, the clay figure of the elephant. He thinks Aurier should have applied the adulation to other painters, to Monticelli above all. Monticelli was the one, says Vincent, who perceived, quoting Aurier writing about Vincent, "the colorations of things with such intensity, with such a metallic, gem-like quality."

He asks Aurier to please go see a painting of Monticelli's flowers at Theo's place. He owes Monticelli a great deal, he says, and also Gauguin, "with whom I worked for a few months in Arles." He tells Aurier he'd have been better off writing about Monticelli and Gauguin than about him.

But Vincent is immensely grateful for the article and is sending Aurier a painting he'd made of some cypresses. He has instructions: The painting won't be dry for a year, but after it dries he should give it a good coat of varnish. Vincent thinks the painting should be framed in a flat, bright orange; that will look good with the blues of the background and the dark green of the trees. Without an orange frame, he fears, the upper part will appear cold.

Vincent works on the painting some more before sending it to Theo to give to Aurier. And then he starts on a painting for the baby.

100.

UNCLE VINCENT'S PAINTINGS

Without you I would be most unhappy.

—Vincent to Theo, April 29, 1890

D EAR MOTHER," Vincent writes. "I've been meaning to answer your letter for days, but didn't get round to writing because I was painting from morning till night, and so the time passed. I imagine that your thoughts, like mine, are with Jo and Theo."

He tells her he wishes they'd named the baby after Pa, "whom I've thought about so often these days."

And he writes that he's making a painting for the baby; he hopes they'll hang it in their bedroom. It's of white almond blossoms against a blue sky, an echo of the Japanese style Vincent loves so much. He paints as spring comes to the South of France, after many dreary winter days, inside and out. The almond trees are beginning to blossom everywhere.

He tells Ma that after the surprise of the Aurier review wore off, he felt heartened by it. And he tells her about the sale in Brussels of his painting *The Red Vineyard* to an artist, Anna Boch.

He hopes to use the money from that sale to go to Paris to visit Theo and meet Jo and the baby. He knows he might not be able to work as easily outside the asylum, but he'd like to try. He wouldn't mind going back to Antwerp—he'd be closer to her and the rest of the family again.

The family bond is still there, the desire to make his mother proud, too.

When he finishes the painting for the baby, he is truly pleased with it. And then he has another breakdown, again after an ill-advised trip to Arles.

It is a month before he can write to Theo. "Work was going well," he told his brother, "the last canvas of the branches in blossom, you'll see that it was perhaps the most patiently worked, best thing I'd done, painted with calm and a greater sureness of touch. And the next day done for like a brute."

A few days later the sixth Exhibition of the Independents begins in Paris. Theo has put ten of Vincent's paintings in it.

Of all the paintings in the exhibition, the ones people talk the most about are those by Vincent van Gogh.

Claude Monet himself tells Theo that Vincent's are the best in the whole show. Gauguin calls them the key to the exhibition. He writes to Vincent that "for many artists you are the most remarkable in the exhibition. With things from nature you're the *only one there who thinks.*" He tells Vincent he hopes he's feeling better after his long crisis.

Jo writes to Vincent that she escaped from the baby briefly to go to the opening of the exhibit. She wanted to see Vincent's paintings hanging in public. "There was a bench just in front, and while Theo talked to all sorts of people I spent a quarter of an hour enjoying the wonderful coolness and freshness of the undergrowth" in *Trees with Ivy in the Garden of the Asylum.* "It's as if I know that little spot and have often been there—I love it so much," she tells her brother-in-law. At home the baby is developing a real personality, she writes. "He always looks with very great interest at Uncle Vincent's paintings."

It is six weeks before Vincent writes again. When he does, it is to wish Theo a happy birthday and to thank him "for all the kindness you've shown me." He is not doing well; he wants Theo to tell Aurier not to write about him again. He is too damaged by grief to be in the public eye. And yet, he's working. He's even thinking about redoing old paintings, such as *The Potato Eaters*, and, if Theo likes, one of the old church tower at Nuenen, *The Peasants' Churchyard*. He thinks he can make something better now.

Vincent also sends Theo some new paintings, the one for Aurier and the one for the baby among them.

Baby Vincent's present is a stunner: an almond tree in bloom, the front branch so alive it reaches out of the canvas as if to invite Theo, Jo, and baby Vincent to grab it, to hold on. Vincent had thought they'd hang it in their bedroom. But they move the harvest scene of yellows and greens and blues from Arles and hang the baby's almond tree in the most prominent place in their flat, above the piano in the drawing room.

101.
VINCENT'S PAINTINGS

OF ALL THE PAINTINGS they have in their apartment, of all the paintings Jo has ever seen, she always understands and admires Vincent's the most. She tells Wil so in a letter.

Theo loves the new paintings Vincent has sent. He sends Vincent more tubes of paint and canvases, and a photograph of Jo and the baby. Vincent is not well enough to go outside right now, but he sets about painting pictures from memory—of their childhood in Zundert. Reminiscences of Brabant, he calls them. He paints not in the colors of the Dutch masters, but in what has become his palette, one full of sun and color, rich and vibrant, the paint thick, tactile, reaching out, begging the viewer to touch Vincent's memories of home.

During his year at the asylum, Vincent paints and draws whenever he is well. He makes almost 150 paintings, some after his favorite artists, like Millet, just as he did at the beginning of his career. The paintings he makes at Saint-Rémy include:

Irises;

Iris; Lilacs;

Field of Spring Wheat at Sunrise;

Field with Poppies;

Cypresses;

Cypresses with Two Female Figures;

Olive Grove; Olive Grove: Bright Blue Sky;

Wheat Field with Reaper and Sun;

Tree Trunks with Ivy;

Undergrowth with Ivy; three self-portraits;

Portrait of Trabuc, an Attendant at Saint-Paul Hospital;

Pine Trees with Setting Sun;

The Spinner; The Thresher; Entrance to a Quarry near Saint-Rémy;

many of the garden at Saint-Paul Hospital;

Portrait of a Patient in Saint-Paul Hospital;

Still Life: Pink Roses in a Vase; more Olive Groves, one with Orange Sky, one with Pale Blue Sky, one with Yellow Sky and Sun, another with Bright Blue Sky, and more; Wheat Fields with Reaper at Sunrise; Olive Picking; Still Life: Vase with Irises; Still Life: Vase with Irises Against a Yellow Background; Olive Trees with the Alpilles in the Background; Wheat Field in Rain; and Starry Night.

102.

TWO MERRY FACES

VINCENT IS READY to leave the asylum. It is the middle of May 1890. He's been feeling better, painting outside again. He's just finished some canvases of roses in a vase and is happy with them. "I hope that the canvases of the last few days will compensate us for the expenses of travel," he writes to Theo.

He wants to be closer to his brother.

"After a last discussion with Mr. Peyron I obtained permission to pack my trunk, which I've sent by goods train. The 30 kilos of luggage one is allowed to take will allow me to take a few frames, easel and some stretching frames &c."

The brothers have made a plan: Vincent will go live in Auvers-sur-Oise, just twenty miles north of Paris. A doctor there, Paul-Ferdinand Gachet, is an amateur painter and likes to spend time with other painters. He will watch over Vincent. The brothers will be able to see each other often.

On the way to Auvers, Vincent is going to stop in Paris and stay with Theo for a few days. He is eager to meet Jo and the baby. Vincent and Theo haven't seen each other for a year and a half. The last time was in the hospital in Arles.

Vincent telegrams Theo: he's leaving Saint-Rémy on May 16 and will arrive in Paris the next morning at ten o'clock. Theo has begged him to travel with an escort, but Vincent insists he's fine to travel alone.

Theo cannot sleep that night, anxious that something bad will happen to Vincent on the journey.

Jo and Theo are thankful when it's time, finally, for Theo to leave to pick up Vincent.

It's a long way to the train station and back again to the apartment on Cité Pigalle; the wait is an eternity for Jo.

The longer it takes the more she worries that something bad has indeed happened to Vincent. She stares out the window, waiting for the carriage that Theo will have hired to bring them home. Finally she sees the open fiacre and then "two merry faces." Vincent and Theo nod to her from below, wave, and come up the stairs.

Jo finally meets Vincent.

Upon looking at him in her apartment, Jo's first thought is that Vincent seems healthy and well, much stronger than Theo. She'd expected someone who looked sick, but instead she is face-to-face with "a sturdy broad-shouldered man, with a healthy colour, a smile on his face and a very resolute appearance." Looking back later at all his self-portraits, she will feel that the one where he is at his easel looks most like him when she met him: trim hair, neat but long red beard, a determined look on his face.

After a few moments, Theo takes Vincent into the bedroom, where the baby is sleeping in his cradle. Vincent and Theo look at little Vincent together, tears in their eyes.

VINCENT IS CHEERFUL, lively, energetic. They do not talk about his time at the asylum at all.

The next morning he wakes up early and looks at his paintings, which are all over the apartment: *The Potato Eaters* in the dining room over the mantelpiece; in the bedroom, *Orchard in Blossom*; in the sitting room, a landscape from Arles and the night sky over the Rhone; the *Almond Blossom* painting for the baby, above the piano.

Theo and Jo have put huge piles of unframed canvases everywhere around the apartment—to the horror of their cleaning woman—and have stored others under the bed, the sofa, and the cupboard in the small spare room. Vincent spreads them all out and studies them. Theo joins him. Ten years of work. Vincent's work. Theo's work.

SOME OLD FRIENDS COME BY, which is nice for Vincent. But he mostly loves spending time with Theo, Jo, and the baby.

And after three days, the noise and bustle of Paris become too much for him; it's time to leave. He tells Theo and Jo he will come back soon and paint their portraits. On May 20, Vincent leaves for Auvers. He's ready to work again.

103.

A HAPPY VISIT

VINCENT WRITES to Theo *and* Jo his first day in Auvers. He tells them he can't imagine writing to just Theo anymore, now that he's met Jo, though he begs her forgiveness for writing in French, not Dutch. He feels better able to express himself in his adopted language. He likes Auvers. It's in the countryside, along a river. He admires the colorful houses, the thatched roofs, and finds both the village and the countryside "gravely beautiful." It's "distinctive and picturesque."

He settles in almost immediately, though it takes him a bit to get used to Dr. Gachet; on first meeting he thinks him quite eccentric. But soon he likes him very much and feels close to him. They resemble each other: both are red haired, fair skinned, though Gachet is much older. Gachet recommends an inn, but Vincent prefers the less expensive Auberge Ravoux. He moves into a tiny room at the top of the stairs. It is an attic room with slanted ceilings, just like their childhood bedroom in Zundert.

VINCENT GETS TO WORK IMMEDIATELY, and the next day has already done a study of "old thatched roofs with a field of peas in flower and some wheat in the foreground, hilly background." After two years of living in the south, he tells Theo, he can see the north more clearly.

Over the next days he paints out in the fields and at Dr. Gachet's house, too. He begins to work on Dr. Gachet's portrait. He wants to make more portraits again; he decides he's most passionate about capturing people. He wants to work again on the human body and asks Theo to send him a book so he can copy the sheets of nude figures, as he had done back in the beginning.

He is determined to improve, to grow as an artist. He even brings out his old perspective frame to help.

And he wants to achieve serenity of mind. He is looking to the future.

A future, he hopes, that will include nearness to Theo, Jo, and the baby. He is certain that baby Vincent would be healthier growing up in the countryside. He starts campaigning for the three of them to visit. He likes Jo a lot; he tells Ma he finds her "sensible and warm-hearted and uncomplicated."

He assures his mother he's doing well, and he has Dr. Gachet to look after him. But he writes to Wil the same day and confesses something he hasn't told Ma: Theo does not seem well. He is coughing more than when they lived together in Paris. Vincent is terribly worried about Theo.

Theo is worried about his own health, as well as the baby's. He wishes he had a friend who was a doctor, too, "for at every turn one would like to know, especially for the little one, where illnesses come from."

———————————

ON SUNDAY, June 8, Theo and Jo and baby Vincent take a train ride north to visit Vincent in Auvers.

Vincent meets them at the station, holding a bird's nest for the baby.

They are invited to Dr. Gachet's for lunch. Vincent insists on carrying the baby as they walk to his house.

At Gachet's, Vincent takes his godson around the yard, introducing him to the eight cats, three dogs, hens, rabbits, ducks, and pigeons. Piercing the quiet country morning, a rooster crows loudly and scares baby Vincent. His face grows bright red, and he begins to cry. Vincent laughs and says, "The cock crows *cocorico*," placating the baby. After Theo and Jo and the baby have gone back to Paris, Vincent writes to his mother that he loved giving his nephew his first real encounter with the "animal kingdom." But, he says, "I don't think he understands very much of it for the present." The baby isn't even five months old.

"Last year I read somewhere that writing a book or making a painting was the same as having a child," he writes to Ma. "I don't dare claim that for myself, though; I've always thought the latter was the most natural and best thing." It feels great to be able to hold a baby again. And not just any baby, Theo's baby. His nephew and namesake.

"Dear brother and sister," he writes a couple of days later. "Sunday has left me a very pleasant memory. In this way we really feel that we are not so far from one another, and I hope that we'll see each other again often."

GALLERY THIRTEEN

A Sense of
the Finite

1890

104.

THEO'S ANGUISH

---

*Lately I've been working a lot and quickly; by doing so
I'm trying to express the desperately swift passage
of things in modern life.*

—Vincent to Wil, June 13, 1890

*I*N AUVERS, Vincent is concentrating mostly on portraits, painting Adeline Ravoux, the daughter of his innkeeper, and Gachet's daughter, Marguerite, playing the piano.

From Paris, Theo reports good news: a Belgian painter, Eugène Guillaume Boch, came to Theo's apartment to see Vincent's paintings. He liked them and *understood* them, which meant a lot to Theo. They arranged a trade, one of Vincent's for one of Boch's. Boch's happens to be a painting he'd made in the Borinage.

But Theo and Jo are terribly worried about the baby. He has been crying and crying, with no relief for him or his poor parents. They've been terrified that he might be dying. Theo writes an anguished letter to his big brother, the only time ever he addresses him as "*Mon très cher frère*," my very dear brother.

"We've been going through the greatest anxiety, our dear one has been very ill." By the time he writes, he is almost sure the baby's life isn't in danger, but he is still upset and anxious. So is Jo.

The baby seems to have gotten sick from cow's milk, which they were using to supplement Jo's nursing. "Here in Paris the best milk one can get is a veritable poison," he writes. "You've never heard anything so painful as this almost continual plaintive crying lasting several days and several nights and with us not knowing what to do."

They've started giving the baby donkey's milk, although it's almost three times more expensive. The change seems to be helping; he's doing better.

But that isn't all Theo is troubled about. Their apartment is too small; he wants to move to a bigger one, on the first floor. They could have a live-in maid. And maybe Andries and his wife, Annie, could move into an apartment just below them, on the ground floor. That would give them some company, and maybe help for Jo. But the rent would be higher and so Theo needs a raise. But "those rats," as Vincent calls Theo's bosses, "treat me as if I'd just started working for them and keep me on a leash." He is thinking once again about leaving the firm and setting up his own art dealership. "What do you say to this old chap?" he asks his brother, but then immediately reassures him: "Don't bother your head about me or about us, old chap, be aware that what gives me the greatest pleasure is when you're well and when you're at your work, which is admirable."

He doesn't want to jeopardize Vincent's health and happiness.

Theo's own health, always precarious, is not getting any better. "Look old fellow," he writes, "do everything for your health, I too will do as much." And then, just as Vincent has done when feeling sick and melancholy, Theo remembers the past and their bond. He thinks of their childhood, of their days together as young men, and of their celebration of nature: "We have too much in our noodles for us to forget the daisies and the freshly stirred clods of earth, and the branches of the bushes that bud in spring, nor the bare tree branches that shiver in the winter, nor the serene skies of limpid blue, nor the big clouds of autumn, nor the uniformly grey sky in winter, nor the sun as it rose above our aunts' garden, nor the red sun setting in the sea at Scheveningen, nor the moon and the stars one fine night in summer or winter, no, whatever happens, that is our possession."

The next morning, after a good night's sleep by all, Theo writes again: he decides they will rent that bigger apartment.

Vincent is worried about Theo, about the baby. He wants them to move to the country, where life is healthier, children are healthier. But in the meantime he wants to visit them in Paris. Theo should let him know when would be a good time.

The next letter from Theo is much more upbeat. The baby is doing well with the donkey's milk. "The animals come to the door, and in the morning he receives warm milk, always from the same animal." Vincent should come visit! "So come if you like on Sunday with the first train."

Theo plans a lunch at their flat. "You can stay with us as long as you want, and you can give us advice on the arrangement of our new apartment."

Vincent gets on the train the next day.

105.

VINCENT'S WORRIES

———————————

VINCENT'S FIRST VISIT to Theo and Jo's apartment had been so happy.

Their visit to Auvers was truly joyful.

But almost from the minute Vincent arrives that Sunday, July 6, he's upset.

He can see how exhausted Theo and Jo still are from the worries over the baby. Theo looks terribly sick.

And both Theo and Jo are preoccupied, thinking about their move to the bigger apartment and Theo's desire to open his own gallery.

They talk about the finances, a subject that has agitated Vincent for so long. He is desperate for his paintings to sell—they are selling some, but many more have to sell so that Theo can recoup all the money he's laid out for Vincent over the years. This is Vincent's focus, not Theo's. Theo doesn't want Vincent to worry about the money he's given him. But Theo *is* focused on starting his own business.

As they talk, Vincent grows more and more tense, though Jo and Theo don't realize it. Jo and Vincent do disagree about where to hang one of

Vincent's paintings, and later Jo worries that she was impatient with him. Vincent is not happy with where Theo is storing the overflow paintings, so they spend time talking about that.

But Theo and Jo don't think the day is going badly. They are happy to see Vincent and happy to welcome friends who stop by to see him, too. Albert Aurier, who'd written the review about Vincent's work, comes over. He and Vincent meet, and Vincent is happy to know that Theo had framed the painting for Aurier just the way Vincent had wanted him to—in an orange frame.

While Aurier is there, Henri de Toulouse-Lautrec comes by, too.

Aurier and Toulouse-Lautrec look at all of Vincent's paintings together, praising them to Vincent.

After ten years, this moment, in Theo's apartment.

TOULOUSE-LAUTREC STAYS for lunch, and he and Vincent have a big laugh together over an undertaker's assistant they had seen earlier on the stairs.

But then Andries Bonger walks in, and he's cranky. Among other things, he's harboring bad feelings, insulted that Theo wants him and Annie to move into the flat beneath them. It's as if Theo wants Annie to be Jo's maid, Dries thinks. He doesn't complain about that outright, but it's bothering him, and it adds to the tension already there about the move, the business venture, the finances.

They even argue about what language to speak: Vincent wants to speak French, but Jo and her brother are more comfortable with Dutch.

Vincent had planned to stay overnight, but he is having such a bad time that he leaves early. He doesn't even wait to see another of his painter friends who is due to visit.

As he goes back to Auvers, worries follow him. Almost a week later he's still upset, and he writes to Theo and Jo about the "rather difficult and laborious hours" they'd spent together. "Once back here, I too felt very saddened," he tells them, "and had continued to feel the storm that threatens you also weighing upon me."

Theo and Jo are shocked. They didn't think it was such a bad visit. They are sad that Vincent seems to have taken on their burdens, something Theo definitely does not want him to do. Jo writes to Vincent immediately, trying to reassure him about everything.

He *is* reassured, he writes back; her letter felt like a gospel to him, like deliverance.

But Vincent still feels upset.

There is, in fact, one worry he hasn't voiced to them, one that Jo could not have reassured him about. It's a huge worry that he cannot dismiss: Theo's health is terribly precarious. Theo could die before him; he could die very soon, from the look of him. What will Vincent do if something happens to Theo?

He tells Jo and Theo he's made three paintings that would show them best how he's feeling: "They're immense stretches of wheatfields under turbulent skies, and I made a point of trying to express sadness, extreme loneliness."

He'll bring the paintings to Paris as soon as possible, he promises, "since I'd almost believe that these canvases will tell you what I can't say in words, what I consider healthy and fortifying about the countryside."

He still wants Theo and Jo and the baby to move to the country. If they lived here, they would all be healthier, he tells them. And he wouldn't be lonely. But he doesn't say what he's most worried about. That Theo will die. So Jo and Theo remain confused.

To Vincent the future is terrifyingly uncertain, and there's one part that Theo could reassure him about but hasn't yet. Theo has asked for a raise; he's given his bosses an ultimatum. Vincent knows this. But what Theo hasn't told him yet is that although his bosses don't agree to a raise, they don't fire him, either. And Theo has decided to withdraw the ultimatum and to stay, given his financial needs.

But as far as Vincent knows, Theo might be out of a job soon. They all might be out of money. And worst of all to Vincent, Theo looks to be out of time.

WHILE VINCENT WORRIES about Theo, Theo worries about Jo and the baby. He takes them back to Amsterdam to Jo's family for a rest.

When Theo returns to Paris, he receives another anguished letter from Vincent. Vincent is seeing the world through a dark haze. Theo is afraid Vincent might be spiraling downward once again.

He writes his brother, "I hope, my dear Vincent, that your health is good, and as you said that you're writing with difficulty and don't speak to me about your work, I'm a little afraid that there's something that's bothering you or that isn't going right. In that case, do go and see Dr. Gachet, he'll perhaps give you something that will buck you up again. Give me news of you as soon as possible."

Vincent writes back on July 23 and says he could write about many things, but he thinks it would be pointless. Again he does not say he can see how sick Theo is. Vincent tells his brother he is going to focus on his work; that will be the best thing for him. It always is. He's mentoring a young painter who is living in Auvers now, too, Anton Hirschig. That's nice for him.

And he's painting a lot. In the nine weeks he's been in Auvers, he's made seventy paintings and thirty drawings. He goes out into the fields day after day, and under the blazing summer sun, devotes himself to his canvases.

106.

THEO ALONE

---

*T*HEO WAKES UP alone on Monday morning, July 28, 1890. Jo and the baby are in the Netherlands. Their time with family and in the fresher air (even Amsterdam is better than Paris) is making them both feel better. Theo wishes he could have stayed with them. He plans to join them in less than a week, this coming Sunday.

He's missing Jo terribly. Two days earlier, on July 26, he'd written to her, "I would rather go for a stroll with you, my love & tell you how much I need you. . . . You asked whether I was pleased to be free for a change. What do you take me for! I am so flustered & don't feel I belong anywhere, so I'm all too aware of your absence. . . . I shall be so happy when we're back in our own little home again, but I do think I need a break from work."

She has written back to him, in a letter he has not yet received, "Who can predict how things will work out? Just promise you'll think of nothing this week except your trip to Holland—you need it so badly, my love, and if you weren't coming on Sunday, I wouldn't manage without you any longer either."

But this is Monday morning, and he has a week of work to get through. So off he goes to the gallery, and that's where he is when the letter arrives.

———————————

THEO IS WRITING A LETTER to Jo when he is interrupted. There is someone there to see him.

It is Anton Hirschig, the Dutch painter whom Vincent is mentoring in Auvers.

Hirschig has a letter for Theo.

107.

THE ENVELOPE

---

*T*HE LETTER is from Dr. Paul-Ferdinand Gachet in Auvers-sur-Oise.

The envelope has no stamp, since it is being hand delivered. Theo's last name is large, the *V* of Van Gogh oversized. The inked word "Paris" is blotched, penned, it appears, in haste.

The eye is drawn to the upper left: in a bold diagonal slash in dark black ink, covering part of the word "Monsieur" and underlined twice, the letters are thick, the words urgent: "*très important.*" On the bottom left corner, also on a diagonal: "*faire suivre*," forward. If Hirschig had not found Theo at the office at 19 Boulevard Montmartre, he was supposed to track him down wherever he was.

The two diagonals of the words "*très important*" and "*faire suivre*" meet on the envelope at a point, an arrowhead—giving an impression of flight, purpose, urgency—or an impending wound.

Theo opens the envelope, reads the letter, and leaves his office immediately.

108.

THE LETTER

Dear Monsieur Vangogh,

It is with the utmost regret that I intrude on your privacy, however I regard it as my duty to write to you immediately, today, Sunday, at nine o'clock in the evening I was sent for by your brother Vincent, who wanted to see me at once. I went there and found him very ill. He has wounded himself.

Not having your address which he refused to give me, this letter will reach you through Goupil.

I would advise you to take the greatest precaution with your wife who is still breast feeding.

I would not presume to tell you what to do, but I believe it is your duty to come, in case of any complications that might occur . . .

Ever yours
Gachet
Auvers-Sur Oise
Sunday 27 July 90

109.

AS IF THROUGH EYELASHES

---

*H*E HAS WOUNDED himself."

It has been a year and a half since Theo rode the night train to Arles to find Vincent lying in a hospital bed drained of life, barely conscious. A year and a half since he laid his head on the pillow next to him and Vincent whispered, "Just like Zundert."

How will he find Vincent this time? Gachet's letter sounds so dire, Theo doesn't even take the time to write to Jo. He gets on the first train he can. It's not a long ride to Auvers, as it was to Arles. This trip will take him under an hour.

But will it be fast enough?

The train passes through green leafy forests filled with oaks, past farmers' fields of wheat and oats. It passes by fields of flowers: red poppies, blue and yellow wildflowers, buttercups, *oeillets*, wild roses, and sunflowers, Vincent's favorite. Vincent has made at least a dozen paintings of sunflowers: sunflowers in a vase, sunflowers on a table, sunflowers alone and with other flowers, sunflowers in full bloom and halfway to death. He started painting them when the two brothers lived together in Paris.

Theo's heart was so empty after Vincent moved out. Now he has Jo and the baby, but as Jo herself knows and had written to Vincent only six months earlier while in labor—"there's no one in the world whom he loves as much."

The train's route runs through small, pretty French villages of stone houses, villages not that different from Zundert. Villages filled with children and old people, midday meals to break up the workday, churches, graveyards, farmers selling crops, town halls with birth records, death notices.

SEVEN YEARS EARLIER, a lifetime ago, writing to Theo from The Hague, when he was still living with Sien, Vincent had said, "There's something of that mysteriousness that one gets by looking at nature as if through the eyelashes, so that the forms simplify themselves into patches of colour."

Back then Vincent was not yet painting the way Theo wanted him to, with the color they both knew he had in him. "It has sometimes surprised me that I'm not more of a colourist," he'd said, "because my temperament would certainly lead one to expect that."

Vincent had been hoping Theo would see his progress back then, hoping for his brother's vote of confidence. . . . "You can imagine how eager I am for you to come, for if you also see that it's changing I'll no longer doubt that we're on course."

Theo hadn't seen progress then, but the last few years, even with Vincent's illnesses, have been spectacular. Vincent's paintings are beautiful. He *lives* color, offers it to the canvas, to the world. He has captured the sun, given a blessing to the world, a benediction of color. His paintings are great impastos of pigment: chrome yellow, Prussian blue, vermilion, carmine, very light cinnabar green, emerald green, veronese green, orange, lemon chrome yellow, geranium lake, silver white, zinc white. . . .

What will Theo find at the end of this journey?

The countryside speeds by, fields of blues and yellows and reds and greens, the patches and swirls of summer. As if through eyelashes, an explosion of colors.

110.

ANOTHER ATTIC ROOM

---

*T*HEO REACHES AUVERS just a few hours after he received Dr. Gachet's letter. He runs the short distance from the train station to the Auberge Ravoux, arriving filled with fear and sorrow.

The innkeeper tells him that Vincent is in his room, number five, on the top floor, opposite the stairs.

Theo runs up.

It's a tiny room, only seventy-five square feet, with a small bed, a chair, a little table, and a built-in corner cupboard. When he was done painting for the day, Vincent would stack his canvases under the bed or put them in the cupboard. He had to be careful; the paint was still wet, the impasto so thick a piece could take weeks or months or a year to dry.

The room has slanted ceilings, just like in Zundert. The only light comes drizzling in from a small skylight.

Theo is expecting the worst, but there is Vincent, sitting up in bed, smoking a pipe. Soon after Gachet examined him on Sunday, the day before, Vincent asked if he could smoke, and the doctor said yes. Gachet found Vincent's pipe in the pocket of the blue plumber's shirt that he wore when he painted. Gachet filled the bowl with tobacco, lit it, and handed it to his friend. Once Vincent had settled, Gachet had written the letter to Theo that had brought him here.

Theo learns that Vincent has shot himself. That's what Vincent had told Gachet and then the police when they'd arrived. He said he had shot himself in a wheat field where he was painting.

The police do not have his gun, or the painting equipment from that day. None of that is found.

Another version of the incident will be floated years later: a group of children were taunting him, a gun had gone off accidentally. Vincent covered up for the children.

Just as some people think he covered up for Gauguin with the ear.

Indeed, why *would* he shoot himself just now? He'd been looking toward the future. He is finally making it as an artist! But he has been stormy inside, worried about Theo. Desperately worried that Theo is dying. He could not tolerate a future without Theo.

And when madness overtakes him, he's not rational. He has tried before, at least twice, eating paints.

But why shoot himself in the body if he meant to kill himself? Why not in the head?

These are unanswered questions.

But on this summer day in Auvers, none of this matters to Theo. Vincent has said he shot himself; Theo has no reason to question. All he cares about is that his brother should live.

Please let Vincent live.

Theo sits with Vincent, then leaves for just a few minutes to write to Jo. He has to tell her where he is, what has happened. Or at least some of it.

"Dearest, dearest little wife, These are trying times for us, dearest, one thing after another that we hadn't anticipated." He tells her about Hirschig coming to his office, and how he dropped everything to go to Vincent immediately.

He has "found him better than I had expected."

But Theo tells her he knows the situation is precarious. Gachet and the village doctor decided they could not remove the bullet. They can do nothing but make sure he is comfortable. To wait and see.

Taking Gachet's advice to protect her, Theo does not tell Jo all. "I shan't go into detail, it's all too distressing, but I should warn you, dearest, that his life could be in danger." If Vincent is better tonight, Theo will go back to Paris early the next morning, he says. If not, he will stay.

Theo doesn't really know what to hope for—for Vincent's sake. His brother "wasn't granted a lavish share of happiness," he tells Jo. And he seems to have given up on that.

But Vincent wants happiness for Theo, and for Jo and the baby. He'd said so, just now, talking in the attic room. Jo is lucky, he'd told Theo—she has "no inkling of life's sadness."

Theo tells Jo that he will manage "no matter what may happen, after all, I have you to live for; I'll not be alone as long as I have my wife & my little boy."

After writing this letter to Jo, Theo goes back to Vincent.

The two brothers talk, Vincent in bed, Theo with the chair pulled up right next to him. Theo does not leave Vincent's side.

Two brothers, a walk together, a pledge, a promise, a shared path.

For many hours, Vincent does not seem too ill. He does not suffer.

He *is* strong. Ma has always said he is her strongest child. His body *has* survived so much.

Theo has been scared before, and he has been surprised by Vincent's survival.

But as the sun starts to set, Vincent's condition worsens. He has pain, trouble breathing. Theo has been sitting with him for twelve hours.

Stars appear in the sky. But the brothers do not look upward. They look to each other.

Vincent's pain gets worse and worse.

As the night goes on, he finds it harder to breathe.

Theo moves onto the bed. He holds Vincent in his arms.

"I've always wanted to die like this," Vincent tells him. It is half past midnight on July 29.

No, Theo says, you will be cured. "You will be spared this sort of despair."

"No," Vincent says, "the sadness will last forever."

Theo understands.

After all those years of struggle, all the hardship, it is a relief for Vincent to know that it is at an end.

In pain, barely able to breathe, Vincent is ready to surrender.

Theo can do nothing but hold him.

Vincent gasps for breath, closes his eyes.

Two brothers, the middle of the night.

An attic room, slanted ceilings, just like in Zundert.

Vincent dies in Theo's arms.

111.

A YELLOW DAY
MADE FOR VINCENT

He found a tremendous peace.

—Theo to Lies, August 5, 1890

WHEN HE HEARS THE NEWS, Dr. Gachet comes to the inn and doesn't leave Theo's side.

Vincent died in the early morning hours of July 29, 1890. Gachet makes sure the word gets out, and the next morning people gather at the inn, friends from Auvers first, then friends from Paris who have taken the early train north: Dries, Émile Bernard, Lucien Pissarro, and others. A few close friends hear the news too late to come in time for the funeral. Toulouse-Lautrec writes to Theo that Vincent was a good friend to him and was always "eager . . . to demonstrate his affection." Toulouse-Lautrec wants Theo to feel as if he's clasping his hand near the coffin.

Camille Pissarro could not quickly catch the train and go to the funeral with his son Lucien, but "I really felt a great affinity for your brother. I feel really sad for you, my dear friend."

Gachet arrives for the funeral carrying a magnificent bunch of sunflowers. These are just the first flowers. By the end of the day there are "masses of bouquets and wreaths."

Émile Bernard directs the hanging of Vincent's latest paintings, "making a sort of halo for him," he later tells the art critic Albert Aurier, who is not there, "and the brilliance of the genius that radiated from them made this death even more painful for us artists who were there."

The friends drape the coffin in a white cloth and surround it with masses of flowers, dahlias and sunflowers, "yellow flowers everywhere." Bernard tells Aurier that yellow was Vincent's "favourite colour, the symbol of the light that he dreamed of as being in people's hearts as well as in works of art."

On the floor in front of the coffin lie his folding stool, his easel, and his brushes.

Villagers gather at the inn, too, to say good-bye to the man who lived with them for only ten weeks. At three o'clock his friends carry the coffin to the hearse.

Waiting that last hour is incredibly hard for Theo. Theo, "who was devoted to his brother, who had always supported him in his struggle to support himself from his art," Bernard writes, "was sobbing pitifully the whole time."

JULY 30 IS A HOT DAY. The sun beats down on the pallbearers as they carry the coffin from the hearse up the hill to the cemetery. As they walk to the grave, Vincent's friends talk about Vincent, how generous and kind he had been to them, how devoted he was to his art.

The cemetery lies among wheat fields ripe for harvest, fields Vincent had loved. Fields he painted. It is a sunny spot and, Theo thinks, a pleasant churchyard.

They all cry as the coffin is lowered into the grave—how could you not, Bernard tells Aurier, "the day was too much made for him for one not to imagine that he was still alive and enjoying it."

A day made for Vincent.

Gachet speaks about Vincent, about his two aims in life: humanity and art. He was, his friend says, an honest man and a great artist. His name will live on, of that Gachet is certain.

Theo is so upset he can hardly speak. He thanks everyone for coming, and they leave.

Back at the inn, Vincent's friends divide up his canvases. Theo somehow manages to leave Auvers and go back to Paris. But he cannot be home alone, so he goes to stay with Dries and Annie.

For Theo there is emptiness everywhere.

112.

THEO'S OWN BROTHER

———————

DEAR THEO!" Ma writes on August 1. "How are you. We are worried that, after the news from Auvers that Vincent was ill but in no immediate danger, your Jo heard nothing more."

Theo hasn't yet written to Jo or Ma to tell them the news. He doesn't want Ma to find out in a letter that her oldest son has died. So he's asked their sister Anna's husband to break the news in person.

His brother-in-law goes to Ma's house and tells her and Wil. Theo writes to Ma when he is sure she will already have heard.

"One cannot write how sad one is nor find solace in pouring out one's heart on paper. May I come to you soon?" Theo asks his mother.

He tells Ma how Vincent died, how the doctors had taken good care of him but couldn't do anything to save his life. He tells her Vincent wanted to go in just that way, and he had his wish. "Life weighed so heavily upon him, but as happens more often everyone is now full of praise for his talent too."

He writes to Jo, too, though she has already heard from the family. He tells her he needs to see his mother first, as much as he longs to be with her and baby Vincent. He knows his mother will want to hear the details. "She's devastated," he tells Jo.

As for him, "it is a sadness which will weigh upon me for a long time," he says, "and will certainly not leave my thoughts as long as I live."

Writing to his mother, Theo tries to be brave, to reassure her. "He has found the rest he so much longed for."

But his grief bursts onto the page:

"Oh Mother, he was so very much my own brother."

113.
LETTERS TO THEO

———————————

*J*O UNDERSTANDS that Theo has to go to his mother first. But she also knows he needs her. So she travels from Amsterdam and is in Ma's house with the baby when Theo arrives.

As Theo is wrapped in the love and comfort of his mother, his sister Wil, and Jo, the letters start pouring in from family, friends, colleagues, people who knew Vincent, and people who didn't.

Lies, who is living about forty miles away, writes to Theo and Jo that she is shocked and distressed. His life had been "far more agreeable of late," she writes. But when she thinks about his life as a whole, it seems to her "that God himself had gently laid him to sleep, having first comforted and soothed him." Still she could not imagine how he could have killed himself, being so close to Theo and Jo and the baby, "all these cheerful little rays of sunshine." He fell, she says, not as one wounded, "but in the fire of battle."

She remembers how all those years ago Vincent journeyed to see their old neighbor who was dying and said afterward, "When I die, I hope I shall be lying just like him," surrounded by family. When their father died, she says, he told a neighbor that "dying is hard, but living is harder still."

She writes, "I have found the paintings"—clearly she didn't have them hanging up—"and they are now even dearer to me."

No one in the family but Theo realizes just how good Vincent's art is. They are beginning to suspect that perhaps there is something to it, but Lies and the rest of the family renounce their claims to Vincent's paintings. They want Theo to have them. He deserves them. And he is the one who will know what to do with them, to show Vincent's genius to the world.

This becomes Theo's mission: to show the world Vincent's work. "People should know that he was a great Artist," he tells Lies. He intends to arrange an exhibit of Vincent's work in Paris in a few months. "He will certainly not be forgotten."

The letters keep coming: from more family members, from the Roos family both brothers had boarded with in The Hague, from Dutch artists, French artists, Australian, Belgian, Danish, English, and Italian artists. Over the next weeks fifty letters arrive, all extolling Vincent's virtues as a painter, as a man, as a friend.

They write to Theo, to Ma, to Theo *and* Jo.

Theo's friend and former roommate Meijer de Haan, the one who made the portrait of Theo with "cokes," "coffee," and "Jo" on his cuffs, writes: "I know what pain this must cause you, who loved him so dearly." He was "an extremely important Artist," a thought he hopes is a comfort to Theo. "He is not dead he lives for you for us—and for everyone, in the work he has left behind."

Paul Gauguin and De Haan are painting and living together in Brittany, and Gauguin writes on the back of De Haan's letter, "I don't want to write the usual phrases of condolence—you know that for me he was a sincere friend; and that he was an artist a rare thing in our epoch. You will continue to see him in his works. As Vincent used often to say—'Stone will perish, the word will remain.' As for me, I shall see him with my eyes and with my heart in his works."

Even Vincent's former friend Van Rappard writes to Ma. He remembers the good times of the visits in Nuenen. He tells her that although they had become estranged, he often thinks of Vincent, "so often volatile and so impassioned, yet for his noble mind and artistic qualities, always worthy of admiration." And he regrets their misunderstanding.

Aurier writes to Theo that he doesn't need to tell him how much he admired Vincent's work, since he's said so publicly, but he wants to tell Theo that Vincent's name will live for eternity. "This will no doubt be poor consolation for you who felt a brother's love for him." But consolation it is. As long as Theo can get Vincent's work to the public.

Other art critics write, including Georges Charles Lecomte: "We have lost a very courageous artist."

Claude Monet writes to say that although he never met Vincent, he knows Theo and had thought Vincent's paintings the best in the most recent Exhibition of the Independents.

––––––––––

DR. GACHET sends a sketch he drew: Vincent on his deathbed. Theo writes and tells him the sketch has given his mother immense pleasure.

Gachet writes back that the more he thinks about Vincent, the more he thinks he was "a *giant*."

These letters and the plan for showing Vincent's work help Theo. He will focus on the show when he gets back to Paris. But he is bereft. A friend writes that it's a good thing he has his wife and child.

It is true. He has Jo. He has baby Vincent. But he does not have his health.

GALLERY FOURTEEN

Remains

1890–1891

114.

THE SHOW

THEO HAS BEEN SICK for so long. Coughing. Bouts of paralysis. Weakness. Now, in the days and weeks after Vincent's death, his health deteriorates further. After being with Ma, he and Jo and the baby go to Amsterdam to stay with the Bongers. It is clear to all of Jo's family how bad Theo's health is. He is near collapse.

Once they are back in Paris, his health improves a bit. He focuses on the exhibit of Vincent's work, which gives him purpose, keeps up his spirits.

But the improvement in his health doesn't last. He starts coughing badly. He becomes agitated often. He has to take medicine to help him sleep at night.

Even though he is so sick, they decide to go through with the move to the bigger apartment. Now that Theo isn't sending money to Vincent, they have enough for the higher rent. So that is something. But the move is exceedingly difficult for Theo, both physically and emotionally. And then the moving men make a huge mess, dumping everything all over the place.

At work he has his usual frustrations, and he is having trouble finding a place to hold the exhibition of Vincent's work.

But he continues to hear from other painters how much they love Vincent's art. This cheers him, keeps him on his task. Dr. Gachet comes down from Auvers to visit, too, and he and Theo have lunch, talking about Vincent. Gachet tells Theo again how much he cared for his brother and what a great painter Vincent was.

All the years of Theo supporting Vincent, carrying his parcel, all Vincent's hard work—it was worth it. Tragically, what Theo worried about—that Vincent wouldn't live to see his acclaim—has come true. But at least Theo will be here to see it. He is determined.

When the place where he'd hoped to mount the show falls through, he decides to hang the paintings right in their apartment. Émile Bernard comes over to help, and in a few days it is done. Bernard even paints the glass panes in the drawing room so that they look like medieval stained glass. Theo is so pleased; it's wonderful to look at so many of Vincent's paintings at once. He can't wait for everyone to come see it.

He writes Wil to tell her all about it. But he tells her something else, too. He is feeling quite crazy, and has been for some time.

115.

NIGHTMARES

---

*T*HEO IS HAVING NIGHTMARES and hallucinations. He thinks maybe it's the medicine he's taking to sleep, so he stops taking it. But a few days after Jo's birthday, on October 4, Theo has a huge argument with his bosses. He is irrational. He quits, but they won't accept his resignation because they can see how sick he is.

And then he has a complete mental and physical collapse.

Jo keeps him at home, determined to take care of him herself.

Dries watches in horror as Theo's condition gets worse and worse.

He can't urinate.

He is delusional.

Finally, when he declares he wants to kill Jo and the baby, Dries insists that Theo be admitted to a hospital.

Jo is furious at Dries for threatening to take Theo away from her. She knows Theo better than anyone and wants to be in charge. But Dries feels there is no choice, and over Jo's objections he takes Theo to a hospital.

Two days later Theo is transferred to a private mental asylum in Passy, on the west side of Paris.

Dr. Gachet comes to see him. So does his old boss, Tersteeg. They aren't allowed in and just watch him from outside the gates. He is walking around the garden.

Wil comes from the Netherlands to help Jo. Theo isn't coming home anytime soon.

The word from the doctor is that Theo's mental condition is much worse than Vincent's ever was. There is no hope of a cure.

The only hope Dries has is that Theo will improve enough that they can take him home to the Netherlands.

116.

NIGHT TRAIN

TWO YEARS EARLIER, Theo had taken a night train because of a medical emergency. He'd traveled from Paris to Arles, where Vincent lay in the hospital, a bandage around his head. That day had started out as one of the happiest of Theo's life. He had been filled with the promise of love and his future with Jo.

Now, on this autumn night, November 17, 1890, he is leaving Paris again, riding another night train to another hospital. But this time he is the patient. He is leaving the asylum in Passy. He is going home to the Netherlands, to a mental institution in Utrecht. His beloved Jo is with him, their baby Vincent in her arms. Theo could not hold his son even if he wanted to; he is bound in a straitjacket.

117.

SCENES IN THE HOSPITAL

Theo in the Hospital, Croquis #1

THEO IS ADMITTED to the hospital, on court authorization officially requested by Jo's father. Theo is cheerful, but completely confused. He has no idea where he is or what time it is. He speaks, but his words are incoherent. He doesn't answer questions correctly, and he mixes up languages. His pulse is weak and fast. He has trouble walking; his right foot is swollen from a fall he'd had back in Paris. "From time to time he is incontinent," reads the medical file. "He has a tendency to destroy his clothes."

He is given a bath, which calms him some, and put to bed in an isolation room. He is restless, agitated. Given sedatives, he falls asleep.

At the end of the day the doctors present the diagnosis to the family, concurring with the doctors in Paris: general paralysis and dementia as a result of a syphilis infection. This is the disease he has had since before he met Jo. Apparently, Theo had no open sores for years and therefore did not pass the syphilis to Jo.

Over the next few days he stops eating and is fed through a tube.

Theo in the Hospital, Croquis #2

ON NOVEMBER 24, Theo seems calm enough for Jo to visit.

But when she arrives, he becomes extremely agitated. He pushes over a table and a couple of chairs.

The visit is stopped.

Jo thinks he *looks* fine, but his emotional condition is quite disturbing to her. The hospital staff thinks both his physical and mental state are "appalling & have said this quite openly."

Theo destroys his straw mattress and his clothes.

Ma and Wil hear about the visit, and Ma writes to Jo: "How painful that visit must have been. Still it is now confirmed. . . . I have been frightened all along. . . . Do you think he suffers much himself? He is not in pain, is he?"

Theo in the Hospital, Croquis #3

IT IS A COLD AND GREY and rainy December in Utrecht.

But inside the hospital the weather makes no difference to Theo. He is in his own world.

Jo and Wil visit the first week of December. Theo is at first reasonably calm. Very quickly, however, he becomes agitated and upset.

The effects of this visit, the hospital staff reports, were felt for days afterward. Jo's presence made him angry and aggressive.

By December 9, the hospital staff have given Theo a dire prognosis. His chances of a recovery, they tell Jo, softening the truth, are poor.

Theo in the Hospital, Croquis #4

JO VISITS at the end of December. She is holding a bouquet of flowers for him. A nurse takes Theo the flowers first, to see how he will react. He destroys them.

Jo is not admitted to see her husband.

118.

THE SHOW, II

PARIS, December 28, 1890.

In Theo and Jo's apartment, the show of Vincent's work is opened to the public.

Neither Jo nor Theo is there to see it.

119.

SCENES IN THE HOSPITAL, CONTINUED

Theo in the Hospital, Croquis #5

JANUARY IN UTRECHT. The sun shines for only a quarter of the day.

Inside the hospital, where Theo van Gogh struggles through the last stages of syphilis, there is no sun at all.

The doctor brings Theo an article from the Dutch newspaper *Algemeen Handelsblad*. It was published a few days earlier, on December 31, 1890. It's on the front page of the paper; the title is "Vincent van Gogh." Theo immediately recognizes the name.

Vincent.

The doctor starts to read: "On this cold short Christmas afternoon, while the crowds enjoyed gathering before the bright market stalls on the boulevard, some Dutch people came together in the somber rooms of a temporarily uninhabited home in Montmartre and admired several hundred paintings there."

Theo gets an increasingly blank expression on his face. The doctor records this in the medical records. He does not record how far into the article he read.

The article continues:

"A sad feeling was mixed with their enthusiasm: the art treasure, which lay and stood assembled here in this dreary cold room, was the bequest of an artist who died too young, and whose younger brother, currently seriously ill himself as a result of that loss, and having been transported to his native country to try to get better, had to leave this great relic which was so dear to him, in the good care of others. May the sick man get well soon, even if only to the extent that his love would allow it, to guard the work of Vincent van Gogh!"

Theo in the Hospital, Croquis #6

JO TRIES TO VISIT on January 6, but she is advised not to. He is unusually excited and noisy today.

Theo in the Hospital, Croquis #7

A WEEK LATER, Wil and Jo are let in to visit Theo. He is calm, but he ignores them completely, as if "he could not care less," reads the medical report.

Theo in the Hospital, Croquis #8

DURING THE THIRD WEEK of January 1891, Theo spends his days and nights heavily sedated in a padded cot, in isolation.

In the article in the Dutch paper, the reporter had said that Vincent's "love of art was a religion, an effusive honoring and sacrificing of himself."

An effusive honoring of the artist's brother as well.

120.

VINCENT'S BROTHER,
JANUARY 25, 1891

VINCENT DIED in Theo's arms.

Theo dies alone.

Mon cher frère, Merci de ta bon...
et du billet de 50 fr. qu'elle contena...
Je voudrais bien t'écrire sur b...
chôses mais j'en sens l'in...
J'espère que tu auras retrouve...
mesdames en de bonnes de...
à ton égard —

Que tu te rassures sur l'état
de ton ménage — c'était pas l...
Je crois avoir vu le bien autan...
l'autre côté — Et suis tellem...
d'ailleurs d'accord que d'élev...
gosse dans un quatrième étag...
une lourde corvée tant pou...
que pour Jo — Puisque cela...
ce que est le principal insister
sur des chôses de moindre i...
ma foi avant qu'il y ait chann...
causer affaires à têtes plus repos...
il y a probablement loin . Voilà
seule chose qu'à présent je puisse di...
et que cela pour ma part je l'ai con...
avec un certain effroi je ne l'ai pas c...
déjà mais c'est bien là tout —

Exit

121.

EPILOGUE

1.

A FEW MONTHS BEFORE they married, Jo Bonger had written to Theo van Gogh: "I'm quite sure that if I stay with you always, you might still be able to make <u>something</u> out of me."

"I have a brother," Theo had written to Jo in his first letter to her.

And when she was in labor, Jo wrote to Vincent that there was no one in the world Theo loved as much as Vincent.

After Theo's death, Jo took up the brothers' cause. She carried that parcel. And she made Vincent van Gogh famous.

She couldn't have had Theo without Vincent. Vincent couldn't have been Vincent without Theo. And the world wouldn't have Vincent van Gogh without Jo.

JO TOOK THE BABY and moved back to the Netherlands, to a town outside of Amsterdam. She ran a boardinghouse. Although some people advised her to get rid of Vincent's paintings, she knew they were valuable. And she knew she should keep as many of them together as possible. She took them with her, too.

Jo learned as much as she could about the art world from Vincent and Theo's friends, and others. She helped to mount shows of Vincent's work in the Netherlands and Belgium, and then in Paris.

Although she got married again in 1901, to a Dutch painter named Johan Cohen Gosschalk, she continued her work to make sure that Vincent's art became known. She had always felt a connection to Vincent's paintings. And she learned how to bring that connection to the world. Vincent's friend Émile Bernard was a great help. He published a short memoir of Vincent soon after his death, and he published the letters that Vincent had written to him.

Jo knew that she had a gift for the world not only in Vincent's paintings but also in his letters to Theo. Theo had kept them all, stuffed in drawers in a cabinet.

She gathered them together, dated them as best she could, and in 1914, two years after her second husband died, she published a collection of Vincent's letters to Theo, in Dutch. She wrote her own introduction, a memoir of Vincent's life, much of which she knew from Theo. Jo's collection of Vincent's letters showed the world what a beautiful writer and thinker he was. His emotion, so evident in his paintings, is in his letters, too.

2.

THE SADNESS of the Van Gogh children did not end with Theo's death. In 1900, the youngest boy, Cor, killed himself while in the army in South Africa. Wil worked as a nurse in a hospital after Theo died, but she also suffered from mental illness. She entered an institution in 1902 and died there in 1941. Lies wrote her own memoir of Vincent, published a few years before Jo's. It was not very well received at the time due to factual errors she made. Ma lived a long time; she died in 1907. Though she lived through the tragedies of Vincent, Theo, Cor, and Wil, she did live long enough to see Vincent get some recognition. Both Anna and Lies lived into the 1930s.

3.

THEO AND JO'S SON, Vincent, grew up surrounded by his uncle's paintings. The walls of the house were covered with them. He watched as his mother made Uncle Vincent's name and paintings famous. He respected art, he said, but thought it was magic, and not for him. He became an engineer, married, and had four children.

He helped to found the Van Gogh Museum in Amsterdam; it opened in 1973, right near the Rijksmuseum and Jo's childhood home.

Millions of visitors go to the Van Gogh Museum every year to see Vincent's paintings.

And tens of millions of people see Vincent's paintings in museums all over the world. Guards have to watch closely so visitors don't touch the paintings, so drawn are people to them. To the color, to the paint, to the raw emotion.

4.

WHEN THEO DIED, Jo had him buried in Utrecht. But in April 1914, she moved Theo's remains to Auvers, his grave placed right next to Vincent's.

Two brothers, side by side, head to head.

Just like in Zundert.

People

THE IMMEDIATE FAMILY

Anna van Gogh-Carbentus,* mother
Anna van Gogh, sister
Cornelis (Cor) van Gogh, brother
Elisabeth (Lies) van Gogh, sister
Theodorus van Gogh (Dorus), father
Theodorus (Theo) van Gogh, brother
Vincent van Gogh, brother
Willemien (Wil) van Gogh, sister

CLOSE FAMILY

Johanna (Jo) Bonger, sister of Dries, wife of Theo
Cornelis (Uncle Cor) van Gogh, brother of Dorus
Hendrik van Gogh, brother of Dorus
Jan van Gogh, brother of Dorus
Vincent van Gogh (Uncle Cent), brother of Dorus
Vincent Willem van Gogh, son of Theo and Jo
Cornelia (Aunt Cornelie) van Gogh-Carbentus, sister of Anna,
    wife of Uncle Cent

FRIENDS, LOVE INTERESTS, HOUSEMATES, COLLEAGUES

Albert Aurier, critic who wrote a review of Vincent's work
Athanase Bague, art dealer to whom Theo sold one of Vincent's paintings
Margot Begemann, Vincent's lover in Nuenen
Émile Bernard, painter and friend of Vincent

* Dutch practice is for the maiden name to follow the married surname.

Andries (Dries) Bonger, friend of Theo, brother of Jo

Hendrik Christiaan Bonger and Hermine Louise Weissman-Bonger, parents of Jo and Andries

Mien Bonger, sister of Jo and Andries

Marguerite Gachet, daughter of Dr. Gachet, subject of paintings

Paul-Ferdinand Gachet, doctor and painter in Auvers-sur-Oise

Paul Gauguin, painter and housemate of Vincent in Arles

Paulus Coenraad Görlitz, roommate of Vincent

Meijer de Haan, painter and roommate of Theo

Annet Haanebeek, Theo's first love

Caroline Haanebeek, Vincent's first love

Anton Hirschig, painter Vincent mentors in Auvers-sur-Oise

Honcoop family, neighbors in Zundert

Clasina Maria (Christien or Sien) Hoornik, Vincent's lover in The Hague

Maria and Willem Hoornik, Sien's children

Willem Laurens Kiehl, housemate and friend of Theo

Arnold Koning, painter and roommate of Theo

Ursula and Eugenie Loyer, Vincent's landlady and her daughter in London

Marie (last name unknown), Theo's lover in Paris

Anton Mauve, painter and cousin by marriage (wife, Jet Mauve)

Claude Monet, painter and founder of Impressionism

Théophile Peyron, doctor in Saint-Rémy

Abraham van der Waeyen Pieterszen, member of the Evangelization Committee and a painter

Camille Pissaro, painter and friend of Vincent and Theo

Lucien Pissaro, painter and friend of Vincent and Theo (Camille's son)

Alphonse Portier, art dealer in Paris

Jan Provily, schoolmaster of boarding school Vincent attended

Rachel (last name unknown), prostitute in Arles

Anthon van Rappard, painter and friend of Vincent

Adeline Ravoux, daughter of innkeeper in Auvers-sur-Oise, subject of paintings

Félix Rey, Vincent's doctor in Arles

Auguste Rodin, sculptor

Willem Marinus Roos and Dina Margrieta van Roos-Van Aalst, couple with
   whom both Vincent and Theo lodged in The Hague
Augustine-Alix Pellicot Roulin, wife of Joseph and model for Vincent's painting
   La Berceuse
Joseph Roulin, postman and friend of Vincent in Arles
S., Theo's girlfriend in Paris
Frédéric Salles, pastor in Arles
Agostina Segatori, woman Vincent sees in Paris
Georges Seurat, painter
Thomas Slade-Jones, pastor and schoolmaster of school where Vincent works
William Port Stokes, schoolmaster in Ramsgate
Julien Tanguy, art dealer to whom Vincent sold early painting
Hermanus Gijsbertus (H. G.) Tersteeg, Vincent and Theo's boss in The Hague
Henri de Toulouse-Lautrec, painter and friend of Vincent and Theo
Cornelia (Kee) Adriana Stricker-Vos, cousin and love interest of Vincent
Johannes Wilhelmus Weehuizen, friend and housemate of Theo

Vincent and Theo's Journey

MARCH 30, 1853 Vincent born.

MAY 1, 1857 Theo born.

OCTOBER 1, 1864 Vincent leaves home for the first time, goes to Mr. Provily's school.

SEPTEMBER 3, 1866–MARCH 19, 1868 Vincent attends Willem II high school in Tilburg.

JULY 30, 1869 Vincent starts work at Goupil & Cie in The Hague, boards with the Rooses.

JANUARY 1871 Theo goes to high school in Oisterwijk.

SEPTEMBER 1872 Vincent and Theo walk to the windmill near The Hague, make a pledge to each other.

SEPTEMBER 29, 1872 Vincent writes back to Theo's thank-you, and a lifelong correspondence begins.

JANUARY 6, 1873 Theo starts work at Goupil & Cie in Brussels.

APRIL 30, 1873 Caroline Haanebeek gets married.

MAY 1873 Vincent is sent to London to work in the Goupil stockroom.

AUGUST 1873 Vincent rooms in Ursula and Eugenie Loyer's house in Brixton, London.

NOVEMBER 12, 1873 Theo moves to The Hague, works at the Goupil branch, boards with the Rooses.

MID-JULY–END OF AUGUST 1874 Anna (sister) is in London with Vincent.

OCTOBER 26, 1874 Vincent is temporarily sent to work at the Goupil branch in Paris.

JANUARY 1875 Vincent moves back to London and works at a new Goupil gallery.

MAY 1875 Vincent is sent to Paris to work at the Goupil headquarters.

MARCH 4, 1875 Theo's friend Johannes Wilhelmus Weehuizen dies.

JUNE 14, 1875 Annet Haanebeek dies.

SEPTEMBER 22, 1875 Theo's friend Willem Laurens Kiehl dies.

JANUARY 1876 Vincent is fired from Goupil's, leaves April 1.

APRIL 1876 Vincent starts work at William Stokes's school in Ramsgate, England.

JUNE 12–17, 1876 Vincent walks to London from Ramsgate.

OCTOBER 1876 Theo is seriously ill.

OCTOBER 29, 1876 Vincent delivers his first sermon in Richmond, outside of London.

NOVEMBER 19, 1876 Vincent starts work at Slade-Jones school.

JANUARY 9, 1877 Vincent begins work at Blussé & Van Braam in Dordrecht, the Netherlands.

JANUARY–APRIL 1877 Theo has an affair with a woman; Ma and Pa disapprove.

MAY 1877 Vincent moves to Amsterdam, lives with Uncle Jan, and attends theology school.

MAY 1, 1878 Theo turns twenty-one and leaves The Hague for Paris, where he works at the Exposition Universelle.

JULY 1878 Vincent quits theology school, moves back home.

AUGUST 22, 1878 Anna gets married.

AUGUST 26, 1878 Vincent moves to Brussels to go to evangelist training school for a trial period.

NOVEMBER 1878 Theo moves back to The Hague from Paris, visits Vincent in Brussels on the way back.

NOVEMBER 25, 1878 Vincent's trial period at evangelist training school ends. He is not accepted.

DECEMBER 1878 Vincent moves to the Borinage without a job.

FEBRUARY 1, 1879 Vincent starts a six-month trial as an evangelist in the Borinage.

FEBRUARY 1879 Pa visits Vincent, persuades him to move out of the hut where he's been sleeping.

JULY 1879 Vincent's appointment is not made permanent.

AUGUST 1–3, 1879 Vincent walks to see Reverend Pieterszen for advice.

EARLY AUGUST 1879 Vincent stays in the Borinage (but changes housing) and concentrates on drawing.

AUGUST 10, 1879 Theo visits Vincent; the two fight and don't have any contact for almost a year.

AUGUST 15–18, 1879 Vincent lives in Etten with his parents, then goes back to the Borinage.

ON OR ABOUT NOVEMBER 1, 1879 Theo starts work permanently at Goupil & Cie in Paris.

MARCH 1880 Theo gives Pa money for Vincent. Vincent walks partway to Courrières and all the way back to the Borinage.

JUNE 1880 Vincent writes to Theo, resuming their correspondence.

AUGUST 1880 Vincent decides to become an artist.

OCTOBER 1880 Vincent leaves the Borinage and moves to Brussels.

FEBRUARY 1881 Theo is appointed manager of the Goupil branch at 19 Boulevard Montmartre in Paris and starts regularly sending money to their parents for Vincent.

END OF APRIL 1881 Vincent moves to Etten and lives with his parents. Vincent asks Theo to give him advice on what to draw and to critique his art.

SUMMER 1881 Vincent falls in love with his cousin Kee Vos.

NOVEMBER 1881 Vincent visits the family of Kee Vos and tries to win her.

LATE NOVEMBER TO ABOUT DECEMBER 21, 1881 Vincent stays in The Hague with painter and relative Anton Mauve, who gives him lessons in watercolor and oil painting.

DECEMBER 24–25, 1881 Vincent has a huge fight with Pa and moves to The Hague.

LATE DECEMBER 1881 Theo starts supporting Vincent directly.

JANUARY 1882 Vincent rents a studio in The Hague; Vincent and Theo have an angry exchange.

LATE JANUARY 1882 Vincent hires Sien Hoornik to become his model. She becomes his lover.

MID-FEBRUARY 1882 Vincent sells a drawing to H. G. Tersteeg.

MARCH 1882 Uncle Cor commissions Vincent to draw twelve views of The Hague.

EARLY APRIL 1882 Uncle Cor commissions a second set of cityscapes.

APRIL 10, 1882 Vincent sends Theo *Sorrow*.

MAY 1882 Mauve breaks off with Vincent.

JUNE 7–JULY 1, 1882 Vincent is treated in a hospital for gonorrhea.

JULY 2, 1882 Sien Hoornik gives birth to a baby boy, Willem.

JULY 15, 1882 Sien and her children move into a larger apartment with Vincent.

JULY 18, 1882 Tersteeg visits Vincent in his studio and criticizes him for letting Theo support him.

LATE JULY 1882 Vincent paints *The Laakmolen near The Hague (The Windmill)*.

NOVEMBER 1882 Vincent practices lithography and hopes to become a working illustrator.

JANUARY 1883 Theo begins seeing a woman named Marie; his parents disapprove.

JULY 1883 Theo is overwhelmed financially and tells Vincent there is little hope he can keep supporting him. (But he does.)

AUGUST 1883 Theo visits Vincent in The Hague and tries to persuade him to leave Sien.

EARLY SEPTEMBER 1883 Vincent breaks off with Sien.

SEPTEMBER 11, 1883 Vincent moves to Drenthe to paint.

DECEMBER 5, 1883 Sad and lonely in Drenthe, Vincent moves to Nuenen to live with his parents. They turn the mangle room into his studio.

DECEMBER 1883 Vincent is angry at Theo, and a visit to Sien makes it worse.

JANUARY 17, 1884 Ma breaks her thighbone while getting off a train.

SUMMER 1884 Vincent and Margot Begemann fall in love.

SEPTEMBER 1884 Margot tries to commit suicide.

DECEMBER 1884 Vincent is furious at Theo and writes that they must split up.

LATE 1884–EARLY 1885 Theo starts a relationship with "S."

MARCH 26, 1885 Pa dies.

MARCH 30, 1885 Pa is buried; it is Vincent's thirty-second birthday. Vincent and Theo make up. Theo likes Vincent's work, takes some of his paintings back to Paris.

SPRING 1885 Theo becomes close to Andries (Dries) Bonger.

MAY 6, 1885 Vincent sends Theo his painting of *The Potato Eaters* and moves out of the house and into his studio after a fight with his sister Anna.

SUMMER 1885 Vincent's friend Anthon van Rappard hates *The Potato Eaters*. The friendship is broken.

AUGUST 7, 1885 Theo meets Johanna Bonger and falls for her immediately. She has no idea.

OCTOBER 1885 Vincent visits the Rijksmuseum for the first time and has a revelation about color. He and Theo begin writing to each other about color theory. Theo encourages Vincent to lighten and brighten his palette.

NOVEMBER 1885 Vincent moves to Antwerp, Belgium. He never returns to the Netherlands.

FEBRUARY 1886 Vincent has many of his teeth pulled.

FEBRUARY 28, 1886 Vincent leaves Antwerp without paying his bills. He arrives in Paris, surprising Theo. He moves in with him.

MARCH–JUNE 1886 Vincent works at the studio of Fernand Cormon. Meets artists there, including Émile Bernard and Henri de Toulouse-Lautrec.

JUNE 1886 Theo rents a bigger apartment at 54 Rue Lepic, and he and Vincent move.

AUGUST 1886 Theo goes to The Netherlands and asks Uncle Cent and Uncle Cor for financial help to start his own gallery. They refuse.

SEPTEMBER 1886 Vincent exhibits his works at different galleries and shops, including one owned by Julien Tanguy. He sells at least one of his paintings to Tanguy.

END OF DECEMBER 1886 Theo has an attack of paralysis and is unable to move for days.

JANUARY–MID-APRIL 1887 The brothers' relationship is strained almost to the point of breaking for good. Theo wants to ask Vincent to move out, but he doesn't.

LATE APRIL 1887 Vincent and Theo make up and decide to live together happily.

MAY 1887 Vincent is painting outside much of the time. His art is improving steadily. Theo is very happy with his brother's paintings.

JULY 1887 Vincent breaks off with the woman he was seeing, Agostina Segatori.

JULY 22, 1887 Theo visits Johanna Bonger in Amsterdam and proposes to her. She is shocked and does not accept.

JULY 26, 1887 Theo writes a letter to Jo so they can get to know each other better. He tells her what has affected him deeply: Vincent.

SUMMER 1887 Vincent paints a portrait of Theo (long thought to be a self-portrait).

FALL–WINTER 1887 Vincent and Theo become closer than ever. They spend time with painter friends, including Camille and Lucien Pissarro, Paul Gauguin, Georges Seurat, Henri de Toulouse-Lautrec. Both brothers organize exhibits of paintings they love, Theo on the entresol at his gallery and Vincent in a restaurant.

FEBRUARY 5, 1888 Anton Mauve dies.

FEBRUARY 19, 1888 Vincent and Theo visit the studio of Georges Seurat; Vincent leaves Paris for the South of France.

FEBRUARY 20, 1888 Vincent arrives in Arles and decides to live there instead of continuing on to Marseille as he had planned.

LATE FEBRUARY 1888 Arnold Koning moves in with Theo.

MARCH 1888 Vincent makes a painting for Jet Mauve in memory of Anton Mauve.

MARCH 22–ABOUT MAY 3, 1888 Three of Vincent's paintings are displayed at the fourth Exhibition of the Independents in Paris.

MAY 1, 1888 Vincent rents the east wing of a yellow house at 2 Place Lamartine in Arles.

MAY 1888 Theo, very sick and exhausted, visits Dr. Gruby, who diagnoses a heart problem. Vincent thinks they should be treating his nervous system instead.

JULY 28, 1888 Uncle Cent dies.

SUMMER AND INTO FALL 1888 Vincent paints furiously. When the mistral is too strong, he stays inside and draws.

SEPTEMBER 17, 1888 Vincent moves into the Yellow House.

EARLY OCTOBER 1888 Theo sells one of Vincent's paintings to Athanase Bague, a Paris art dealer.

OCTOBER 1888 Vincent worries about how much money he owes Theo for all the years he's supported him. Theo reassures him.

OCTOBER 23, 1888 Paul Gauguin arrives in Arles and moves into the Yellow House with Vincent.

OCTOBER 28, 1888 Meijer de Haan moves in with Theo.

ON OR ABOUT DECEMBER 10, 1888 Theo runs into Johanna Bonger on the street in Montmartre.

DECEMBER 11, 1888 Gauguin writes to Theo and says he has to leave Arles; he can't live with Vincent. Vincent persuades him to stay.

DECEMBER 21, 1888 Theo writes to his mother that he and Jo are in love.

DECEMBER 23, 1888 Vincent and Gauguin have a fight, and Vincent slices off his left ear.

DECEMBER 24, 1888 Theo writes to his sister Lies that he and Jo Bonger are engaged to be married. That same day he gets a telegram from Gauguin that Vincent is gravely ill. He takes a night train to Arles.

DECEMBER 25, 1888 Theo visits Vincent in the hospital in Arles, then takes Gauguin back to Paris.

JANUARY 3, 1889 Gauguin gives Theo a portrait he made of Vincent painting sunflowers.

JANUARY 5–13, 1889 Theo is in the Netherlands with Jo. On January 9 they hold their engagement reception.

JANUARY 7, 1889 Vincent leaves the hospital.

JANUARY 13–MARCH 30, 1889 Jo and Theo write letters to each other.

FEBRUARY 7, 1889 Theo's Monet show goes up in the gallery. Vincent is admitted to the hospital again; he is placed in isolation.

FEBRUARY 18, 1889 Vincent leaves the hospital, goes back to the Yellow House.

FEBRUARY 26, 1889 Vincent's neighbors write a petition asking that he be committed to a mental hospital. Instead the police take him to the hospital where he'd been before.

FEBRUARY 28, 1889 Wil would like to bring Vincent to the Netherlands and take care of him; Ma does not agree to it. He stays in the hospital.

APRIL 18, 1889 Theo and Jo marry in the Netherlands and a few days later move into the apartment that Theo found for them.

MAY 1889 Vincent packs up some paintings he made in Arles and sends them to Theo. When they arrive in Paris, Theo says there are superb paintings in the batch. He tells Vincent he is certain his work will be appreciated.

MAY 8, 1889 Vincent checks into the Saint-Paul-de-Mausole asylum in Saint-Rémy-de-Provence. He has a room to sleep in and a room to paint in.

JULY 5, 1889 Jo writes to Vincent that she is pregnant, knows the baby will be a boy, and wants to name him after Vincent. Theo's health is deteriorating.

ON OR ABOUT JULY 16, 1889 Vincent has a breakdown and eats paints.

SEPTEMBER 1889 The fifth Exhibition of the Independents goes up with two of Vincent's paintings in it. People notice them; a critic calls him a colorist.

JANUARY 1890 Jo worries terribly about Theo's health as a flu epidemic hits Paris. Albert Aurier writes the first critical appraisal of Vincent's work, calling him a worthy successor to the Dutch masters.

JANUARY 20–21, 1890 Vincent has another breakdown and eats his paints again. He is sick for a fortnight.

JANUARY 29, 1890 Jo writes a letter to Vincent while she is in labor.

JANUARY 31, 1890 Vincent Willem van Gogh is born.

JANUARY–FEBRUARY 1890 Vincent has six paintings in a show in Brussels and one of them, *The Red Vineyard*, is sold to artist Anna Boch.

MARCH 20–APRIL 27, 1890 Vincent has ten paintings at the sixth Exhibition of the Independents in Paris; visitors talk about his paintings the most.

APRIL 1890 Vincent sends paintings to Theo, including an almond tree in bloom for the baby; Theo and Jo hang it above the piano in the drawing room. Theo is arguing with his bosses.

MAY 16, 1890 Vincent leaves the asylum in Saint-Rémy.

MAY 17–19, 1890 Vincent visits Theo and Jo in Paris, meeting Jo (and the baby) for the first time.

MAY 20, 1890 Vincent moves to Auvers-sur-Oise, meets Dr. Paul-Ferdinand Gachet, and takes lodgings at the Auberge Ravoux.

JUNE 8, 1890 Theo and Jo and the baby visit Vincent in Auvers.

JUNE 30–JULY 1, 1890 Theo writes to Vincent that the baby has been very ill. He is also worrying about his job and feels his apartment is too small. He is distraught.

JULY 6, 1890 Vincent visits Theo and Jo in Paris. The baby is better, but Vincent is upset by the visit.

JULY 15–18, 1890 Theo is in the Netherlands taking Jo and baby Vincent to stay with her family.

JULY 23, 1890 Vincent writes the last letter he will mail to Theo.

JULY 27, 1890 Vincent shoots himself.

JULY 28, 1890 Anton Hirschig delivers a letter to Theo from Dr. Gachet. Vincent is very ill. Theo immediately takes a train to Auvers.

JULY 29, 1890 Vincent dies.

JULY 30, 1890 Friends gather in Auvers for Vincent's funeral. Theo heads back to Paris, bereft.

AUGUST 3, 1890 Theo goes to the Netherlands and stays with his mother and sister Wil. Jo and the baby are there.

AUGUST 1890 Letters of condolence pour in for Theo. Theo decides to mount a show of Vincent's work.

ON OR ABOUT SEPTEMBER 16, 1890 Theo and Jo move to a bigger apartment in their building. Theo's health deteriorates.

SEPTEMBER 22–24, 1890 Émile Bernard helps Theo mount a show of Vincent's work in Theo and Jo's new apartment.

SEPTEMBER 27, 1890 Theo writes to Wil that he's been feeling crazy for some time.

OCTOBER 1890 Theo has a mental and physical collapse.

OCTOBER 12, 1890 Dries has Theo hospitalized against Jo's wishes.

OCTOBER 14, 1890 Theo is transferred to a mental asylum in Passy, on the west side of Paris.

NOVEMBER 17, 1890 Jo and Dries take Theo back to the Netherlands on a night train. He is hospitalized in Utrecht.

DECEMBER 28, 1890 The show of Vincent's work in Theo and Jo's Paris apartment is opened to the public.

JANUARY 25, 1891 Theo dies.

MAY 1891 Jo moves to Bussum, the Netherlands, where she runs a boarding-house.

1892–1893 Jo helps to organize exhibits of Vincent's work.

AUGUST 21, 1901 Jo marries Johan Cohen Gosschalk.

1905 Jo organizes a successful exhibit of Vincent's work in Amsterdam. Her husband writes an essay about Vincent for the catalog.

APRIL 29, 1907 Ma dies.

MAY 18, 1912 Gosschalk dies.

1914 Jo publishes a collection of Vincent's letters to Theo, which she has painstakingly organized.

APRIL 1914 Jo moves Theo's remains to Auvers to lie next to Vincent's.

SEPTEMBER 2, 1925 Jo dies.

JUNE 1973 Van Gogh Museum opens in Amsterdam.

Author's Note

I've always loved Vincent van Gogh. *Starry Night, Sunflowers*, his self-portraits—so many of his paintings were the backdrop of my teenage years. Don McLean's song "Vincent (Starry Starry Night)" came out when I was just thirteen, and by then I'd already read Irving Stone's novel about him, *Lust for Life*. I thought I knew the most important things about Vincent. It turned out I did not.

In June 2011, my husband and I went to the Van Gogh Museum in Amsterdam. Walking around, I was bowled over to be in the presence of so much of Vincent's art. Then, next to one of his paintings, I read a brief mention of Theo. I hadn't remembered that Vincent had a brother. The note said that Theo had supported him. I definitely had not known that. It was a eureka moment. I probably gasped. I knew nothing more than that, but I realized at once that I had to write a book about the brothers.

I took some notes that day. I wrote: "What does everyone remember about him? The ear, killing himself. And some paintings, of course. But what about his religion and his decision to become a painter so he could leave the world a souvenir?" And then I wrote: "Story of brothers. (And sister-in-law.)"

I did not grow up with siblings near my age and always wished I had. So when my sons were born three years apart, I was thrilled to watch the beauty of their brotherhood. Aaron and Benjamin are very different from each other, but they have always benefited from their closeness as well as their differences. My writing the story of Vincent and Theo seemed meant to be.

As I always do, I began with primary sources. I read the letters between Vincent and Theo. I quickly saw that it was not just a love story. Their relationship was filled with anger and sacrifice and love and hurt and more sacrifice and even more love. Then I read the letters between Theo and Jo. It was all so much better than I had thought.

While I read the letters, I also painted. I am not an artist, but some friends gave me watercolors, and so for months I played with paints and got to know color. I started to get an inkling of what it feels like to be a painter.

Only after I had met Vincent and Theo and Jo in their own words did I turn to secondary sources. And that's when I hit trouble. Everyone has an opinion about Vincent van Gogh, an agenda of some kind. This was overwhelming. But I benefited from two great pieces of wisdom at this time. My editor told me: "We want *your* tour of Vincent. Nobody else's. When friends come to New York City," she said, "I can't take them everywhere. So I take them to *my* favorite New York places."

And then, over lunch in a museum café, an artist friend said this: a work of art on a wall is an open question.

I thought about both of these things as I visited museums and looked at Vincent's paintings. I looked at other artists' paintings. And soon I realized that when we look at a work of art, we look at it from where we stand—who we are, where we've been, what we've seen, how we feel. A work of art is an open question, a question that invites you in.

A life lived is also an open question.

When we look at a person—alive or dead—we do so from our own perspective. We bring our own particularity to art and also to biography.

In some ways, it is easier to know a person after death. We can look back over deeds and misdeeds, work and relationships, love and hate. On the other hand, we can't ask the questions we really want to ask: *Why did you leave? Whom did you love most? What made you sad, angry, joyful? Who were you really?*

A famous person can be easier to know—or harder. Easier because there is more material to peruse—letters, journals, diaries, interviews, books, and articles. But we can be misled by others, by misinterpretations, and even by falsehoods.

After years of careful research and thought, I have given you my view of

Vincent van Gogh and the relationship that I think was at the center of his life. You will take away what speaks to you. And maybe you will want to know more and will do your own research. I hope so.

I want to tell you about another moment, one I had while writing this book. It was the day I discovered Vincent's painting *The Laakmolen near The Hague (The Windmill)*. I happened upon it while I was looking up information about the walk the brothers took to the mill and the pledge they made to each other. I found old photographs of the windmill, and then I was shocked to see that Vincent had painted it. I had never seen that painting. I was amazed to see that this painting is barely written about. Nobody, to my knowledge, has ever described it as central to Vincent and Theo's relationship. It took me hours to determine that I had discovered something unique and important. When I did, I threw myself down on my office floor and stared at the ceiling, saying "Oh my God" over and over. Fortunately I live with a writer, and when he saw me lying on the floor, he wasn't terribly worried. When I told Jonathan (from the floor) what I had discovered, he said, "This is the moment. This is the moment when you found your book. I will remember this." He was right; I had found my book, but I didn't know it yet. That was another moment, a year later, while I was revising a draft. I said aloud (I seem to do a lot of talking to myself when I write), "These boys are *mine*!"

In these pages, you meet Vincent and Theo as if you are walking through a museum show of their lives—a collection of paintings, drawings, and sketches. Because Vincent van Gogh drew as much as he painted, and because his style evolved and changed over the years, I wrote in different styles, changing as it fit the topic, the time of Vincent's life, or the amount of knowledge we have. There are traditional pieces, sketches, impressions, scenes filled with great emotion, pictures where the emotion is in the white spaces, or in the details, pieces where it's all in the black line, others where the passion is in the color and the light.

Vincent van Gogh referred to many of his works as *studies*, not finished, not final. Even some of his most famous paintings, the ones people from all over the world stare at and take photographs of in museums, guards keeping a watchful eye so visitors don't get too close—but how can you not! Vincent's art draws you to him, whether or not he himself thought it was finished.

Vincent's life was not finished when it ended, either. But it was a work of art. So was Theo's. And their relationship was a masterpiece.

Bibliography

BOOKS AND ARTICLES

Auden, W. H. "Calm Even in the Catastrophe." *Encounter*, April 1959, pp. 37–40.

Aurier, Albert. "Les isolés: Vincent van Gogh" [The isolated: Vincent van Gogh], *Mercure de France*, January 1890, pp. 24–29.

Baedeker, Karl. *Baedeker's Paris and Its Environs*. Leipzig, Germany: Karl Baedeker, 1878.

Borg, Marlies ter, and Dorothée Kasteleijn-Nolst Trenité. "The Cultural Context of Diagnosis: The Case of Vincent van Gogh." *Epilepsy & Behavior* 25, no. 3 (2012): pp. 431–439.

Cassee, Elly. "In Love: Vincent van Gogh's First True Love." In *Van Gogh Museum Journal 1996*, pp. 109–117. Zwolle, Netherlands: Waanders, 1996.

DeVita-Raeburn, Elizabeth. *The Empty Room: Understanding Sibling Loss*. New York: Scribner, 2007.

du Quesne van Gogh, Elizabeth. *Personal Recollections of Vincent van Gogh*. Translated by Katherine S. Dreier. Boston: Houghton Mifflin, 1913.

Eksteins, Modris. *Solar Dance: Van Gogh, Forgery, and the Eclipse of Certainty*. Boston: Harvard University Press, 2012.

Gauguin, Paul. *Letters to His Wife and Friends*. Edited by Maurice Malingue. Translated by Henry J. Stenning. Cleveland, OH: World Publishing, 1949.

Gogh, Theo van, and Johanna van Gogh-Bonger. *Brief Happiness: The Correspondence of Theo van Gogh and Jo Bonger*. Edited and translated by Leo Jansen and Jan Robert. Amsterdam: Van Gogh Museum, 1999.

Gogh, Vincent van. *The Letters of Vincent Van Gogh*. Edited by Mark Roskill. New York: Touchstone, 2008. This volume also contains the memoir by Jo van Gogh-Bonger.

————. *Van Gogh: A Self-Portrait; Letters Revealing His Life as a Painter*. Selected by W. H. Auden. London: Thames & Hudson, 1961.

————. *Vincent van Gogh: The Letters; The Complete Illustrated and Annotated Edition*. 6 vols. Edited by Leo Jansen, Hans Luijten, and Nienke Bakker. New York: Thames & Hudson, 2009.

————. *Vincent van Gogh—The Letters*. Edited by Leo Jansen, Hans Luijten, and Nienke Bakker (2009). Version: November 2014. Amsterdam: Van Gogh Museum and Huygens ING. vangoghletters.org.

Gogh-Bonger, Johanna Gesina van. "Memoir of Vincent van Gogh." December 1913. Van Gogh's Letters, webexhibits.org/vangogh/memoir/sisterinlaw/1.html.

Gopnik, Adam. "Van Gogh's Ear." *New Yorker*, January 4, 2010, pp. 48–55.

Holy Bible, New International Version. Colorado Springs, CO: Biblica, 2011. BibleGateway.com.

Homburg, Cornelia, ed. *Van Gogh Up Close*. New Haven, CT: Yale University Press, 2012. Exhibition catalog.

Hulsker, Jan. "The Elusive Van Gogh, and What His Parents Really Thought of Him." *Simiolus: Netherlands Quarterly for the History of Art* 19, no. 4 (1989): pp. 243–270.

————. *Vincent and Theo: A Dual Biography*. Edited by James M. Miller. Ann Arbor, MI: Fuller Publications, 1990.

————. "What Theo Really Thought of Vincent." *Vincent: Bulletin of the Rijksmuseum Vincent van Gogh* 3, no. 2 (1974): pp. 2–28.

Jamison, Kay Redfield. *Touched with Fire: Manic-Depressive Illness and the Artistic Temperament*. New York: Free Press Paperbacks, 1993.

Jansen, Leo, Hans Luijten, and Erik Fokke. "The Illness of Vincent van Gogh: A Previously Unknown Diagnosis." In *Van Gogh Museum Journal 2003*, pp. 113–119. Amsterdam: Van Gogh Museum, 2003.

Kaufmann, Hans, and Rita Wildegans. *Van Goghs Ohr: Paul Gauguin und der Pakt des Schweigens* [Van Gogh's ear: Paul Gaugin and the pact of silence]. Berlin: Osburg Verlag, 2008.

Kools, Frank. *Vincent van Gogh et zijn geboorteplaats Als een boer in Zundert* [Vincent van Gogh and his birthplace, as a farmer in Zundert]. Zutphen, Netherlands: De Walburg Pers, 1990.

Mast, Michiel van der, and Charles Dumas, eds. *Van Gogh en Den Haag* [Van Gogh in The Hague]. Zwolle, Netherlands: 1990, pp. 34, 36, 37. Translated for the author by Susanna Mitton.

Meester, Johan de. "Vincent van Gogh." In *Algemeen Handelsblad*, December 31, 1890. Translated for the author by Susanna Mitton.

Meyers, Jan. *De jonge Vincent. Jaren van vervoering en vernedering* [The young Vincent. Years of rapture and humiliation]. Amsterdam: De Arbeiderspers, 1989.

Naifeh, Steven, and Gregory White Smith. *Van Gogh: The Life.* New York: Random House, 2011.

Nordenfalk, Carl. *The Life and Work of Van Gogh.* New York: Philosophical Library, 1953.

Op de Coul, Martha. "Der Laakmolen in Den Haag door Vincent van Gogh" [The Laakmolen near The Hague by Vincent van Gogh]. In *Oud Holland*, 104, no. 3–4 (1990), pp. 336–340. Translated for the author by Susanna Mitton.

Pickvance, Ronald. *"A Great Artist Is Dead": Letters of Condolence on Vincent van Gogh's Death.* Edited by Sjraar van Heugten and Fieke Pabst. Amsterdam: Van Gogh Museum, 1992.

———. *Van Gogh in Arles.* New York: Metropolitan Museum of Art, 1984.

Righthand, Jess. "The Woman Who Brought Van Gogh to the World," Smithsonianmag.com, November 1, 2010.

Silverman, Debora. *Van Gogh and Gauguin: The Search for Sacred Art.* New York: Farrar, Straus and Giroux, 2000.

Standring, Timothy J., and Louis van Tilborgh, eds. *Becoming Van Gogh.* Denver: Denver Art Museum, 2012. Exhibition catalog.

Stolwijk, Chris. "'Our Crown and Our Honour and Our Joy': Theo van Gogh's Early Years." In *Van Gogh Museum Journal 1997–1998*, pp. 42–57. Zwolle, Netherlands: Waanders, 1998.

Stolwijk, Chris, Richard Thomson, and Sjraar van Heugten. *Theo van Gogh 1857–1891: Art Dealer, Collector and Brother of Vincent.* Amsterdam: Van Gogh Musuem, 1999.

Tilborgh, Louis van, and Teio Meedendorp. "The Life and Death of Vincent van Gogh." *Burlington Magazine*, July 2013, pp. 456–462.

Tralbaut, Marc Edo. *Vincent van Gogh*. New York: Viking, 1969.

Verhaegen, Marc, and Jan Kragt. *Vincent Van Gogh: An Artist's Struggle*. Translated by Laura Watkinson. Amsterdam: Eureducation/Van Gogh Museum, 2011.

Voskuil, P. H. A. "Het medische dossier van Theo van Gogh" [The medical files of Theo van Gogh]. *Nederlands Tijdschrift voor Geneeskunde* 136, no. 36 (1992): pp. 1777–1780. Translated for the author by Susanna Mitton.

Voskuil, Piet. "Diagnosing Vincent van Gogh, an Expedition from the Sources to the Present 'Mer a Boire.'" *Epilepsy & Behavior* 28, no. 2 (2013): pp. 177–180.

Wilkie, Ken. *The Van Gogh File: The Myth and the Man*. London: Souvenir Press, 2004.

Wolk, Johannes van der. *The Seven Sketchbooks of Vincent Van Gogh*. New York: Harry N. Abrams, 1987.

Wylie, Anne Stiles. "Vincent's Childhood and Adolescence." *Vincent: Bulletin of the Rijksmuseum Vincent van Gogh* 4, no. 2 (1975): pp. 4–27.

WEBSITES

There are many websites about Vincent van Gogh. However, many of them are inaccurate. In addition to the website for the letters (vangoghletters.org), I found these most useful:

Van Gogh Museum, Amsterdam: vangoghmuseum.nl/en

The Metropolitan Museum of Art: metmuseum.org

Van Gogh Gallery: vangoghgallery.com

For additional resources, please visit DeborahHeiligman.com.

Thank You

Many people helped me carry the heavy parcel that became this book. Thanks to all of my friends and family who supported me with laughter, love, and Vincent-related articles, e-mails, and gifts.

Deepest thanks to these spectacular friends and family who read drafts of the book: Laurie Halse Anderson, Daphne Benedis-Grab, Judy Blundell, Barbara Kerley, Susan Kuklin, Nancy Sandberg, Rebecca Stead, Benjamin Weiner, Jonathan Weiner, Aaron Zinger, and Sarah Zinger.

Susanna Mitton provided translations for articles and books written in Dutch and answered many questions about the Netherlands. Myrna Gunning helped with Dutch translation, too, and talked to me about the Netherlands early in the morning in the park. Andrew Fink helped with German translation, as did Rick Sams and Sebastian Rettlbach. Marie Rutkoski and her in-laws, Christiane and Jean-Claude Philippon, consulted about French flowers. With the help of their parents, Harry and Desi Saunders found and photographed all the places where Vincent and Theo lived and worked in Paris. Deborah Freedman gave me an essential understanding of what it means to engage with art. Sheri Mason taught me about art sales and auctions. Thanks to Alix Finkelstein and Neil Watson and David Wiesner for discussions about art process, materials, and the art world.

Thanks to Christine Haynes, history professor at the University of North Carolina Charlotte, for help with currency comparisons. Thanks to Sree

Sreenivasan, then chief digital officer of the Metropolitan Museum of Art, for good advice and for a before-hours visit with the Met's Van Gogh paintings.

Many people at the Van Gogh Museum in Amsterdam helped with this book. Thanks especially to Martine Blok, Monique Hageman, Hans Luijten, Lucinda Timmermans, and Marije Vellekoop. Thanks also to Ron Dirven, director of the Van Gogh House, to Charlotte Joosten of Van Gogh Brabant, and to Wim Monté of the outdoor museum of Vincent van Gogh in Nuenen.

Thank you to William Rau for his insights about *The Laakmolen near The Hague (The Windmill)* and for letting me spend so much time staring at it. Because I couldn't afford to buy it (!), the painting is now in a private collection in England. Thank you to the owner for verifying some details. If you ever want to give it away, please let me know.

Much gratitude to Alex Weintraub, Fulbright Fellow (for his work on Vincent van Gogh), for his extremely insightful expert reading reading of the manuscript. And thank you to Timothy Standring, curator of *Becoming van Gogh* at the Denver Art Museum, for his helpful comments.

Ken Wright, formerly my agent, still dear friend, helped me start on this journey. To Susan Ginsburg, fabulous agent and friend, a Vincent-sized thank you for carrying so much of the parcel for such a long way. Thank you also to Stacy Testa at Writers House for help I'm aware of, and more help that I'm not.

The team at Henry Holt Books for Young Readers is stellar. Huge thanks to Jennifer Healey, managing editor, who keeps it all running, to Tom Nau, production manager, for his skill and wisdom, and to Anna Booth for her exquisite design of this book. Heartfelt thanks to Sherri Schmidt, copy editor and fact-checker extraordinaire, and to proofreader Barbara Bakowski. Thanks to Angus Killick, Lucy Del Priore, Katie Halata, Johanna Kirby, Amanda Mustafic, Teresa Ferraiolo, Melissa Zar, and Allison Verost for making the magic happen when the book is finished.

A huge thank-you to Julia Sooy for her indefatigable help with and attention to this book, and for the sunlight that emanates from her on even the cloudiest day. And thank you to my brilliant editor, Laura Godwin, who encouraged me to trust my vision of Vincent and Theo and helped me put the frame around the story.

I am so very lucky to have my husband, Jonathan Weiner, next to me on this path we call life. As Vincent said, "What a mystery life is, and love is a mystery within a mystery." I am grateful every day for these mysteries.

Endnotes

THRESHOLD

3   "There was a time when I loved . . .": Theo van Gogh to Willemien van Gogh, March 14, 1887, FR b908, in "Concordance, Lists, Bibliography: Documentation," vangoghletters.org.

3   "almost intolerable for me at home": Theo to Willemien van Gogh, March 14, 1887.

3   Goupil & Cie: The art dealers where Theo worked had officially changed names by then, but people kept referring to it as Goupil's. To make things easier, I refer to it as Goupil's as well.

4   "He loses no opportunity . . .": Theo to Willemien van Gogh, March 14, 1887.

5   "O Lord, join us intimately . . ." Letter 113, Vincent to Theo, April 30, 1877.

6   "particularly in my spirit . . .": Theo to Elisabeth van Gogh, April 19, 1887, FR b910, in "Concordance, Lists, Bibliography: Documentation," vangoghletters.org.

ENTRESOL

12   "Just like in Zundert": Johanna van Gogh-Bonger, "Memoir of Vincent van Gogh," December 1913, Van Gogh's Letters, webexhibits.org/vangogh.

GALLERY ONE: BEGINNINGS

21   "I again saw each room . . .": Letter 741, Vincent to Theo, January 22, 1889.

21   When he was cold, Vincent . . . : Kools, *Vincent van Gogh et zijn geboorteplaats*, p. 17. Wil remembered this.

22   pea vines . . . beech hedge: Du Quesne van Gogh, *Personal Recollections of Vincent van Gogh*, p. 3.

22   "primitive memories of all of you . . .": Letter 741, Vincent to Theo, January 22, 1889.

24   "black fields with the young green wheat": Letter 109, Vincent to Theo, March 23, 1877.

24   After showing Theo . . . : Du Quesne van Gogh, *Personal Recollections of Vincent van Gogh*, p. 5.

24   "Copying nature absolutely isn't . . .": Letter 291, Vincent to Theo, December 4–8, 1882.

26   "Our father and our mother. . .": Letter 741, Vincent to Theo, January 22, 1889.

27   "We thought so much of him . . ." and "severe" and "a proper little Protestant pope": Tralbaut, *Vincent van Gogh*, p. 17.

30   "It is better to be fervent . . .": Letter 143, Vincent to Theo, April 3, 1878.

31   "more or less irresistible passion": Letter 155, Vincent to Theo, June 22–24, 1880.

36   "I wish I didn't love home so much": Elisabeth van Gogh to Theo, January 10, 1875, in Meyers, *Dejonge Vincent*, p. 58.

36   "I stood on the front steps . . .": Letter 90, Vincent to Theo, September 2–8, 1876.

39   His blue eyes . . . : Van Gogh-Bonger, "Memoir of Vincent van Gogh," webexhibits.org/vangogh.

41   "they came to tell" . . . around Pa's neck: Letter 90, Vincent to Theo, September 2–8, 1876.

41   He has years of pilgrimage: Letter 90, Vincent to Theo, September 2–8, 1876.

43   "No, thank you . . .": Tralbaut, *Vincent van Gogh*, p. 25.

48   We walked "through the raindrops": Letter 1, Vincent to Theo, September 29, 1872, trans. Susanna Mitton.

49   "Both you and I thought then . . .": Letter 413, Vincent to Theo, December 15, 1883.

50   "It was strange for me . . .": Letter 1, Vincent to Theo, September 29, 1872.

GALLERY TWO: DANGERS

53   "The years between 20 and 30 . . .": Letter 90, Vincent to Theo, September 2–8, 1876.

55   "But precisely because love is so strong . . .": Letter 183, Vincent to Theo, November 12, 1881. Elly Cassee mentions this letter in "In Love: Vincent van Gogh's First True Love," which is where I first learned of it.

55   "My dear Theo . . . We must correspond often": Letter 2, Vincent to Theo, December 13, 1872.

56   "Be brave. You have now taken . . .": Anna van Gogh-Carbentus and Reverend Theodorus van Gogh to Theo, March 1, 1873, in Stolwijk, "Our Crown," p. 46.

56   "Theo, I must again recommend . . .": Letter 5, Vincent to Theo, March 17, 1873.

57   "It's cold here . . .": Letter 4, Vincent to Theo, January 28, 1873.

58   He was terrified of his family: Letter 234, Vincent to Theo, June 1–2, 1882.

58   When he returns to the Roos house . . . : Pieter Boele van Hensbroek, "Uit," in *Verzamelde Brieven van Vincent van Gogh* (1955), eds. J. van Gogh-Bonger and V. W. van Gogh, pp. 334–335; in Naifeh and Smith, *Van Gogh: The Life*, p. 79.

58   "You'll have heard that . . . as well as I'd like": Letter 5, Vincent to Theo, March 17, 1873.

60   eventually they will be called Impressionists: The term *Impressionists* was applied derogatorily at first. Monet's painting was accused of being unfinished, merely a sketch or an impression. For more information you can start here: metmuseum.org/toah/hd/imml/hd_imml.htm.

61   "You cannot be in London . . .": Reverend Theodorus van Gogh to Theo, May 31, 1873, trans. Robert Harrison, in Van Gogh's Letters, webexhibits.org/vangogh.

62   "It was glorious": Letter 13, Vincent to Theo, September 13, 1873.

63   He's comforted to be reminded of home: Anna van Gogh-Carbentus to Theo, July 2, 1873, in Stolwijk et al., *Theo van Gogh*, p. 193.

64   "The Family rests upon . . .": Jules Michelet, *Love*, trans. J. W. Palmer (New York, 1860), p. 7.

64   "A book like that . . . that I believe": Letter 27, Vincent to Theo, July 31, 1874.

65   "I gave up on a girl . . .": Letter 183, Vincent to Theo, November 12, 1881.

65   "when the sun's setting behind . . .": Letter 39, Vincent to Theo, July 24, 1875.

68   "Anna is managing well . . .": Letter 27, Vincent to Theo, July 31, 1874.

69   Vincent "has illusions about people . . .": Anna van Gogh to Theo, April 28, 1875, FR b2333, in Letter 33, n4.

70   "I hope and believe I'm not what . . .": Letter 33, Vincent to Theo, May 8, 1875.

71   "How is the patient?": Letter 33, Vincent to Theo, May 8, 1875.

71   Annet is "still so young to have to die. . . .": Elisabeth van Gogh to Theo, April 26, 1875, FR b2332, in Letter 33, n2.

71   "He thought it so beautiful": Letter 45, Theo to Vincent, September 7, 1875.

71   "She stayed with me 30 years . . .": Letter 35, Vincent to Theo, June 19, 1875.

71   "happy and jolly": Reverend Theodorus van Gogh to Theo, July 8, 1875, FR b2346, in Stolwijk, "Our Crown," p. 50; and in Letter 36, n1.

71   "We are hard hit by the news . . .": Reverend Theodorus van Gogh to Theo, September 25, 1875, FR b2363, in Letter 52, n1.

72   "trials and tribulations": Reverend Theodorus van Gogh to Theo, October 7, 1875, FR b2366, in Stolwijk et al., *Theo van Gogh*, p. 29, n63.

72   "Let us trust in God . . .": Letter 50, Vincent to Theo, September 25, 1875.

72   "Be careful, old boy . . .": Letter 52, Vincent to Theo, September 29, 1875.

GALLERY THREE: MISSTEPS, STUMBLES

75   "After all, we're in the midst of life. . .": Letter 118, Vincent to Theo, May 31, 1877.

77   "breakfast together or drink a cup . . .": Letter 52, Vincent to Theo, September 29, 1875.

78   "The packages of chocolate marked X . . .": Letter 61, Vincent to Theo, December 10, 1875.

78   "You can imagine that . . .": Reverend Theodorus van Gogh to Theo, January 3, 1876, in Hulsker, "The Elusive Van Gogh," p. 248.

79   "Through the small window I saw . . .": Letter 78, Vincent to Theo, April 21, 1876.

79   "And now we picture him . . .": Anna van Gogh-Carbentus to Theo, April 16, 1876, in Hulsker, "The Elusive Van Gogh," p. 249.

80   "When you were baptized . . .": Reverend Theodorus van Gogh to Theo, April 29, 1876, in Stolwijk, "Our Crown,"p. 44.

81   "He walks great distances . . .": Reverend Theodorus van Gogh to Theo, July 1, 1876, in Hulsker, "The Elusive Van Gogh," p. 250.

81   "full of all kinds of ships . . .": Letter 77, Vincent to Theo, April 17, 1876.

81   "The sea was yellowish, . . .": Letter 83, Vincent to Theo, May 31, 1876.

82   "Many a boy . . . that causeth shame": Letter 83, Vincent to Theo, May 31, 1876.

83   "A clergyman's son . . . such a situation": Vincent to probably Edmund Henry Fisher, in Letter 84, Vincent to Theo, June 17, 1876.

83   "exaggerated and overwrought, quoting . . .": Reverend Theodorus van Gogh to Theo, September 8, 1876, in Hulsker, "The Elusive Van Gogh," p. 251.

84   "Don't worry about your wanton life . . .": Letter 86, Vincent to Theo, July 8, 1876.

84   "How much I'd like to be . . .": Letter 92, Vincent to Theo, October 3, 1876.

84   "Besides wanting so much to sit . . .": Letter 94, Vincent to Theo van Gogh and Anna van Gogh-Carbentus, October 13, 1876.

85   "When I stood in the pulpit . . .": Letter 96, Vincent to Theo, November 3, 1876.

87   Görlitz's Portrait of Vincent: The details and quotes in this section come from P. C. Görlitz to Frederik van Eeden, ca. December 1890, in *Van Gogh: A Self-Portrait; Letters Revealing His Life as a Painter*, ed. W. H. Auden (Greenwich, CT: New York Graphic Society, 1960), pp. 37–42.

88   "bond that never lets go of us . . .": Letter 124, Vincent to H. G. Tersteeg, August 3, 1877, after the death of his third child, a baby girl three months old.

88   "few secrets as possible . . .": Letter 103, Vincent to Theo, February 26, 1877.

89   "two brothers who slept together . . .": Letter 104, Vincent to Theo, February 28, 1877.

89   "Your heart will need to trust itself . . .": Letter 111, Vincent to Theo, April 15, 1877.

90   "We have improved his appearance . . .": Reverend Theodorus van Gogh to Theo, May 7, 1877, FR b959, trans. Robert Harrison in Van Gogh's Letters, webexhibits.org/vangogh.

90   "Would you be so kind . . .": Reverend Theodorus van Gogh to Theo, May 7, 1877. I combined the translations of the FR b959 letter by Robert Harrison and the *Complete Letters* editors in Letter 114, n42.

91   "write him from time to time . . .": Anna van Gogh-Carbentus to Theo, June 7, 1877, trans. Robert Harrison in Van Gogh's Letters, webexhibits.org/vangogh.

91   "Your love is based on sensuality . . .": Anna van Gogh-Carbentus to Theo, May 21, 1877, FR b2533, in Letter 117, n1.

91   "You can and must have pleasure . . .": Reverend Theodorus van Gogh to Theo, May 21, 1877, FR b2532, in Letter 117, n1.

92   "I should really like to get away . . .": Letter 117, Vincent to Theo, May 30, 1877. Vincent is quoting Theo's letter back to him.

92   "as much as the hedges . . . in store for us": Letter 118, Vincent to Theo, May 31, 1877.

93   "Don't spoil things . . .": Reverend Theodorus van Gogh to Theo, June 16, 1877, FR b2537, in Letter 120, n2.

93   "Who knows . . .": Anna van Gogh-Carbentus to Theo, ca. October 1877, FR b2559, in Stolwijk, "Our Crown," p. 53.

94   "May Vincent not only have blessing . . .": Anna van Gogh-Carbentus to Theo, January 6, 1878, in Hulsker, "The Elusive Van Gogh," p. 252.

95   "He is so awfully impractical . . .": Anna van Gogh-Carbentus to Theo, February 2, 1878, FR b966, in Letter 140, n1.

95   "put my mind at ease a little . . .": Reverend Theodorus van Gogh to Theo, February 2, 1878, FR b965, in Letter 140, n1.

95   When he goes back to his room . . . : Letter 140, Vincent to Theo, February 10, 1878.

95   "the worst time I've ever gone through": Letter 154, Vincent to Theo, August 11–14, 1879.

97   "more of a wooden lion than ever . . .": Anna van Gogh to Theo, August 13, 1878, FR b989, in Letter 147, n2.

97   "far from being as one would like . . .": Letter 146, Vincent to Theo, August 5, 1878.

100 "those who work . . .": Letter 148, Vincent to Theo, November 13–16, 1878.

100 "How much there is in art . . ." and "I wish you well . . .": Letter 148, Vincent to Theo, November 13–16, 1878.

102 "There are sunken . . . chimney-sweeps": Letter 149, Vincent to Theo, December 26, 1878.

103 "a very grim letter from him . . .": Anna van Gogh-Carbentus to Theo, February 27, 1879, FR b2463, in Letter 150, n2.

104 "in a kind of basket . . . beautiful recently?": Letter 151, Vincent to Theo, April 1–16, 1879.

105 "Wouldn't you consider spending a day . . .": Letter 152, Vincent to Theo, June 19, 1879.

105 "as though it were . . . what will become of him?": Anna van Gogh-Carbentus to Theo, July 2, 1879, FR b2484, in Letter 152, n16.

106 "to have some keepsakes . . .": Letter 153, Vincent to Theo, August 5, 1879.

107 "types from here, not that they alone . . .": Letter 153, Vincent to Theo, August 5, 1879.

GALLERY FOUR: FISSURES

112 "wise counsel given with the best . . . struggle against despair": Letter 154, Vincent to Theo, August 11–14, 1879.

114 "Hello, Father, hello, Mother": Anna van Gogh-Carbentus to Theo, August 19, 1879, FR b2492, in Letter 154, n2.

114 "His father saw him and was filled with compassion for him . . .": Luke 15:20 (New International Version). The parable of the prodigal son is told in Luke 15:11–32.

115 Ma and Pa are in no hurry . . . : Anna van Gogh-Carbentus to Theo, August 19, 1879, FR b2492, in Letter 154, n2.

115 For the next year, he sends no letters home: There are no extant letters between Vincent and Theo, or from the whole family during this next year. Some scholars think that there were such heated quarrels in that time period that it was potentially embarrassing, so they destroyed the letters. It is certain, however, that there was a silence between Vincent and Theo for a long time, almost certainly that whole year.

119 trudging "rather painfully": Letter 158, Vincent to Theo, September 24, 1880. Ten francs would be the equivalent of about forty-five dollars in 2017.

120 "a point of destitution . . .": Letter 391, Vincent to Theo, September 28, 1883.

120 "I earned a few crusts of bread . . .": Letter 158, Vincent to Theo, September 24, 1880.

121 "Oh, Theo, if only some light . . .": Reverend Theodorus van Gogh to Theo, March 11, 1880, FR b2496. Letter 155, n2.

121 "Vincent is still here. . . .": Reverend Theodorus van Gogh to Theo, March 11, 1880.

GALLERY FIVE: THE QUEST

127 "Everything has changed for me": Letter 158, Vincent to Theo, September 24, 1880.

127 "It's with some . . . this person and that": Letter 155, Vincent to Theo, June 22–24, 1880.

128 "You should know . . . as soon as possible": Letter 156, Vincent to Theo, August 20, 1880.

129 "the Courrières countryside then . . . good minds succeeding": Letter 158, Vincent to Theo, September 24, 1880.

131 the painter "thought my drawing good . . .": Letter 163, Vincent to Reverend Theodorus van Gogh and Anna van Gogh-Carbentus, February 16, 1881.

132 "For this accept my heartfelt thanks . . .": Letter 164, Vincent to Theo, April 2, 1881.

134 "Sometimes I'll find it useful . . .": Letter 166, Vincent to Theo, April 30–May 1, 1881.

134 Vincent and Van Rappard paint together . . . : Anthon van Rappard to Anna van Gogh-Carbentus, date unknown, in Pickvance, *"A Great Artist Is Dead,"* p. 103. Original letter lost; published by Johanna van Gogh-Bonger (in excerpts) in 1914.

GALLERY SIX: STORMS

could not buy it). I am also indebted to Alex Weintraub for his confidence in my claims here, and for his important clarifications.

167   "Do you think . . . those days in drawings": Letter 250, Vincent to Theo, July 23, 1882.

168   "privileged above a thousand . . . gamboge": Letter 253, Vincent to Theo, August 5, 1882.

168   They are part of each other . . . : I owe these insights to Elizabeth DeVita-Raeburn, a friend and the author of *The Empty Room: Understanding Sibling Loss* (New York: Scribner, 2004).

169   "on the beach . . . look through it": Letter 254, Vincent to Theo, August 6, 1882.

172   "doing that kind of old church . . .": Letter 259, Vincent to Theo, August 26, 1882.

173   He makes one of his first oil paintings, *View of the Sea at Scheveningen*: This painting was stolen from the Van Gogh Museum in Amsterdam in 2002.

173   "There's something infinite . . .": Letter 259, Vincent to Theo, August 26, 1882.

173   "a blond, soft effect . . .": Letter 260, Vincent to Theo, September 3, 1882.

173   "Success is sometimes the outcome . . .": Letter 270, Vincent to Theo, October 1, 1882.

175   Meanwhile in Paris, Theo has met a woman. Marie: Marie's identity is not known.

175   "What a mystery . . .": Letter 310, Vincent to Theo, February 8, 1883, trans. Myrna Gunning.

176   "As for the future . . .": Letter 363, Vincent to Theo, July 22, 1883. Vincent is quoting Theo's letter.

176   "I don't know how you . . .": Letter 363, Vincent to Theo, July 22, 1883.

176   "I don't really have . . . heart on it": Letter 364, Vincent to Theo, July 22, 1883.

177   "living beings": Letter 366, Vincent to Theo, July 24, 1883.

177   "My studies and everything . . .": Letter 367, Vincent to Theo, July 25, 1883.

179   "What you write . . . cleverer than I am": Letter 368, Vincent to Theo, July 27, 1883.

180   "can't count on living . . .": Letter 371, Vincent to Theo, August 7, 1883.

181   "This year I've been completely . . .": Letter 375, Vincent to Theo, August 18, 1883.

182   His "heart yearns to be together": Letter 377, Vincent to Theo, August 20, 1883.

182   "I am indifferent and lazy . . .": Letter 379, Vincent to Theo, August 23–29, 1883.

183   "I can't help but make progress . . .": Letter 396, Vincent to Theo, October 15, 1883.

183   "Do you know . . . straight as possible": Letter 380, Vincent to Theo, September 2, 1883.

184   "Neither you nor I must *ever* do that . . .": Letter 401, Vincent to Theo, October 31, 1883.

184   "If something in you yourself says . . .": Letter 400, Vincent to Theo, October 28, 1883.

186   "There's a similar reluctance . . .": Letter 413, Vincent to Theo, December 15, 1883.

187   The dog will "get in everyone's way . . .": Letter 413, Vincent to Theo, December 15, 1883.

187   "At first it seemed to be hopeless . . .": Reverend Theodorus van Gogh to Theo, December 20, 1883, FR b2250, in Letter 416, n1.

187   "eccentricities of dress etc.": Reverend Theodorus van Gogh to Theo, December 20, 1883.

187   "very much for her well-being . . .": Letter 417, Vincent to Theo, December 26, 1883.

188   "What is crueler than . . . the poor woman": Letter 418, Vincent to Theo, December 28, 1883.

GALLERY SEVEN: ENDINGS AND BEGINNINGS

193   "I do so hope that his work . . .": Reverend Theodorus van Gogh to Theo, February 10, 1884, FR b2252, in Letter 428, n1.

194   "Vincent remains exemplary . . .": Reverend Theodorus van Gogh to Theo, February 10, 1884.

194   "You have *never yet* sold . . .": Letter 432, Vincent to Theo, March 2, 1884.

195   "something different from what I thought . . .": Letter 450, Vincent to Theo, mid-June 1884.

197   "acted extremely imprudently . . . call the others": Letter 456, Vincent to Theo, September 16, 1884. I substituted "immediately" for "straightaway."

199   "It seems to me that we must split up . . .": Letter 474, Vincent to Theo, December 10, 1884.

201   "His short temper prevents . . .": Reverend Theodorus van Gogh to Theo, February 19, 1885, FR b2267, in Letter 482 n4.

201   SUDDEN DEATH, COME, VAN GOGH: Letter 486, Vincent to Theo, telegram, March 27, 1885.

201   OUR FATHER FATAL STROKE . . .: Letter 487, Vincent to Theo, telegram, March 27, 1885.

201 OUR FATHER FATAL STROKE. VAN GOGH: Letter 488, Vincent to Theo, telegram, March 27, 1885.

202 "Pa went out in the morning . . .": Willemien van Gogh to Line Kruysse, August 26, 1886, FR b4636, in Letter 486, n1.

203 "Never have I taken a friend . . .": Andries Bonger to H. C. Bonger, March 31, 1885, FR b1811, in Letter 486, n1.

204 In a letter Vincent offers this painting . . . : Letter 490, Vincent to Theo, April 6, 1885. You can see the first painting by looking at an X-ray of the second, Letter 490, n5.

204 "I'm still very much under the impression . . .": Letter 490, Vincent to Theo, April 6, 1885.

204 someone he'd met a few months earlier, "S.": We don't know her name or her identity. She is always referred to simply as "S."

204 "He is a charming companion": Andries Bonger to H. C. Bonger, April 4, 1885, in *Brief Happiness*, p. 13.

205 She thinks he gives in "to all his desires". . . : Anna van Houten-van Gogh, memoir of her sister Lies, ca. 1923, in Van Gogh Museum Documentation, Amsterdam, bd57, in Letter 490, n9.

206 "quite glad that I could give Vincent . . .": Theo to Anna van Gogh-Carbentus, April 22, 1885, FR b900, in Letter 494, n3.

207 "The last days are always hazardous . . .": Letter 497, Vincent to Theo, April 30, 1885.

210 "You'll agree . . . for a nose?": Letter 503, Anthon van Rappard to Vincent, May 24, 1885.

210 "I just received your letter . . .": Letter 504, Vincent to Anthon van Rappard, May 25, 1885.

210 "How dare you to invoke . . .": Letter 503, Anthon van Rappard to Vincent, May 24, 1885.

211 "I'm too absolutely . . . to do it": Letter 528, Vincent to Anthon van Rappard, August 18, 1885.

212 "an inexhaustible topic of discussion": Andries Bonger to his parents, April 4, 1885, in *Brief Happiness*, pp. 13, 53, n16.

212 "wanted life; life at all costs . . .": Jean Gigoux, *Causeries sur les artistes de mon temps* (Paris, 1885), p. 65, in Letter 496, n3.

212 "like a lion devouring . . .": Gigoux, p. 174, in Letter 526, n5.

213 "Even if the world is the greatest . . .": Theo to Andries Bonger, August 6, 1885, FR b889, in "Biographical & historical context," vangoghletters.org.

213 "Won't it be enriching . . .": Theo to Andries Bonger, August 6, 1885, inv. b885V/1975, in *Brief Happiness*, p. 13.

214 "far-reaching consequences": Theo to Johanna Bonger (hereafter Jo), July 26, 1887, in *Brief Happiness*, p. 63.

GALLERY EIGHT: AN EXPANDED PALETTE

217 "When his work comes right . . .": Theo to Elisabeth van Gogh, October 13, 1885, FR b903, in Letter 536, n1.

219 "The longer you know him . . .": Andries Bonger to his parents, August 25, 1885, inv. b1820 V/1970, in *Brief Happiness*, p. 14, n21.

219 "flawless character . . . in a village": Theo to Elisabeth van Gogh, December 28, 1885, in *Brief Happiness*, p. 14, n24.

220 "the trip to Amsterdam well worth while . . .": Letter 534, Vincent to Theo, October 10, 1885.

221 "Here we are on the way . . .": Letter 536, Vincent to Theo, October 20, 1885.

222 "My palette is thawing . . .": Letter 537, Vincent to Theo, October 28, 1885.

222 "I read your letter about black . . .": Letter 537, Vincent to Theo, October 28, 1885.

222 "If you put your mind to it . . .": Letter 537, Vincent to Theo, October 28, 1885.

223 "*Colour Expresses something in itself*": Letter 537, Vincent to Theo, October 28, 1885.

224 "Who hath believed our message? . . .": Isaiah 53:1–3 (New International Version).

225 "one must work and be bold . . .": Letter 492, Vincent to Theo, April 9, 1885.

225 "it really comes quite readily . . .": Letter 537, Vincent to Theo, October 28, 1885.

225 "What bad luck for Vincent! . . .": Theo to Anna van Gogh-Carbentus, September 8, 1885, FR b902, in Letter 531, n3.

226 "cubby-hole . . . in the city?": Letter 545, Vincent to Theo, November 28, 1885.

227 "splendid old man": Letter 546, Vincent to Theo, December 6, 1885.

227 "the same conventional eyes . . .": Letter 547, Vincent to Theo, December 14, 1885.

227 "they still think women's heads . . . charming sister": Letter 548, Vincent to Theo, December 17, 1885.

228 He's lost "no fewer than 10 teeth". . . : Letter 557, Vincent to Theo, February 2, 1886.

228 "I am most definitely literally exhausted . . .": Letter 558, Vincent to Theo, February 4, 1886.

231 "My dear Theo . . . as soon as possible": Letter 567, Vincent to Theo, February 28, 1886.

232 "Van G.'s brother . . .": Andries Bonger to his parents, March 17, 1886, FR b1838, in "Concordance, Lists, Bibliography: Documentation," vangoghletters.org.

232 "Theo's brother is here for good . . .": Andries Bonger to his parents, April 12, 1886, FR b1841, in "Concordance, Lists, Bibliography: Documentation," vangoghletters.org.

232 "They now have a large . . .": Andries Bonger to his parents, June 23, 1886, FR b1843, in "Concordance, Lists, Bibliography: Documentation," vangoghletters.org.

233 He looks "awfully haggard. . . .": Andries Bonger to his parents, June 23, 1886.

235 "angelic patience . . . or the eraser": in Émile Bernard, *Lettres de Vincent van Gogh à Émile Bernard*, Paris: Ambroise Vollard, 1911. Preface pp. 10–11 quoted in Nicole Myers, "Van Gogh and Thinking Nude" in *Becoming Van Gogh*, eds. Timothy Standring and Louis van Tilborgh, p. 75.

236 "Hardly a day passes . . .": Theo to Anna van Gogh-Carbentus, June–July 1886, FR b942, in "Concordance, Lists, Bibliography: Documentation," vangoghletters.org.

238 "Courage and composure": Letter 568, Vincent and Andries Bonger to Theo, August 18, 1886.

238 "good things about Vincent . . .": Willemien van Gogh to Line Kruysse, August 26, 1886, FR b4536, in "Concordance, Lists, Bibliography: Documentation," vangoghletters.org.

239 "the effect of that on you . . .": Letter 568, Vincent to Theo, August 18, 1886.

239 "The issue is to open S.'s eyes. . . .": Letter 568, Andries Bonger to Theo, August 18, 1886.

242 "It's a long time since . . . when the sun shines": Theo to Elisabeth van Gogh, April 19, 1887, FR b910, in "Concordance, Lists, Bibliography: Documentation," vangoghletters.org.

GALLERY NINE: BONDS

247 he and Vincent have "made peace . . .": Theo to Willemien van Gogh, April 25, 1887, FR b911, in "Concordance, Lists, Bibliography: Documentation," vangoghletters.org.

248 "Vincent is still working hard . . . it's enviable": Theo to Elisabeth van Gogh, May 15, 1887, FR b912, in "Concordance, Lists, Bibliography: Documentation," vangoghletters.org.

250 "Myself—I feel I'm losing the desire . . .": Letter 572, Vincent to Theo, July 23–25, 1887.

250 Jo gives him "the impression . . .": Theo to Elisabeth van Gogh, April 19, 1887.

251 "You girls usually think . . .": Theo to Elisabeth van Gogh, April 19, 1887.

251 "I was pleased he was coming . . . could I?": Johanna Bonger, diary, Van Gogh Museum, inv. b4550 V/1986, quoted in *Brief Happiness*, pp. 9, 19.

252 "for your health . . .": Letter 572, Vincent to Theo, July 23–24, 1887.

253 "Having just found a quiet space . . .": Theo to Jo, July 26, 1887, in *Brief Happiness*, pp. 63–65. All the quotes in this chapter are from this letter as well.

255 "I realise you haven't made up . . .": Theo to Jo, August 1, 1887, in *Brief Happiness*, p. 66. All the following quotes in this chapter come from this letter as well.

260 "young painters' Bohemia": From diary of Johanna van Gogh-Bonger, quoted in Stolwijk et al., *Theo van Gogh*, p. 44.

260 "When he came here two years ago . . .": Theo to Willemien van Gogh, February 24 and 26, 1888, FR b914, in "Concordance, Lists, Bibliography: Documentation," vangoghletters.org.

GALLERY TEN: PASSIONS

265 "During the journey I thought . . .": Letter 577, Vincent to Theo, February 21, 1888.

266 "Don't worry," he writes Theo . . . : Letter 578, Vincent to Theo, February 24, 1888.

266 "it's not easy to replace . . .": Theo to Willemien van Gogh, February 24 and 26, 1888.

266 "It seems to me that my blood . . .": Letter 578, Vincent to Theo, February 24, 1888.

266 "He has such a big . . . on my own": Theo to Willemien van Gogh, February 24 and 26, 1888.

268 "I'm inclined to place slightly . . .": Letter 582, Vincent to Theo, March 2, 1888.

269 "I attach importance . . .": Letter 585, Vincent to Theo, March 16, 1888.

270 a Post-Impressionist . . . : He is also referred to as a father of Expressionism, or a Proto-
     Expressionist. For more on this, start here: metmuseum.org/toah/hd/poim/hd_poim.htm.

271 He'd like to paint "a starry sky . . .": Letter 596, Vincent to Émile Bernard, April 12, 1888.

272 "rooked by those . . . gentlemen": Letter 601, Vincent to Theo, April 25, 1888.

272 "which contains 4 rooms . . .": Letter 602, Vincent to Theo, May 1, 1888.

274 "My poor friend . . . see few women": Letter 603, Vincent to Theo, May 4, 1888.

274 "If you could now have . . .": Letter 611, Vincent to Theo, May 20, 1888.

275 "suffer from unaccountable, involuntary . . .": Letter 615, Vincent to Theo, May 28, 1888.

276 "At the same time that he's an excellent artist . . .": Émile Bernard to his parents, July 1888, in
     Laure Harscoët-Maire, "Lettres d'Émile Bernard (1888): à Saint-Briac," *Le Pays de Dinan 17*
     (1997), pp. 177–178, quoted in Letter 641, n1.

276 One critic praises . . . : Stolwijk et al., *Theo van Gogh*, p. 79, quoting Gustave Geffroy.

277 "And look . . .": Letter 635, Vincent to Theo, July 1, 1888.

278 "Vincent's becoming very good": Émile Bernard to his parents, July 1888.

278 "a sense of the infinite": Letter 652, Vincent to Theo, July 31, 1888.

279 "You're enough of a judge . . .": Letter 662, Vincent to Theo, August 15, 1888.

279 "sees in the future . . .": Letter 670, Vincent to Willemien van Gogh, August 26, 1888.

280 "That's a really good one, about Bague": Letter 699, Vincent to Theo, October 8, 1888. Sadly,
     we don't know which painting it was, but probably one from his time in Arles.

281 "I very often think that all the costs . . .": Letter 702, Vincent to Theo, October 10–11, 1888.

281 "This time it's simply my bedroom . . .": Letter 705, Vincent to Theo, October 16, 1888.

283 "You talk about money that you owe . . .": Letter 713, Theo to Vincent, October 27, 1888.

284 "I'd be very glad to see you . . .": Letter 711, Theo to Vincent, October 23, 1888.

284 "I can see that . . .": Letter 713, Theo to Vincent, October 27, 1888.

284 Theo has been giving Vincent about 15 percent of his income: Van Gogh Museum,
     "Biographical & historical context: The financial backgrounds," vangoghletters.org.

284 "He's very, very interesting as a man . . .": Letter 712, Vincent to Theo, October 25, 1888.

285 "something of a dual nature . . .": Letter 709, Vincent to Theo, October 21, 1888.

285 "a simple worshipper of the eternal Buddha": Letter 695, Vincent to Paul Gauguin, October 3,
     1888, and Letter 697, Vincent to Theo, October 4 or 5, 1888.

286 "continue as in the past and create . . .": Letter 713, Theo to Vincent, October 27, 1888.

288 "has proved to me a little . . .": Letter 721, Vincent to Theo, November 19, 1888.

288 Monet "had made of sunflowers . . .": Letter 721, Vincent to Theo, November 19, 1888.

290 "if I manage to do *this entire family* . . .": Letter 723, Vincent to Theo, December 1, 1888.

290 "It is certainly me, but me gone mad": Hulsker, *Vincent and Theo*, p. 317.

290 "It was indeed me, extremely tired . . .": Letter 801, Vincent to Theo, September 10, 1889.

291 "Vincent and I can absolutely not live . . .": Paul Gauguin to Theo, December 11, 1888, in
     Victor Merlhès, *Correspondance de Paul Gauguin* (Paris, 1984), p. 301, in Letter 724, n1.

291 Gauguin will either "definitely go . . .": Letter 724, Vincent to Theo, December 11, 1888.

291 "The discussion is . . .": Letter 726, Vincent to Theo, December 17–18, 1888.

293 honorable discharge for "health reasons": *Brief Happiness*, p. 22, n66.

293 "My married life so far . . .": Andries Bonger to Jo, September 12, 1888, in *Brief Happiness*,
     p. 23, n72.

294 "Recently I wrote to you . . .": Theo to Anna van Gogh-Carbentus, December 21, 1888, in
     Hulsker, *Vincent and Theo*, pp. 328–329.

294 tells her that he loves her . . . : Theo to Anna van Gogh-Carbentus, December 21, 1888.

295 "a very beautiful & very young . . .": Theo to Jo, August 1, 1887, in *Brief Happiness*, p. 66.

295 "such peace together": Theo to Jo, January 1, 1889, in *Brief Happiness*, p. 77.

296 "Vincent and I do not find . . .": Paul Gauguin to Émile Bernard, December 1888, in Gauguin, *Letters to His Wife and Friends*, pp. 115–116.

296 "I answer . . . in the medium": Paul Gauguin to Émile Bernard, December 1888.

298 "You are one of the first to hear . . .": Theo to Elisabeth van Gogh, December 24, 1888, in Hulsker, *Vincent and Theo*, p. 329.

300 Wrapped in the cloth is Vincent's left ear: Some eyewitnesses reported Vincent had severed his whole ear. The family maintained it was the lobe and a little more. A recently discovered drawing by Dr. Rey indicates the whole ear was sliced off.

300 Some historians postulate that Gauguin cut Vincent's ear (by accident) and Vincent agreed to keep quiet: Hans Kaufmann and Rita Wildegans, *Van Goghs Ohr: Paul Gauguin und der Pakt des Schweigens* [Van Gogh's ear: Paul Gauguin and the pact of silence] (Berlin: Osburg Verlag, 2008). This is not a widely held belief.

301 "I received sad news today. . . .": Theo to Jo, December 24, 1888, in *Brief Happiness*, p. 67.

302 "been showing symptoms . . .": Theo to Jo, December 28, 1888, in *Brief Happiness*, p. 70.

302 "Just like in Zundert": Johanna van Gogh-Bonger, "Memoir of Vincent van Gogh," webexhibits.org/vangogh.

303 "Will he remain insane? . . .": Theo to Jo, December 28, 1888, in *Brief Happiness*, p. 70.

GALLERY ELEVEN: ABUNDANCES

305 "I've been wavering . . .": Theo to Jo, December 30, 1888, in *Brief Happiness*, p. 74.

307 "My thoughts were . . .": Jo to Theo, December 25, 1888, in *Brief Happiness*, p. 69.

307 "the prospect of losing . . .": Theo to Jo, December 28, 1888, in *Brief Happiness*, p. 70.

308 "In his night-shirt . . . in an asylum": Félix Rey to Theo, December 29, 1888, FR b1055, in "Concordance, Lists, Bibliography: Documentation," vangoghletters.org.

308 "My assessment," the doctor writes . . . : Félix Rey to Theo, December 30, 1888, FR b1056, in "Concordance, Lists, Bibliography: Documentation," vangoghletters.org.

308 "What would become of me . . .": Theo to Jo, January 1, 1889, in *Brief Happiness*, pp. 76–77.

308 "Reception Wednesday!!!": Theo to Jo, January 3, 1889, in *Brief Happiness*, p. 83.

308 "He was pleased to see . . .": Joseph Roulin to Theo, January 4, 1889, trans. Robert Harrison, in Van Gogh's Letters, webexhibits.org/vangogh.

308 "I am, my dear brother, so *heartbroken* . . .": Letter 729, Vincent to Theo, January 4, 1889.

309 "Tell me. Was my brother . . .": Letter 730, Vincent to Paul Gauguin, January 4, 1889.

309 "which I regard as a perfect . . .": Paul Gauguin to Vincent, January 8–16, 1889, Letter 734.

309 "Engaged Theodorus van Gogh and Johanna Bonger": Letter 731, Theo and Jo to Vincent, January 6, 1889, vangoghletters.org/vg/letters/let731/letter.html.

310 "I hope that I've just had . . .": Letter 732, Vincent to Theo, January 7, 1889.

310 "Would you be so good . . .": Letter 733, Vincent to Anna van Gogh-Carbentus and Willemien van Gogh, January 7, 1889.

310 "each path, each plant . . .": Letter 741, Vincent to Theo, January 22, 1889.

311 "Oh Theo, must the year end . . .": Anna van Gogh-Carbentus to Theo, December 29, 1888, FR b2425, in "Concordance, Lists, Bibliography: Documentation," vangoghletters.org.

312 "My dearest Theo . . . little about him": Jo to Theo, January 13, 1889, in *Brief Happiness*, pp. 84–85.

314 "I'm delighted with it . . .": Jo to Theo, January 22, 1889, in *Brief Happiness*, p. 103.

314 "like to lay my head . . .": Theo to Jo, January 24, 1889, in *Brief Happiness*, p. 110.

314 "a person's state of mind . . .": Theo to Jo, January 27, 1889, in *Brief Happiness*, p. 116.

315 "Yesterday I went . . . lose your head": Letter 745, Vincent to Theo, February 3, 1889.

315 "I promise I shall stop . . .": Theo to Jo, February 6, 1889, in *Brief Happiness*, pp. 141–142.

317 "Let us keep our hopes up": Theo to Jo, February 11–12, 1889, in *Brief Happiness*, p. 155.

317 "This afternoon I received . . .": Theo to Jo, February 9, 1889, in *Brief Happiness*, p. 145.

317 Vincent "has withdrawn into absolute . . .": Frédéric Salles to Theo, February 7, 1889, trans. Robert Harrison, in Van Gogh's Letters, webexhibits.org/vangogh.

318   "had for so long . . . That is the question": Theo to Jo, February 9, 1889, in *Brief Happiness*, p. 146.

318   "The same expression of suffering . . .": Theo to Jo, February 9, 1889.

319   "Your letter came at exactly . . .": Theo to Jo, February 11–12, in *Brief Happiness*, p. 153.

320   "Dear Mr Mayor . . . women and children": Residents living near Place Lamartine to Jacques Tardieu, petition, shortly before February 27, 1889, in "Concordance, Lists, Bibliography: Documentation," vangoghletters.org.

321   "prone to interfering with women" . . . : Police summons by Joseph d'Ornano, February 27, 1889, in "Concordance, Lists, Bibliography: Documentation," vangoghletters.org.

321   "a hammer-blow full in the chest": Letter 750, Vincent to Theo, March 19, 1889.

321   "It's unnatural that other people . . .": Willemien van Gogh to Theo, February 28, 1889, in *Brief Happiness*, p. 187, n2.

323   "In arranging my new apartment . . . about you": Letter 749, Theo to Vincent, March 16, 1889.

323   "I seemed to see so much restrained . . .": Letter 750, Vincent to Theo, March 19, 1889.

324   "Your work and . . . brotherly affection . . .": Letter 762, Theo to Vincent, April 24, 1889.

324   "key myself up a bit to reach . . .": Letter 752, Vincent to Theo, March 24, 1889.

325   "It's an absolute farce . . . it would be so good": Jo to Mien Bonger, April 26, 1889, in *Brief Happiness*, pp. 27–28, 55, n84.

326   "you and your wife": Letter 760, Vincent to Theo, April 21, 1889.

328   "It's high time your new little sister . . .": Letter 771, Jo to Vincent, May 8, 1889.

328   "straight at that beautiful flowering peach tree of yours . . . when we don't speak of you": Letter 771, Jo to Vincent, May 8, 1889. It was most likely a pear tree.

329   "continually hears shouts and terrible howls . . .": Letter 772, Vincent to Jo, May 9, 1889.

329   "Your latest paintings . . . mysterious regions": Letter 781, Theo to Vincent, June 16, 1889.

330   "dead tired in the evenings": Jo to Mien Bonger, May 25, 1889, in *Brief Happiness*, p. 56, n95.

331   "This winter, around February . . .": Letter 786, Jo to Vincent, July 5, 1889.

332   "Let's not be *too* concerned . . .": Letter 790, July 14–15, 1889, Vincent to Theo.

332   "If you were living . . .": Letter 793, Theo to Vincent, July 29, 1889.

334   "It's like a sword . . .": Jo to Mien Bonger, January 9, 1890, in *Brief Happiness*, p. 35.

GALLERY TWELVE: FUTURES

339   "Dear Vincent," she begins . . . : Letter 845, Jo to Vincent, January 29, 1890. All quotes that follow are from this letter, unless noted.

340   "I would feel I were . . .": Theo to Jo, July 26, 1887, in *Brief Happiness*, pp. 63–65.

340   Vincent had six canvases in the [Brussels] show, one of which sold . . . : It is often said that this was the only painting of Vincent's sold in his lifetime, but that is not true. He had the commissions from Uncle Cor. He sold his first painting to Julien Tanguy, and Theo sold at least one other to a gallery in London. There was the one that the art dealer Athanase Bague bought in 1888. It is likely that other paintings sold for which there is no record. Since he also traded his paintings for other artists', the number of paintings owned by others during his lifetime was quite large. As to the price, that would be about $2,000 in 2017. For perspective, *The Laakmolen near the Hague*, not a famous painting, sold for $3,669,550 in 2015. Another of Vincent's paintings, *L'allée Des Alyscamps*, also sold in 2015—for $66.3 million.

340   "This morning Theo brought . . .": Letter 845, Jo to Vincent, January 29, 1890.

341   "strange, intense and feverish": Albert Aurier, "Les isolés: Vincent van Gogh," *Mercure de France* (January 1890), pp. 24-29, in Letter 845, Jo to Vincent, January 29, 1890, n2. For the text, with commentary and an English translation, see Ronald Pickvance, ed., *Van Gogh in Saint-Rémy and Auvers* (New York: Metropolitan Museum of Art, 1986), exhibition catalog, pp. 310–315.

341   "too simple and at the same time too subtle . . .": Aurier, "Les isolés: Vincent van Gogh."

342   "It sounds sentimental . . .": Letter 845, Jo to Vincent, January 29, 1890.

343   "It touches me . . . he sees you recovering": Letter 846, Vincent to Jo, January 31, 1890.

343 "brought into the world . . . courageous as you": Letter 847, Theo to Vincent, January 31, 1890.

344 "Today I've just . . . mired in flattery": Letter 850, Vincent to Theo, February 1, 1890.

344 "Thank you very much . . . months in Arles": Letter 853, Vincent to Albert Aurier, February 9–10, 1890.

346 "Without you I would be most unhappy . . .": Letter 863, Vincent to Theo, April 29, 1890

346 "Dear Mother," Vincent writes. . . . : Letter 855, Vincent to Anna van Gogh-Carbentus, February 19, 1890.

347 "Work was going well . . .": Letter 857, Vincent to Theo, March 17, 1890.

347 "for many artists you are . . .": Letter 859, Paul Gauguin to Vincent, March 20, 1890.

347 "There was a bench just in front . . .": Letter 861, Jo to Vincent, March 29, 1890.

348 "for all the kindness you've shown me": Letter 863, Vincent to Theo, April 29, 1890.

352 "I hope that the canvases . . . stretching frames &c.": Letter 872, Vincent to Theo, May 13, 1890.

353 "two merry faces": Van Gogh-Bonger, "Memoir of Vincent van Gogh," webexhibits.org.

353 "a sturdy broad-shouldered man": Johanna van Gogh-Bonger, ed., *Vincent van Gogh, Brieven aan zijn broeder* (Amsterdam, 1914), quoted in Letter 872, n1.

355 "gravely beautiful . . . distinctive and picturesque": Letter 873, Vincent to Theo and Jo, May 20, 1890.

356 "old thatched roofs with a field . . .": Letter 874, Vincent to Theo, May 21, 1890.

356 "sensible and warm-hearted and uncomplicated": Letter 878, Vincent to Anna van Gogh-Carbentus, June 5, 1890.

356 "for at every turn one would like . . .": Letter 876, Theo to Vincent, June 2, 1890.

357 "The cock crows *cocorico*": Johanna van Gogh-Bonger, "Memoir of Vincent van Gogh," webexhibits.org/vangogh.

357 "I don't think he understands very much . . .": Letter 885, Vincent to Anna van Gogh-Carbentus, June 13, 1890.

357 "Dear brother and sister . . .": Letter 881, Vincent to Theo and Jo, June 10, 1890.

GALLERY THIRTEEN: A SENSE OF THE FINITE

361 "Lately I've been working . . .": Letter 886, Vincent to Willemien van Gogh, June 13, 1890.

361 "*Mon très cher frère* . . .": Letter 894, Theo to Vincent, June 30 and July 1, 1890. All the following quotes in this chapter are from this letter, unless noted.

363 "The animals come to the door . . .": Letter 897, Theo to Vincent, July 5, 1890.

365 "rather difficult and laborious hours": Letter 898, Vincent to Theo and Jo, July 10, 1890.

366 Theo could die before him; he could die very soon, from the look of him: Piet Voskuil in "The Medical Files of Theo van Gogh" [in Dutch] makes the argument that Vincent would have been able to see just how sick Theo was. I agree with this.

366 "They're immense . . . the countryside": Letter 898, Vincent to Theo and Jo, July 10, 1890.

367 "I hope, my dear Vincent, that your health . . .": Letter 901, Theo to Vincent, July 22, 1890.

368 "I would rather go . . .": Theo to Jo, July 26, 1890, in *Brief Happiness*, pp. 265–266.

369 "Who can predict . . .": Jo to Theo, July 27, 1890, in *Brief Happiness*, pp. 267–268.

370 The two diagonals of the words . . . : The envelope is reproduced in Pickvance, *"A Great Artist Is Dead,"* p. 21.

371 "Dear Monsieur Vangogh . . .": Paul-Ferdinand Gachet to Theo, July 27, 1890, in Pickvance, *"A Great Artist Is Dead,"* p. 27.

373 "There's something . . . we're on course": Letter 371, Vincent to Theo, August 7, 1883.

376 These are unanswered questions: For more about this theory, see Naifeh and Smith, *Van Gogh: The Life*. Appendix: "A Note on Vincent's Fatal Wounding." The question of where he shot himself is also unresolved. Some people say stomach, some chest.

376 "Dearest, dearest little wife . . .": Theo to Jo, July 28, 1890, in *Brief Happiness*, pp. 269–270. All the following quotes come from this letter unless otherwise noted.

378 "I've always wanted to die . . . the sadness will last forever": Theo to Elisabeth van Gogh, August 5, 1890, in Pickvance, *"A Great Artist Is Dead,"* pp. 72–73.

379 "He found a tremendous peace": Theo to Elisabeth van Gogh, August 5, 1890, in Pickvance, *A Great Artist Is Dead,"* p. 73.

379 "eager . . . to demonstrate his affection": Henri de Toulouse-Lautrec to Theo, July 31, 1890, in Pickvance, *"A Great Artist Is Dead,"* p. 114.

379 "I really felt a great affinity . . .": Camille Pissarro to Theo, July 30, 1890, in Pickvance, *"A Great Artist Is Dead,"* p. 109.

379 "masses of bouquets . . .": Theo to Jo, August 1, 1890, in *Brief Happiness*, pp. 279–280.

380 "making a sort of halo for him . . .": Émile Bernard to Albert Aurier, July 31, 1890, in Pickvance, *"A Great Artist Is Dead,"* pp. 34–35.

380 "who was devoted . . . and enjoying it": Émile Bernard to Albert Aurier, July 31, 1890.

381 For Theo there is emptiness: Theo to Jo, August 1, 1890, in *Brief Happiness*, pp. 279–280.

382 "Dear Theo!" Ma writes . . . : Anna van Gogh-Carbentus to Theo, August 1, 1890, in Pickvance, *"A Great Artist Is Dead,"* p. 55.

382 "One cannot write how sad one is . . . praise for his talent too": Theo to Anna van Gogh-Carbentus, August 1, 1890, in Pickvance, *"A Great Artist Is Dead,"* pp. 56–57.

383 "She's devastated . . . as long as I live": Theo to Jo, August 1, 1890 in *Brief Happiness*, pp. 279–280.

383 "He has found the rest . . . my own brother": Theo to Anna van Gogh-Carbentus, August 1, 1890, in Pickvance, *"A Great Artist Is Dead,"* p. 57.

385 "far more agreeable of late . . . even dearer to me": Elisabeth van Gogh to Theo and Jo, August 2, 1890, in Pickvance, *"A Great Artist Is Dead,"* pp. 67–69.

385 "People should know . . .": Theo to Lies, August 5, 1890, in Pickvance, *"A Great Artist Is Dead,"* pp. 72–73.

385 "I know what pain . . .": Meijer de Haan to Theo, ca. August 2, 1890, in Pickvance, *"A Great Artist Is Dead,"* p. 83.

385 "I don't want to write the usual phrases . . .": Paul Gauguin to Theo, ca. August 2, 1890, in Pickvance, *"A Great Artist Is Dead,"* p. 133.

386 "so often volatile and so impassioned . . .": Anthon van Rappard to Anna van Gogh-Carbentus, date unknown, in Pickvance, *"A Great Artist Is Dead,"* p. 102.

386 "This will no doubt be poor consolation . . .": Albert Aurier to Theo, August 1, 1890, in Pickvance, *"A Great Artist Is Dead,"* p. 122.

386 "We have lost a very courageous artist": Georges Charles Lecomte to Theo, August 1, 1890, in Pickvance, *"A Great Artist Is Dead,"* p. 124.

386 "a *giant*": Dr. Paul-Ferdinand Gachet to Theo, ca. August 15, 1890, in Pickvance, *"A Great Artist Is Dead,"* p. 144.

GALLERY FOURTEEN: REMAINS

396 "From time to time he is incontinent . . .": Voskuil, "The Medical Files of Theo van Gogh" [in Dutch]. All these scenes, unless otherwise noted, are from Theo's medical file.

397 "appalling & have said this quite openly": from Theo's admission file in the Utrecht municipal archives, cited in *Brief Happiness*, p. 49.

397 "How painful that visit . . .": Anna van Gogh-Carbentus and Wil van Gogh to Jo, November 25, 1890, in *Brief Happiness*, p. 49.

400 "On this cold short Christmas afternoon . . . Vincent van Gogh!": Johan de Meester, "Vincent van Gogh," *Algemeen Handelsblad*, December 31, 1890, retrieved by the Van Gogh Museum and trans. by Susanna Mitton for the author.

400 Theo gets an increasingly blank expression: *Brief Happiness*, p. 50.

401 "A sad feeling was mixed . . . sacrificing of himself": Johan de Meester, "Vincent van Gogh."

EXIT

407 "I'm quite sure that if I stay . . .": Jo to Theo, January 13, 1889, in *Brief Happiness*, pp. 84–85.

Index